Praise for *Dead Man Walking*

'A compulsive thriller with pace, brilliant plotting, and characters who are credible, despite the extraordinary situations in which they find themselves' **Ann Cleeves**

'An unstoppable and addictive thriller. Clear your diary, you'll want to read this in one sitting' **Michael Wood**

'Tension bristles on every page on this rollercoaster of a read. I couldn't put the book down' **Sarah Wood**

'Rich with tension and action, there are surprises at every plot twist' **Marni Graff**

'Always exciting to meet a new detective, especially when they're as kick ass as DS Rick Turner' **Dan Malakin**

'I loved this. An immediately gripping, compelling and emotionally wrought thriller . . . Clear your diary and get reading!' **Gytha Lodge**

Photo credit: Murf

M. K. MURPHY writes internationally acclaimed and bestselling psychological thrillers under her own name, and forensic thrillers as Ashley Dyer and AD Garrett. She is a past Chair of the UK Crime Writers Association (CWA), founder of Murder Squad, and a former RLF Writing Fellow and Reading Round Lector. She's been a country park ranger, biology teacher, dyslexia specialist and visiting professor in creative writing. A Short Story Dagger, HRF Keating, and CWA Red Herring award winner, she has also been shortlisted for the 'First Blood' critics award and CWA Dagger in the Library.

Dead Man Walking

M. K. MURPHY

ONE PLACE. MANY STORIES

HQ
An imprint of HarperCollins*Publishers* Ltd
1 London Bridge Street
London SE1 9GF

www.harpercollins.co.uk

HarperCollins*Publishers*
Macken House, 39/40 Mayor Street Upper,
Dublin 1 D01 C9W8

This paperback edition 2023

2

First published in Great Britain by
HQ, an imprint of HarperCollins*Publishers* Ltd 2023

Copyright © M. K. Murphy

ISBN: 9780008618254

MIX
Paper | Supporting
responsible forestry
FSC
www.fsc.org
FSC™ C007454

This book is produced from independently certified FSC™ paper
to ensure responsible forest management.

For more information visit: www.harpercollins.co.uk/green

Printed and Bound in the UK using
100% Renewable Electricity at CPI Group (UK) Ltd

For Murf, always.

NOW

Chapter 1

Sunday evening

DETECTIVE SERGEANT RICK TURNER eased through the crowd to the bar. The place was heaving, but he was tall and broad-shouldered, and people gave way readily.

'He's here!' someone shouted.

This prompted others to turn. 'Oi-oi – thought you weren't coming, Sarge!'

Soon he was running the gauntlet of backslapping congratulations from his colleagues. It was the night before the biggest day of his career and here he was, in a pub, smiling his thanks for compliments from people who a few months earlier would have crossed the street to avoid him.

I could be at home, watching a film, sharing a takeaway with Jess, he thought. But the boss had said he'd be here, and Rick had enough of a grasp of office politics to know that there are some invitations you can't wriggle out of.

Relax – it might be fun.

Rick's inner voice sounded a lot like Sam, his older brother. Mum, Dad, Granddad Turner – even DS Stott, his former mentor – would be more appropriate counsellors, but of all the people who might drop a word of advice in his ear, for some reason it always seemed to be Sam's voice he heard.

'Here he is, man of the moment!'

Jim Stott, in the flesh. In the last year, he'd turned grey, gained weight around the middle and lost a few centimetres of hairline. Glass-eyed, tie askew, top button popped, his booze-induced rosacea was aflare across his nose and cheeks.

Rick acknowledged him with a nod. 'Jim.' Catching the barman's eye, he said, 'Glass of Coke when you're ready, mate.'

'Put your money away.' Stott waved a fiver at the barman. 'Give him a proper drink – we're celebrating, aren't we?'

The barman raised his eyebrows in question. 'Coke's fine,' Rick said.

'You've landed yourself a big fish in this stagnant little pond, son,' Stott said. 'Let your hair down for once.'

The fish in question was Thomas Unwin, a barracuda of a businessman whose criminal interests had been impossible to pin down until very recently.

'Thanks, Sarge,' Rick said, knowing that Stott would be flattered by the use of his title, 'but we're some way off a verdict, and anyway, I'm driving.'

'It's a poor do if a man can't buy his protégé a pint. This is *huge*, Rick – you're playing with the big boys, now.' Stott grabbed him by the shoulders and laughed hard into his face.

Rick caught whisky fumes, beer, and a whiff of desperation. But he smiled and tried not to grit his teeth. 'I'm fine, honest, Sarge.'

'Give him a pint of lager, mate.'

Rick opened his mouth to protest, but Stott cut him off: 'It's *one bloody drink*, Ricky.' He forced another laugh, and this time the man's anger and resentment was barely veiled.

As the barman began pulling Rick's pint, Stott slapped a box of mint Tic Tacs on the bar. 'Anyway, I've got you covered, mate—' He leaned in close. 'Just in case you get pulled over.'

Rick glanced down at the pack. 'You do know mints won't beat a breathalyser?'

'Well, you're the expert.' Stott smirked, catching the eye of a few others bellying up to the bar.

This was an unsubtle reference to Rick having once arrested a fellow cop for drunk driving. Four times over the legal limit, the idiot had tried to mask the reek of whisky on his breath with half a pack of breath fresheners. Since then, the rattle of Tic Tac boxes had become a standing joke in certain quarters.

Rick grinned obligingly, tucking the packet into Stott's top pocket. 'Looks like you'll be needing those yourself, Sarge.'

A spatter of laughter from the onlookers and DS Stott flamed red from the collar of his shirt to his hairline.

The barman set the pint on the bar and eyed each of them in turn. 'Everything all right here, gents?'

'Fine, mate,' Rick said. 'Just a bit of banter. Joke without a punchline.'

The barman's mouth twitched, but he quelled the smile. 'Let's keep it that way.'

Rick ordered Stott a whisky chaser and carried the pint away to show there were no hard feelings.

DCI Kath Steiner was keeping a low profile at a table in the corner. It was standard protocol for a senior ranking detective to head up homicide inquiries, and Steiner was nominally in charge of the investigation. But she had been parachuted in late in the game, and only after it became obvious that Rick had a serious chance of making the case that two 'accidental' deaths were actually contract killings, commissioned by Unwin. In her early forties, a trim, strawberry blonde, her hair was cut in a neat bob and her makeup was, as always, perfect. Unlike most female detectives Rick knew who bought their workwear from Marks & Spencer, Steiner favoured Hobbs and Ted Baker.

She raised her glass to Rick, turning away immediately, and

Rick was relieved to have escaped the awkward necessity of making conversation.

Detective Superintendent Ghosh appeared two minutes later. Grey-haired, trim, fit, and smooth-shaven despite the late hour, he looked as much politician as senior police, which of course he needed to be at his rank. Rick left his drink on one of the tables before edging through the crowd towards his boss, doing his best to be gracious, counting the minutes till he could escape without raising too many eyebrows.

'Good turnout,' Ghosh said, shaking Rick's hand.

'You know this lot, sir,' Rick said. 'Any excuse for a booze-up.'

'Neil is fine – we're off duty now.' Ghosh's given name was Anil but, as the only Asian child in the rural Cheshire community where his father practised medicine, he had quickly adopted the anglicised 'Neil' – much to the chagrin of his parents. Or so he'd told a reporter for *The Job*, London Met Police's newspaper. 'And don't sell yourself short,' the superintendent went on. 'The National Crime Agency's been after Unwin for *years*.'

It was common knowledge in the job that Unwin's criminal enterprises ranged from drug smuggling to people trafficking. But knowing something and proving it were two very different things. Until Rick Turner had linked those two apparently unconnected deaths. Tomorrow, Thomas Unwin would stand in the dock at the Old Bailey charged on two counts of 'soliciting to murder'.

'Get a conviction, it could drive a wedge between Unwin and his associates, give the Serious Fraud Office a way in.'

Ghosh was all but rubbing his hands at the prospect, but Rick's stomach did a slow roll; putting a man in front of a jury was a long way from securing a conviction.

Surveying the room Ghosh said, 'Where's Steiner – keeping her head down, is she?'

'She's here,' Rick said, noncommittally.

'I'll bet she hasn't congratulated you?'

Rick wasn't sure what to say; he didn't want to disrespect his line manager, but couldn't really take his boss to task, either.

Ghosh chuckled at his embarrassment. 'She's just sore that you managed what she couldn't. You know she took a run at Unwin herself, last year?'

'No,' Rick said, but it did explain some of her resentment of him: Steiner was a fast-track promotee without the ambition or imagination to make a quality investigator.

'Kath'll do all right, though,' Ghosh said, as though he'd spoken his thoughts. 'With looks like hers she'll make a move sideways into media and communications in a year or two, then land a nice job fronting true crime on TV before the bloom fades.'

Ghosh was one of just four Met officers who had achieved the rank of detective superintendent before the age of forty, and the first of Indian origin. He was widely tipped to make chief superintendent in the next couple of years, so who was Rick to argue?

'Not that I'm sexist,' Ghosh added, and Rick realised that he'd left an uncomfortable silence.

He shook his head as though his thoughts had been elsewhere. 'I was just wondering if there's anything we've missed.'

Ghosh patted his arm. 'It'll be fine; you're thorough. Not one in a thousand cops could have done what you did – seeing connections – following up, ignoring the naysayers.'

He sounded sincere, but Rick hadn't forgotten that Detective Superintendent Ghosh had been one of those naysayers up until a few months ago.

Meet him halfway, Sam counselled. *This is modern policing, Rick – mavericks need not apply.*

Like it or not, Rick would need Ghosh's goodwill in the future, so he nodded his appreciation, though the bones in his neck crackled. 'I couldn't have pulled the case together without support,' he said.

'That's the spirit,' Ghosh said, relief flooding his face. 'It's all about the team.' He leaned in and lowered his voice. 'You know, there could even be a promotion in this for you.'

Smile, Rick – it won't break your face.

He obliged, muttering something about not thinking beyond the trial, for now.

After an awkward moment, Ghosh said, 'You're not drinking. Can I get you one?'

'I'm good, thanks, sir – I mean Neil,' Rick amended in response to the superintendent's chiding look.

Ghosh beamed his approval and moved on, putting in another ten minutes, doing the rounds of the troops like the good politician he was, shaking hands, delivering praise, asking after wives and kids and grandkids – and then he was gone.

That wasn't so hard, was it? Five more minutes, you can be on your way.

Sam again. But the cold reality was that Rick had no family he could talk to. His parents were both dead – his brother Sam, too, for all he knew. Despite the noise and beery camaraderie, he felt completely alone. His phone buzzed and he slipped it from his pocket. A message from Jess:

—How's it going?
—It's hell, he replied, tapping the message in with both thumbs.
—But I'll be home in fifteen.

She sent a sad-face emoji, then:

—Cheer up. I'll have something nice on.

He smiled, because she wasn't talking about food, and all the tension of the last half-hour dropped away.

Chapter 2

A MAN SITS IN AN ARMCHAIR just beyond the restaurant area of a London hotel. In thirty seconds, a waiter will wheel a trolley from the kitchen and head to the bank of lifts nearby. The man has acquired many skills in his thirty-plus years, the most useful being the knack of invisibility. It's a nice hotel, in an affluent area of London, so he's smartly dressed to blend in. His black trilby hat and cashmere overcoat suggest that he's about to leave; he is well padded, even paunchy: the inevitable weight gain of ten years of business lunches and constant travel, perhaps. He seems purposeful and focused, scrolling through his mobile phone, his body language sending a clear message to the ever-vigilant waitstaff that he does *not* require their attention.

And here he is – right on time.

The man hears the trolley's merry jingling a moment before it turns the corner. It is decorously linen-draped; white wine in a bucket, plated food a tantalising secret under the gleaming dome.

He times his arrival at the lift doors to the second, moving with surprising agility for a fat man, darting inside with a cheery, 'Going down?'

Startled, the waiter reaches to hold the doors, but the businessman parries the move with practised grace.

'No need,' he says. 'I'm quite safe.' Although that would depend on your point of view.

He slides past the trolley and stands behind the waiter, his hands clasped behind his back. 'Haven't I seen you before?' He has a pleasant voice – cultured and musical – hinting at someone who is easily moved to laughter. 'George, isn't it?' He'd read the name on the waiter's lapel badge as he stepped into the lift.

'Yes, sir.' George has a high-pitched voice, somewhat nasal in tone. 'I have been working here since two years.'

Since two years, the guest notes.

Well mannered and beautifully trained, George begins to turn to his interrogator.

'Did we miss our floor?' the guest says, to redirect his attention.

George glances at the floor indicator. 'No, sir,' he says. 'Four more to go.' He pronounces the word 'four' as 'foor', which means the name on his lapel badge has been anglicised. But the accent is hard to place. Slavic, maybe? Or Portuguese? They can be oddly difficult to distinguish.

'Ah, here we are,' the guest says, as if he is delighted by their timely arrival.

He watches George rattling the trolley over the lift door sill, turns sharp right as George turns left, returning when he hears the trolley rattle around the corner into the west corridor. He glides like a shadow after the waiter, ducking into the fire escape stairwell at the end of the lift bank. Easing the door open a crack, he has a good line of sight to room 612, the first door at the end of the west corridor, where the waiter is headed.

George knocks and announces, 'Room service, Mister King.'

The door opens. A glimpse of King's grey head, then George rolls the trolley inside. A minute later, the room door opens again, and a rather flustered George exits, apologising – apparently not for the first time – promising to return in two minutes. Mr King must have noticed the absence of a wine glass.

The man allows the fire escape door to close under its own weight and raises his left hand from which hangs, inverted like a bell, Mr King's glass, filched from the trolley. He flicks his nail against the good crystal, and it rings a perfect middle-E.

George makes his way back to the lift, muttering, and the man waits until he hears the lift doors open, then close. George is an optimist – it will take him at *least* four minutes to make the journey to the kitchen and back – even so, there's no time to waste.

The man sets the timer on his watch, walks swiftly to Mr King's door, and knocks softly. Standing erect, holding the glass upright by its base in his left hand, he tucks his right hand, waiter-style, in the small of his back.

'Your wine glass, Mister King,' the man says, in a passable imitation of the waiter.

A rumble of noise from within: the toilet flush. Then: 'Wait a minute.'

King is wearing a white bathrobe as he opens the door. He looks puzzled to see a man dressed in overcoat and hat, holding a wine glass in one hand.

The man offers King the glass with a courteous bow, and King accepts it, as he'd known he would.

The assassin swings his right hand from behind his back and aims a semi-automatic pistol at Mr King's chest. The gun coughs, twice, and as King staggers back into the room, the gunman steps inside, closes the door, and shoots his victim in the face. King falls forward and the man moves nimbly aside; a second shot to the back of the head ensures the job is done.

He removes the suppressor from the pistol and pockets both items inside his overcoat, then takes out a mobile phone, clicks off a few photographs of the body, sends them, and turns the room thermostat up to its highest setting. His phone buzzes: payment made, contract completed. He retrieves the glass, happily still intact, and takes a napkin from the table. Suddenly ravenous, he checks under the dome on the service trolley. What he sees disappoints him: bland fried food in prodigious quantity – and the wine isn't up to much, either. His background checks had King pegged as something of an epicure but apparently he had been more gourm*and* than gourm*et*.

The assassin covers the food again and wipes the dome for prints, then wraps the glass in the napkin and slides it into the flap pocket of his overcoat – no sense in making it easy for investigators to connect the affable gentleman in the lift to Mr King's mysteriously truant wine glass.

He checks the corridor through the peephole before opening the door, hooking the Do Not Disturb sign from the door handle, and heads for the fire escape, not wanting to bump into George on his return journey. As the fire escape door closes behind him, he stops the timer. All done in under ninety seconds.

Chapter 3

RICK TURNER WAS GETTING READY to say his goodbyes and head for home when his phone buzzed again.

The caller introduced himself as Detective Inspector Irons from MIT4, one of the major investigation teams that worked in rotation on serious crimes across London. 'Am I talking to DS Turner?'

'You are. What can I do for you?' he yelled over the noise.

'Bad news, I'm afraid,' Irons said, then something Rick couldn't quite hear; it sounded like 'The King is dead,' and for a second, he thought it was another wind-up. But DS Stott was holding forth to a group of young detectives a little way off, apparently oblivious, and no one else seemed to be watching for his reaction.

Rick was standing shoulder to shoulder with an older detective who was regaling a couple of admin staff with a story about five cops trying and failing to handcuff a one-armed druggie off his head on PCP.

Rick turned away, stuck a finger in his right ear and pressed the phone to his left. 'Say again?'

'I said we've got a DB,' Irons repeated. 'Looks like Austin King.'

King dead? No.

'How?'

'Shot.'

Jesus. The noise of the bar seemed suddenly overwhelmed by the rush of blood in his ears.

'Looks like a professional hit,' Irons continued.

'Where?'

'The Royal Somerset on the Strand.'

Rick knew it: an ex-mansion house, recently converted to a high-end hotel.

'You said "looks like". Don't you have a positive ID?'

'It's his room, but the face is a bit of a mess,' the inspector said. 'We're checking his prints. We do know that King ordered room service shortly before he was found, and the waiter who delivered the order says a guest rode up in the lift with him. He had to go back to the kitchen for a wine glass he *swears* he'd put on the tray before heading up.'

'The "guest" swiped it,' Rick said. 'King was expecting the knock, so he didn't bother to check before opening up.'

'That's the way I see it,' Irons agreed. 'I've requested CCTV recordings, the Crime Scene Unit is already searching the lift for trace, and the pathologist is on his way.'

'I'm in Richmond, right now.' Rick checked his watch: seven-forty-five, traffic shouldn't be too bad. 'I can be there in forty minutes – an hour, at the most.'

'Okay,' the inspector said. 'We're rounding up everyone who interacted with King at the hotel as we speak.'

'Can you hold off interviewing them till I get there?'

'Sure. I won't be here, but I'll let my team know to expect you.'

Rick ended the call and the noise swelled around him again. He'd need to let Ghosh know, but until he was sure that King really was the victim, the others might as well enjoy their celebrations.

'You all right, mate?' The yarn-spinning detective was staring at him with some concern.

'Gotta go.' Rick was already looking for the quickest route out, but he only managed to get a few feet towards the exit when he was confronted by DS Stott.

'You can't be leaving already, mate,' Stott bellowed over the clamour of voices and laughter.

'Something came up,' Rick said.

'What could be more important than this?'

Rick hesitated, and Stott squinted at him. 'Wassup, son?'

If he was sober, Rick might have taken Jim Stott aside and told him – even have asked for his advice – but drunk, Stott was not a man to share confidences with.

'Nothing. I'll see you in the morning, Jim,' Rick said.

'Nah, nah, nah . . . You finished your pint. I'm just going for one—' He waved in the general direction of the bar. 'Lemme getchoo another.'

Slurring, and it's not even eight o'clock.

'Have one for me, Sarge,' Rick said. 'I've really got to go.'

Stott wasn't having that. He flung his left arm over Rick's shoulder in an action that was meant to look friendly, but he was already tightening it into a headlock. Rick acted without thinking, bringing his right arm up, under Stott's grip, squeezing the sergeant's palm with his right hand as his left held the wrist. With his right elbow now at Stott's chest height, Rick turned his whole body, ducking free of the lock.

Off balance, Stott barged into someone's back. Beer was spilled and a couple of shouts went up. Rick held the wrist lock just long enough to prevent Stott from pitching headfirst through the crush of bodies, and as he released it, he put a steadying hand on the sergeant's shoulder.

Heads were turning, so Rick pasted a smile on his face and shouted, 'Oopsy, Sarge – I've got you! Someone make sure Stotty gets home safe, eh?'

He was out of the door before Stott's addled brain could work out exactly what had just happened.

The voice in his head said, *Would it have killed you to have one drink with him?*

Sam, the voice of reason.

Probably not, Sam, Rick thought. *Probably not.*

There again, the last time Rick saw his brother, he'd watched Sam calmly slide a knife into the heart of an unconscious man, so who was he to talk?

Chapter 4

THE HOTEL MANAGEMENT HAD QUIETLY cleared the rooms on the sixth floor, upgrading the occupants from executive to premier standard and arranging to have their belongings packed and moved with minimum fuss and maximum discretion. Nevertheless, Rick Turner heard a hum of conversation as he stepped out of the lift. A constable in uniform was waiting to shepherd disorientated guests and hopeful journalists back inside, but he gave way when Rick showed his warrant card and announced that he was expected. The lift car in which the suspect had ridden with the waiter stood open, and fully kitted CSIs were busily fingerprinting its burnished bronze interior. Rick knew that they would already have vacuumed every inch of it with even greater rigour than the hotel's punctilious cleaning staff in the hope of gathering tell-tale traces of the killer.

The fire escape door was propped open, as was the door to 612, and he noted grey-black smudges of fingerprint powder on the key touch-points of both. Rick registered mechanically the dull metallic scent of blood in the air. The west corridor was cordoned off with scene tape, and he wouldn't be allowed inside the room until the CSIs were done, but he had a good line of sight to 612 where one CSI, looking like a curled white grub in his Tyvek coveralls and mask, knelt with his back to Rick, blocking his view of the interior.

A detective sergeant from MIT4 was hovering at the edge of the tape, and he turned on hearing Rick's name.

He was winter-pale, despite the seven days of unseasonably warm October sunshine they'd just had, and Rick guessed that he was one of the unlucky types who copped more than their fair share of night duty.

They shook hands and Rick said, 'Pathologist been, yet?'

The sergeant grunted. 'Been, stated the bleedin' obvious, took a few snaps for his memoirs, and left the CSIs to it.'

Rick nodded. Obvious or not, the law required a qualified doctor to pronounce life extinct. The CSIs would process the body as far as possible before they shifted it – too much evidence could be lost in lifting and bagging it.

The sergeant eyed him curiously. 'This must be a sickener for you. Wasn't King your star witness?'

Rick looked into the sergeant's face. It was broad and apparently innocent of all consciousness that a question relating to a sensitive prosecution on the brink of trial might be impertinent. His bland expression might even fool some into thinking he was a little slow, but his small dark eyes were sharp and inquisitive, and Rick wasn't fooled.

'I expect we'll manage,' he said, switching his gaze to the huddled figure collecting evidence in the doorway of the murder scene.

The CSI suddenly stood and backed into the corridor, revealing the body lying face down just inside the doorway. There was a lot of blood; the man's white bathrobe was steeped in it, and more of it pooled on the plush grey carpet around him. In the room beyond, Rick glimpsed two more CSIs bagging evidence and speaking in low murmurs.

'Do we know if it's King, yet?'

'It's him all right,' the sergeant said. 'Fingerprint results came through just before you got here.'

Rick stared gloomily through the doorway. King was Unwin's right-hand man – so hardly a friendly witness – but since there was no chance that Unwin would take the stand, King had been the closest they would get to questioning the man himself. The prosecution barrister's case relied heavily on the questions he'd planned to fire at King as Unwin's surrogate. Questions that had been carefully worded to construct the narrative around Unwin's criminal empire. It wouldn't have mattered if he'd lied – the jury would draw their own conclusions.

Rick stared at the mess inside the doorway of 612 and felt a familiar chill, recalling another body in a hotel room almost eighteen months earlier, and his conflicting sense of dread and longing as he'd braced himself to look at that other scene.

THEN

Chapter 5

Eighteen months earlier

A COLD AND SHOWERY APRIL EVENING, still light at eight p.m., and Rick Turner was off duty. Even so, he turned up uninvited, just as he'd turned up uninvited to many other suspicious deaths since becoming a detective. He'd made excuses and lied to gain access to scenes, and if that failed, he'd found ways to steal a look at the body in a mortuary, or via the investigating teams' records. When he was challenged – and he had been, several times – he'd claimed crossed wires, snafus at the Force Control Room – anything that would keep him the right side of a disciplinary sanction.

Rick showed his warrant card to the constable taking names at the hotel room door.

The pathologist, dressed in a beautifully tailored tuxedo, stood at the entrance to the en-suite bathroom and he turned at the sound of Rick's voice.

Rumour was that in his younger years Dr Pritchard had been quite the heartbreaker. But age and alcohol had taken its toll and with his staring eyes, untamed brows and boozer's nose he would be a fair double for a gargoyle at Westminster Abbey.

'Sergeant Turner,' he said, his expression sour. '*Must* you turn up to every sudden death like a sin-eater at a wake?'

This was an exaggeration – it wasn't *every* sudden death – Rick's interest lay solely in white, male victims, aged mid-twenties to thirties.

Aware that he was here under sufferance, Rick answered with a civil: 'Dr Pritchard.' He made a quick visual sweep of the hotel room. No signs of disturbance; no tell-tale odours. So the body was fresh, and the mode of death perhaps gentler and less bloody than he had feared.

'I suppose you'll want a squint at him?'

'If you wouldn't mind,' Rick said, choosing his words carefully. This wasn't his case, and he might have to account for anything he said if his inappropriate presence came to the attention of his superiors.

'Oh, I *mind*,' Pritchard grumbled. 'I mind being dragged out of a Rotary Club bash I've been looking forward to for months. I *mind* letting down the fellow Rotarians to whom I promised an after-dinner speech. But nobody seems to care what I *mind*.'

Rick suspected that the pathologist was more disgruntled by the fact that he had been called away from an evening of good food and a captive audience, than by a genuine concern for having let anyone down. But he knew better than to comment, and instead gave the pathologist a sympathetic look.

'Must be some sort of death obsession,' Pritchard muttered.

Rick accepted this dark pronouncement with a tilt of his head. Pritchard had a point: no matter how many times Rick told himself that he was being unprofessional, that what he was doing was madness, he could never let an opportunity pass.

Finally, shaking his head, Dr Pritchard stood aside.

Rick hesitated, his heart thumping painfully in his chest. *What if this is it? What if it's him? Do I really want to know? Can I live with knowing that he's dead?*

In truth, he couldn't have answered that last question if he'd had a gun to his head.

You can do this, he chivvied himself. *It's just another body.* But there again, it might not be. It might be that of all the sudden deaths he'd attended like some thrill-seeking rubbernecker, this body really was Sam, his brother, dead.

Pritchard vented an irritated snort at the delay, and Rick realised that he couldn't bear *not* knowing. So he took a breath and peered inside the small hotel bathroom.

He swallowed a gasp of relief.

Not Sam. He stared at the corpse a moment longer. *It's not Sam.*

Rick let his breath go slowly, keeping his shoulders squared, and forced himself to assess the scene.

The tub was sunk into a marble-tile surround, creating a shelf, on which lay a steel-barrelled pen. A small towel was folded at one end of the tub, as though the dead man had been leaning back against it, sitting up to read. A second towel, now siphoning water from the bath, was draped over the side. The man's left arm was flung out over the tiled rim, and a broadsheet he'd been reading had dropped to the tiles; the distinctive pink sheets identifying it as the *Financial Times*. The corpse was partially submerged, his eyes wide open.

'Do we have a name?' he'd asked, looking at the body to avoid Pritchard's busy gaze.

'The hotel has him registered as Charlie Haskins.'

'Who was he?'

The pathologist considered the remains. 'Nobody.'

'Nobodies die in bar fights, or crossing the road,' Rick said, stepping back into the main room. 'They fall downstairs; they take a dive off a hotel balcony because they're so drunk they forget which way is up and which is down. Nobodies do *not* die after a slip in a bath in a five-star hotel, circling rising stocks in the *Financial Times*.'

The pathologist shot out his lower lip. 'Did you see the empty wine glass by his bedside?'

Rick nodded.

'And did you happen to notice how much was in it?'

The glass was empty, and Rick said so.

'Suggesting he'd had a drink. Maybe one too many.'

'I don't see a bottle anywhere.'

'Well, perhaps it's in the fridge,' the pathologist said with testy pragmatism.

'So, you think he drowned?'

The doctor gave him a disparaging look. 'When will you police learn that the science of forensic pathology requires a post-mortem examination to establish cause of death?'

Rick was on the point of apologising and quietly withdrawing, but the great man turned to the body and began to expound: 'Empty wine glass. No blood. No signs of struggle . . .' He paused and inclined his head as if conceding a point. 'He is, clearly, under water . . . But there is a definite depression in the region of his right temporal lobe.' He tapped the side of his own head, just above his right ear, and shot Rick a quick, humorous glance.

'Note the bath towel.' He jerked his chin towards the sopping towel trailing over the side of the bath. 'There's a towel rail on the wall above the taps.'

Rick edged forward again but Pritchard waved him away.

'Take my word for it,' he said. 'The rail . . . is empty. Like the wine glass,' he added with heavy emphasis.

Rick quirked his eyebrows in question and Pritchard gave another impatient snort.

'Mr Haskins drinks his fill, decides – somewhat intoxicated – to take a bath, but as he stands to get out, he slips, cracks his head on the deplorably sharp edge of the tile bath surround, slides under the water—' he pursed his lips in an insincere gesture of regret '—and stays there.'

Rick regarded him with quiet interest. 'Alternative scenario: someone cracked Haskins over the head with the wine bottle, posed him in the bath, and took the murder weapon away.'

Chapter 6

THE CAUSE OF DEATH WAS DROWNING. Two months after Rick had gate-crashed the death scene, he'd attended Haskins's inquest – also uninvited. Dr Pritchard testified that Haskins had suffered a depressed fracture of the temporal lobe during his slip-fall in the hotel bath, had lost consciousness, and slipped under the bath water. His blood alcohol was virtually zero when he died – Pritchard had been wrong about him being drunk – but Mr Haskins had worked a long day and tiredness might have been a factor. He'd also had a slight ear infection at the time of his death, which Pritchard said might have resulted in dizziness. The coroner ruled Charlie Haskins's death a tragic accident.

Rick tried to let it go – he really did. Working punishing shift rotations as well as covering for staff absences, he could do without the extra work. But he kept coming back to that little tableau in the hotel bathroom: the dead man, his arm flung out, the towel draped over the edge of the bath, wet and sagging, seeping water onto the floor. It reminded him of a painting – he didn't know what – something he'd seen on TV maybe; one of the arts programmes Jess liked so much. It looked dramatic – artistic, even – and Rick had attended enough sudden deaths to know that mostly they were sad, ugly, and often sordid. There was nothing tangible, nothing to suggest that anyone else had been involved, but it troubled Rick, and he couldn't let it pass.

The detective tasked to investigate Haskins's death would not be pleased to learn that someone was snouting around his nicely boxed-off case, so Rick had to base his investigation on information gathered from the public domain.

The coroner had touched upon Haskins's finances at the inquest. As a senior adviser for one of the city's big wealth management firms, the accountant's client list included successful business types, footballers, TV celebrities, an artist, bankers – even an earl – yet his earnings didn't seem a true reflection of his status.

Rick couldn't approach Haskins's old firm in an official capacity, but Haskins's acrimonious divorce had been touched upon by the coroner and excluded as irrelevant to the circumstances of his death. Local news sites had reported on his arrest for breach of the peace eighteen months earlier and his divorce had followed soon after. Up to that point, he'd broken no rules and spoken to no one directly, relying on the sad truth that death lays bare a man's life. Contacting Haskins's ex-wife would take him over the line, but his inquiries would stall without details of Haskins's business and finances, so Rick went in search of Ms Haskins.

She'd kept the marital name, which helped. *Name-dropping her ex's glittering client list to business associates must have been worth the pain*, Sam whispered in his ear. Rick was just grateful he didn't need to access the Police National Computer to find her – that would be illegal, and could get him sacked.

Ms Haskins was eager to talk. She told him that her ex had rented a flat while the divorce went through. She smelled a rat when he vanished the day after she'd signed the consent order that would effectively sever their financial affairs permanently and irrevocably.

Always suspicious of his comparatively meagre declared earnings, Ms Haskins had immediately hired a private investigator.

The PI, a man named Wilson, had traced Haskins to a tiny studio flat in Harlesden, paid for on a fifteen-year mortgage. Two months after the divorce settlement, he'd bought the rest of the occupants out and purchased the leases. By the time he'd died, Charlie Haskins owned the entire house and work was well under way to convert it back to a single dwelling with a loft extension.

It crossed Rick's mind that knowing all of this, Ms Haskins might have wanted her ex-husband dead, but armed with the evidence the PI had gathered, she was certain that her challenge to the divorce court would succeed – she even gave Rick her divorce lawyer's contact details.

So, Charlie Haskins had been hiding money – a lot of it. And if the PI had uncovered Haskins's illegal accounting, he might have exposed the accountant's clients to scrutiny as well. In Rick's experience, people with wealth and power did not like exposure. Was that what had got him killed?

Rick couldn't talk to the solicitor without first telling his boss about his highly irregular off-the-books inquiries, and all he had right now was a divorcee hiding assets from his embittered ex-wife. He wouldn't risk losing his chance at reopening the inquiry into Haskins's death on so slight a premise. So he'd smiled and thanked Ms Haskins, tilted his head on one side and said, 'You wouldn't happen to have the PI's address, would you?'

Chapter 7

THE PI'S OFFICE WAS ABOVE A TINY Portuguese coffee shop in Old Compton Street. Rick buzzed but got no answer. He tried ringing the mobile number Ms Haskins had given him, but it went straight to voicemail.

Access was via a door to the right of the coffee shop; three doorbells, one for each floor, he guessed: PRW Investigators, a chartered accountant, and a third bell with no name on the buzzer. He bought a coffee and hung around. Forty minutes later, a woman came out, and he caught the door before it closed, flashing her a winsome grin. 'Mr Wilson about?'

'How would I know?' she'd answered with a cold look. 'I'm not his secretary.' He thought himself lucky that she didn't slam the door on his fingers.

Wilson's place was locked up as tight as a drum. Rick peered through the frosted glass at the top of the door, cupping his hands to reduce the glare, but could only make out a few blurred shadows. Back downstairs, a few months' worth of mail was stacked on top of the meter cupboard in the communal hallway.

Returning to the coffee shop, he asked for the manager.

The boss was a small, clean-shaven man in his mid-forties.

Kitted out in white T-shirt and trousers, he came to the counter wiping his hands on a pristine towel.

Rick flashed his warrant card. 'Can't get an answer at Mr Wilson's office,' he said.

Suspicion flashed across the man's face. 'Show me card again,' he said.

This time, Rick held it up next to his face, knowing that this guy would not forget Sergeant Turner snooping around asking questions. Still, he needed to see this through to the end – whatever that might be.

Finally, the manager nodded, and Rick pocketed his ID.

Now, he seemed more outraged than suspicious. 'How you don't know Mr Wilson is dead?' he demanded.

Rick's heart slowed. 'What happened?'

'A car! Ran him down. Right in front of here.' He gestured angrily, as though the violence of Wilson's death were a personal insult.

'When?'

'Four months ago. Hit-and-run – how you don't *know* this?' the manager repeated.

Rick shook his head, mumbled, 'Different investigation, sir.' He asked for the name and number of the landlord, thinking, *How the hell didn't we know? Wilson was investigating Haskins, now both men are dead and nobody made the connection?*

Forty minutes after that, he was standing outside Wilson's widow's flat; the ground floor of a house in Shepherd's Bush.

Answering the door, Mrs Wilson checked his ID then looked past him as if half-hoping to see her husband lingering in his shadow. A dark-haired, tousled boy of seven or eight clung to her legs, staring up at Rick with solemn brown eyes. She introduced the child as Ethan.

'Say hello to Sergeant Turner.'

The child detached himself from his mother and stamped through to the kitchen. They followed him and she sent the scowling child to play in the back yard – a paved area of no more than twenty feet square, but with a small table and chairs and a few plant pots brimming with spring flowers. She watched her son through the patio doors for a few seconds, her shoulders slumped, then she seemed to gather herself, straightening to her full height and turning to face Rick.

'Why did you want to speak to my—' Her mouth twisted – clearly the word 'husband' had too many emotional connections, and she stammered. 'To Kirk?'

'He was investigating a person of interest in a case I'm working on,' Rick said carefully.

'Well, that would be in his work files – he didn't keep them at home.' She glanced forlornly at her tiny kitchen and her hand went to a heart-shaped locket around her neck. 'No room, you see.'

She seemed to drift off for a moment, and Rick asked, 'Your husband's name was Kirk?'

A frown creased her forehead, and he realised his mistake – as a cop investigating the case, he should have known her husband's first name. 'Only I thought – seeing the firm's name is "PRW Investigations", they would be his initials?' he hurried on.

'No, PRW was Peter Woodcroft – he owned the agency before. He employed Kirk, and when he retired, Kirk bought the business. Said it would help, not having his actual name over the door.' Her eyes began to brim, and she dashed the tears away impatiently. 'Look – why don't I give you the keys? You can take a look, bring back the mail. There's probably bills I should've paid ages ago.'

It didn't take long. Rick gloved up and took a photo log on his mobile every step of the way from the front door through to his search of the filing cabinets. The desktop computer was gone, leaving only the mouse mat and a slightly thinner layer of dust where it had sat. There was no sign of the laptop Mrs Wilson said her husband had always taken with him to work, nor the backpack he carried it in. There were high-definition photos in some of the files, but no camera. There was also a gap in the filing cabinet labelled "A–N" where Rick would have expected to find Haskins's file.

An hour later, Rick was back in Mrs Wilson's kitchen, having left the box of mail in her hallway. The boy sat at the table, slowly working his way through fish fingers and chips. He chewed thoughtfully, eyeing Rick between each bite.

Rick scrolled through the images he'd taken, and Mrs Wilson's consternation grew with each shot. 'The police didn't ask to see the office,' she'd said, staring at the empty desk. 'I'd imagined everything would be as he left it.'

'So, you've no idea what had happened to the computer?'

'Not a clue. And the laptop and backpack definitely weren't among his—' she glanced at Ethan '—personal effects?'

The boy's brows gathered briefly, and he gazed from his mother to Rick.

Rick felt a tightening knot in his stomach. 'Did Kirk back up his files?'

'I – I don't know.'

'Maybe on the Cloud?'

'No – I'm sure of that – he didn't trust Cloud security.'

'How about memory sticks? External hard drives?'

She brightened. 'Yes – he was looking them up online before—' Another quick look at her son. He seemed to be concentrating on spearing peas on one prong of his fork, and Mrs Wilson gave Rick a nervous smile. 'I suppose he *might* have bought one, but I didn't see it.'

Rick took a breath. 'I'm afraid there was no electronic equipment in his office.'

'Oh!'

'Mrs Wilson?'

'Can we, um . . .' She stood and led him through to the hallway.

'Mum . . .'

'Finish your dinner, love,' she said, shutting the kitchen door after her.

She edged Rick a little further down the narrow hallway. 'The house was broken into the day Kirk – the day of the accident,' she murmured. 'The police came and asked me to come and – you know, make sure it was – was him.

'They dropped me at home, after. But as soon as I opened the front door, I could see something wasn't right. The doors were open, and I could feel a draught.' Her eyes widened, remembering. 'The place had been turned upside down. The officer who brought me back thought we must have disturbed them, but they'd had a good rummage – emptied the wardrobes and drawers—'

'Did they take much?'

She shook her head. 'Just a couple of credit cards, my ancient iPad, a Sonos player.'

'Did Kirk have a safety deposit box?'

'No . . .' She frowned. 'At least, I don't think so.'

'Maybe a storage facility for old files?'

'I don't know – but if he did, he would keep receipts.'

'And they would be at his office?'

'Like I said, he didn't keep any of that stuff here.' She paused, reading his face. 'There were no receipts?'

'Not unless there are some in the letters I brought back.'

'Why are you asking all these questions?' she asked suddenly.

'Like I said – your husband was investigating—'

'Don't do that, Sergeant Turner. Don't assume I'll swallow whatever guff you come up with. If you think that Kirk's investigation got him—' She swerved away from the word 'killed', and said instead, 'That I lost my husband – that Ethan lost his *father* because of this "case" you're working on – I think I've a right to know.'

'Mum, why are you shouting?'

The boy was standing in the kitchen doorway, his brown eyes wide and frightened, but fearful or not, his small hands bunched into fists, ready to defend his mother.

'I'm not, shouting, sweetie, I was just making a point, very firmly, that's all. Why don't you get a Petit Filous from the fridge, and I'll be through in a minute.'

He flushed. 'I'm not a *baby*.'

'I know, love,' she'd said. 'But you're not a grown-up, either, and this is grown-up stuff. Just go back in the kitchen and close the door.'

He folded his arms. 'NO.'

'Ethan Wilson!'

He ignored his mother and fixed his gaze on Rick. 'Are you going to find who killed my dad?'

Alarmed, Mrs Wilson said, 'Nobody *killed* your dad.'

'Well, *somebody* was driving the car.'

'Yes, but it was an accident. Nobody . . . Daddy wasn't—' She'd floundered, looking to Rick for support he couldn't, in all conscience, give. Her face twisted in concern, and her hand went again to the little locket around her neck.

'My dad was careful when he crossed the road,' Ethan told Rick. 'Dad taught *me* to cross the road,' he added, puffing his little chest out, 'and he *always* said you have to keep your wicks about you—'

'Wits, darling – keep your wits about you.'

'What*ever*. What I'm saying is, Dad wasn't STUPID. He could cross the road without getting KNOCKED DOWN.' Now Ethan was shouting, craning his neck to look up at Rick. 'So, ARE you GOING to CATCH him?'

Rick crouched so that he could look the boy in the eye. 'I don't know, Ethan,' he said quietly. 'I don't have much to go on, and the other police who investigated said it was an accident. But I am going to try to find out what really happened.'

The boy threw his mother a triumphant look. 'I TOLD you, Mum. Those police was *hopeless*. They didn't even look at Dad's cases.'

'*Sergeant*,' Mrs Wilson said, sharply. 'Stop filling his head with nonsense. He has a childish notion he can catch the coward who did this and you're encouraging him.'

'I'm NOT childish!' Ethan thundered.

'No, Ethan, you're not,' Rick said. 'But you *are* a child, and your mum is right – it's my job to catch criminals, not yours. Look . . .' He settled back on his heels, wondering if he'd regret what he was about to say, but understanding on a visceral level this child's need to seek justice for his father's death. 'How about we make a deal?'

Ethan narrowed his eyes, waiting.

'*You* let me investigate, and *I* tell you what I find out?'

A flash of excitement flared in Ethan's eyes. 'Like a briefing?'

'Not exactly. You see, I have to swear an oath not to tell anyone things about an investigation while I'm actually doing it – even other police officers, if they're not on my team – because if I do, it might mess things up. And the law says if you mess up an investigation, you can't take the bad people to court, even if you're *sure* they've committed a crime.'

The stubborn set of the boy's mouth returned, and he looked up at his mother for corroboration. 'It's true, love,' she said.

Ethan drooped physically.

'But if I *do* find something,' Rick went on, 'I could call round – if your mum says it's okay – and we could have a special signal so you know if things are going good.' He looked up at Mrs Wilson.

'I don't know . . .' she said. 'What makes you so sure you *need* to investigate?'

The boy slapped his forehead. 'Mu-um! The baddies stole Dad's *stuff*. His big computer *and* his laptop. They got his *case files*. Dad said his case files were Top Secret, and somebody *got* them.'

'You little spy!' she exclaimed, a hint of merriment in her eyes. 'You were earwigging the whole time!'

'I *wasn't*.' He seemed offended by the accusation. 'But you never tell me *anything*. I didn't even know they'd broke in and took all our stuff.'

She raised a finger and opened her mouth to tell him off, but suddenly her face softened and with a look of wonder that shed months of worry and tension from her face, she said, 'You know, they didn't get *everything*.'

'What, Mum?' Ethan demanded. '*What* didn't they get?'

She took a breath, one hand resting lightly on her chest as though to still her heart.

Ethan shifted impatiently, and Rick gave a warning shake of his head, almost afraid that she would change her mind and shut down again. Ethan responded by putting his hand over his mouth and Rick had to turn away to cover a smile.

'Would Kirk's mobile phone be of any use?' she asked at last.

Rick shot to his feet. 'You have Kirk's mobile phone?' *Why hadn't she handed it over to the police?*

'It wasn't in his personal effects when I went to the hospital,' she said, forestalling his question. 'But the accident investigators found it later.' She meant the CSIs, but the police would want to keep from the grieving wife the fact that they'd had to scrape up bits of human tissue from a thirty-yard track at the scene. 'They returned it after the inquest.'

Rick wondered if he'd missed something. 'It was used in evidence?'

'No.' She held his gaze, and he read in the widow's steady, calm look that she understood that this had been a serious oversight in the inquiry into her husband's death.

No one thought to access the phone? Rick thought. Surely, the lead investigator would want to satisfy his own curiosity about what the PI had been investigating? Then he remembered Dr Pritchard's pronouncement that Charlie Haskins was 'nobody'.

Hate to remind you, little bruv, Sam's voice whispered in his ear. *But it was* you *who said, 'Nobodies die crossing the road.'*

Rick stole a guilty glance at Mrs Wilson. She was fully occupied, rummaging through a small cabinet near the front door. A moment later, she handed him a smartphone, still in an evidence bag. 'I'm afraid it's broken.'

The screen was cracked. But there was broken, and then there was broken. If the SIM was intact, they could get a list of contacts, and if the gubbins of the phone was unharmed, the techs might get a whole lot more.

But Rick was in the widow's home without official sanction, investigating – what? In all honesty, he didn't know exactly. And to make things worse, his unofficial presence meant that CSIs, tech support and data recovery specialists were way beyond his reach.

'I don't suppose you could try turning it on . . .?' he heard himself say.

'It won't work,' she said, dismayed.

'Perhaps the battery's just flat,' Rick suggested.

'I'll get your charger, Mum.' Ethan bounded off and was back moments later, handing the lead shyly to Rick.

Attached to the mains, the screen sprang to life, and Rick gently slid a finger over an intact section. 'It's asking for a PIN,' he said. 'You wouldn't happen to—'

'Try 1512,' Mrs Wilson interrupted.

'That's my birthday!' Ethan exclaimed.

She ruffled the boy's curls. 'He said he needed a number he would never forget.'

Ethan gulped and looked down, fighting back tears.

'I'm in,' Rick said, to distract the child from his misery. It did the trick: the boy danced on his tiptoes, trying to steal a glimpse, until his mother reminded him that Sergeant Turner had to keep his investigation private and confidential.

Recent calls were accessible, which was a good start. A slew of texts, many from disgruntled clients demanding to know if progress had been made with their inquiries.

He opened the photo gallery. The first image was a group of four men, Thomas Unwin standing at the centre. Rick recognised him immediately; Unwin had been notorious for as long as Rick had been a cop.

He turned the phone to show Mrs Wilson. 'Do you know any of these men?'

She shook her head. 'But I think you do.'

He didn't answer. Scrolling through a few more pictures, it was clear that the men were unaware of the photographer, so these must be covert surveillance photos.

'Is it important?' Mrs Wilson prompted.

'I think it could be,' he said, hearing the cautious tone in his voice, although he knew he'd hit the jackpot.

NOW

Chapter 8

Sunday night

THOMAS UNWIN LAY IN THE TOP BUNK of his small cell, staring at the dark rectangle of its barred window, his phone to his ear as he listened to Callum Mounsey, his solicitor. Few slept well here – least of all those on remand – and the wing was alive with the restless energy of the shut-in. Muttered conversations, occasional groans, a shout of terror from someone awakened by a nightmare, and somewhere down the landing a recent admission sobbed on and on, like a child unconsoled.

Unwin had spent seven months in the squalor of this cell; by government decree, it should be called a 'room', but to the inmates and the screws, it was a cell or a cage. His mobile phone had been smuggled in by one of the screws. Unwin expected privacy and the freedom to make calls whenever the need arose, so the shared phone on the wing was out of the question.

Only his mother could have read in Unwin's face the shock and anger he felt hearing of Austin King's murder.

'Who?' he said.

'No one has claimed responsibility,' Mounsey said, with the careful diction and cautious language of a lawyer.

'That's not what I asked.'

'Unknown,' Mounsey replied, and Unwin heard a rasp in that one word which said, *I am not one of your thugs – do not test me.*

Unwin's mind raced: who would gain from his accountant's death? Not the cops, for sure. A rival? Well, if any one of them thought that killing his accountant would stop Unwin operating his business inside these four walls, they were in for a rude awakening. Hadn't he done just that, over the last two-hundred-plus days?

But if they knew he was getting out, then Austin's death would certainly slow him down – perhaps even enough to give an enemy the edge they would need to gain territory and power.

'Who would know I'm about to get a . . . *room upgrade,*' he asked, falling into coded wording out of habit.

Mounsey hesitated, gave a polite cough. 'I really couldn't speculate.'

'Find out,' Unwin said. 'Those bastards just tried to cut off my right hand – there's got to be a reason.'

'I would have thought an internecine conflict would be the first avenue to explore.'

'If that means they're after my turf – thanks, I'd already worked that one out. But any fool would know I'm going to be kept busy with the courts for the foreseeable. King's testimony would've taken a week – more if I told him to take it slow. So, someone must've heard about my . . . contingency plans. I want to know who.'

'Ah,' Mounsey said. 'I'm afraid news of your impending release has been rather widely broadcast.'

'By who?' He injected a sliver of ice into his voice.

'Um,' the solicitor said, 'I fear that Mrs Unwin has been perhaps a little—' another cough '—precipitate in making arrangements for your return home.'

Unwin closed his eyes and cursed softly; Zoe never could resist the chance to throw a party. This time, her passion for celebration might just have crashed the biggest deal of his career – *and* got his lieutenant killed. He would have words with his wife about this, and there would be consequences, but for now, he needed to focus on his immediate situation.

He ran his fingers through his hair. The wing barber had done a fair job, and it would pass muster in court, but it certainly wasn't up to Joe & Co, his favourite Soho barber.

'Did King make the transfer?'

'The . . .?'

He wanted to reach down the phone and grab the solicitor by his scrawny throat. 'The *transfer* – for the shipment,' he said between gritted teeth.

'Payment isn't due till ten this morning, so I wouldn't have thought so.'

Shit. With all eyes on him, Unwin had given direct control of money for the purchase to Austin King, and it wouldn't be a simple task to take back that control. If King hadn't completed the transaction, things could get complicated.

'Maybe he scheduled the payment to send automatically,' Unwin said, knowing it sounded like wishful thinking.

'It's *possible . . .*' Mounsey said, in a tone Unwin sometimes used himself to soothe Zoe's anxieties; a tone that said, *King would have to be a rank amateur to automate an illegal payment on an illegal shipment to the unreliable and dangerous men who'd organised it.*

'Well, find out,' Unwin said, roughly. 'But be subtle,' he warned. 'I don't want to spook the buyers.'

'Of course.' Mounsey seemed shocked that his client felt the need to say it.

'So,' Unwin said. 'The hit – anyone spring to mind?'

A slight movement behind the modesty panel at the end of the cell caught his eye: Laser, his cellmate, the top of his head just visible.

'Wait.' He craned to look over the edge of the bunk to check what the kid was up to behind the toilet partition.

Laser – named, not for his burning intellect, but for his surname, Lasovsky – was wedged into the farthest corner of the cubicle, between the tiled wall and the toilet bowl, knees, elbows, shoulders and bony wrists slotted together at impossible angles. He wore earplugs connected to a CD player on the floor in front of him, and Unwin could hear the tinny rasp of heavy rock playing at full volume. Tears seeped from under his eyelashes, but he kept his eyes shut tight.

Unwin leaned back. 'Go ahead.'

'I suppose the Algerian rabble has been making somewhat of a nuisance of itself . . .' the lawyer mused.

Unwin had businesses all over London – north and south of the river – but the Peckham-based Algerian gang had raided one of his garages in the borough shortly after he was banged up and had disrupted normal operations at one of his clubs in recent weeks by intimidating the punters.

'Skinny kid, Saidi, is head of the crew, isn't he?'

'He is,' Mounsey said. 'The most recent insult was in Bermondsey. They snatched two of the girls from the Tingle Touch salon.'

Unwin experienced a flash of hot rage. 'First I've heard – when was this?'

'Minutes after news of the shooting went up on the web.'

'Cocky little bastard.' By targeting a massage parlour well beyond the borders of his own territory, Saidi had sent a message to every other wannabe: Unwin was fair game.

Meanwhile, men with greater power than Saidi could ever imagine were eagerly awaiting that shipment. Once payment was made and the cargo divided and distributed, Unwin was planning to step away from his old business operations. The new market he'd eased into would be infinitely more lucrative and a lot safer from the Rick Turners of this world. If he could get the deal done, Unwin would be untouchable.

Until that time, he had a reputation to defend and businesses to protect.

'You know, Mr King's death might yet play to your advantage,' Mounsey ventured.

'I don't see how.'

'People will wonder who took out the contract on Mr King.'

'They will. And like you, they'll probably come up with Saidi's name.'

'True . . . but that might stay the hand of lesser men with ambitions in your direction.'

Meaning that someone brazen enough to take down Austin King might make the less cocky alphas hesitate, wanting to size up the competition before pitching in, while the beta dogs would be watching to see who they should align with, and the omegas who they should fear.

'This isn't like you lawyers fencing with words, Mounsey; this is real blood warfare. If I let a jumped-up kid get away with assaults on my property, snuffing out *my right-hand man*, who d'you think he'll come for next? Hm? I might as well drop my trousers right now and bend over.'

He stopped and waited for the silence to have an effect. Finally, Mounsey murmured an apology.

'All right,' Unwin said. 'Here's what you do: send Zoe away for a couple of weeks – not to one of the holiday properties – find her a nice hotel in Paris. Or Vienna – she likes Vienna. Double security on everything – the clubs, the salons, the garages, the lot – keep a lid on this till I'm out and can deal with it.'

'I'll have to bring in extra personnel.' Mounsey sounded doubtful.

'Do it.'

'The ongoing costs are squeezing the budget.'

Disturbed, Unwin said, 'What happened to the contingency fund?'

'As you know, there are thousands of pages of materials relating to your case. Aside from your barrister's fees, a trial defence of this magnitude requires insider intelligence at every level, from police to prison transport, to the courts. That doesn't come cheap. Add in the cost of additional security—'

'Okay, you've made your point.' Unwin sucked his teeth. 'What'll it take?'

'Barrister's fees – £300k for six days; security – upwards of two thousand a day, for all your venues. And assuming twenty-four-hour personal security for Mrs Unwin—'

'Goes without saying,' Unwin interrupted.

'—Another couple of thousand a day.'

'You're telling me I need to liquidate assets.'

Mounsey made an incoherent sound Unwin imagined was supposed to sound like he was being sympathetic.

'And without Mr King on hand, you will need to appoint someone you trust to – um – facilitate matters. Mrs Unwin, perhaps?'

'No. I don't want Zoe involved.'

'Well then . . .' With those two words Mounsey, in his ambiguous, insinuating way, put himself forward for that privileged position.

Unwin smoothed his carefully clipped beard as he thought. Trusting Mounsey was risky, but he had emergency funds squirrelled away in numerous accounts under a range of fake business names. He could give his lawyer access to one of the smaller stashes; any potential losses would be limited to the relatively modest value of the funds. If all went well, he'd be back at the helm in a few days – and if Mounsey tried to screw him, the little weasel would live only long enough to regret it.

'Don't write this down,' he said. 'Memorise it and repeat it back to me.'

'Shall I make payment for the cargo from this?'

'No,' Unwin said, allowing himself a smile at the lawyer's sheer nerve. '*You* get me out of here so *I* can make payment on the cargo. When I'm out, all of this goes away – including my barrister's frankly outrageous fees.'

'Very well.'

Unwin's smile broadened hearing the stiffness in Mounsey's tone.

'Cheer up,' he said. 'There's enough in that account to take care of our Algerian friend. Permanently.'

'I'll make discreet enquiries,' Mounsey said.

'Nah, I want an example made. I want this to go viral. Think Piccadilly Lights, DeepScreen – the whole 3-D experience. Saidi thinks he can come after my right-hand man—'

'We don't know that,' Mounsey jumped in. 'Not for certain.'

'Doesn't matter. Perception matters. He steals two of my girls right after King is shot – that sends a message I can't ignore. Well, I'm sending one back – full volume.'

'Consider it done.' Mounsey hesitated before adding, 'As to the . . . other matter. Do you think it might be wise to postpone – just until we've had time to assess—'

'That goes ahead, as planned,' Unwin interrupted.

There was a pause – a definite pause – before Mounsey said, 'As you wish,' sounding like a greasy politician, disapproving even as he agreed, implying that Unwin was wrong – was making a gross error. Unwin simultaneously despised the man's spinelessness in not coming out and telling him straight, and furiously resented his condescending tone.

'Talk me through the plan,' he said, knowing that the little man with his coded language and paranoid belief that someone, somewhere was always listening, would hate putting the plan into words. 'Step by step.'

He listened to Mounsey's plan of action, thinking he would like to tear out Saidi's heart with his own hands for what he did to Austin King.

Five minutes later, he ended the call and peeped over the edge of his bunk again, to where Laser sat, trembling, tears dripping from his chin as music blasted out at ear-splitting volume into his ears. Unwin clicked his fingers, but the kid's eyes remained shut, so he sighed and picked up a book to read. He'd work it out eventually.

Chapter 9

THE ASSASSIN EXITS A TAXI outside a Michelin-starred restaurant in Mayfair. The Tudor frontage has a smart pairing of red brick and creamy Bath stone ashlar, warmed by golden uplights at this time of night.

He's dressed in an Edward Sexton suit – his third change of clothing since completing the contract on Austin King, having emerged from the hotel's fire escape stairwell in a bomber jacket and baseball cap, his wool overcoat carefully packed into the foldaway backpack he'd worn around his midriff to create the impression of a middle-aged paunch. Blending in with a knot of American tourists, he'd made his way out with a party of seven, breaking away only when they headed into the underground. Now, showered and beautifully tailored, he could be a lawyer or an actor, a sportsman, a banker – perhaps even a Whitehall mandarin.

The restaurant is lively with a low buzz of conversation and laughter, and immediately he relaxes. He greets the maître d' by name and is in turn greeted by one of his aliases. Someone appears at his side to take his raincoat and he hands it over with a smile of thanks.

He makes do with a small glass of white Burgundy to accompany the lobster mousse starter. He had selected a red for the main course and called ahead of his arrival so that it would be decanted and ready to serve with a Cumbrian rose veal fillet. He chats in French to the waiter, Jean-Marc, discovering that he is from the city of Bordeaux.

'*Ah, connaissez-vous La Salle à Manger des Chartrons?*' It's a small restaurant on the left bank, off the tourist route.

Jean-Marc is delighted: apparently, he had landed his first job at the restaurant.

As he is dining alone, the assassin has foregone the bolder choice of a Margaux and ordered a more modest 2009 Château Péby Faugères St-Émilion. It does not disappoint. The waiter smiles at his approval and pours a generous glass.

'*Malheureusement, je dois me limiter à un verre ce soir.*'

'*C'est dommage!*' the waiter exclaims.

'*Il faut que travailler pour gagner sa vie,*' he says, with a wry smile.

In the next hour, he reflects that the 'life earned' for this day's work is worth it. The veal is delicious, the morel mushroom sauce intense and nutty, and he savours every bite, taking time to observe the other diners. They are privileged and affluent, for the most part, but as he finishes his meat course, a young couple is shown to a nearby table. They seem nervous and out of their depth. The man looks uncomfortable in a suit and tie, and the woman is shy, but he senses excitement, too. He glances over a little later as the couple exchange a dismayed glance over their menus, and she mouths, 'Oh, my *God,*' at the prices. They settle for a jug of water rather than wine with their meal.

Newlyweds. He sips from his glass and a thought occurs to him. He catches Jean-Marc's eye and asks him to offer his two-thirds-full decanter of wine with his compliments to the couple.

'Oh, no – we couldn't,' the young wife protests. He hears a Lancashire burr in her accent.

'Nonsense, you'll be doing me a favour.' He pats his perfectly flat stomach. 'And I hate to see a good wine go to waste.'

51

She turns to her husband, who blushes deeply and can't lift his gaze from his plate. The woman seems to decide that she has to take the initiative. 'Well, if it helps save the planet . . .' She looks the assassin in the eye. 'Thank you,' she says, and to the waiter: 'I think we'll be needing those wine glasses after all.'

He laughs delightedly at her brio, wishes the couple *bon appétit*, and forgets them. The assassin often performs random acts of kindness after a killing; right now, his entire focus is on the choice of dessert: pear *tarte Tatin* or apricot Cointreau soufflé?

He has ordered coffee and is contemplating a brandy to round off the evening, when his mobile phone buzzes in his inside breast pocket. He uses several – all of them burners. The assassin prefers his phones simple, rather than smart, under the GPS radar – and entirely untraceable.

He has received a text:

—Chat? Urgent.

He would have ignored the message if he'd just started his meal, but he's eaten well, and it's late to drink coffee. Also, a message tagged 'Urgent' and sent to this untraceable phone usually means something lucrative. The only way to be sure is by contacting the prospective client, and to do that, the assassin needs to log in to a secure chatroom via his laptop, which is back at his hotel.

He looks up and Jean-Marc is at his side in an instant.

'*Je suis désolé,*' the man says. '*Je dois partir tôt.*'

'*J'espère que rien de grave, monsieur?*'

Grave? He thinks. *Almost certainly, for some unhappy soul.* But he gives the waiter a droll look. '*Travail,*' he says.

Chapter 10

THE ASSASSIN SITS IN FRONT OF HIS LAPTOP in his hotel suite near Covent Garden. He is logged into a private chatroom on the dark web, accessed through a virtual private network and the Tor browser. Tor will connect him using end-to-end encryption to his potential client via relays that will bounce their conversation randomly from one volunteer router to another, anywhere in the world – and then permanently erase all trace of the exchange when he closes the browser.

He opens the message, headed, URGENT ATTENTION. There are two attachments: an image of the target, and background information, including some of his favourite haunts. The message is most particular that the hit must be public, highly visible, and calculated to 'make a splash' on social media.

The target is a lowlife by the name of Hakim Saidi.

The assassin has had dealings with this particular lowlife; in fact, it was Saidi who had engaged him to assassinate Austin King – presumably to move in and fill the void caused by Unwin's inevitable detention at Her Majesty's Pleasure. It seems that Saidi's grand scheme is to be cut short.

Musing on this interesting development, Austin King's killer pushes his chair back from the desk and contemplates a framed photograph of Margot Fonteyn striking a classic ballet pose. *So beautiful*, he thinks, yet so much pain is masked by a ballet dancer's serene elegance, so much ugliness and injury bound tightly inside those delicate silk shoes.

Is this commission from another criminal, aiming to capitalise on Austin King's death? It's entirely plausible; a whole slew of empire builders would literally kill to take over Unwin's byzantine criminal endeavours.

But a would-be usurper would be wise to bide his time, let the scene play out for a few days – perhaps even for a week or two. Unwin's inevitable reprisals on whomever he blamed for King's death would inevitably weaken any other opposition, allowing a smoother, less bloody takeover. So why the urgency? Unless . . .

. . . Unless Unwin *himself* is commissioning the hit on Saidi. If so, the same question applies: why the urgency? Even before he'd accepted the hit on Austin King, the killer had researched Unwin, who had held on to power in a highly competitive market for almost two decades. He is known to hold back, working out his adversaries' weak points and the best means of attack before he strikes, meting out revenge with tactical intelligence and cold-blooded precision. So if Unwin *is* financing the hit, the rush on this commission is all the more puzzling.

Does he feel he has to strike early to prevent a takeover? Surely Unwin isn't so weakened by imprisonment that he feels intimidated by a small-time criminal with overblown ambitions?

The assassin's attention is dragged away from the lovely image of Fonteyn by the caterpillar crawl of three dots in the chat bubble.

—Problem?

He considers; there is a pleasing symmetry in the proposal – especially given the part he played in King's death – but he doesn't like acting blind, and he doesn't want to fall into a trap. He types:

—If I am to be involved in a turf war, I'd like to know on whose behalf I'm acting.

A pause, then:

—Austin King's.
—Austin King is dead.
—And that cannot go unpunished.
—That seems a desperate response, the assassin replies.
—Street cleaning, ready to string up the bunting for Mr Unwin's homecoming.

Well, that couldn't be more explicit – this is most definitely Unwin's commission, and he wants it known.

—Isn't it a little early for celebration?
—Not in the least. He is expected home imminently.

Even more puzzling. Unwin – considered a danger to witnesses and the wider public – has been denied bail all along; there's no reason on earth that the CPS would let him go home as the trial gets under way. Unless Unwin is expecting the charges to be dropped.

But is that likely? King's death will be a setback, but surely it wouldn't be enough to crash the trial?

No, if Unwin expects to be freed, he must have found leverage. Witness tampering? That seems unlikely – the witnesses have been sequestered. The judge? But this judge has tried a dozen high-profile cases involving seriously bad men and never flinched. Which leaves one other possibility: Unwin must have something on one of the lead cops.

The killer swiftly opens a new browser and searches for reports on Unwin's arrest and impending trial. One face is featured heavily in the press images – Detective Sergeant Rick Turner, poster boy for the Met, envy of every ambitious career cop south of the Wash.

He experiences a prickling discomfort in his chest; it radiates downwards to his abdomen for a fleeting moment – indigestion caused by his rushed meal? But then he recognises the unfamiliar sensation. Anxiety.

Surprised and intrigued, he examines the phenomenon, turns his hands over and observes the slight tremor in his fingers, and notices the strong pulse in his throat.

Extraordinary. Perhaps he should decline the commission – this could become a complicated mess – and what good could come of it, after all?

He stares at his laptop in astonishment.

—Triple standard fee, half in advance, non-negotiable, has appeared on the screen without his conscious involvement.

It seems his fingers have made the decision for him. He could change his mind, send a second message – second thoughts, no reasons given – but he knows he will not. He is a man of few principles, but having made a commitment to a contract, he always sees it through.

The cursor blinks noncommittally for half a minute. Then the caterpillar crawl of the ellipsis begins again . . . Unwin's negotiator is typing.

—Terms accepted.

He sends details of the method and route for payment, waits only until the transaction has completed, then packs his belongings, pays his hotel bill, and leaves.

Chapter 11

Monday, early: day 1 of trial

RICK TURNER WAS SHOWERED, DRESSED, and ready for work, but Jess was still asleep. He flicked on his bedside light, and she groaned, flinging an arm across her face.

'Bloody hell, Rick – turn it off!'

'Sorry, love,' he said. 'I need to choose a tie and the judge might take it amiss if I turn up wearing that Scales of Justice one you bought me.'

'Oh, God . . .' She shifted her arm and opened one eye. 'Is it tomorrow already?'

'Exactly five hours and forty minutes into tomorrow, which officially, is today.'

'Oh, Rick,' she said. 'I meant to wait up for you.'

'I'm glad you didn't. Haven't you got that audition?' Jess had bagged a few minor roles in TV soaps but hadn't yet landed a regular spot.

'It's an early call. Maybe I'll skip it.'

'You've plenty of time,' he said.

'I'm feeling a bit rough.' She snuggled under the duvet. 'Think I'll stay in bed.'

'Here—' He sat next to her and picked up a mug from the bedside table. 'I made coffee . . .'

She eyed the proffered mug suspiciously. 'Instant?'

'Filter.'

Easing to a sitting position, she took it, inhaling the aroma.

'It'd probably do more good if you drank it,' he confided. 'You look like you could use the caffeine.'

She shot him a look. 'That bad, huh?'

Her hair was flattened on one side and a bird's nest at the back. He tucked a stray brown strand behind her ear. 'Runway perfect.'

Jess pulled a face. 'I opened a bottle of wine last night; I've got a horrible feeling I might've finished it.'

He tilted his head. 'You left me a good half-glass.'

'Ugh!' She slid a hand down her face. 'So, tell me about the party – how'd it go?'

'The boss hinted at a promotion if everything pans out.'

Her face lit up. 'See – I told you it'd be worth it. I bet Jim Stott was glowing like a proud dad.'

'The only glow was from his boozer's nose.'

'Honestly, Rick.' She laughed. 'You're such a puritan! So *what* if he likes a drink?'

'He doesn't *like* it, he *needs* it – and he doesn't know when to stop.'

'Well, maybe he's got problems.'

'Wouldn't know,' Rick said, reaching a couple of ties from their hanger.

'Radical idea, but have you tried *asking* him?'

'Can we do this some other time?' he said, irrationally annoyed that she was taking Stott's side. 'I've got other things on my mind, right now.'

She sighed. 'I'm just saying; he's been good to you, and if he's struggling, maybe he could use your help.'

He turned to face her. 'Okay . . . I'll talk to him, after the trial's finished—'

She was already shaking her head. 'You can't just postpone your life till a more convenient moment!'

In fact, Rick had done exactly that for most of his life in his hopeless search for his brother; Jess had an uncanny knack for seeing through his BS – although she called it, 'reading the subtext'.

'Look, Jess,' he said. 'I'm starting the biggest murder trial of my career today—'

'I know,' she soothed. 'I know, babe. But try to be kind, okay? He's not the enemy.'

He took a breath, ready to argue, then let it go. She was right – Jim Stott was one of the few who had backed him in the early days of his investigation, and he'd never given his old mentor credit for his support.

'Yeah,' he said, 'I know.' He slid one palm over his face. 'I've been wound so tight, recently, and now with this . . .' He realised that he was making excuses and stopped. 'I'll talk to him.'

'When you do, could you *pur-lease* refrain from kicking his arse?'

Jess was smiling, now, and he marvelled at her acceptance of him. His intense focus seemed to fascinate her; she'd never complained about the long hours he kept and had so many friends that she was never at a loss for something to do if he had to cancel dinner or a night out. She trusted him so absolutely, believing in him without question, that Rick felt unworthy of her trust. Which was why, a month ago, he'd confessed to Jess something he'd never even told his parents.

She'd brought home the Scales of Justice novelty tie, and seeing her beaming at him, the sparkle in her eyes somewhere between glee at her own joke and pride in him, he'd felt a miserable fake. Stupid, really – it was just a tie, after all – but that was all it took: a silly joke tie and that big, full-beam smile of hers for him to realise that he was crazy in love with her, and he could not try to win her love under false pretences.

He'd set Jess's gift to one side, and sat her down, and had done the riskiest thing with their relationship so new and at such a delicate stage. He'd told her the truth about the awful moment, thirteen years ago, when he'd witnessed his brother coldly, deliberately, stab a defenceless man to death.

'My brother's older than me by eight years,' he'd said. 'He'd got himself in a mess with the law and—' he'd stopped himself just in time; Jess didn't need to know Lockleigh's name '—let's say his former boss. This guy was dangerous. I mean deadly – like a shark. He should've just run, but Sam—' He'd realised he was babbling and forced himself to take a breath. 'Sam was a risk-taker, you know?'

Jess had been staring up at him, her brown eyes puzzled. 'Rick,' she'd said, 'I don't care what your *brother* did. I care about *you*.'

'No,' he'd said. 'This *is* about me – about what I did.'

Her eyes had widened. 'Rick, babe – please, don't—'

He'd touched a finger gently to her lips. 'I need to say this.' He'd thought she might argue, but after a few seconds, she'd nodded and Rick sat next to her, staring at his hands as he went on.

'So, Sam's supposed to be in a police safe house, but he's got away. His boss has people out looking for him. He's got scouts waiting for Sam to show up on the estate.' He'd paused, realising he'd have to explain. 'See, before the family moved here, we lived in a shit tenement in Lewisham – I mean really horrible. Sam did some dodgy business there for his boss. I knew he'd go back – he'd left some stuff at the old flat – valuables and that . . .'

The room faded, and Rick was on the public landing of their old flat – not visualising it – actually *there*. He heard the rumble of traffic, which sometimes made him feel like they were living inside a great machine, its cogs and wheels constantly grinding, day and night. He couldn't imagine what this machine churned out unless it was dirt and misery. The drone of traffic on the A20 was punctuated by the sudden wail of a police siren, a dog barked frantically nearby, and the smell of cooking drifting from an open window on the landing made him feel sick.

The front door stood open, and one of Lockleigh's thugs – a huge ape, bloated on steroids – loomed just inside. Rick could see Sam beyond him, bouncing on his toes, ready to fight. There was no way out except through the front door; Sam was cornered. Light glanced off something in the thug's hand: a ten-inch butcher's knife, honed for carving.

Pumped on adrenaline, Rick yelled, 'Get out of the way!' It had no more effect than the distant barking of the dog in one of the flats below.

Rick raised the baseball bat he'd carried all the way from Putney and whacked the doorframe, hard. 'Oi, Meathead!' he screamed, and his voice cracked. 'Leave my brother alone!'

Ape-man barely glanced over his shoulder.

'Jog on, little boy,' he'd said. 'Come back when your voice has broke. I'm gonna cut your big brother's nuts off, take 'em to the boss in a Ziploc bag.'

Driven by impotent fury, Rick swung the bat again, putting a dent in the frame, but the end cap clipped the thug behind the left ear and Rick heard a *zzziing* as the knife fell from his hand. Rick danced back, ready to go again, but the man crumpled, falling forwards, and Sam sprang out of his way.

For a few seconds, the brothers had stared down at the stricken man, Rick, still on the outdoor landing, taking hold of the bat in a double-handed grip, daring the big ape to get up, *willing* him to try.

Then Sam grabbed his upper arms, shoved him inside the flat, and slammed the front door. Shocked, Rick stood with the bat still in his hand.

'What the *hell* are you doing here?' Sam demanded.

'I thought—'

'No, you didn't – you never do, Rick. You shouldn't be here, man!' He twisted the bat from Rick's grip, set it down.

'Sam—'

'Shut up.'

61

Sam never snarled at him like that.

Rick stepped forward and Sam straight-armed him into the wall, winding him. 'Shut the *fuck* up and stay where you are.'

Sam bent and checked the thug's pulse like it was something he did routinely, every day. Twitching at his side, Rick felt mildly reassured. Sam knew everything – he'd know what to do about the unconscious *quadzilla* blocking the hallway – and how to get off the estate without being spotted by Lockleigh's lookouts.

Sam probed the man's chest with his fingertips, and when he found the sternum, he reached for the dropped knife and positioned the point on the man's chest, directly over his heart.

'No!' Rick screamed. 'Don't!'

But Sam pressed hard, slicing through clothing and flesh in one quick movement.

Faint with horror, hyperventilating, Rick whispered, 'What are you *doing*?'

Sam said, 'Giving us time.'

The story told, Rick had come to, faintly surprised that he was in the bedroom of his house in Putney. He blew air out of his nose, purging himself of the phantom stench of blood. He hadn't looked at Jess as he'd told the story, but now he was finished, he glanced into her face.

Her look of dismay had sent a shaft of grief through him.

'Why'd you *tell* me that?' she'd said, and it sounded like an accusation.

It's over, he'd thought. *We're finished*. And when he'd reached for her, Jess jumped up, backing away.

'You didn't have to *tell* me that,' she'd wailed.

It had felt like every muscle in his chest was fighting to keep his heart from being torn from his body, but he'd forced himself to go on:

'I did,' he'd said. 'I *had* to tell you.'

She'd shaken her head, staring at him as though he was insane.

'You think I'm this irreproachable fighter for truth and justice,' he'd persisted. 'I'm not. I stood and watched my brother kill a man, and I did nothing. And I don't want this to be built around a lie.'

'This?'

'Us,' he'd said simply.

Hearing those words, Jess had frozen, her hands bunched into fists, a stunned look on her face.

'I – I couldn't do that to you, Jess.'

Then her eyes had filled with tears and she'd sat down again, had even taken his hands in hers. For the longest time she didn't speak, and when she did, his whole body juddered with the shock of it.

'God,' she'd breathed. 'I *so* effing wish you hadn't told me that. But okay, I get it. And it's sweet that you want to be honest – a bit "eve of self-destruction", given we've only known each other for, like, a nanosecond – I mean, didn't you read *Tess of the d'Urbervilles* at school?'

'I . . . what?'

'Never mind.' She had smiled at his incomprehension, then, taking a deep breath had exhaled slowly. 'All right . . . Fine . . . You want to look at this, let's look: you say you did nothing to stop Sam?'

Rick had nodded, his palms damp with sweat in her cool, dry fingers.

'D'you think you could've, if you'd tried?'

'No,' he'd said, surprised by the answer. He'd never really considered that he might not have had a choice. 'It was – I was in shock, and it happened so—' He'd taken a breath. 'No, Jess, I couldn't have stopped him.'

'Well then.'

'It's not that simple. I should've told someone.'

'Who?'

'I dunno. My parents maybe? The police?'

Her dark eyes shining, Jess had cupped his face in her hands. 'You were *fifteen*, Rick. A *kid*. You thought you had to protect your brother. But you can't be held responsible for his actions. Not then. Not now.'

A month on, almost to the day, Rick hadn't for one second regretted entrusting Jess with his darkest secret.

Sam had bought the house in Putney fifteen years earlier, and gifted it to his parents. Rick had considered selling it after they'd died – what was he going to do with a four-bedroom house? But recently, he'd begun to dream about making it a family home again.

'Earth to Rick, come in, over.'

He was standing at the mirror straightening his tie; behind him, reflected in the glass, Jess was watching him with a quizzical frown.

'You looked a million miles away.'

'Counting my lucky stars,' he said, turning to her.

'Aw, sweet . . .'

She pouted, and Rick impulsively went to her and kissed her on the lips. She responded, grabbing his tie with her free hand.

'Sorry,' he said, disengaging reluctantly. 'I've got to go – briefing.'

'Briefing? I thought the investigation stuff was all done. Aren't you in court today – isn't that what you meant about the tie?'

'I am, and it is.'

As he straightened his tie for the second time, she said, 'Oh, I get it. The shooting last night. Will it mess up the trial?'

'How d'you know about the shooting?'

'You were talking in your sleep.' She laughed, making a face in a monstrous parody of his look of horror. 'Only joking. It was all over social media.' She grinned at him over the rim of her coffee cup.

Jess had been asleep when he'd got home, her iPad on the covers next to her.

'King, they said his name was,' she said, finishing her coffee and setting the mug aside. 'A key witness in the trial of suspected underworld boss Thomas Unwin.'

She laughed and kicked off the duvet delightedly. 'How cool is that? "Underworld boss" – and *my Rick* caught him! Was King going to testify against Unwin? They said it was a professional hit. Was it horrible? It must have been. God, I wish I could've been there.' She flushed, realising what she'd just said. 'For research, I mean – not in a creepy way. They do it all the time in America – "ride-alongs". Sounds like the Wild West, doesn't it? D'you think your boss might let me – you know, *ride along*, if you asked him?'

Rick grinned. She did this all the time, bombarding him with questions, not waiting for the answers, piling on inconsequential observations.

Her brow creased. 'What?' she said.

'Nothing.' He shrugged into his jacket and headed for the door. 'Just pleased the caffeine's working.'

From the corner of his eye, he saw Jess launch a pillow at him. He deflected it with an elbow and back-heeled it onto the bed.

'Great reflexes,' she said.

He picked up his phone, keys, wallet and notebook, stashing them in various pockets.

'Seriously, though – will it? Mess up the trial, I mean?' She looked anxious, now.

'No,' he said, though really, he wasn't sure.

Jess looked unconvinced, and he said, 'Don't *worry* – it's a setback, but we'll handle it.'

After a few seconds she shrugged and caught the corner of her lower lip in her teeth. 'So, this really is the big one,' she said, eyeing his mid-section, teasing.

He glanced down, giving her a slow smile. 'Nice of you to mention it.'

She crawled to the foot of the bed and, despite the hangover and the bed hair, Jessica Oakes was sexy.

She hooked her fingers in the belt of his trousers and pulled him towards her. As she started to wrap herself around him, he responded, succumbing to the moment. He wanted her *so* much . . . But as she reached for this belt buckle, he grabbed her hands.

'Sorry,' he said. 'You can't *know* how sorry . . . But I won't lie to you, Jess: King was a key witness – his murder is going to make it a rough start to the trial – I can't be late.'

She ruffled his hair in revenge and, smiling, he turned once more to the mirror for a quick tidy-up. Halfway through the door, he changed his mind and popped back in, phone in hand.

'Maybe you could WhatsApp me later with a little something to keep my pecker up?' he said, waggling the phone. He darted out before the pillow hit the door.

It was a sombre bunch of detectives and admin staff who gathered in the major investigation room. Most of the desks were empty, many of the team having moved on to new deployments, the investigation being wound down as the court hearing began. The few remaining looked monstrously hungover; it seemed the party had gone on for a while after Rick left the pub. DS Stott looked about as sick as a man could look outside of a hospital ward, his skin a nasty slug-grey; a sheen of cold sweat completing the look.

DCI Kath Steiner stood at the front of the room, looking grave. She was nicely suited, as always, but her neck was blotched with red, and raised welts suggested that she'd raked her nails under her chin. They locked gazes, and as Rick joined her, Steiner murmured, 'I'll hand over to you as soon as I've gone through the formalities – okay?'

'No problem.' Rick had brought Steiner and Superintendent Ghosh up to speed in the early hours of the morning, after he'd finished interviewing hotel staff alongside DI Irons's crew.

Superintendent Ghosh arrived and, on his nod, Steiner tapped the nearest desk. The murmur of voices fell away, and she introduced DI Jake Irons from the Homicide and Major Crime Command, then broke the news of King's death. Most would have seen it in the news feeds on their phones already, but it was a shock to one or two of the more seriously hungover.

'Rick has the best overview and in-depth of knowledge of the Unwin case,' Steiner said. 'So I'm going to hand over to him. Rick?'

Generous intro, Rick thought, but his cynical inner voice added, *unless she's distancing herself, in case Unwin slips through our grasp.*

'I'm grateful to DI Irons for letting me know about the shooting soon after it was discovered,' Rick said.

Irons was standing to the side of the room looking fresher than any of the existing team, despite his late night. He acknowledged the courtesy with a lift of his chin.

'Forensic techs are already working on King's laptop and phone,' Rick continued.

'Some of the hotel's security cams were out of commission – possibly nobbled,' Irons added. 'So we've got nothing in the lifts, or on the sixth floor, where King's room was located. But King ordered a room service meal – I believe you spoke to the waiter, DS Turner?'

All eyes turned again to Rick. 'He says a middle-aged white male stepped into the elevator on the restaurant floor at the last moment, then got off with him on the sixth floor and turned in the opposite direction.' He saw a couple of half-shrugs. 'The odd thing,' he went on, 'is the wine glass – which the waiter *swears* was there when he left the kitchen – was missing from the food trolley when he got inside the room. He went for a replacement but couldn't raise Mr King when he returned.'

'It's likely the killer used the missing glass to fool King into opening the door,' Irons said, 'but if he did, he took it with him.'

'Professional hit,' someone murmured.

'Almost certainly,' Rick said. 'And he was thorough: two shots to the chest, one in the face, a fourth to the back of the head.'

Stott glanced up, and Rick wondered if he was about to ask a question, but he quickly looked away.

'Are we doing an e-fit of Mystery Guy with the waiter?' someone asked.

Rick spoke up before Irons could reply. 'HMCC will run the investigation into King's murder.' This was the Met's Homicide and Major Crime Command. 'But they'll share intel with us, and we'll reciprocate. What we need to focus on, is how King's death affects the Unwin trial.'

That was the question on everyone's mind, and there was a general shuffle as people sat up and picked up pens or phones to make notes.

'We've still got the money trail,' someone said.

Rick nodded. 'The digital evidence is compelling, but Unwin's defence might argue that King's testimony would have exonerated him.'

This raised a few snorts of derision from the team.

'I know,' Rick said, holding up his hands, 'but all he needs to do is create a reasonable doubt – and you know how juries hate tech evidence.'

'Where's the prosecution barrister?' Steiner demanded. 'Shouldn't we be hearing strategy from him?'

That was a question Steiner should be answering herself, but Rick took it in his stride. 'Mr Kildoran is doing a bit of fire-fighting at his end. For the first few days of the trial, he'd intended to lean heavily on King's testimony, so he's rewriting his opening arguments as we speak.'

'He should ask for a short deferral,' Steiner said.

'It's already ticked off on his to-do list,' Rick said. 'I'm expecting a text any minute. And he's considering bringing in a couple of extra jury-friendly experts who can explain the technical aspects of forensic accounting to people who might have trouble balancing their own bank accounts.'

That raised a pained chuckle from those on the team who had wrestled with the financial evidence.

He glanced towards Superintendent Ghosh. 'I'm hoping we can persuade the Serious Fraud Office to loan us Dave Collins for the duration.'

'I've a call scheduled with Collins's boss at nine-fifteen,' Ghosh said.

Rick's phone fizzed in his pocket and he took it out. 'Mr Kildoran,' he said. 'The judge has given us until eleven a.m. to make a start – he says she'll hear arguments for further deferral then.' Which gave them a scant hour of extra time.

Steiner raised a hand to her cheek and gouged along the line of her jaw with a thumbnail, raising a fresh wheal. 'Well, let's hope Kildoran can convince the judge to open and adjourn the case, at least for a few days.'

'I'm meeting him at his chambers before he heads over to Court Number Two,' Rick said, thinking that Steiner needed to work on her poker face.

By nine-thirty, the briefing long over, those with tasks allocated were hard at work. Just a couple more emails to send, then Rick planned to head off to the barrister's chambers. He glanced up and saw Jim Stott across the room, watching him nervously. Stott took a gulp of coffee as a man might take a shot of liquor for courage, then weaved between the desks to where Rick was seated.

'Well, this is a real sickener,' he said.

Rick tilted his head. 'It does look like the celebrations were a bit premature.'

'About that . . .' Stott scratched the back of his head. 'I think I was a bit out of order last night – I'd had a few; you know how it is.'

Rick didn't honestly know how anyone could get pickled every night and call it 'one of those things', but the memory of Jess's gentle rebuke made him bite his tongue.

'Is everything all right with you, Jim?' he asked.

Immediate bluster: 'Yeah. 'Course. Why wouldn't it be?'

'Come on, Sarge,' Rick said. 'This is me . . .'

The sardonic smile faded from Stott's face, and he said, 'Ah, you know – family stuff.'

'The boys—?' Rick said, feeling a quick spasm of alarm.

'They're fine.'

'Oh, God, not Maddie?' He'd been a regular visitor to the Stotts until relatively recently, and Maddie was like the big sister he never had.

'Nah, she's breaking my balls, as usual.' Stott laughed, but Rick felt a shift of mood, and saw a flare of the anger he'd read in his mentor's eyes the previous night, quickly followed by a crease of pain.

Rick opened his mouth to speak, but his mobile buzzed on the desk beside him and, muttering an excuse, Stott bumbled off.

Rick glanced down at his mobile and couldn't help smiling. It was a WhatsApp message from Jess, and she'd sent an attachment. He tapped to open the message, and the world stopped turning. The room tilted sideways, and he was falling so fast he grabbed the edges of the desk to save himself.

In the photograph, Jess was bound and gagged. Tears stained her face, and her left ear was bleeding.

The text message read:

—Log out. Tell no one. Await further instructions.

Chapter 12

HIS HEART STILL RACING, RICK checked the room. Laid out like a commercial office, it was abuzz with quiet activity, detectives and clerical staff working on their allotted tasks with purposeful and business-like focus. As he watched, he began almost unconsciously to search for signs of guilt or malice or glee in the faces of his team. He knew he had enemies – the handshakes and hearty congratulations of the previous night were not entirely sincere in all quarters – and while he felt sure that Jess had been taken to create leverage on Unwin's behalf, he couldn't stomach the thought that one of his colleagues might be involved.

He speed-dialled Jess's phone. It was switched to voicemail. For all he knew, whoever took her had already ditched it, but he spoke into the phone anyway, hoping that somehow, she would get the message: 'Jess, stay calm,' he murmured quietly. 'Do as they say. I promise, I'll get you home safe—'

Someone passed his desk and he paused, waiting till they were out of earshot before adding, 'Whoever you are, don't do anything I'll make you regret.'

As he disconnected, his phone fizzed in his hand, and he felt it like an electric shock straight to his heart. Still, he managed to greet a member of the clerical team and point her towards the detective she was looking for in a calm and measured tone before opening the text.

—Head towards the flyover on foot.

Although Rick's main base was in Richmond, the Major Incident Room worked out of Hammersmith Police Station, so whoever sent the text meant Hammersmith Flyover, about five minutes' walk away.

He grabbed his coat, notebook and tie and made his way to the door.

'Off to see Kildoran, Sarge?' someone called.

'Better hear the worst sooner, rather than later,' he said, avoiding an outright lie. 'Tell the DCI I'll meet her at the Old Bailey?' he added, balking at calling Steiner 'the boss'. He shrugged into his jacket, stuffing his tie and notebook into his pockets. The phone, he kept in his hand.

Hurrying down the concrete steps of the fire exit stairwell, he acknowledged the few people he passed with a nod or a smile. Nobody observing him would suspect his inner frenzy; Rick had learned young how to mask fear with seeming indifference. Even so, he suspected every glance and mistrusted every greeting.

Stepping out into watery autumn sunshine, he was deafened by the angry surge of traffic pounding along the A4 and would have missed the next message except for the buzz of his phone against his palm.

—Keep going down Fulham Palace Road.

He glanced around. Were they watching him? Impossible to say – any one of the people on the street; any in the shopfronts, office buildings or delivery vehicles he passed might be observing him, relaying information.

At the Duke of Cornwall pub, another message:

—Back of the Apollo.

The Apollo was a huge venue, and he knew there was an extensive area at the rear, large enough to accommodate trucks delivering equipment for the bands and theatre companies that used it. But it was gated. He ran the length of the street, praying to the gods of rock that there was a delivery happening right now.

The first gate was closed. He kept running – along the wide frontage of the building, dodging pedestrians, his head booming with the reverberation of traffic on the flyover to his right. The second gate was open. He scooted through, ignoring a shout of protest from a security guard, heading to the back of the building.

Nothing. No one.

He scouted the tar-black fire escape zig-zagging down the side of the building. It was empty.

His phone buzzed and he checked the screen again.

—Over the wall with the fence.

He couldn't see it.

He ran a little further, turned a corner and there it was, a low wall topped with fence panels. He scrambled over, pausing at the top. It was a good twenty-foot drop on the other side. He slipped the phone inside his jacket, lowered himself as far as he could and then let go, reaching for his phone even as he landed.

—Jiffy bag in a black recycler bin – the big type. Best get a wiggle on – collection's on its way.

Rick heard the distant rumble and grind of a bin lorry and took off in that direction. He was at the back of a modern four-storey low-rise which housed a care home, but coming out from the shadow of the building, he realised he'd made a mistake. There was no sign of the lorry on the road outside – the noise bouncing off the high walls of the Apollo and the nursing home had echoed and re-echoed, and he didn't know where to turn.

He ran through the entrance gate onto the street, looking right and left, straining to hear the sound again. A second later, the engine coughed and revved. *But where?* He cast about wildly. *The housing estate across the road?*

A taxi pulled away from the kerb in the street opposite, revealing a black recycling container on the pavement. He jogged to it. It was empty.

Shit.

A shout to his right made him turn, and on the other side of a six-foot grey aluminium gate, he saw a man beckoning, and heard the unmistakable groan of heavy-lifting hydraulics. He vaulted the barrier, skidding to the corner of the building as the bin lorry began heaving a weighty container off the ground.

'Whoa, whoa, whoa!' he yelled.

The man directing the operation waved his arms, trying to block him, but he leapt onto the running board of the cab and hammered on the driver's window. Startled, the man halted the hydraulics.

'What the bloody hell d'you think you're doing?' he demanded.

'Police,' Rick shouted. 'Lower it.'

'Do *what*?'

Holding on to the wing mirror for support, Rick fished for his wallet and slapped his warrant card against the side window. 'Lower it!'

Cursing, the driver did as he was told, and Rick hopped down.

He moved to the back of the truck and peered inside the dumpster at a jumble of glass and plastic bottles, drinks cans, paper and card. He couldn't see the jiffy bag. *God had they already collected it?* He'd never find it in a lorry full of this crap.

'*Oi*, mate!' The driver had wound down his window and leaned out of the cab to get a look at him. 'I haven't got all day, you know.'

Rick reached into the bin, moving aside a box, corrugated card, old copies of *The Metro*, an empty bottle, sticky and soiled. Under it, a small white jiffy bag. It was addressed to him; turning it over, he saw a smear of blood on the seal.

'Jesus,' he breathed. '*Jesus . . .*'

'You all right, mate?'

Rick looked up and saw that the refuse collectors had gathered to see what all the fuss was about.

He swallowed, braced up, and slapped the side of the lorry with the flat of his hand. 'Thanks, mate,' he called. 'You can get on with it, now.'

The driver replied with a sarcastic, 'Oh, well, fuck you *very* much, guv'nor,' as Rick walked away fast, looking for somewhere out of their sight where he could open the envelope. Cutting through the grounds of the borough housing department, he found himself under the flyover, in the staff parking bays. He crossed to one of the overpass pillars and ducked behind it, out of view of the office building's reflective glass frontage.

For a moment, he hesitated. He should turn this in for forensic examination, ask for help. But he wouldn't, because if he did, he would be told to go home and let others get on with the job of finding Jess – and she wouldn't live to see another day. With shaking hands, he opened the padded bag and looked inside.

What the hell . . .? It seemed to be empty.

Holding his breath, he tipped the package carefully into his hand, and something gold slipped into his palm. It was one of a pair of double-loop earrings he'd given Jess only a week ago. It, too, was stained with blood.

He sagged against the pillar and for one confused second, he wasn't sure if it was the vibration of traffic he felt or a seismic tremor within himself that threatened to shake his entire world apart.

Chapter 13

THE PROSECUTION BARRISTER'S CHAMBERS were housed in a nineteenth-century building on a broad street lined with robinia trees, their penny-round leaves shining buttery yellow in the autumn sunshine. Rick announced himself to a video camera above the gleaming front door and was buzzed into the foyer, where a receptionist sat behind a polished oak desk. She took his warrant card and looked him up and down with something like disdain before handing it back and pressing a button, which gave access through a set of etched glass doors to the offices.

'It's—'

'I know my way,' he interrupted.

The lawyer rose from his desk to greet Rick and shook his hand. 'Forgive the clutter.' His office was large and roomy by the standards of others in the building, yet every surface was crammed with files, folders, boxes and papers in readiness for the trial. He lifted one of the boxes and stacked it on top of three others, inviting Rick to be seated with a wave of his hand. 'Well,' he said, leaning with his back to the window, 'this is . . . unprecedented.'

Anthony Kildoran QC had suffered from complete alopecia since childhood. His pate was as smooth and polished as a billiard ball, and his flat cranium, thick neck and Roman nose gave him the profile of an American bald eagle. This hawkishness extended far beyond his looks, and Rick could only hope that the pressure of this substantial roadblock to his trial preparation would keep the barrister from noticing that he was nervous.

'What's the plan?' he asked, not trusting himself to say more.

'In the short term, containment and buying time,' the lawyer said. 'Before the jury is sworn in, we have to establish how your sequestered witness will give evidence.'

This witness, PA to one of the major players in Unwin's financial dealings, had come forward with vital evidence when it looked like they'd hit a wall in the investigation.

'I'll argue for a video link,' the lawyer went on. 'I don't think we'll get it, but at the very least I would want her to be allowed to sit behind a screen. I will also ask that Mr King's interviews recorded under caution be allowed into evidence. Defence counsel will scream the house down, but we have to try – as I recall, Mr King would have made a terrible poker player, so it would be instructive for the jury to see him sweating.'

Rick nodded his approval. Kildoran wasn't exaggerating. King really had sweated freely under pressure – he'd looked as shifty as a weasel caught in a henhouse on the video recordings.

'After the jury is settled in, I'll do my best to carry opening remarks into the afternoon,' Kildoran went on. 'I will see what I can do to emphasise the importance of Mr King's testimony, and plant in the jury members' minds the seed of a suspicion that he might have been *done in* by one of his former employer's shady rivals. The Honourable Ms Justice Latymer does not suffer any shenanigans in her courtroom, but I trust she will allow me *some* latitude under the circumstances. The defence lead is a windbag, so his opening statement should take us safely over into tomorrow morning.' He glanced around at the mounds of paperwork. 'Tonight will be when the real work begins.'

'I had a call on the way over from Superintendent Ghosh,' Rick said. 'The SFO have given us Dave Collins for however long it takes.'

'Mr Collins's skills are admirable,' Kildoran said, with nothing more than a twitch of one smooth eyebrow to indicate his dismay, 'but his social graces are not likely to endear him to a lay jury.'

It was a fair comment. Dave Collins had virtuosic skills as a forensic accountant, but if you rushed him, his brain seemed to seize. It was like steel shutters clanged down behind his eyes and he retreated into a fortress of introversion.

In the early stages of the investigation, when Rick had asked for help with the financials, Superintendent Ghosh had been doubtful that the Serious Fraud Office would 'squander valuable resources on a *fishing* expedition'.

Rick had insisted that he just needed someone to show him where to look.

Two days later, the message came back that the SFO was over-stretched, but they had someone who was willing to advise in his spare time. That someone was Dave Collins.

He showed up, sweating in a suit and tie on a warm summer's day at Twickenham Police Station, out in the leafy London borough of Richmond upon Thames.

Completely out of his comfort zone in a building populated by gregarious, fit and physically intimidating types, Collins looked like a very large, very awkward teenager hauled in after being caught smoking dope behind the bike sheds. Guilt came off him in waves, and he mumbled and stammered his way through fifteen minutes, unable to string a coherent sentence together under the disparaging gaze of Rick's boss.

Ghosh seemed to take it personally that the financial whizz they'd been offered was inarticulate, seemed completely out of his depth, and was apparently incapable even of making eye contact.

'Well, if this is the best the SFO can offer, we might as well pack up and go home now,' Ghosh said, his face bunched with fury.

Collins opened his mouth, closed it again, then jammed his hands into his lap and stared at them as though only willpower was keeping him from falling apart.

'Sir—'

Ghosh silenced Rick with a furious glance.

'*Mister* Collins. Would you mind stepping into the corridor while I have a brief chat with Sergeant Turner?' He held the door and waited with icy control as Collins lumbered through, then closed it firmly. 'You see what you get when you piss off the SFO with a half-baked idea?' He bugged his eyes. 'The *Pillsbury Doughboy*, is what you get!'

Rick had no idea who the Pillsbury Doughboy was, but it was a fair bet it wasn't a compliment. He lowered his voice out of consideration for the man standing just the other side of the door. 'I asked around; he comes highly recommended, sir.'

Ghosh snorted as though Collins had left a bad smell after him. 'I'd be surprised if he can tie his own *shoelaces*,' he hissed.

'I'd be happy to give him a try-out.'

'Well, of course *you* would – it's not like you have a choice in the matter, is it?'

It was his brother's phantom voice that persuaded Rick to hold his tongue. *I know he's a dickhead, but give him a sec, Rick*, his superego said. *I believe he's about to come around.*

A second later, Ghosh let out an irritated sigh. 'Oh, all *right*. Give it a go; see if you can get any sense out of him.'

Rick stood, thanking him, eager to get out before the superintendent changed his mind.

'I want a daily report, and if you've made no progress by the end of next week, I'm shelving the whole thing.' Rick began to thank him, but Ghosh waved him off impatiently. 'You'd better pray he's some kind of *idiot savant* – but I have to tell you, Sergeant, I'm not seeing it.'

When Rick opened the door, he could tell from his defeated posture that the forensic accountant had heard most of what had been said. He guided Collins back to his car, saying that he'd like to take up his offer of help. Collins looked so demoralised that Rick proposed having a chat over a beer later that evening. Collins declined, head down, a picture of misery – he worked lates, couldn't spare the time.

'Any time to suit you, mate,' Rick said easily. 'You're the one doing the favour.'

A frown creased the forensic accountant's brow. He lifted his head a little, still avoiding Rick's eye.

'Five o'clock, upstairs at the Bear & Staff on Charing Cross Road?' he said, as though he expected Rick to laugh in his face.

Rick arrived early and found Dave Collins already tucking into a huge plate of fish and chips. Slowly, over a mountain of food and prodigious quantities of beer, Dave Collins explained in detail how he intended to 'join the dots', as he called it.

Rick realised with increasing wonder that given the time and space he needed to think, Collins was creative, analytical, wily and totally unstoppable.

That was over a year ago and Rick had become even more convinced of the man's genius. He looked Kildoran in the eye. 'I'll admit Dave operates better on the interface than face to face,' he said, and Kildoran inclined his head, amused.

'So I've asked him to take a look at the evidence, see what we can still use in King's absence, and where the focus should be. And I'm sure he can recommend a few forensic accountants who could step into King's shoes, so to speak – explain the money angle.'

The lawyer considered the idea. 'That would be most helpful.' He paused, staring past Rick.

Rick turned and saw that a little group of young lawyers, already gowned ready for the courtroom, were clustered on the other side of the office door.

'Yes, yes,' the barrister said, beckoning them forwards. 'Come and make a start.'

They entered apologetically, and silently began loading files into boxes and boxes onto trolleys. Rick watched them, burning with rage against Unwin, thinking bleakly, *I'm lying to this man – to all of these people.*

'I may need to call you earlier than planned,' Kildoran said, breaking into Rick's thoughts.

'Oh?' It was the safest response Rick could make under the circumstances. His testimony had originally been scheduled for the second week of the trial – how could he find Jess if he was corralled in Court Number Two at the Old Bailey?

'I know we pencilled you in later – and I know that the events of last night will have increased your workload,' the lawyer said, apparently reading a lot more than Rick had intended from his one-word response. 'I had a whole slew of questions for King that would have thrown a spotlight on Unwin, whether or not he answered them. In King's absence I need *someone* to address those questions to—'

'I don't see how I can help with that – I can't answer questions on banking practices or accountancy, Mr Kildoran.'

'No, and I wouldn't dream of asking you, but I need to focus the jury's minds, and for now, you're my best chance of achieving that.' Rick took a breath, ready to object, but Kildoran raised a placatory hand. 'The murders are your province,' he began. 'So, I'll take you through your investigation and how you connected the deaths to Unwin, to set the scene. When we have a jury-friendly expert witness in accountancy who can hand-hold our twelve good persons through the numbers I *would* have put to Mr King, your testimony will be the roadmap to guide them along the money trail.'

Rick had to admit it was a good strategy. 'Got a date in mind?' he asked, keeping his breathing steady.

'I'll let you know tomorrow – it's on my to-do list for this evening,' the lawyer said, with the merest hint of humour.

After the juniors had left, Rick made a move, and Kildoran checked his watch. '*Tempus fugit*,' he remarked, following Rick to the door. He paused to pick up his robe and a bag that Rick assumed would contain his wig.

He must have noticed Rick's glance because he said, 'Wouldn't trust them to the Old Bailey – the place is rife with villains. And the robing room is practically *awash* every time it rains. See you at eleven, then. You might want to give yourself a quick spruce-up beforehand . . .'

Rick glanced down and realised his jacket was speckled with wood splinters and a few flecks of paint from the barriers he'd vaulted. No wonder the receptionist had given him a dirty look.

'I trust all is well, Sergeant?' Kildoran said, his tone suddenly sharp.

'No, it's not.' Rick avoided the prosecutor's scrutiny by picking a few paint flecks off his jacket lapels, but he felt the man's close attention in his stillness.

'We just lost a key witness to a contract killing, so no,' he repeated, 'all is not well.'

He felt, rather than saw, Kildoran relax. 'Strange times,' he said. 'Speaking of which—'

Rick looked up from his grooming and, with the ghost of a smile, the lawyer lifted his chin to indicate a grim-faced man waiting in the reception foyer. 'For the first time in my career I have what I believe is termed "close protection". Doesn't look much, does he?' he added in a low voice, 'but I'm told he is adept in several martial arts – and those eyes! Cold steel.'

If Rick hadn't fully understood just how much trouble he was in, he knew it now. Kildoran had prosecuted sex offenders, serial murderers and terrorists. He'd been lead prosecutor on inde-pendent inquiries into government policies, police incompetence and major corporate malfeasance. He was not a man who rattled easily, yet for Unwin's trial he'd accepted a bodyguard.

Rick followed the lawyer and his escort out to the car idling at the kerb but refused the offer of a lift. He had no intention of attending counsels' opening speeches; he needed time to think.

The A40 blared with mid-morning traffic as he reached the end of the street. He crossed and ducked down Chancery Lane, heading for the quiet of Lincoln's Inn Fields. It would be easier to see if he was being followed in the green spaces and wide squares of that seventeenth-century enclave.

He'd hardly walked fifty yards when a small, scurrying figure crossed the narrow lane and hailed him.

Callum Mounsey was a skinny, dough-faced man with a wide mouth, protruding eyes, high shoulders and no discernible neck, so that his face seemed to sit squat on his shoulders. His taste for expensive tailoring and bright silk ties gave him the look of a toad in a Savile Row suit.

Rick considered turning back, but pride made him plough on, avoiding the little man, and acknowledging him with only a contemptuous glance.

Mounsey fell in step, taking two paces to each of his strides.

'I can't talk to you,' Rick said.

'Oh, but I think you should – since you will be first up after opening statements.'

'What makes you think that?' Rick said, tightly. *I've just stepped out of Kildoran's office – how the hell could Mounsey know already?*

'It's what *I* would do.' Mounsey had a light voice, which seemed to come from the back of his throat, giving it an unpleasant, strangulated tone. 'A nice, personable young detective could make a strong impression on a jury. But that would put my client in a very bad light.'

'Newsflash – Unwin is on trial for two murders – he's already in a bad light. And you don't get to dictate the prosecution's trial strategy.'

'Oh,' Mounsey said, 'I think I do.'

Rick stopped dead. *Is this little shit threatening me?*

With a grateful 'Oof!' Mounsey came to a halt a step ahead of him.

'Are you in on this?' Rick demanded.

'I'm not sure I follow. We're just having a civilised conversation about how things might . . . develop in the coming days. For my client – and for you.'

He knows, all right . . .

'What d'you want from me, Mounsey?'

'A simple *quid pro quo*,' Mounsey said.

'You're going to have to get specific.'

Mounsey stared at him with what looked like disappointment, then with a sigh and a shake of the head that said, *I was hoping to avoid this*, he began slowly: 'You have received a package, I understand?'

Rick noted the careful choice of words, and a giddying wave of paranoia washed over him. *Are they recording this?*

'I was *directed* to a jiffy bag dumped in a bin. Inside the "package" was a bloody earring belonging to my girlfriend.'

A soft, vertical fold appeared between the lawyer's eyebrows, and for a few seconds he seemed genuinely perplexed. Suddenly, his face cleared, and he gave a nasty, gurgling chuckle. 'Yes, of course – I could see how you might misconstrue . . . That is, I didn't mean to imply you were taking a *bribe* – what an outrageous notion.' He covered his mouth with his hand as if to stifle a guffaw at the silliness of the proposition. 'Well. Now we've got *that* misunderstanding cleared up, let's not be coy. We have something you want, and you have something *we* want.' The round, pink tip of his tongue flicked obscenely onto his lower lip. 'We are willing to make an exchange.'

'You have my *girlfriend*—' Rick growled, bunching his hand into a fist.

Heads turned.

'Ah-ah-ah.' Mounsey raised one spoon-ended finger. 'That would *not* be wise, Sergeant. Impulsive actions have consequences.' The despicable little prick sounded almost playful.

Rick stared down into the solicitor's pale, merry, almost colourless eyes and felt suddenly weak. 'What d'you expect me to do? I can't just walk off the case.'

'No. No, *indeed* you can't – that certainly wouldn't do.' He actually sounded flustered. 'They'd only bring in that dreadful woman, Steiner – a person of no imagination. It's you we want.'

'I have literally *nothing* I can give you,' Rick said. 'Most of the evidence in this trial is digital: money transfers, CCTV, emails, texts. You *know* this – all the relevant documents were passed to you under duty of disclosure.'

'You underestimate your own importance, Sergeant Turner,' Mounsey said, his tone oily. 'The leads you followed, the questions you asked, the people you spoke to. Doggedly collecting and sorting and pondering, peeling back the onion layers to reveal that two *apparently* accidental deaths were in fact cold-blooded murders. Mr Kildoran will want you to tell the jury all about that – and why not? It reads like a detective novel – and you a hero of the action!' He grimaced, turning the corners of his wide mouth down. 'Unless, of course, it *doesn't* . . .'

Rick felt a cold sweat break out on his face and neck. 'You want me to screw up my own testimony? You're crazy. Kildoran wouldn't fall for it. Neither would the judge.'

'You're probably right,' Mounsey said. 'But who cares what they think? It's what the *jury* thinks that matters.'

Rick had seen enough clumsy presentations and shifty-looking testimony in the witness box to know how easy it was to lose a jury's trust. A surprising number of ordinary, law-abiding citizens thought the police incompetent and worse – corrupt. But Rick had built this case fact by painstaking fact, finally connecting the murders to Unwin and his co-conspirators. If he fumbled this in court, his bosses would know. Kildoran would know. The judge, the expert witnesses, Dave Collins and every member of his team would *know* that he had deliberately set about destroying his own case; that he'd been bought or compromised by some past sin. He would be finished in the job.

Mounsey checked his watch. It was fancy, gold, too large for his skinny wrist. 'Opening statements begin in twenty-five minutes,' he said. 'What shall I tell my client?'

Rick jammed his hands in his pockets to hide their shaking. 'I'll give it some thought,' he said, hardly recognising his own voice. 'But I need time.'

'Time and tide wait for no one,' Mounsey said. 'Not even a lovely girl who set out this fine morning to audition for her dream job and ended up in a nightmare not of her making.'

Jess, Jess . . .

'Look, if I make it too obvious, they'll know I've been nobbled, kick me off the trial, bring someone else in. Unwin could face additional charges of attempting to pervert the course of justice.'

After a moment's rumination, Mounsey jutted out his chin. 'Fair point.'

'Since we're talking man to man, let's get this straight.' Rick stooped and stared into the little man's ugly face. 'If *anything* happens to Jess—'

'Anything *else*, you mean?' Mounsey hissed.

A spray of spittle peppered Rick's face and he had to steel himself not to flinch.

'Let me save you the trouble of enumerating,' Mounsey went on, his pale eyes unblinking, never leaving Rick's face. 'You will come looking for me; you will take me apart strip by bloody strip; you will do unspeakable things with knives or pincers – possibly involving my genitals. Or hammers – hammers are popular. Or you'll simply make me disappear.' He raised one hand level with his face, fingertips to thumb, then splayed them, 'Poof! Like a puff of smoke.'

Rick stared at him, convinced by the liquid fear in his gut that Mounsey had imagined Jess in each horrifying scenario.

The little man's pale eyes seemed to harden to stone, and Rick saw again the blood smear on Jess's earring, felt the small packet inside his jacket as a heavy, heavy weight. It must have shown in his face, because after a few moments, Mounsey gave a curt nod.

'I've been threatened by professionals, Sergeant Turner,' the little man said pleasantly. 'I don't scare easily.'

Rick couldn't hold his gaze, and Mounsey seemed satisfied.

'I'll pass on your message, but Mr Unwin is not a patient man.' He turned abruptly and walked away with a jaunty swagger.

Watching him leave, the shaking threatened to convulse Rick's entire body and he had to hold himself rigid for fear he would collapse.

Chapter 14

RICK HEADED WEST, AWAY FROM the Central Criminal Court and the prying eyes of colleagues and press. Though sick at heart, his instincts were ablaze and – ever watchful – he was certain he was being followed. Taking evasive manoeuvres, he ducked in and out of lanes packed with gleaming bijou shops, occasionally sidestepping into rank-smelling alleys, where only the foolhardy or those with malicious intent would follow. Cutting through the glass-roofed Apple Market at Covent Garden, he weaved through the press of tourists, avoiding too-obvious glances over his shoulder and instead stopped suddenly at jewellery stalls, or stole glimpses reflected from the plate glass windows of shops on the perimeter of the market, but he saw no one suspicious. Still, he felt eyes on him like an itch between his shoulder blades.

Emerging opposite the Romanesque stone frontage of St Paul's Church, he hesitated for a second. A shout of alarm went up, and from his left, a helmeted cyclist with a messenger bag slung crossways tore across the stone sets and skidded in a half turn in front of him.

'Rick Turner!' he shouted, no hint of a question in those two words. He thrust his arm out and slapped an envelope square into the centre of Rick's chest. Rick staggered one step back before regaining his balance, clutching at the envelope and steadying himself, ready to launch after the courier. But he was already ten yards away, zig-zagging through the crowds, quickly out of sight.

Rick did a fast three-sixty turn to check but only a small family group of shocked Japanese tourists were paying him any attention. An older woman in the group was leaning heavily on a young woman, and Rick realised that she must have been injured trying to avoid the bike.

'Is she okay?' he asked.

The older male in the group, clearly the patriarch, scowled at him. 'Crazy man,' he shouted angrily; Rick wasn't sure if he meant the messenger, or Rick himself. The family moved off to one of the open-air seating areas and a waitress was at their table in seconds, offering high-priced tea and sympathy.

For a long, horrible moment, Rick stared at the envelope, wondering if Unwin had sent another grisly warning.

Sod this! He tore it open and found a single slip of paper inside. It read, '*Bakker Books, Cecil Court.*'

Rick cursed under his breath. *Another wild goose chase?*

He knew the place: a cut-through between St Martin's Lane and Charing Cross Road, Cecil Court was like stepping back into the nineteenth century, the narrow, pedestrianised street crowded on both sides with Victorian shop frontages accommodating bookstores, fine art galleries, antique dealers and the like. Three minutes later, he was standing, slightly out of breath, in front of a four-storey building.

He looked again at the slip of paper. The handwriting seemed vaguely familiar. He turned it over and saw that two words had been written in tiny print in the bottom left corner: 'Self-Help'. An instruction to find the relevant section in the store? A twisted joke?

The shop was narrow but deep, extending a good forty feet from the bowed display window to an opening at the rear, curtained off with what looked like a sheet of chain mail. The walls on either side were lined with shelving, and further bookcases were ranked, row on row, at right angles to the walls. A desk on which rested a cash register and card swipe device was crammed into a tiny space to the right of the door and seated there was a woman with short, cropped hair and a pleasant expression.

'Can I help?' she said, with a slight emphasis on the last word, and – could it be – a flicker of humour?

'Self-Help,' Rick said.

'Fourth floor. Stairs are halfway down on the left.'

Wide enough for two to pass up to the second floor, the wooden steps narrowed at the third and wound in a tight spiral to the eaves of the old building. A sign in yellow and black above the door lintel read, 'CAUTION – mind your head!'

Rick ducked, stepping at a crouch over the threshold into a slanting room. The bookshelves here were mostly restricted to the outer walls, and the middle of the floor was open. Feeling a faint tremor in the floor joists as he walked across the space towards a single bookcase jutting into the space near one of the small, latticed windows, he understood why.

He stopped short of the stack and listened, sensing he was not alone.

'Don't make me come around there,' he said.

A faint whisper of sound, as of someone replacing a book on the shelf, then a man came out of the shadows—

And Rick came face to face with the assassin.

Today, the human chameleon wore a good charcoal-grey suit over a gunmetal-grey T-shirt. Freshly shaved, light-brown hair in a short businessman cut, he was lean and loose-limbed – the very picture of a wealthy man about town.

Rick glared at him with searing rage in his heart. '*Bastard.*'

He threw a punch with his right; the assassin blocked with his left and moved in, bringing his right forearm hard against Rick's chest. He followed through with his right hip and leg, turning and dropping, using his weight and Rick's own to bring him down.

Rick rolled and was on his feet in a second. He attacked again, furious to have been so easily thrown. This time with a jab punch, feinting first with his left and striking with his right – and ended up flat on his back, winded, having missed the man's defensive move entirely.

'I just want to talk,' the suited man said.

'*Fuck* that.'

Frowning, the man moved into a defensive stance as Rick rolled left, ignoring the pain and bouncing to his feet, attacking again and again, but the man just kept blocking and turning, blocking and turning, blocking and turning, giving Rick a little contemptuous shove after each attempt, keeping him off balance and sending him a few steps away. Rick, panting, felt like the new kid at the dojo being taught a lesson by the sensei.

Finally, he rushed at the older man, roaring, head down, and felt himself turn under the sensei's hands, swinging almost a full three-sixty degrees until he slammed into a bookshelf.

'Rick – stop fighting,' the man said, breathing hard now. '*Please.*'

'Let me *go*, you bastard.' Rick struggled but was in a lock so strong that every muscle and tendon shrieked as he fought it.

'I'll let you go when you stop fighting.'

'I'll stop fighting when you tell me where she is.'

Was it shock, or a loss of concentration that caused the man to ease his grip? Rick didn't care, he played his advantage, twisting and pushing, using his momentum to topple books and create the space he needed to turn. He grabbed a book from the shelf, striking hard at the man's larynx, but was blocked again. Rick felt a sharp tap to his upper arm. A shooting pain tore down the radial nerve and his fingers flexed involuntarily, dropping the weapon.

Immediately he was floored, and the man had Rick in an armlock. 'You're making a *mistake*,' he growled.

'No – *you* made the mistake when you took her.'

'Took *who* for pity's sake?'

His face mashed into the dirty lino of the floor, humiliating tears squeezing from his eyes, Rick still threatened: 'Tell me where she is, or I swear I'll *kill* you.'

'Jessica?' the man said. 'Did someone take Jessica?'

The tension released and in the time it took Rick to gather himself and struggle to his feet, the man had retreated to the far end of the room.

'Jesus, Rick,' he said. 'You thought it was *me*?'

'Why the hell else are you here?' Rick yelled.

'I'd heard that Unwin was about to be released and guessed he must have something on the lead investigator.' The man flicked at the dust on his good suit. 'And although officially it's not your name over the door, it's definitely your show, isn't it, Rick?'

The two men stood staring one at the other, neither speaking, neither sure what to believe, but tied to each other by bonds that could never be broken.

The assassin has many names, and well-thumbed passports for nationalities across Europe and the Americas. Although he doesn't know any of these aliases, Rick is one of only a handful of people who know his true identity. His voice is different, his hair too, his eyes are not quite as blue as Rick remembered, and there is no lingering trace of London's East End in his accent, but he would know this man anywhere. For this is Sam Turner, the brother who vanished out of his life more than a decade ago.

Chapter 15

THE SHOP MANAGER SEEMED UNTROUBLED by the violent argument that had raged for some minutes on her premises, although Rick noticed that the sign on the door had been turned to 'CLOSED'. The woman looked up from her book and asked, 'Rearranging the furniture, gents?'

'There's no serious damage, but my apologies for the mess, Mila,' Sam said, and Rick thought, *Sam on friendly terms with a bookseller – this just keeps getting weirder.*

'Oh, don't trouble yourself, Adam,' the unflappable Ms Bakker said. 'The fee will no doubt defray any expenses.'

Sam Turner nodded his thanks. 'And you'll be in touch about the Chandler?'

Her eyes sparkled with excitement. 'I expect to have news within the week.'

They left the bookstore via the chain mail curtain, which gave on to a pinched and grimy corridor with a cluster of tiny rooms off it, and finally to a back door.

'Is that what I call you, now?' Rick asked with a sly look. '"Adam"? Or is that a surname?' He tried it out: '*Mr* Adam?'

'I'd prefer you didn't call me anything at all,' Sam said.

'But since I only use Adam when I'm buying first editions, it wouldn't be relevant anywhere else.'

'I never saw you as a reader.'

Sam lifted one shoulder. 'People change.'

'No,' Rick said. 'They don't.'

'You can call me Sam. But for your own sake – and Jessica's – do not refer to me as your brother.'

'All right, then. Sam it is.'

An hour later, Rick and Sam Turner were sipping coffee in a private dining room above a small restaurant near Leicester Square. At around five-ten, Sam was a little shorter, his face a little rounder than Rick's. He was pleasant and inoffensive looking, though Rick knew that dangerous currents ran beneath his still, somewhat bland expression. He also carried less muscle, but he was fast and ruthless – Rick's bruised ribs and shoulders were evidence of that.

'So,' Sam said, 'what makes you so sure Jessica has been abducted?'

'Where did you hear that Unwin was getting out?' Rick countered. *You don't just stroll into my life after all this time and expect me to spill my guts.*

Sam gazed back at him with a mild, empty expression, which was far from innocent.

'Was it Unwin?' Rick asked, after a few seconds of silence.

'No.'

'I don't believe you.'

Sam raised his shoulders: *Take it or leave it.*

'Why, Sam?' Rick demanded. 'Why show yourself *now*? It's been thirteen years – and I'm guessing this isn't your first visit to London since you ran.'

He caught a flicker in Sam's eyes and took it for an admission.

'You vanish, leaving me to deal with the mess you made, and stay gone – even when Mum got sick. I sent a message, like you said I should and – nothing.' He caught a flash of pain in his brother's eyes and gained a fierce satisfaction in seeing it.

'Let's say I thought you could use some help,' Sam said at last.

Rick felt his fists clench and he forced his hands flat on the table in front of him.

'Mum was sick for *three years*. I could have used some help then. And when Dad sank into the depression that killed him, it would've *helped* to have someone to talk to.'

Sam lifted his chin, accepting the argument, it seemed.

'Explain to me why it is you can't show up to help with family stuff – you know, like families do. But in a situation where I've got people I can actually call on for help, you magically appear, wanting to be all hands-on, using my girlfriend's name like you know her. Talking to *me* like you know me.'

Sam took a breath, and for a second Rick thought he might get an unguarded response but, always the strategist, his brother stopped and seemed to reconsider.

'Honest answer?'

'That would be a first,' Rick said, adding with a shrug, 'But what the hell – go for it.'

Sam held his gaze. 'When I heard that Unwin was getting out, I knew he must have something on you, and you always played things straight, so I knew it must be bad. I can help, if you'll let me – unless you'd prefer to rely on the people you say you can call on?'

Rick shook his head. 'She wouldn't survive the night.'

'What do you plan to do?'

'Give them what they want,' Rick said, a lump as hard as granite settling in the pit of his stomach.

'That'd be a career-killer.' Sam tilted his head, appraising him. 'Although there are other, more financially rewarding ways to earn a living.'

'So this what you do now – recruitment?'

'Among other things,' Sam said with an easy, untrustworthy smile.

No further information forthcoming, Rick prompted, 'What happened to the strong-arm stuff you used to do for Lockleigh?'

Theo Lockleigh was the bent lawyer who had given Sam his chance to move up from tenement boyo to a more rarefied and infinitely better paid job catering to big-city criminals.

'There was a man Lockleigh hired from time to time,' Sam said. 'Ex-Para – must have been about forty-five – still hitting the gym every day in the hopes of being hired for a gig that involved getting beaten up to save lesser men a beating. His knees were giving out and he had scars all over him. That poor sod was living proof that a career that involves putting your body through that kind of punishment isn't sustainable in the long term.' He shrugged. 'So I shifted focus.'

'To what, exactly?' Rick asked.

'Investigator, computer specialist, hacker, occasional fixer – skills like that never wear out – in fact, they just keep getting better.'

Well, the ego certainly hasn't shifted, Rick thought. *The 'focus' was still on Sam the Man and all his marvellous talents.* 'There's more to it than that, though, isn't there?' he said. 'I mean you've still got those street moves, so I'm thinking there's got to be something physical involved.'

Even as he said it, he was re-evaluating. Watching Sam's formal and respectful exchange with the bookstore owner, his easy manner negotiating with the restaurant manager for a private room, he'd known that this was not the Sam Turner who the hard lads on their horrible council estate had nicknamed Bam-Bam Sam. And when the restaurant waiting staff had come to take their order, he was relaxed and chatty, accepting their efforts to please with courtesy, despite all the unspoken emotion going on between the two of them.

He's doing what he always did, Rick realised. Sam had a genius for being what people needed him to be. He would modify his accent, his vocabulary – even his posture – depending on who he was with. Confronted by authority on their childhood escapades, Sam could charm his way out of trouble, laying it on so thick, you'd swear he was minor aristocracy. Cornered by dangerous youths on unfamiliar territory, he'd brazen it out – get such a mad look in his eye that even Rick was afraid of what he might do.

Sam was watching him keenly, as though he could read every thought as it appeared, and to evict that uneasy notion from his mind, Rick leaned forward aggressively. 'What, no answer?'

'Oh, you know I *hate* talking about myself.' The quirk of Sam's eyebrow said he acknowledged the outrageousness of the lie. 'Now, what makes you so sure that Unwin has Jessica?'

Rick handed Sam the small, padded envelope containing the earring Rick had bought for Jess only weeks earlier, watching as Sam peeked inside it, then tipped it into his hand, examining it closely.

'It looks good quality,' Sam said.

'Well of course it is – what d'you take me for?'

'I meant that it wouldn't be something that any thug with twenty quid spare could pick up on a market stall to put the frighteners on a boyfriend.'

'It's *hers*, Sam. Unwin's slimy brief confirmed it.'

'All right.' Sam returned the earring to the jiffy bag and slid it over the table to Rick. 'Do you want to bring Jessica home safely?'

Rick gritted his teeth. 'Her name is *Jess*, and I don't think I need to answer that.'

Sam looked over the gleaming white rim of his coffee cup. 'And if I can work out a way for you to find Jess *and* keep your job?'

His heart thudding thickly, hardly daring to hope, Rick said, 'Got a plan?'

Sam returned the cup delicately onto the saucer. 'Not yet. But I have contacts, resources and money. The three things that make the world turn.'

'Did these contacts tell you who shot Unwin's right-hand man last night?'

Sam looked him in the eye. 'No.'

'Blimey,' Rick said, with a blink of surprise. 'No hesitation – I think that might've been the God's honest truth.'

'It is. And – think about this, Rick – if they got to Austin King, who are they coming for next?'

Rick stared at him. 'You think they'll come for Unwin? Is this a *takeover* bid?'

'I don't know what it is,' Sam said, 'but I do know that he's desperate to get out, and when a man like Unwin cries, little children die in the streets.'

'What is that – a quote or something?'

'A misquote.'

'From one of your first editions? Don't try and tell me you actually read them.'

He expected Sam to shrug that off, but after a few moments, he said, 'D'you still have my Marvel comics collection?'

'What? I dunno – in the loft, maybe.'

'You might want to dust them off – some of those are first editions – worth quite a bit, too.' He paused. 'I was *always* a reader, Rick. My tastes have matured, that's all.'

Rick experienced a ripple of shame. He'd resented Sam so long for abandoning him after the killing that it had become easier to label him thuggish and stupid, rather than accept his disappearance as a smart move. The fact was, Sam had always been cleverer than Rick: cleverer and more at ease with himself and with others.

The silence stretched and Sam waited a second or two longer before saying, 'My point is, we need to find Jess before Unwin gets too desperate. And if he *has* got enemies breathing down his neck, that will be soon.'

'All right—'

'I haven't finished. If his enemies get to Unwin *before* you find Jess, she won't stand a chance.'

Rick felt his breath becoming ragged. 'You're telling me it's a no-win situation.'

'I'm telling you we need to act fast.'

They locked gazes, and Rick nodded. A tacit truce had been drawn; for now, their common goal was to find Jess.

'Just don't expect me to trust you.'

'You'll warm to me,' Sam said. 'Everyone does.'

Over the next twenty minutes, Rick talked Sam through the sequence of events, pausing occasionally to field texts from the Incident Room. Most of the team thought he was in Court No. 2, and for those who had actually shown up at the Old Bailey, he'd just nipped back to the office, or was in conference with Mr Kildoran's crew, or was out on a coffee break.

His phone buzzed again; Kildoran this time. He swiped the screen to reject the call.

'What d'you want me to do?' he demanded.

'Get yourself a burner phone,' Sam said. 'Pay cash.' He jotted a number onto a corner of a paper napkin. 'That's my mobile number. Text me as soon as you have the burner; I'll let you know what I need, evidentially.'

'I'll get over to the office now.'

'No,' Sam said. 'Right now, you need to show your face in the courtroom.'

'Not a chance.'

Sam tapped Rick's phone, lying on the tabletop. 'You must've had a dozen texts since we sat down, and if I'm not mistaken, the last call was from the lead prosecutor. Your colleagues need to think it's business as usual.'

Rick began to argue, but Sam spoke over him. 'Meanwhile, get word to Unwin's go-between that you're working on a way to get him what he wants. Tell him you could maybe throw in an attack of nerves on the stand, but it has to be cumulative – one mistake piled on top of another.'

'Thanks, Sam, I know what cumulative means, but the prosecution's gonna call me to give evidence in the *next few days* – I haven't got *time* to piss about.'

'Understood. And the sooner you're out of here, the sooner I can get to work.'

Rick stood. 'Okay, I'll do it. But don't cut me out, Sam,' he warned.

'Not a bit of it,' Sam said. 'We two desperados will set the world to rights together – it'll be quite like old times.'

Given that a man died the last time they met, Rick wasn't sure he relished Sam's take on setting the world to rights.

Chapter 16

Monday afternoon

NUMBER TWO COURT AT THE OLD BAILEY was reserved for high-security trials. Additional airport-style checks were in place at the doors, and the security staff were thorough. Rick sent Sam a quick text from his newly purchased burner phone before switching all his mobile phones off.

The court was hushed when Rick arrived, everyone's attention fixed on Unwin's defence barrister, in mid-flow.

Rick made a formal bow to the royal coat of arms carved into the oak pediment above the judge's head – the symbol of justice in English and Welsh courts – and took a moment to assess the room. Counsels for the defence and the prosecution sat on the same row of dark oak seating to the judge's left, arrayed like church misericords at right angles to the judicial bench. All of the lawyers, including Ms Justice Latymer, were robed and wigged.

As one of the key investigators, Rick was allowed access to the slightly racked seating behind the lawyers, rather than having to fight for a seat in the gallery where, despite reporting restrictions on the trial, every available space was jammed with press and media, many of whom had queued early for a spot. Under the overhang of the gallery, he recognised the faces of a few TV journalists who had been given privileged spots in the main body of the courtroom.

The dock dominated the space, standing front and centre, high above the lawyers and court personnel. Unwin, dressed in suit and tie, his grey hair neatly trimmed, looked every inch the successful businessman. Mounsey sat behind the defence team. Seeing Rick, he glanced towards Unwin in the dock and gave a slight nod.

The proceedings were moving faster than he had expected, and during the next hour, the defence counsel completed his opening speech and counsel for the prosecution requested an adjournment so that his team could reorganise their witness schedule. Anthony Kildoran was granted the leeway he had hoped for by Ms Justice Latymer. She'd allowed mention of Austin King's 'gangland-style murder' and 'his boss, Thomas Unwin, who stands in the dock', not once, but three times. But Kildoran's fourth attempt broke the charm. The judge admonished Kildoran, saying that a King's Counsel should know better and added that, as he'd had over six months to gather his evidence and prepare his case, rescheduling witnesses should be the work of a minute.

With a slight bow, Mr Kildoran ventured, 'While I am gratified by my lady's faith in my abilities, I am neither a miracle worker, nor a time traveller.'

Rick took this ungracious response as a sign of the pressure the prosecutor was under. The judge was not in a forgiving mood; she chastised Kildoran rather crossly and underlined her displeasure by announcing a fifteen-minute break.

Unwin was taken down, and at the top of the steps leading to the maze of tunnels under the courts he paused, looked Rick in the eye, and deliberately tugged his left ear. Rick held his gaze without flinching, though his guts clenched, and every inch of his scalp seemed to prickle.

He dived in his pocket for his personal phone on the way out, but hearing his name called, he left it there and waited for a breathless lawyer to catch up with him. Rick recognised the woman as one of Kildoran's junior barristers.

'Sergeant,' she said. 'Mr Kildoran would like a word, if you can spare a minute?'

The anguish of not knowing if he'd been messaged was excruciating, but he couldn't really refuse. He followed the woman to a room off the main corridor, where Kildoran and his team had spread out an array of papers and laptops over a series of scuffed and ill-assorted tables that had been crammed together. Coffee cups and sandwich wrappers littered their surfaces, and four young trainees, still in their black robes, were hunched over their files like a murder of crows, jotting notes onto legal pads and into their computers.

Kildoran seemed in good spirits for a man who had just been publicly rebuked by the presiding judge in the trial he was prosecuting. He moved with energy and excitement, pointing to relevant lines of text and giving instructions to his team as he circled the tables. He'd shed his wig, and as he peered over shoulders, his bald head gleamed under the artificial lights.

Seeing Rick, he straightened.

'Sergeant Turner! Glad you could make it.' He threw both arms wide, as if inviting Rick into a party, then brought his hands together in a clap. 'Well, that worked nicely.'

'Your little outburst was a ploy?'

'Oh, I wouldn't call it an *outburst*, as such,' Kildoran said. 'A gentle needling, perhaps – m'lady abhors sarcasm; it offends her dignity. But after tea and biscuits her good humour will be restored. The thing about a fifteen-minute break: it's too long to sit and do nothing and too short to do anything useful. So half the jurors will ask for the loo, the other half for a glass of water, or whatever, and I'd be surprised if they are all where they should be at the allotted time. And when they *are* safely reinstalled, I'll faff about for a bit before asking the judge to consider a point of law which – as we speak – my learned colleagues are looking up. Ms Latymer will ultimately dismiss it as spurious, but she'll have to send the jury out while we barristers argue the point. That should take us to four o'clock, and she won't want to overshoot on the first day, so with fair weather and a following wind, we *could* be back at chambers by four-thirty.'

Rick smiled despite himself. 'Looks like you won't be needing me, then.'

'Not *just* yet,' Kildoran said. 'But Mr Goodlass does seem to be in a fearful hurry, so you might want to read over your notes, and do some bathroom mirror rehearsals over the next couple of days.'

'Of course.' Rick hoped the sudden heat he felt didn't show in his face. 'Is that why you wanted to see me?'

'Partly. I saw that you weren't around for much of the proceedings – quite understandable, under the circumstances,' he added reassuringly. 'You'll have a full breakdown from one of my team by six p.m., but in sum: video testimony is *out* for your sequestered witness; video recordings of King's interviews are *in*.' He must have seen the surprise on Rick's face, because he added, 'Ye-es, I was expecting to do battle over that, but counsel for the defence capitulated *very* readily – I fear he might be trying to rush the proceedings.'

The guilty thought occurred to Rick that the defence's cooperation could hang on knowing that the trial would be over before they got to the dead accountant's interview recordings. He might be doing Unwin's barrister, Goodlass, an injustice, but complicit or not, he had just cranked up the pressure.

'The other thing I wanted to mention,' Kildoran added, 'and I don't mean to nag – is that we could do with Mr Collins's expert witness recommendations so that we can make approaches sooner, rather than later. I *could* ask one of the existing experts to double up, answering the questions I would have put to King, but it wouldn't serve the narrative as well as having a surrogate standing in for the guilty party.'

'I'll have a chat with Dave this evening, let you know,' Rick promised, his hand straying to his pocket. Even as he left, he was checking for messages.

There was nothing from Jess on his personal phone. His work mobile logged Kildoran's voicemail and three more from DCI Steiner, wanting updates. The burner had one text message from Sam; he needed background on Unwin, his crew and associates, names, addresses – photos, too, if he could get them. He also asked for Jess's phone number and the name of the production company whose audition she was supposed to attend that morning. Rick forwarded both, adding the name and number of the agent who had set up the audition. The rest would take longer.

He checked his watch, and with a sinking sense of time running out, saw that he was overdue a trip to the Incident Room to report back to DCI Steiner.

Chapter 17

STEINER DEMANDED TO KNOW why her lead investigator had been AWOL most of the day. Rick made an excuse of having to chase Dave Collins about an expert witness to stand in for Austin King; then court in the afternoon and a post-session conference with Kildoran.

She listened impatiently to his summary of the meeting, eyeing him suspiciously.

'All right,' she said. 'I expect a written report by this evening.'

'I'll forward Kildoran's to you as soon as I get it.'

'No-o,' she said in a patient tone that was anything but. 'You will read his report, assimilate, and feed back to me with your *own* impressions and any suggestions.'

'I won't get it before six at the earliest,' Rick said, hearing the strain in his voice. 'I've still got to head over to the SFO to see Dave Collins, and Kildoran wants me to rehearse my testimony – he might call me early—'

'*This evening*,' she said sharply.

It took him until after seven p.m. to finish and by then, the office was quiet. He pulled up the files he had on Unwin and his crew. A specialist surveillance team had added a fair number of images, building on the core that the murdered PI had gathered.

Rick had bought a small thumb drive on his way back from the Old Bailey. He slotted it into the USB port and for ten minutes sorted, copied, and transferred images and compiled a list of names, addresses, and vehicle registration numbers, his eyes flitting busily between the screen and the door, his heart jumping in his chest every time someone passed along the corridor.

He heard DS Stott clear his throat at the very instant he removed the tiny drive from the USB port. Closing his fist on the drive, he swung his chair around.

'All right, mate?' Stott said – a greeting, rather than an enquiry after his health – and Rick responded with a shrug and a slight grimace.

Stott's gaze flicked quickly from Rick's eyes to the hand that held the drive. Or maybe it didn't, and it was just Rick's guilty conscience.

'I heard Steiner chewing your ear off earlier. You doing okay?'

'Yeah . . . I'm good,' Rick said, hearing the hesitation in his voice and seeing too much sympathy in Stott's gaze.

'Can't be easy, all this going on.'

For one dizzy second, Rick thought he was talking about Jess. He covered the flurry of emotion he felt with a cough. 'We'll manage.'

'You might,' Stott chuckled, 'but I'm not sure the rest of us will – Steiner's been hormonal all day, screaming like a fishwife—'

'You'd better not let Maddie hear you talking like that.'

Stott's mouth twisted into a smile. 'Right – she'd tear my balls off and . . .' He petered off into silence and glanced anxiously over his shoulder as if his wife might storm into the room with murderous intent. Coming out of his reverie, he gave himself a little shake.

'Steiner shouldn't be asking you to do her job for her on top of everything else, though. Why hasn't *she* been in court? It's supposed to be her case. I'll tell you why: she's embarrassed to face Unwin.'

'Embarrassed?' Rick said.

'You do know she was chasing Unwin for a year? Thought she had him, an' all. But it turned out she was only chasing her own tail.' He laughed.

Rick nodded. 'Ghosh mentioned it at the pub last night. Unwin's a slippery bastard, that's for sure,' he said, his jaw clenched.

Stott's eyes searched Rick's face. 'Anything I can do?'

'Nah, thanks for the offer, but I've got it covered,' Rick said.

For a second, it looked like Stott might try again, but then he sighed and said, 'Well, if you want to talk, I'm here.'

As a rookie detective, and even up to a year ago, Rick had invariably turned to Jim Stott for help. He couldn't say when that had changed; perhaps when he'd noticed Jim's drinking had encroached into daytimes and weekdays. He felt a stab of guilt: Jess was right, he had been judgemental, bound up in the rules. Had there been a degree of arrogance too, believing himself too experienced – too *savvy* – to ask for guidance from his old mentor?

It was tempting to blurt it all out, to tell Stott everything – to confess how terrified he was at the thought of losing Jess.

What gave him pause was he knew that Stott would feel morally bound to report Jess's abduction – would urge him to trust the Met to bring her home safely. But in the early stages of the Unwin inquiries, Rick had done battle with colleagues who'd called his professionalism into question – and many of those he'd proved wrong had made it very clear that they bitterly resented him for exposing their mistakes. How could he rely on any of them?

So, he smiled, shoving his hand into his pocket, releasing the thumb drive from his sweaty palm, and said, 'Yeah. Thanks, Stotty.'

They stood for an awkward moment.

Finally, DS Stott cleared his throat. 'Fancy a quick half?'

'I've still got a meeting with Dave at the SFO,' Rick said, adding with a weak smile, 'And I need to get a mirror practice in.'

Chapter 18

Monday night

SAM HIRED A PRIVATE KARAOKE ROOM in a dive bar near Tower Bridge for their next meeting. Dressed down in a short, black peacoat and pork pie hat in deference to the strict 'no suits' house rule, he blended well with the hipster clientele.

Rick arrived late, looking frazzled, and handed him a thumb drive. Sam slotted it into his laptop without comment; Rick was boiling with such suppressed rage that Sam could practically hear the rumble of the oncoming eruption.

With the dull thud of karaoke music pounding the walls either side of them, Rick talked him through the images, beginning with those Wilson, the private investigator, had taken. Wilson had been thorough, snapping not only the obvious bosses, but the men who hovered in the background. Sam listened attentively, making perfunctory notes although he knew Unwin, of course. He'd been acquainted with Haskins and King, too – although only very briefly, and neither had survived the encounter. Some of the others were familiar as types: the men who flanked Unwin or Haskins in a crowd, those who held doors, the drivers and flunkeys, eyes constantly on a swivel. Their build, bearing and demeanour marked them out as bodyguards, bruisers, henchmen.

He stopped at a grouping of four men.

'We think that's the image that got Wilson killed,' Rick said. 'He took it inside a five-star hotel near Hyde Park. The man in the centre is Alan Hugenot, CEO of Laligne private bank; he commissioned the contract on Wilson.'

Sam tapped the figure on the left of the frame. 'Who's this?'

'Charlie Haskins, Unwin's financial adviser.'

'Ah, one of the victims in your conspiracy trial.' Sam felt Rick's gaze on him but didn't look up. Instead, he zoomed in on the fourth figure in the group, a broad-shouldered man with black hair and a watchful gaze. 'This one has the build of a minder, but that suit must have cost a fortune.'

'Yeah,' Rick said. 'He's a conundrum. We have a witness who says he spoke with an Eastern European accent, but that's it.'

'Surely *Hugenot* could identify Mr Tall Dark and Dangerous – if only to earn himself a few brownie points, shave a few years off his sentence?'

Rick shook his head. 'Seems he'd rather do the time.'

'Eastern European criminals can be very persuasive in that way,' Sam said, swiping through the images a second time. 'How traceable are these back to you?'

'Completely,' Rick said.

'The police run regular checks on use of the system, don't they?'

'Yep.' Rick took a breath, and Sam realised with some wonder how much this small criminal act must have cost his brother.

'Yeah,' Rick said again, 'but I reckoned you'd want hi-def, so I didn't really have a choice. The checks are random, so I'll just have to hope it works the same way as the lottery.'

Sam looked at him in question.

'I've never even won a lucky dip.'

Sam chuckled. 'Fingers crossed your bad luck holds, then.'

Rick remained grim-faced. 'I'll deal with any fallout if it happens.'

He gave his head a small, irritated shake and said, 'So, what've you been up to while I was flushing my career down the toilet?'

'Gathering a team,' Sam said.

'And what're they going to do?'

'You don't need to know the details.'

'Yeah, Sam, I do.'

'Oh, Rick,' Sam said. 'You know what you're like with rules.' As a kid, Rick always needed to know the rules of the game, their individual roles in it, before he would get involved. Sam usually thought them up on the spur of the moment, and mostly it was all right, but if they didn't fit Rick's parameters of acceptability, he would abstain. 'Remember that time at London Zoo?'

Rick folded his arms. 'You mean the time we *broke in* to London Zoo?'

'I suppose, *technically*, it was after hours,' Sam conceded. 'But you had to make a huge deal of it.'

'It was *one o'clock in the morning*, and we were supposed to just take pictures, but *you* decided you wanted to take a koala home, broke into the marsupial enclosure, set off the alarm, and brought security *and* the police down on us.'

Sam shrugged. 'I got us out, didn't I?'

Rick snorted. 'Good to see that selective memory's still working for you – *I* got us out after *you* froze on that wall like a virgin jockey.'

It was true. They'd run to the perimeter. With the surefooted-ness of a mountain goat and a steeplejack's head for heights, Rick was up and straddling the sheer structure in seconds, ready for the climb down. Sam scrambled to the top after him but balked at the long drop on the other side, and Rick had to coax him down, guiding him to every foothold till he was safely on solid ground, and with only seconds to spare.

'My fourteenth birthday challenge,' Rick said, adding with malicious glee, 'So that would make you, what – twenty-two?'

'Don't change the subject,' Sam said, and was gratified to hear Rick laugh.

'I never had a problem bending rules, Sam,' Rick said. 'I had a problem with doing things that hurt people.'

Also true. Rick had always had an overabundance of empathy. But when it came to exploring abandoned buildings to active railyards, tunnels and fairground roller coasters, he'd been totally fearless.

Rick fixed him with a look, in full earnest again. 'Listen to me. I'll do *whatever* it takes to bring Jess home.'

Sam knew that Rick's respect for the rules of engagement was inbuilt in his psyche. If he laid out what his crew were willing to do – the rules they would not only bend but break into tiny shards to find Jess – Rick would likely call a halt. So, he sidestepped, giving his brother something else to think about:

'We know Unwin took Jess. Chances are he's got her stashed at one of his properties. So—'

'He owns a frigging *empire*,' Rick interrupted. 'How're we going to narrow that down?'

In answer, Sam pinched the image on his laptop screen, zooming in on two flint-eyed men behind Unwin. 'By targeting Unwin's team.'

'Good luck with that,' Rick said, with a twitch of his eyebrows. 'Unwin has a *lot* of employees – and he has been known to use kids as lookouts and carriers.'

'Currently?' Sam said, picking up on the use of the past tense.

Rick tilted his head. 'It's debatable. Either he's scaled back on drug trafficking, or he's more careful – the surveillance unit didn't pick up any activity they felt we could act on. He brings in extra muscle when he needs it, but the men he keeps closest have been with him since he was a Young Turk, building his criminal enterprises.'

'And those men are . . .?'

Rick slid the laptop to face him and selected the relevant images.

'The man on the left of this group is Tommy Novac. Ex-boxer, lives in a high-rise with his old mum. The other one is Darren Mays – lives in a maisonette in Barking with his wife, two kids and a boxer dog named Pudge. Those two are the longest-serving members of Unwin's crew.'

'Is it feasible Unwin has placed Jess with one of his crew?' Sam asked.

'Tommy takes his shoes off before he's allowed in the flat – I don't see Mrs Novac allowing him to bring a stray girl home – let alone one in handcuffs. As for Darren, there isn't enough room at his house to stash the odd spliff he's partial to, never mind a full-grown kidnap victim.'

Sam watched his brother, thinking Rick was thorough. 'Wherever they're keeping Jess, it takes manpower. So, we need to look at who's missing from Unwin's crew.'

'They're not exactly clocking-in types, Sam.'

Sam nodded. 'Okay . . . but while the boss is away, *someone* must be keeping tabs, making sure the business keeps ticking over.'

'That would be Austin King,' Rick said. 'Only, as of last night, King is unavailable. Permanently.'

'What about the brief – the one who had you followed?'

'Mounsey,' Rick said. 'He knows a lot – and yeah – he might even know where Jess is. But we can't touch him, Sam – it's too dangerous.'

'Agreed.' Sam had heard things about Callum Mounsey. 'But Mr Mounsey isn't the only one who can have people followed.'

Rick looked doubtful. 'Mounsey won't go anywhere near the actual location.'

'No. Which is why we'll follow the men.'

'That'll take a hell of a lot of bodies.'

'It will.'

Rick's eyes widened. 'You have the personnel for that?'

Gratified by the surprise on his brother's face, Sam said, 'Ready to go as soon as they have names and addresses.'

'How – I mean how can you afford that?'

'Worried there's blood on it?' Sam asked. 'No man alive ever earned that kind of money from bloodshed – except, maybe, an arms dealer – and I'm no arms dealer,' he added, quelling an angry response from Rick.

'So where'd the money come from?'

'I suppose I've Theo Lockleigh to thank, once again. He was moving into transatlantic waters with some of his dealings, and he asked me, as his resident computer geek, to look into new ways of making secure, anonymous payments. Shortly after we parted ways, I saw some exciting stuff about a new cryptocurrency called Bitcoin.'

'You got in early,' Rick said.

'Got in early, stayed in till just before the crypto crash.' He caught a slight flicker in Rick's eyes. 'You seem surprised. Did you think I'd blow it all, Rick?'

'Well . . .'

He smiled. 'Okay, back then I did have little a problem with impulse control, and at first I did burn through a lot of it. But I left enough in my wallets to make me stupendously wealthy.'

'Is that how you paid for the house?'

'Which house? Oh – you mean the family home.'

'You got so many you're confused?' Rick shot back.

Sam had several under different identities, but he left the question unanswered. 'As I said – Bitcoin happened *after* I split with Theo.' He saw the emotional struggle on his brother's face and added, 'The house was payment for a gambling debt.'

'Someone bet their *house*?'

'Literally.'

Rick didn't look reassured, but Sam had said all he was going to say on the subject. He checked his watch. 'I have somewhere I need to be. Are we doing this, or not?'

Rick nodded, still looking slightly stunned by the revelation. Sam took back control of his laptop and opened a VPN to access a chatroom he'd set up for the purpose. While he waited for confirmation that his instructions had been received, he asked, 'What was the PI's angle?'

'I told you,' Rick said. 'He was investigating Haskins's ex – trying to track down assets he'd hidden during their divorce.'

'Come on, Rick – Wilson ended up a bloody smear on a roadway – that isn't the action of a sneaky accountant who's squirrelled away a bit of cash.'

'I'm always amazed at what people will do for a bit of cash,' Rick said, fixing him with a hard and unforgiving look. 'He found some of the shell companies Haskins had set up for Unwin.'

'Blackmail,' Sam said. 'He went after some of the big players in these shots.'

'We checked Wilson's mobile phone, home number, and office landline,' Rick said, his tone cautious and official-sounding. 'There were no calls logged to any of Unwin's contacts.'

'I know evasion when I hear it,' Sam said. 'And this is the digital age – there are other, more secure means of communication.'

Rick stared at him from across the table. He seemed to be considering, and after a moment he gave a slight shake of his head. 'Wilson handed over the pictures to Haskins's ex. Why would he do that if he intended to blackmail the people in them? As for Unwin – Wilson would have to be a fool to go after a known gangland boss – and his widow says Kirk Wilson was no fool.'

'So,' Sam said patiently, 'what got him killed?'

No answer.

Sam watched his brother closely. 'I know you've got a theory.'

Rick's expression was unreadable – and Sam prided himself on his ability to read others. Was he calculating the risks of voicing his suspicions, or wondering why Sam should be so interested?

After a long pause, Rick said, 'Wilson made one call from his mobile through to the main switchboard at New Scotland Yard two days before he was killed. We couldn't establish who he spoke to, or what it was about.'

'So, he tried to report what he knew to the police, and went to the wrong cop?'

'Not that we can prove. We got the hit-and-run driver, though – after I got the inquiry into Wilson's death reopened. Bastard had dumped the stolen car a couple of miles away, on a side street around King's Cross. Thought he'd been clever, knowing it'd get towed pretty fast. It did, but he got caught on a video doorbell. Good image, too.'

Sam sighed. 'Technology will be the death of honest criminality.'

'I'm sure Wilson's widow and eight-year-old son would find that reassuring,' Rick said coldly.

'You do take yourself seriously these days, don't you?' Sam said. 'Let me guess – the hit-and-run driver was police?'

'He was head of security at Laligne Bank,' Rick said, with a scowl that could curdle milk. 'In exchange for witness protection for his wife and kids, he gave us his boss's name. He was paid cash for the hit-and-run, but our forensic accountant traced the exact amount back to the bank's CEO – it seems that in his panic, Hugenot sidestepped the protocols designed to hide the paper trail.'

'And the CEO was acting under Unwin's orders?'

Rick gave a brief nod.

'Who paid for the hit – the mystery Eastern European?'

Rick gazed at him, his face impassive. 'The PI's murder is being tried right now in Southwark Crown Court. Different investigation team, different prosecution team. It's nothing to do with me.'

Sam leaned forward, peering into his eyes. 'Except for the fact that Unwin is charged with conspiracy in that very same death. A death *you* identified as murder, which means it's got a *lot* to do with you. I know you're not naïve, Rick – please don't assume that I am.'

His brother's flat gaze did not waver, and Sam tried a different approach. 'So, Wilson was killed for poking his nose in, but why Haskins? It doesn't make sense.'

'It does if Haskins was hiding more than his marital assets.'

'Ah, he was skimming Unwin's accounts.' Sam sat back. 'He wouldn't take kindly to that.'

Rick nodded. 'Unwin left a decent interlude so nobody would see the link between Haskins and the PI.'

'But you *did* see the link,' Sam said, coming to the question that had been tormenting him since the previous night. 'You're called out to a sudden death – a drowning – sad, but you know, accidents happen. The case was closed. And then you *reopen* it.'

'How're your team shaping up?' Rick said.

There was a lot going on behind Rick's eyes that Sam still couldn't read. *It never used to be like that*, he thought. Time was, he'd had to teach Rick how to tell a convincing lie.

'Sam – the team?' Rick said. 'I haven't got all night.'

Sam glanced at the screen. 'One still to confirm. Humour me – I know it takes a lot to reopen a closed case. Didn't that make you look a bit of an idiot?'

Nettled by Sam's calculated attack on his skills, Rick said, 'First of all, it wasn't *my* case, so it wasn't me who looked like an idiot. Second, it got reopened because I found the link between Haskins, Unwin, and the private investigator. With Unwin linked to both men, two tragic accidents started to look like something much more sinister.'

Sam laughed. 'You always were like a dog with a bone.' Rick bristled, but Sam pressed on: 'Seriously. The pathologist, the CSIs, the police inquiry, *and* the coroner all concluded that Haskins's death was an accident. Why didn't *you*?' He was asking out of professional curiosity, but also because he needed to know where he had blundered.

Rick seemed to debate how much he could safely say. Finally, he shrugged. 'What the hell. After the inquest verdict, I kept seeing Haskins dead in that hotel bathroom.'

He described the scene that Sam remembered very well.

'I kept thinking, it's like a picture. You know, a famous one – from an art gallery.'

'The Death of Marat,' Sam said, absently. 'A decorous murder.'

'Death of who?'

'It's a painting by Jacques-Louis David. Marat was a radical of the French Revolution, stabbed to death in his bath by Charlotte Corday. Ironically, *she* was a moderate.' Sam regarded his brother with new respect. 'Got to hand it to you, Rick, you tore down a criminal empire from one slightly off-kilter accidental drowning.'

Rick glared at him, clearly not flattered by the compliment. 'It wasn't an accident; Haskins was murdered. And Unwin's empire might be showing a few cracks, but he's using me to do the remedial work.'

'True enough. One final question: if Haskins's death wasn't your case, what were you doing at the scene?'

Before Rick could answer, his smartphone gave a shrill notification beep. Glancing at it, Rick paled. 'From Jess,' he said.

She was chained to a radiator in an empty room. Her eyes were swollen and red, and she had a shadow of bruising just above her jaw, as if a very large hand had gripped her face, hard.

'Type an answer,' Sam said. 'Tell them you want to talk to her. Try to keep the line open – I've got people monitoring it.'

Rick sent a message and waited. 'No reply,' he said. 'I think they've gone.'

Sam typed a question onto his laptop and sent it to his team. 'You're right – it's switched off again.' A second message popped up on the screen. 'But they think she's still in central London.'

'We need to do better, Sam.' Rick's voice was shaking, and as he set down the phone, Sam was intrigued to see that his hands were, too.

'Tell me about her.'

'What d'you want to know?'

'How will she respond to this? Is she strong? Does she have courage? Will she fight?'

Rick's hands were clenched in front of him, but now he relaxed a little, fingers still interweaved, but open. 'We met in a pub. Her date had stood her up, though God knows why any man would do that to Jess. *Everyone* noticed her: huge brown eyes, hair curling to her shoulders, perfect figure, slinky dress, killer heels – and a glow about her, you know?' He gazed at his hands as though the memory was playing out on his upturned palms. 'A guy tried to buy her a drink. She turned him down, he tried to cop a feel, and she broke his finger.' Rick tilted his head. 'Then the groper turned nasty . . .'

'Let me guess – you stepped in.'

'Didn't go down well.' He gave a rueful smile. 'I turfed the guy out, advised her to leave in case he came looking for payback. She said, "Thanks, Sir Lancelot, but I've got a drink to finish – and I can take care of myself."'

'What a woman!' Sam was enjoying this.

'When she finally did leave, I followed her for a bit, just to make sure she was safe. She pounced on me as I turned a corner, shoe in hand, ready to gouge my eye out with her stiletto.'

'Love at first sight, then,' Sam deadpanned.

Rick didn't disagree.

'All right, she's a fighter. That's good, because she won't give up – but it's bad if she doesn't know when to accept that she's outgunned. Can she play the damsel in distress?'

Rick's forehead creased in pain as he thought it through. 'She's clever. She'll play whatever role works to her advantage.'

'Good,' Sam said. 'Very good. So – let's look at this new picture they sent you.'

Rick sent it via Bluetooth, and Sam enlarged it on his laptop screen, sliding it right and left, up and down. 'I'll get someone to analyse this,' he said. 'The skirting board and that small slice of coving look Victorian. The radiator, too – and look at the width of the floorboards.' He felt Rick's impatience like heat coming off him. 'I know, I know – half of central London is Victorian. But look at this . . .'

He slid the image on the screen to focus on the window above the radiator. Through it, across the street, a glimpse of a red

119

brick wall, and three windows opening onto a balcony of black wrought iron. Each window was edged with cream stone lintels and fancy plaster mouldings.

'You think you can identify it?' Rick asked.

The seen-it-all cop persona slipped for a moment and Sam saw Rick at fifteen, a couple of growth spurts from his final height, and a good thirty pounds below his fighting weight, hope and anxiety flickering back and forth in his eyes.

'This is specialist work,' Sam said. 'But I know people who live for this kind of nerdy detail. And that does look like premium real estate – just the sort of properties your buy-to-leave money launderers go weak at the knees for.'

Rick was looking at him with an odd gleam in his eye. 'I didn't mention money launderers.'

Sam gave a joyful shout of laughter. 'Bent bankers, fraudulent financial advisers, international criminals – it takes a lot to wash that kind of money clean. Of *course* there are money launderers.'

Chapter 19

JESS OAKES GINGERLY TESTED THE BRUISED FLESH along her jawline and glared at the man holding her mobile phone. He was big – a rugby player's build, though running to fat – and she could still feel the imprint of his fingers on her skin.

'You got your picture,' she said. 'Now take these off.'

The blond man grinned. 'Sure you don't want me to take a few more for your whatjamacallit – portfolio?'

'Take them *off*.' She fought back tears – she would not show this brute any weakness. 'I want to speak to the older guy.' The one they called Tommy seemed all right – he'd said she needn't be bound all the time – it wasn't like she could tiptoe out of the place with the front door double-locked and three of them on guard.

'He's busy.' The creep waggled the phone in her face. 'How about a selfie? Give your boyfriend something to think about.'

He reached for her. She lashed out with her foot, but he dodged away, laughing.

'Pig,' she spat. 'You bloody *pig*.'

Then he was on her, physically crushing her against the radiator, his bulk suffocating, wiry strands of his hair scratching her face, the sour reek of him a sickening invasion. She reached with her free hand, her fingers ready to gouge, but he caught her wrist, forcing her hand down to his crotch.

'*No.* Leave me alone, you *animal*,' she shrieked. *Oh, God, please make it stop!*

She closed her eyes and a second later, she heard a thud. When she dared to look, the creep was lying on his back, winded, whooping for air. The bigger surprise: it was the female guard who'd put him down, not Tommy. The creep lumbered to his feet, his fists bunched, and Jess flinched.

The woman laughed. 'Go for it, I could use the workout.'

He dropped his gaze and she moved in close, her forehead almost grazing his. 'Any more trouble,' she said quietly, 'I'll put you to bed early.'

He backed away, head down. 'I was only having a laugh.'

Shaking, now, Jess began to sob.

As the woman turned and walked away, Jess caught a glint of impotent hate in the creep's eyes.

'Don't go,' she pleaded.

The woman didn't even look at her. 'I'm not your chaperone,' she said. 'Now stop snivelling; he hardly touched you.'

Chapter 20

SAM TURNER CHECKED HIS WATCH; he had plenty of time to get to his next task.

Hakim Saidi liked to be seen at an industrial-style nightclub under the railway arches. The venue was convenient in two ways: it had a multitude of pillars and dark corners where Sam might observe unnoticed, and CCTV was only used at the entrances and in the bar areas; the rest of the building was free from the obnoxious intrusion of cameras and monitors.

He'd slipped one of the doormen a few notes earlier in the evening and, as arranged, the man was waiting at a side door at the designated hour. He admitted Sam and secured the door before heading around to the main entrance, where Sam was confident he would say nothing of his bonus.

Sam wore shades and kept his head down until he was seated in an alcove a good thirty feet away. The boy who would be king was older than he seemed at first glance. Mid-twenties maybe, his slight frame and wispy tuft of beard giving a falsely youthful impression. Saidi had swapped his sports streetwear for chinos and a button-down shirt, even shedding his trainers for gleaming Oxford shoes to conform with the club dress code. He had two girls with him, and two minders were stationed nearby.

Saidi's arms rested along the back of the couch, his legs spread wide. His attention kept straying to the bar on the left side of the space where a group of women were drinking cocktails and making a lot of noise.

Sam shifted out of his direct line of sight, partly concealing himself behind one of the iron pillars, and when a couple of girls asked if he would share the table, he agreed graciously: he would be less conspicuous if he appeared to be with company, and the music allowed few opportunities to chat, which suited him well.

He watched Saidi drinking beer steadily and eyeing the women at the bar. After thirty minutes, he sent the smaller, less intimidating minder to order drinks and as the man returned with a tray of beer bottles and brandy glasses, the group of women were presented with a bottle of champagne by one of the serving staff, who indicated the banquette where Saidi sat. They glanced across and he raised his glass to them, then, turning to the escort on his right, he pressed the flat of his hand against her cheek, drawing her to him. His mouth close to her ear, he said something that made her jerk away, a look of shock on her face. Saidi grabbed her chin with his right hand, forcing her to look at him. He mouthed something and she gave a feeble nod, dropping her gaze. Then, slowly and quite deliberately, he leaned across and bit her earlobe. She gave a little yelp, but didn't resist, and laughing, Saidi stood.

Over the noise, Sam heard him say, 'I need a piss, then I'm having a chat with them fine-looking ladies over there.'

Sam was at a sink, tap running, looking like he was finishing up when one of Saidi's minders popped his head around the door to check the area was clear. He gave his boss the nod and Saidi swaggered in, not quite steady on his feet. Sam could have told him that his low body mass made him more susceptible to intoxicants, but Saidi wouldn't be in need of the advice after tonight, so he didn't comment.

'You,' the minder said. 'Out.'

'Just washing my hands, mate,' Sam said, pure cockney vowels coming out of his mouth, his tone reasonable, polite. 'Be out of your way in a jiffy.' Although he made no eye contact, he could gauge that this was the larger of the two men, the other one presumably having remained to keep an eye on Saidi's two girls in case they made a break for it.

Saidi unzipped his trousers as the minder reached for Sam's shoulder to eject him forcibly. Sam ducked and turned, sliding his left foot back, while seizing the minder's wrist with his left hand and delivering a punch to his groin with the right. Then pivoting on his left foot, he turned one-eighty degrees, using the minder's own weight and momentum as he fell, executing a takedown that finished with the big man's face hitting the opposite wall. He was down and out for the count.

Saidi turned away from the urinal, frantically trying to zip up. Before he could yell, Sam punched him open-handed in the throat, following through with an elbow strike to the side of his head. He dragged the minder across the tiles to act as a doorstop, then, as Saidi staggered backwards clutching at his throat, Sam grabbed a handful of hair, tilted Saidi's head to expose the internal jugular vein, and sliced lengthways along it before changing the angle of the blade to cut into the artery. He eased Saidi to the floor as he passed out.

Sam folded the knife and carefully stripped off the nitrile gloves he had put on as he'd made his way to the restroom. He folded the gloves inside each other, enveloping the bloody knife, then with one clean hand he took a Ziploc bag from his coat pocket and dropped gloves and knife inside, sealing it and placing it inside his laptop bag before putting on a new pair of nitriles. Phone in hand now, he eyed the spreading pool of blood around the young pretender with distaste – he deplored a messy scene – but the client had ordered bloody and obvious, and Sam provided a bespoke service. He snapped a few shots of the dead man, slid the groaning minder out of the doorway and stepped over him.

Someone was waiting outside, but he moved to let Sam pass. Sam lowered his head, offering the man a perfect view of the crown of his hat as he tapped in the message to his client and attached the images to confirm the killing.

'You don't wanna go in there, mate,' he growled, blocking the way as the customer made a move to edge past him. 'Try the khazi upstairs – this one's in a shocking state.'

THEN

Chapter 21

Sixteen months earlier

RICK FOUND THE HIT-AND-RUN CAR at the car pound in Tower Hamlets. While he waited for the vehicle to be forensically checked, he spoke to the house owner who had reported it. She was disgusted that it had taken so long for anyone to speak to her – the car thief had dumped the car in her parking space and run off. Rick empathised and soothed and flattered, and finally she gave him the biggest break he needed: she'd saved her doorbell videocam footage – if he was interested.

The car had been impounded for months, but there was plenty of evidence that it was the hit-and-run vehicle, and although the driver thought he'd been careful, they found DNA all over it. It took a lot of legwork, but two weeks on, Rick found the man: Toni Sereni, head of security at Laligne Bank.

Sereni claimed that he'd hit Wilson 'by accident' and had panicked. He wouldn't explain why he'd stolen the car, or what had brought him to Wilson's place of business that day. After that, he'd given three 'no comment' interviews.

Rick had been granted an extra twelve hours to fact-check the confession and re-interview Sereni before he was charged.

Certain that Wilson had been deliberately targeted, Rick pleaded for more time, but Ghosh wanted the case wrapped up quickly.

The maximum sentence for causing death by driving was fourteen years, and that wasn't enough – not nearly enough. It was a surprise, then, when Rick received an urgent call from the custody sergeant four hours later saying that the prisoner was demanding to speak to him.

Sereni was red-eyed and pale. He sipped from a paper cup with a tremulous hand and avoided eye contact as Rick started the interview recording. Formalities concluded, per PACE regs, Rick made a start: 'You asked to speak to me, Toni.'

Sereni gave a jerky nod of his head in answer.

'Is there something in your statement you'd like to clarify?'

'Yeah, clarify – you might say that.' Sereni spoke with a pronounced Glasgow accent. 'See, I killed that poor bastard, right enough. But it was no accident – it was an execution.'

Rick felt his heart slow as, perversely, it sometimes did in times of stress.

'Are you now confessing to the murder of Kirk Wilson?' he asked.

'Aye, murder, yes – that's what it was.'

'Can I ask why you didn't tell me the whole truth before now?'

'Because I thought it would protect them.' Sereni's mouth twitched and tears started in his eyes. 'I would've gone to prison and done my time – kept my mouth shut. I *would've*.' He seemed outraged that his loyalty had been doubted.

'What happened to change your mind?' Rick asked gently, already anticipating the answer.

'They threatened my family!' Sereni's dark eyes were racked with torment. He clasped his hands in front of him, as if to still their shaking.

His solicitor placed a reassuring hand on his forearm, but Sereni shook him off angrily.

'They stopped my wife in the street, pointed at Lorenzo, my wee boy, asked her how would she feel losing the two men who meant most in her life. He's *five years old* for fuck's sake!'

Seven-year-old Ethan flashed into Rick's head, his small fists clenched as he demanded a promise that Rick would find out who killed his dad. But he nodded sympathetically and murmured his regret. Sereni would have time enough to reflect on the harm he'd done to Wilson's family and his own during the long years he would spend in prison; right now, Rick needed the man's cooperation.

'I'm no' a bad man,' Sereni protested. 'I fought for my country – three eight-month tours of duty in Afghanistan, one in Iraq – I don't scare easy. But this is my *family*.'

'Why did you murder Kirk Wilson?' Rick asked. 'And who is threatening your family?'

Sereni sat back and with a sideways glance, handed over to his solicitor. 'Mr Sereni will tell you all he knows in exchange for relocation and witness protection for his wife and children.'

The Crown Prosecution Service didn't do quid pro quo deals with criminals. If a witness genuinely feared for his own, or his family's safety, the police and the Director of Public Prosecutions had a duty to offer advice and protection. But everyone in the room knew how this worked – if the police said that the threat was credible, the DPP would listen – if not, the witness and his family could be left to twist in the wind.

Rick spoke to Superintendent Ghosh, who put in the request, and within hours, Sereni's wife and child were in protective custody.

As good as his word, Sereni named names. He said that Alan Hugenot, the CEO at Laligne Bank, had commissioned the hit on behalf of Thomas Unwin. Sereni confessed to the theft of Wilson's laptop and desktop computers, as well as the break-in at the PI's flat on the day he was killed – all under Hugenot's orders.

Rick typed up his notes and went straight to Ghosh's office.

Superintendent Ghosh, on his way to a meeting, refused point-blank to ask for a warrant to access Hugenot's bank transactions and phone records.

'The financial evidence Wilson collected was illegally obtained – it's tainted,' he said. 'As for Sereni – he could be acting out of pure malice.'

Grappling with his frustration, Rick said, 'With respect, sir, you wouldn't have signed off on witness protection for Sereni's family if you believed he was just trying to stick it to the boss.'

'It doesn't *matter* what I believe,' Ghosh said. 'It's what you can *prove* that matters.'

'Get me access to Hugenot's financials – I'll *find* the proof.'

Ghosh shook his head. 'You can't go looking for proof to fit your theory – the DPP won't stand for it, and neither will I.'

'Sir, Kirk Wilson was mown down by the head of security at Hugenot's bank. Sereni – his head of security – has now admitted that it was a contract killing. He gave us access to his accounts; he was paid fifteen thousand the day Wilson died.'

'Well,' Ghosh said, 'if that was a cheque or transfer from his boss's accounts, you might have a case—'

Rick closed his eyes. 'It was cash. But I'll find the paper trail if—'

'Stop, Rick. Stop. Laligne Bank's client list reads like a who's who of British politics – an ex-government minister is chair of the board, for God's sake! Stop complicating things when you've already got your result. Sereni confessed to the hit-and-run – you got your man.'

Sickened, Rick shook his head. 'Sereni's just a foot soldier; we can't let Unwin and Hugenot get away with it.'

Ghosh sighed. 'That's how it works, sometimes. Unwin has outfoxed some of the best on the job. The joint NCA and Border Force raid I mentioned? They opened every container, X-rayed the goods. Nothing. Brought in detector dogs, had them sniff out that ship inch by inch. *Not one* item of contraband. Kath Steiner was SIO on the Met side of that embarrassing mess; cost us a bloody fortune – stalled her career and a few others into the bargain.'

So, this was the real reason why Ghosh was havering: he didn't want to jeopardise his own promotion prospects.

'So you're saying Unwin's clean?' Rick heard the contempt in his voice.

Ghosh sucked his teeth, staring at Rick with such malevolence that he had to look away.

Bloody hell, Rick! There's speaking truth to power, and there's plain suicidal. This was Sam-as-alter-ego.

After a few more agonising seconds, Ghosh spoke slowly and clearly: 'I'm saying he's clever, and he's careful.' He raised a finger and pointing it squarely at Rick's face added softly, 'And don't you *ever* take that insubordinate tone with me again, Sergeant.'

Chapter 22

THE NEXT EVENING, RICK was trudging towards Hammersmith Underground station having spent the last nine hours filling forms and writing a report on his investigation into the death of Kirk Wilson. After his set-to with Ghosh, he was under strict orders to focus on securing Sereni's conviction. Hugenot and Unwin were strictly off-limits.

A woman was drinking coffee outside the Café Nero on the corner. Seeing him, she half stood, and called his name. Rick walked to her table but declined her invitation to sit.

'My name is Annita Yalman,' she said. 'I am PA to Mr Hugenot at Laligne Bank.'

'I know who you are, Mrs Yalman,' Rick said.

She had been their first contact at the bank when Rick and two other detectives had shown up looking for Sereni, three days earlier. Then, she had seemed formal, efficient, cool. The staff deferred to her, which she apparently accepted as her right, and at first Rick had mistaken her for a senior executive. She'd shown them through to her office adjacent to Hugenot's and explained that her boss was away, but she could help them with whatever they needed.

'We need to speak to Toni Sereni,' Rick had said.

134

She'd considered his request. 'May I ask what this is about?'

'Police business.'

'I'll ring his mobile,' she'd said, clearly piqued by his tone. 'You may wait in the lobby, and I'll direct him there.'

Rick had shaken his head; one glance at the three men waiting for him across the marble expanse of the bank's lobby would be enough to warn their suspect. 'It was quite busy when we came through,' he'd said. 'You wouldn't want to embarrass yourself – or your boss – in front of clients, would you?'

Her eyes had widened, but she'd kept her composure. 'What would you have me do?'

'Just say you need to speak to him in your office.'

On that day, Mrs Yalman had worn her dark brown hair loose to her shoulders; a simple gold chain glowed against her olive skin, and her dress, in a flattering shade of green, was fitted to the waist and slightly flared at the hips – not flamboyant, exactly, but feminine and confident.

This evening, she wore a black trouser suit with a creamy silk blouse. Her hair was covered with a scarf, and Rick got the sense that she had dressed down, perhaps even disguised herself.

'May we talk somewhere private?' she said.

'Sure, why not? The police station's only two minutes' walk.' Rick gestured back the way he'd come.

'I should very much prefer somewhere more neutral,' she said, remaining firmly seated. 'A place where we might speak privately and'– she glanced past him –'unobserved.'

Her English was impeccable, faintly accented, grammatically correct, if slightly over-formal. The poise was still there, but she seemed less self-assured, and anxiety flittered behind her dark eyes.

Remembering his superintendent's angry words the last time they had spoken, Rick hesitated and – clearly uncomfortable under his scrutiny – Mrs Yalman reached inside a large leather shoulder bag and retrieved a pair of sunglasses. Her hands trembled as she put them on and the lenses all but eclipsed her face.

'Please, Sergeant,' she murmured, her head lowered. 'I am risking a great deal, just being here.'

That decided it; Rick took her by the elbow, steered her around the corner, and flagged a taxi.

'So,' he said, once they were inside.

She gave her head a vehement shake. 'Not here.'

'Furnival Gardens, mate,' Rick said to the driver. 'By the boat club.'

On the riverfront, they turned their backs to Hammersmith Bridge and walked into the gardens, finding a quiet spot where they could sit and talk in private. It was a warm July evening, and they found a shady corner sheltered by a beech hedge.

For half a minute, the silence was broken only by the roar of traffic on the Great West Road behind them. Rick felt it resonate with the anxiety in his chest and abdomen. But the musical chug of boats on the river, and occasional shouts and laughter from children playing on the lawns out of sight, seemed to calm her, and at last, she began:

'As soon as you left on Monday, naturally, I called Mr Hugenot. He returned to the office, cutting a meeting short. He wanted to know the reasons you had given for Mr Sereni's arrest.'

Rick had gone with suspicion of failing to stop after an accident and the theft of a car, keeping his options open for further charges.

'Mr Hugenot is usually a calm man,' she said, frowning. 'But he became extremely agitated. He went to his office and closed the door – said he did not want to be disturbed.'

She seemed astonished, even now, by her boss's behaviour.

'I could see that he was making calls, because the lines lit up on my phone – and I know that one of the calls was to a client named Thomas Unwin because Mr Unwin called back, and was mistakenly put through to me, first.'

Unwin! Rick felt a fizz of excitement.

'He was so *angry*. Before I could say a word, he said, "They've arrested Sereni for Wilson." Of course, I told him there'd been a mistake and put him through to Mr Hugenot straight away, but . . .'

She stopped, suddenly clasping her hands in her lap, knotting and twisting her fingers. 'But I kept thinking what you'd said when you arrested Mr Sereni; I couldn't get the words "accident" and "car" out of my head. So I searched online for "Wilson" and "car accident" . . .'

'And found "hit-and-run",' Rick supplied.

A sudden rustling in the hedge behind them made her start to her feet with a little exclamation. She peered about her, wild-eyed, and for a moment it looked like she would flee.

'Birds,' Rick said. 'It's just birds,' he said gently.

'Oh, this is awful,' she said, sinking onto the bench again and loosening the scarf at her throat.

Rick gave her a moment and gradually her breathing became less ragged.

'What is awful, Mrs Yalman?' he asked.

In answer, she reached again into her shoulder bag.

'Mr Hugenot has a regular email account for day-to-day office communications, which I have access to – I even send routine replies on his behalf. But he also has a private account.'

Her hand shook violently as she handed him a sheet of paper. It was an email from Unwin to Hugenot.

—I want those photos, Unwin wrote. —And you'd better put a stop to that bastard PI Wilson.

Hugenot replied:

—I'm afraid I don't have that class of contact.

Seconds later, Unwin shot back:

—You can save the high-handed crap for someone who gives a shit. And don't try and tell me that you can't find someone handy – you got more security than Fort Knox.

How had Unwin known about the images? Was Unwin tipped off? Was the PI spotted as he took them, or had Wilson tried to blackmail Unwin?

Rick would investigate every possibility, but right now, he wanted to revel in the moment. His exhaustion evaporated and he experienced a soaring elation: this email linked Unwin, Hugenot, and the murdered private investigator. On its own, it might not have been enough, just as Sereni's testimony alone was not enough. But this confirmed Sereni's claim; this was the new evidence Ghosh had demanded. Rick could demand his warrant, and with it, a good chance of proving the conspiracy.

'This is from Hugenot's private email account?' Rick asked.

She nodded mutely.

'Does he know you have it?'

'I – I don't think so. I sneaked into his office when he'd gone out for a moment – he's terribly lax about logging off – I didn't want it to be *true*, you see. I was praying that I was mistaken, but—' She broke off, clasping her hands. 'Oh, God – what shall I *do*?'

'Go back to work, act as normal—'

'No. *No*—' She snatched the sunglasses from her face. 'I can't. I *can't* go back.' She pressed a hand to her forehead. 'I was so *frightened* – I thought he'd come in at any second – that he'd see me, going through his things like a – a thief! He'd know as soon as he set eyes on me. No, I *couldn't* face him.'

'All right,' Rick soothed. 'Can you take a few days off – call in sick, maybe, or take some personal days?'

She frowned. 'I have been meaning to take my mother for a check-up . . .'

'That's ideal,' Rick said. 'Is there somewhere out of London you could stay for a few days – somewhere Hugenot wouldn't think to look – just until I've had the chance to talk to my boss?'

'Yes.' She held herself erect, but her thin gold chain jittered in the hollow of her neck.

'Tell no one where you're going; switch off your mobile phones.' He scribbled his personal mobile number and tore it out of his notebook. 'Ring me on this number when you're settled.' She grasped the folded sheet, but he held on to it a moment longer.

'This is very important, Mrs Yalman: do *not* try to contact me via the police switchboard.'

She looked into his eyes, and he saw a shiver of terror. 'You can't trust your own people?'

'I don't know,' Rick admitted. 'But I don't want to take any chances with your safety.'

She pressed a hand to her chest and took a few sips of air, her eyes darting right and left, as if she were watching her future on a screen, and what she saw filled her with horror.

NOW

Chapter 23

Monday night

THE SERIOUS FRAUD OFFICE WAS based at Canada House, within shouting distance of Trafalgar Square. The grand portico with its massive Ionic columns and creamy Portland stone symbolised empire and the institutions of governance, and Rick was conscious that his actions since that morning had betrayed those institutions, undermining the years of honest work he'd done in policing.

He showed his warrant card and Collins shambled into the entrance hall as Rick was pinning his guest ID to his jacket. The forensic accountant was a giant landslide of a man. Off duty, his preferred gear was a triple-XL Metallica T-shirt and jogging bottoms, but tonight he wore his work uniform of chinos, shirt and tie.

That first meeting with Dave Collins at the Bear & Staff, the day that Superintendent Ghosh had verbally abused him and virtually kicked him out of his office, Dave had had a beaten look. By then, Mrs Yalman's testimony had given them access to Hugenot's computers and phones. Dozens of companies were named in exchanges on his private email account, of which only a scant few were registered at Companies House in the UK; the rest were most likely overseas shell companies. While such companies weren't necessarily illegal, they were a byword for tax evasion and money laundering – hence the need for SFO input.

Laying out the sheer volume of data he'd been trying to tackle single-handed, Rick had grown more and more despondent. But as Rick's mood had darkened, Collins's face became flushed with boyish enthusiasm. The meal finished, he outlined a plan of attack, suggesting creative measures to trace the 'untraceable' account Hugenot had used to pay his head of security for the hit-and-run murder of Kirk Wilson, even predicting the evasive measures Hugenot might have used.

Collins, Rick had learned, was incapable of empty boasts: if he was making a wild suggestion, he would tell you. But if he said he was ninety-nine per cent certain something would work, you could be ninety-nine-point-five per cent sure it would. And the tactics Collins had outlined over that gargantuan pub meal had secured Thomas Unwin's arrest.

Despite Ghosh's concerns that the SFO had sent them a dud, it had taken Collins less than twenty-four hours to track Sereni's hit money from a shell company in Jersey to Alan Hugenot's personal account at Laligne, via his wife's business account. Hugenot had withdrawn the cash himself – they'd got security video to prove it – plus a text to Sereni's phone from his boss five minutes later that read,

—I have it. My office, now.

Hugenot had tried to claim that the payment to Sereni was a bonus. But there was no paperwork for it, and the firm had strict rules of transparency on how bonus payments were awarded. Hugenot blamed his PA for the missing paper trail, but since Mrs Yalman was currently in hiding under police protection from her boss, that defence strategy didn't stand up to scrutiny.

It was ironic that in trying to guarantee Sereni's silence with the threat against his family, Unwin had implicated himself in the murder. If he'd left it alone, he might have been safe.

Rick followed Collins through to the open-plan office where he worked, stopping at the kitchen – a spare room equipped with fridge, microwave and kettle.

'Coffee?' he asked. 'It's only instant.'

'Instant's fine,' Rick said, watching his friend load his own mug with four spoons of sugar before reaching into the far corner of the topmost cupboard and retrieving a pack of Jaffa Cakes. Rick declined the offer and Collins settled one buttock on a stool and began studiously dunking a Jaffa Cake in his coffee. His concentration was so intense that he seemed almost to have forgotten Rick was there.

'Any luck with the experts?' Rick asked, to start him off.

'Yeah,' Collins said, his eyes on a second cake, which was just on the point of disintegrating into his drink. He slurped it in one go, wiping his chin before saying, 'Bit of a turn-up, King getting croaked like that, eh?'

Rick's heart lurched, but he managed a tight, 'Yep. Appreciate your help on this, Dave,' he said.

For a millisecond, Collins glanced up and Rick saw delight in his grey eyes, but the accountant looked away quickly; he wasn't good with eye contact.

Rick listened as Collins talked him through three possible experts who could hand-hold the jury through the trickier data.

'Can you send their names, profiles and contact details over to Mr Kildoran now? I know he'll be reworking his evidence strategy most of the night.'

'Sure. I've still got a bit to do – crossing Ts and that.' Modesty and honesty were always a dual burden to the forensic accountant. 'But I'll send it over in the next half-hour.'

'Sounds like you've got it covered. In which case . . .' Rick stood and stretched some of the tension out of his shoulders. 'I'd better leave you to get on with it. I've got a bit of homework myself – I still haven't done a proper read-through of my notes and Kildoran keeps threatening to call me in early.'

Chapter 24

RICK GOT HOME AT ELEVEN, DEAD ON HIS FEET. The voicemail on the hall phone beeped, letting him know he had two new messages. He picked up and hit the key to listen to the first. It was from Jess.

'Hey, handsome! I figured you'd have your mobile switched off, so I thought I'd catch you at home. Just to let you know if the audition goes well, I might not be back till after six. Oh, and I hope you knocked their socks off in court today – see you tonight, lover man – wear something sexy!' She hung up with a throaty laugh, and Rick swayed on his feet.

Jess had started the day excited, full of confidence, brimming with the possibilities of the future. And now—

The second message had nearly finished by the time he realised it was from Jess's agent. She sounded puzzled and a little exasperated. He pressed the key to hear the message again, and the agent said she'd tried Jess's mobile, and got no reply. 'The casting director said you'd messaged them about a mugging? It must have been a good audition because they want to know how long you'll be out of action. Call me.' Then, almost as an afterthought, 'Hope you're okay.'

Rick stared at the phone. Jess had made it to the audition. He ran through to the kitchen. Jess had stuck a note with the date, time and location on the fridge door. He took out the burner phone. Sam had warned him that he wouldn't pick up calls on the mobile number he'd supplied, so Rick dropped him a text with the address of the venue where the auditions had taken place – a church hall in Spitalfields.

—First audition scheduled @ 08:45am, he texted.
—Jess was there. After, producers had msg to say she'd been mugged. Will talk to them tmrw.

The reply came seconds later:

—DO NOT GO NEAR VENUE. LEAVE TO ME.

Jeez, Sam— Rick thumbed in a quick message.

—I can't just—

The next message came through before he'd finished typing.

—You need to stay low. Look like you're doing as they say. Attract attention, you put Jess at risk.

A pause, then the phone buzzed with another new message.

—Tell me you'll stay away.

Rick closed his eyes for a second, exhaled, cursing quietly, then deleted his half-finished message and started again:

—Will stay clear. BUT KEEP ME INFORMED.

Hand shaking, he set the burner phone down on the counter. The kitchen felt cold and soulless without Jess's energy and her constant bubbling conversation to enliven it. He paced restlessly from room to room, finding reminders of her in every one. Her coffee cup was still by the bedside, the bed unmade, and her makeup cluttered the dressing table. He removed the cup, but left the rest as it was, finding comfort in the disarray.

Hard as it was, he had to look like he was following instructions. The trick would be in satisfying both the prosecution *and* the defence that he was acting in their interests. Returning to the kitchen, he brewed coffee, whipped up an omelette, and started reading through his notes for the trial.

Sam was right – the hit-and-run trial and the charge of conspiracy to murder against Unwin had *everything* to do with Rick. When he'd got the doorbell video image of the driver dumping the car, they still hadn't known who he was, because the trace DNA they'd found in the car didn't match anything in the national database.

But Rick refused to give up. The photos of Unwin with the CEO of Laligne Bank gave Rick a starting point. He'd staked the bank out on his off days and off-duties, and after two weeks of nothing, the man in the doorbell video footage walked through the front door of the bank. Sereni was ex-army; his skills had guaranteed a rapid rise from part-time adviser to full-time head of security at Laligne. Rick later discovered that while Ethan and his mother mourned the loss of a father and husband, his murderer had taken his own family on holiday to the Caribbean.

UK policing was still rigidly hierarchical, and at his rank, Rick would never be allowed to run two major investigations concurrently. He'd been given a stark choice: complete the investigation into Wilson's murder or continue with Unwin. Rick had reluctantly handed the Wilson case off to another team. But he'd only agreed to step away when he was certain they had enough evidence to convict Sereni – and on condition that he would have the privilege of telling the Wilsons the good news. The look of mingled pain and joy in seven-year-old Ethan's eyes when Rick said they had arrested a man for his father's unlawful killing would be seared on his memory forever.

If Rick's interference in the trial were discovered, it could mean that Unwin would go free as well as all the crooks and gangsters, accountants and bankers who'd stolen or defrauded under his instruction. Unwin and men like him would win – as they always won – because their greed and cruelty and amorality gave them the power to take whatever they wanted and destroy things they had no use for – like trust, and innocence, and hope.

Rick dumped the rest of his meal in the bin, nauseated by the smell, and grabbed a beer from the fridge.

He wondered how close he'd come to being rumbled earlier that evening as he'd downloaded the images of Unwin's crew onto a thumb drive. Even blunted by drink, Jim Stott's instincts were good, and Rick had the strongest impression that his old mentor had known exactly what he'd been up to. Had Stotty's ostentatious throat-clearing as Rick palmed the thumb drive been a warning?

Is he protecting me? Rick wondered.

In Rick's early years as a detective, Jim and Maddie Stott had invited him for barbecues in the summer, and for a while, Friday curry nights had become a regular thing. The invitations to dinner had dwindled to nothing over the past two years, but if he was honest, Rick had been unavailable on many weekends as he'd conducted his unofficial inquiries into the murders, and after Jess came into his life every spare minute had been spent with her.

During one of those boozy curry-night Fridays at the Stotts' home, Jim said that he saw his younger self in Rick.

'You're a resourceful and tenacious investigator, and you can think outside the box,' he'd said.

Maddie Stott was ex-police, and Rick had warmed instantly to her seen-it-all manner and dry humour. Having put away a few glasses of wine herself, she'd rolled her eyes, leaned across the table and, laughing, delivered an affectionate facepalm to her husband. 'Sorry, Rick. He always was a sloppy drunk. And that, my dear husband, was the most outrageous humble brag since Khloé Kardashian tweeted, "I still can't believe I have a *Cosmo* cover!"'

Jim had protested that he was in earnest, but Maddie scoffed, 'Forget "resourceful and tenacious". *Your* best asset is *you* are bloody *nosy*, Jim.' Emphasising her point with three sharp taps on his best asset, she'd added: 'Cur-i-osity – that's *your* biggest strength.'

If Stott *had* seen what Rick had done, that innate curiosity would drive him to ferret out the truth – and there would be limits to the secrets Jim Stott would be prepared to keep on Rick's behalf.

His face burning with shame, Rick took the tiny piece of traitor electronics out of his pocket and placed it on the kitchen counter, rifled the kitchen drawers till he found a pair of tongs, lit the gas, turned on the extractor fan, and held the drive in the flames till the metal warped and the plastic bubbled and caught, sending acrid fumes into the extractor hood.

Chapter 25

Tuesday morning

RICK WOKE AT FIVE O'CLOCK after a scant three hours of fitful sleep.

Scooping up his phone, he disconnected the charger and checked WhatsApp and his texts. Nothing. The burner was also blank. He brewed coffee and toasted a slice of bread. As he topped up his cup, his mobile rang and he jerked, spilling hot coffee onto his hand. Cursing, he answered the phone, turning on the cold tap with his scalded hand and plunging it under the flow.

'Sorry, did I wake you?' It was Kildoran.

'No.' He set the phone down and switched to hands-free while he wiped up the mess. 'What can I do for you, Mr Kildoran?'

'I thought you'd like to know that Mr Collins's recommendations were most helpful. I've settled on Harriet Alnwick – her credentials are impressive, and having viewed the video links Mr Collins sent, I think she'll charm the jury.'

'Great that it worked out,' Rick said.

'Anyway, you'll be glad to know that it lets you off the hook for today at least.'

'Well, whenever you're ready,' Rick said, working hard to disguise his relief.

'I've emailed Mr Collins with my thanks, but could you tell him again that I'm very grateful for his work on the evidence overnight?' Kildoran added. 'Ms Alnwick says it's first class.'

'I'll be sure to tell him,' Rick said, pleased that Dave Collins's skills and brilliant work were appreciated.

It was still only five-twenty and pitch-dark outside, but the office would be empty, and there was nothing he could do there in any case, so he decided to go for a run. He needed to see Sam, and for that, he needed a clear head.

He jogged at an easy pace towards the river at Wandsworth Park. The area might not have the cachet of nearby Barnes, but it was a stratosphere above the tenements where they'd been born and raised, and – even fifteen years ago and in need of a complete rewire and refit – it had cost a lot more than his father could ever have afforded on his wages as a motor mechanic.

Rick was thirteen years old when Sam had financed their move away from the council estate. At first, he'd acted tough at his new school. By that time, he'd learned how to handle himself and knew how to look intimidating. The other kids would stare at him and whisper about him on the playground, but nobody bothered him. He'd studied hard, told his parents that school was great, that he'd made loads of friends, helped his father with the repairs and renovations to the house, proud of what they had, proud that his big brother had made it possible. It was Sam who'd made things right for them and Rick had worshipped him for that.

But Sam wasn't around much, and he'd never even lifted a paintbrush to aid the renovations. So it was a surprise to see him one day, parked near the school gates, leaning against the gleaming paintwork of his latest car – an Audi A3 Sportback.

He'd said he wanted to surprise their mother with a new washing machine she'd had her eye on, and he needed Rick to get her out of the house for an hour or two while he organised the delivery.

Sam would have been around twenty-one, then. He dressed well and some of the girls filing through the gates had given him the eye. He'd reciprocated with a smile or a genial 'Afternoon, ladies'. But everyone – boys and girls alike – had avoided Rick's gaze, and of course, Sam had noticed. He'd waited until they were in his car, before he'd said, 'You're not on the estate now, Rick.'

Rick had known instantly what he meant. He'd hunched in the seat and glowered out of the window. 'Yeah, well, I'm the new kid; gotta be sure they don't take the mickey.'

Sam had watched the knots of teenagers drifting past. 'No danger of that, bruv. These kids are soft, after what you're used to. They bruise easy – and you—' He elbowed Rick, to illustrate the point. 'You're rock hard.'

Instantly Rick had seen that he'd made a colossal mistake.

'Oh, shit – what'm I gonna *do*, Sam?' he'd cried, dismayed that he'd messed up his chance to make a fresh start.

'You could try smiling once in a while—'

Rick had shot his brother a searing look and Sam held his hands up.

'See, now you got *me* scared.'

That was so blatantly ridiculous that Rick couldn't help laughing. 'No, but seriously, bruv . . .'

'Join an after-school club,' Sam had said. 'Join two. You're good at sports; the girls'll love you for it, and when the boys see you're not all East End attitude, you won't have no trouble at all.'

Sam had always dispensed good advice – when he wasn't encouraging Rick to take risks that could get them both in hot water. He'd been proved right, as usual, and apart from a couple of run-ins with schoolyard bullies, Rick had learned to fit in, and had made some good friends.

Rick slowed to a walk now and paused for a few minutes to stare across the river towards Hurlingham. From where he stood, the north side was mostly dark, except for a few low-rise apartment blocks to the east and west. The river, too, was ink-black and still. He caught a sulphurous whiff of river mud; the tide was just on the turn, ebbing eastward to Chelsea Docks and winding on to central London, jostling the boats at their mid-river concrete moorings and setting their rigging a-jangle. Rick heard a soft splash and focused on a silky swirl of movement near one of the wide concrete slabs; a seal, maybe, drawn nearly forty miles up the Thames from the North Sea.

He sometimes wondered how things might have turned out if Sam had stayed. But Sam's sights were always set much higher than the ordinary life his parents lived; even if things hadn't turned bad between him and Lockleigh, he would have gone eventually. Which didn't make the pain of those years any easier to bear: Sam had burdened him with a secret that had almost crushed him as a kid. He'd lost count of the times he'd woken screaming, shocked into wakefulness by the dull crunch of a knife blade piercing cartilage. It was always Mum who had come to his bedside, calmed him, held him till the shaking subsided. She'd begged Rick to tell her what was tormenting him, and he had lied – for Sam's sake, but also for hers – because he was sure that the awful knowledge would destroy her.

Perhaps it had, he reflected, now. Perhaps the steady onslaught to her peace of mind had slowly eroded her health until the cancer took her.

Why had Sam come back now, when he'd stayed away after Mum had got sick? That was something Rick would have out with his brother, when all this was done.

He picked up the pace on the way back, stopping only to order a bacon roll at a little coffee shop near the Tube station. Suddenly ravenous, he ate it standing outside the café and, as he dumped the wrapper in a waste bin, a black Jaguar XJ drew up alongside him. He stepped back from the kerb and ducked to take a look. The driver, big-bearded and long-haired, looked like an ex-roadie

154

for The Strokes; the clean-shaven man in the passenger seat was family man Darren Mays, one of Unwin's trusted inner circle. Rick made a mental note: clearly, *he* wasn't guarding Jess – at least, not today.

Mounsey was seated comfortably in the back. He wound down the window.

'You lost, Mounsey?' Rick said.

Mounsey smiled his toad-faced smile. 'I need a word.'

'I'm listening.'

'Get in.'

Rick looked at the two men in the front of the car.

'You really want Han Solo and Chewy to hear this?'

He saw a momentary, intensely satisfying uncertainty in the lawyer's eyes – then Mounsey opened the door and climbed out.

Rick walked away at a brisk pace, causing a scramble for doors as the driver and Darren Mays exited to keep an eye on their boss's lawyer.

Mounsey caught up with him on a street corner. He was slightly out of breath and looked less complacent than he had a few moments earlier.

'So,' Rick said, keeping an eye on the two goons now standing by the car. 'What's the word?'

'Mr Unwin is interested in the sequestered witness from the bank.'

'I bet he is,' Rick said.

Mounsey stretched the corners of his mouth; it might have been a smile.

Rick stared down at the little man. 'She's in witness protection. You know that I have *no idea* where she is, or who is guarding her.'

Mounsey gazed back as though seeing Rick through a mist.

'I didn't ask for an address,' Mounsey said at last. 'The final leg of her route to court would do nicely – and the exact date and time she'll be called to the witness box.'

'I don't think even Kildoran knows that – how the hell would I?'

'Mr Kildoran intends to call the expert witness who will act as stand-in for Mr King, today, so you're off the hook, for today, free to do a little information gathering,' Mounsey said. 'You *might* be called on Thursday, but my guess is the prosecution will want to have brave Mrs Yalman talk to the jury while their brains are still warmed up and half-comprehending the financial hocus-pocus.

'Now, I accept that there are a lot of variables and imponderables: how long will your expert drone on, for instance – and Mr Unwin's barrister might want to call experts of his own. But as soon as Kildoran makes a decision on Mrs Yalman, you need to let me know.'

Rick stared at the man. How did Mounsey know so much? It was just after six in the morning – only Kildoran and his team would know his revised strategy.

And exactly how many poorly paid, student-loan-crippled junior barristers does Kildoran have on his team? This question came to Rick in Sam's most incredulous tone. He mentally shoved the phantom away but couldn't escape the disturbing thought that this was the second time in twenty-four hours that he'd wondered if the defence team had been infiltrated.

'Kildoran doesn't give me a blow-by-blow account of his itinerary,' he said, keeping his tone neutral.

'You've already proved that you're resourceful, Sergeant. Show an interest – *find out*.'

Rick shook his head slowly. This was too much.

'Think of it as insurance. If you're called to give your testimony before Mrs Yalman, and you do what's necessary, it won't matter – if you do your job *right*, the prosecution will have no use for her – and she'll be safe.'

'No,' Rick said. 'I won't put anyone else at risk—'

'Not even for Jess?'

'Why do you even want Yalman when you have Jess?' A terrible thought crossed his mind: no messages, no images of Jess since yesterday. What if she'd tried to escape? What if—

'I want to speak to Jess,' he said, interrupting the thought. 'I want proof she's alive.'

'I'm so sorry,' Mounsey said, wide-eyed, 'didn't you get last night's snapshot?'

The image of Jess, bruised and frighted, chained to a radiator would be seared in his memory forever, but Rick forced himself to stay calm. 'I got it. But there's no time or date reference, no context. I want proof of life, or this ends here.'

Something dangerous slithered across the solicitor's colourless eyes. 'I'll convey your . . . stipulation to my client and see what can be arranged.'

Rick walked the final quarter mile home, feeling too nauseated to run, obsessing over the inside information Mounsey had on the trial. Should he talk to Kildoran – tell him he might have a mole on his team?

Yeah, and while you're at it, you might put in a word about yourself. It was weird, hearing Sam's advice in his head, now that Sam was a real and tangible presence in his life again – especially as the here-and-now Sam sounded nothing like the Sam of his teenaged years. But Rick couldn't deny that his amoral superego had a point – Rick himself was as much an inside man as any of the bent coppers who took backhanders from Unwin.

Rick felt for the burner phone in his pocket and checked around. By now he was on a side street, and he couldn't see anyone who might be watching. Even so—

He darted into a side entry and dashed off a quick text:

—Need to talk – asap.

A moment later he was back on the street. Twenty-five yards away, a man was jogging. Seeing Rick, he pulled up, then made as if to answer a call on his mobile. But Rick had seen that *Oh, shit,* look on his face, and they'd made eye contact. Knowing that

Unwin's goons were fallible, Rick felt more in control. He took out his camera and clicked off a photo of the jogger, then smiled and waved before walking on.

Mounsey was right about one thing – Rick's reprieve from the witness box would give him time to gather intel – but on Unwin's men, not on Mrs Yalman. He stopped, a cold band of sweat suddenly chilling the nape of his neck. Mounsey had said, *You're off the hook, for today.*

Hadn't Kildoran used those exact words, *You're off the hook, for today*? And hadn't he switched his mobile to speaker after he'd scalded his hand when Kildoran rang?

He broke into a sprint.

Thirty minutes later, he had located listening devices in his kitchen, sitting room and master bedroom. Which explained how they'd known about Jess's audition – and Kildoran's trial strategy – Rick had leaked the information himself.

Jesus – how long have they been listening? Rick never discussed details of this case, or any other with Jess, but he'd taken calls at home from his team and from prosecuting counsel. He tried desperately to remember those conversations.

Sam! His stomach twisted so hard he felt like he'd been kicked. He'd told Jess about Sam – about the man her brother had murdered. And that he, Rick, had seen it all and told no one.

Chapter 26

BY SEVEN-FIFTY, RICK TURNER HAD TRAVELLED from Putney to Camden, driving part of the way, then taking a bus for a couple of stops before jumping off to hail a taxi to drop him at the nearest Tube station. Once underground, he bounced around like a squash ball, changing direction, even switching lines to make sure he wasn't followed.

Sam had texted the address of an Italian restaurant that served breakfast. He was sitting in a booth at the back, savouring his first espresso. A waiter was by their side in an instant.

Rick ordered a cappuccino while Sam went for a café latte and a sweet pastry.

Rick began by telling him that his house had been bugged.

'Video or audio?' Sam asked.

'I didn't find any cameras. And I took the place apart.'

Sam wiped his hands thoughtfully on his napkin. 'I could send someone in to do a sweep – but if you missed even one—'

'Unwin would know I've had help,' Rick finished. He blew out a shaky breath. 'Give me the equipment, I'll do it.'

Sam nodded. 'You destroyed what you found?'

'No.'

He glanced sharply at Rick. 'Why not?'

'Because when I do that bloody rehearsal Kildoran's nagging me to do, I'll make it sound like I mean to screw up the case for the prosecution.'

Sam brightened. 'Well played.'

He took a final sip of his coffee and set the cup squarely on the saucer. 'So, I'm curious . . . what made you go grubbing for bugs in the first place?'

'I just had an encounter with that little weasel, Callum Mounsey. Unwin's upped the ante – he wants the location of a witness for the prosecution. She was PA to the banker who paid for the hit on Kirk Wilson.'

'The deceased PI . . .' Sam tapped the handle of his cup thoughtfully. 'Can you give him what he wants?'

'What? No!'

'You mean you *can't* because you don't know, or you *won't* because you think it wouldn't be right?' He made the second option sound like the naïve rationale of a child.

'As it happens,' Rick said, 'I *don't* know, but—'

'Ah, then you *could* find out?'

'I've no intention of even trying. Jeez, what is *wrong* with you?'

Sam seemed perplexed by Rick's outrage. 'Unwin wants to get to this PA,' he said. 'If he gets what he wants on the PA, it'll buy us time – keep Jess safe for longer—'

'You're talking like it's a simple logistical problem.'

'It kind of *is*, Rick. I thought this was about saving Jess.'

'Not by throwing someone else under the bus!'

Sam glanced past him, into the body of the restaurant, and Rick realised he'd raised his voice.

He took a breath. 'Look, this woman stood up when her bosses, her work colleagues, Unwin, his crew – *everyone* was against her. She's spent the best part of a year in crummy witness protection accommodation. She and her elderly mother were given thirty minutes to pack everything they needed and get out of their house, and they haven't been back since. She doesn't know if she'll *ever*

160

be able to go home again. But despite every shitty thing that's happened to her, she *still* wants to do the right thing.' He paused. 'I gave her my word that I'd protect her, and I will.'

'Since you don't know where she is,' Sam said quietly, 'I don't see how you can do anything of the sort.'

Rick stared at him. Sam had always been hard, but he hadn't thought him so cold.

'This is the sort of work you did for Lockleigh, isn't it?'

'Finding people?'

'Threatening and intimidating people,' Rick said with mounting anger. 'Delivering good people into the hands of bad men.'

'To be fair, most of my targets weren't exactly top drawer, but yes, I did some of that for Theo.' He didn't even seem offended.

'Yeah, well maybe you should be working for Unwin – it'd be a lot more lucrative.'

Sam raised his eyebrows, apparently amused by some private joke. 'You have no idea.'

Rick swung out of his seat and Sam raised his hands, a faint smile playing on his lips.

'Look, I can see that you feel strongly on this point – if it's a problem, we'll find a workaround.'

'The *problem* is you seem to think this is funny.' Rick's hands curled into fists. 'You really haven't changed, have you?'

'Oh, I have – in ways you don't want to know,' Sam said softly, his face set, his dark blue eyes dulled to slate-grey. 'Which is precisely why you need me. Because I'm everything you say: a liar, a manipulator, a heartless bastard – and a lot more you couldn't even begin to guess. In your predicament, that's good, because I understand men like Unwin. Even better – I'm one of them. And like Mrs Yalman, you are *on your own*, Rick.'

Rick stood by the booth, his shoulders hunched, knowing that everything Sam said was true, and hating him for it.

But Sam wasn't finished. 'And for the record,' he went on, 'I do care – about you. I care about Jess because *you* care about her. I care about a woman who for some unfathomable reason is willing to risk her life for someone she never even met – not because I admire her – but because *you* care about her. Okay?'

'Ever the bloody orator, eh, Sam?' he said, unwilling to admit that Sam's words had moved him.

His brother chuckled. 'Now, d'you want to hear *my* news?'

With a sigh of resignation Rick sat down. He wouldn't change Sam – no one could. And he did need Sam's unique combination of dispassion and ruthlessness.

Sam had got a little closer to identifying the building in the last image of Jess. Apparently, the exterior plasterwork was a pattern called palmette, a Queen Anne revival style that had been popular in the late 1800s.

'It's distinctive, which helps,' Sam said. 'My contact believes the building is located in the Royal Borough of Kensington and Chelsea. On the downside, there's a fair number of properties of this style in the area, but he thinks he can narrow it further.'

'How's he going to do that?'

'Ask his pals on Twitter, I suppose.' Sam must have read the alarm on Rick's face because he said, 'Relax. You see thousands of queries like this on social media every day, but you'd have to be following some obscure account or be alert to weird hashtags – I mean, seriously, would "hashtag PargeterFreak" mean anything to you?'

'I don't even know what a pargeter is,' Rick admitted; Sam looked ready to explain, and he raised a hand. 'Never mind, I get the idea – it isn't exactly on the "trending" sidebar. So, how long will it take?'

'Hard to say. But he got this far overnight, so I'm optimistic.'

Rick tapped the table with his fingertips. The waiting was killing him; his skin itched, and he could feel his heart racing. 'What about the auditions – what did the production company say?'

'As you said: Jess did the audition. Then production team got a text to say she'd been mugged, was in A&E, and to contact her agent if she wasn't answering her phone.'

'The kidnappers sent the text.'

'It would seem so.'

Rick ran a hand over his face. 'Okay . . . The audition was at eight-forty-five; I got the first WhatsApp at nine-thirty. Even if they were on schedule – and they usually aren't – she was probably there till after nine.'

'She signed out at nine-twenty,' Sam said promptly.

'Which means she was snatched near the venue.'

He accessed Google Maps on his smartphone, finding the church hall tucked down a narrow street. 'This is the audition venue.' He pinched and enlarged, switching between map and street views.

'There are a lot of coffee shops and restaurants nearby,' Sam said. 'Which could complicate things.'

Rick shook his head. 'She doesn't usually eat before lunchtime.' He squinted at the map. 'But she'd probably duck into Spitalfields Market for a bit.' He moved the map so that the market was at the centre of the screen and checked for entrances and exits. 'And clothes shops. There's one she really likes . . .' He couldn't remember the name, but he kept searching.

'Forget pedestrianised sections,' Sam said. 'You'd need a van, and from what you've told me, Jess wouldn't go quietly.'

Rick noted that Sam had said, '*You'd* need a van,' like he'd done this himself at some time.

Sam produced a tablet from a backpack on the seat beside him, and slid it onto the table, deftly calling up a map and selecting the same section while Rick continued his search. 'One-way streets are unlikely,' he said, and Rick heard a tense excitement in his voice. 'Not enough flexibility for grabbing someone up – and too easy to get boxed in.'

'Oh, wait a minute,' Rick said, reading the details from his smartphone. 'The market doesn't open till ten on a Monday, so that's out.'

'Actually, that's helpful,' Sam said. 'I'll have someone check opening times for clothes shops. If she was window-shopping, rather than inside, we'll be able to track her more easily. We'll start with the two-way streets around the market and work out in a spiral from there.'

'Access to Transport For London's traffic jam cams would be an asset.'

'Already on it,' Sam said.

'I demanded proof of life, too – so whoever you've got monitoring my phone better not nod off – I'll keep her on the line as long as I can.'

'Anything else I should know before you go?'

Should he tell Sam that Jess knew about him – and about what he did? If his house had been bugged for a while, Unwin might have heard him confess about the murder. But he couldn't be sure, one way or the other. Sam had been more than willing to use Mrs Yalman as a pawn in his logistical chess game; what if he concluded that the personal risk was too high, and decided to cut his losses? Rick couldn't afford to lose his brother's help.

'Why the hesitation, Rick?' Sam demanded.

'I'm not sure about this – it's just a gut feeling,' Rick said, hedging to cover his deception. 'But if I'm right, then it's not just me being spied on – Kildoran might have a mole in his chambers.'

Sam tilted his head. 'It's only to be expected. Student loans, pupillage costs, Inns of Court fees and God knows what else to pay – it's a wonder there's a straight barrister among them.'

Rick stared at him; Sam-as-superego had told him more or less the same thing.

'What?' Sam said.

'Nothing. Just – I thought you'd say that,' Rick said.

'Well, I'll try not to be so predictable in future.'

'What am I going to tell Mounsey about the PA?'

'Tell him Kildoran has told you in confidence that he's going to hold off bringing her in as long as possible.'

'And if he decides to call her to give evidence in the next twenty-four hours?'

'He changed his mind,' Sam said. He lied so glibly, so *easily* – without a thought for Mrs Yalman, or the threat that Jess was living under hour by dreadful hour.

'A couple more things . . .' Rick recited Mounsey's Jaguar XJ plate number and pinged an image to his brother's burner, telling him about the man who'd been following him on foot. 'For info, Darren Mays was minding Mounsey today, along with a hairy guy I didn't recognise. Couldn't get a shot of him, but I'll see if I can find him in the files when I go to the office.'

'I'll be in touch. In the meantime . . .' Sam typed a message on his burner, and a moment later Rick's own burner phone buzzed. 'That's the name and number of an electronics specialist in Tottenham Court Road. Ask for Ahmed. Tell him you're there to collect a bug detector for Julian – it will be paid for already, so don't take any crap from him. He'll show you how to use it – but make sure you turn off any RF devices, or you'll get a false positive. So, mobile phones, central heating thermostat, radios, microwaves – if you're not sure, google it. Sweep the house every time you've been out. *Every* time, Rick.'

'Roger that.' Rick waited a couple of seconds. 'So, who's Julian?'

Sam smiled. 'You know better than to ask me that.'

Chapter 27

RICK TURNED ON HIS PHONE as he reached Camden Town Tube station. It buzzed and his heart jumped. It was a text message from Dave Collins:

—Meet me at work. Urgent.

He was about to pocket the phone when it rang.

'Jake Irons, MIT4.' DI Irons was leading the investigation into Austin King's murder. 'I thought you'd want to know – Hakim Saidi was found dead in the toilets of a nightclub near London Bridge, last night.'

'His name came up in some of the texts messages we recovered from Unwin's mobile,' Rick said. 'He's just a small-time thug, isn't he?'

'Apparently he had ambitions. According to the gang's command unit, he's been snapping at Unwin's heels ever since his arrest. And his crew snatched a couple of Unwin's girls from his salon in Bermondsey on Sunday night.'

'Talk about taking liberties,' Rick said. 'How did he die?'

'Throat slit,' Irons said. 'And I mean *slit* – lengthwise. Pathologist says the killer cut the jugular vein to reduce blood pressure before he went for the artery. Less spray, that way. A lot of blood, but very little spatter.'

'Second professional hit linked to Unwin in a week,' Rick said.

'Yeah – this guy was *slick*. No witnesses, except Saidi's minder, who was laid out cold on the floor next to him.'

'How's he doing?'

'He'll live.' Irons gave a dry chuckle. 'But he'll never live it down. He said the guy looked small, harmless, caught him off guard. Didn't get a good look at his face, but he was white.'

'You're thinking this is retaliation for the girls?' Rick asked, recalling Mounsey's words about Unwin's retribution coming swift and hard.

'That'd be my guess.'

'Well, thanks for letting me know, Jake,' Rick said.

'Rick?'

'Yep?'

'Watch your back, mate.'

'Will do.' Rick closed the phone, keeping a rein on his emotions. He dithered for a moment but finally switched off the mobile and turned back the way he'd come. Dave Collins would have to wait; Sam needed to hear this.

Chapter 28

SAM TURNER ORDERED MORE COFFEE and set to work organising his associates. It had occurred to him that he might resolve his brother's predicament by taking out Unwin himself. But with their boss dead, there was a chance that Unwin's men would panic and kill Jess, and he couldn't take the risk. It wouldn't hurt to do some background on Unwin's inner circle, however, and having the names and addresses of key members of his crew would certainly help speed the process if he changed his mind. He already had surveillance on Zoe Unwin. She'd decamped suddenly to a hotel in Vienna, with a couple of minders in tow. Sam had people watching her and monitoring her calls.

He took out a new burner phone from his shoulder bag and rang the only number in its contacts folder.

'Where did Mounsey go after speaking to the sergeant?' he asked.

'His office, and then the Old Bailey,' the man replied promptly. 'I've had confirmation he's with his client now.'

'He'll almost certainly be tied up at the court till lunchtime,' Sam said. 'But have your insider keep an eye on him, in case he slips out. What about the driver and Mays?'

'Mays went in with Mounsey. The driver went back to the office.'

'Who's sitting on that?'

'The two Jackies.' This was a male-female pairing. To a casual observer, they looked like a settled and rather dull married couple. Combined, they had the hunting instincts of trained gundogs.

'Tell them I need the driver's name, and whatever else they can get on him.'

'Will do.'

'Has Tommy Novac surfaced, yet?' This was the ex-boxer who'd been with Unwin from the start.

'He's still off the radar, but I've got someone on his flat, and as of this morning, a substitute carer will be going in to look after his old mum. Proper chatty, she is; if Novac's mum knows anything, she'll find out.'

'Excellent. Who followed the sergeant this morning?'

'Ollie.'

'New, is he?'

'Recent, yeah . . .'

Sam heard the question in the man's tone.

'He was spotted.'

'Hell.'

'I just sent you a text. That him?' He waited for his accomplice to open the image Rick had taken of his stalker.

'Fuck.'

'Get rid of him. And put someone *less* recent on Turner, eh?'

'Sure. Sure, Boss.'

Sam stopped. Rick had just come through the door, looking worried.

'I'll call you back.' He cut the line and waited for Rick to be seated.

'Problem?' he asked.

'Maybe,' Rick said. 'Possible retaliation hit from Unwin.'

'Who's the victim?'

'Hakim Saidi.'

Sam puckered his brow. 'And he is . . .'

'A lowlife with his heart set on taking over Unwin's manor.'

'Ah, well.' Sam nodded as if enlightened. 'When you swim with sharks—'

'This happened in a club full of people,' Rick said, hardening his voice.

'Was anyone hurt? Apart from Mr Saidi, I mean.'

'His minder – but he's recovering. It looks like a professional, Sam.'

Sam gave a sombre look. 'Professionals usually shun the lime-light. A hit in a busy public setting sends a message.'

'That's what I was thinking.'

'And what does the Met think?' Sam asked, watching his brother closely.

'The general feeling is it's payback. Saidi scooped up two of Unwin's girls on Sunday night.'

The two frightened-looking teenagers Saidi brought into the club. 'That seems like overkill,' Sam said aloud.

Rick nodded. 'Unwin has kept a low profile since he was banged up. I don't see him lashing out like this, unless—'

'He's desperate,' Sam finished for him.

'I was going to say unless Saidi took out the contract on Austin King,' Rick said.

'Are you investigating *another* murder, Rick?' The very last thing Sam needed was Rick investigating the hit on Austin King. 'Because I want to be clear – I'm only in this to help you find Jess,' he added, feeling a little put out.

'I know. I'm just trying to work out what it means, okay?'

'It's damage limitation,' Sam said. 'Unwin's been challenged. He expects to get out of prison soon, but he knows that if he loosens his grip even a little bit, he'll lose everything.'

Rick nodded slowly. 'He made an example of Saidi.'

'It also explains why he upped the ante, asking you to compro-mise the sequestered witness's security. He's desperate to get out, and he'll do anything to make that happen. Which is not good for Jess.' Anxiety flared briefly in his brother's eyes. Sam didn't feel good about it, but he couldn't have Rick investigating his professional activities.

'We need to find Jess,' he pressed on, relentless, knowing he was stating the obvious, but wanting Rick's entire focus on that one, single goal. 'So *you* need to let me get on with organising that.' He paused. 'Okay?'

'Yeah. Yes,' Rick said.

'Okay,' Sam repeated, satisfied. 'Off to court, now?'

Rick gave a brief shake of his head. 'Serious Fraud Office. The forensic accountant wants a word.'

Sam waited until his brother was through the door before calling his associate back.

'Turner is on his way to the SFO – Canada House – get someone there fast. If you need a tag team, I'll fund it. As of now, I want to know what he's up to, night and day.'

'Sure, if that's what you want, Boss . . .' He sounded doubtful; DS Rick Turner was not their primary target, but it wasn't his business to question the paymaster's strategy – only to implement it.

'It's exactly what I want,' Sam said, 'And no more screw-ups.'

'Understood.'

'If Mays leaves the court, stay on him. He's one of Unwin's most trusted minders, so he's likely to be talking to key people; he could even lead us to Jess. I want a report on every stop he makes: locations, times, durations – and a background check on anyone he talks to.'

'Goes without saying, Boss.'

'You got a tap on his home landline?'

'Done. But he doesn't use it. I got someone chatting up the wife at the dog park – he's tried to hack the mobile, but the missus is careful – Bluetooth's been switched off both times. He thinks he's got another way in, though – Mrs Mays is mad about boxer dogs, so he's gonna tempt her with a pic of his puppy.'

'I do hope that's not a euphemism.'

'Nah, he got it off of Facebook.'

Sam suppressed a smile. 'Well, text me if you get anything useful.'

Chapter 29

Tuesday morning: day 2 of Unwin's trial

IN A NARROW CELL AT THE OLD BAILEY, Thomas Unwin was in conference with his solicitor advocate. The white metro tiles on the walls were faded to a dingy grey with age, and the small, poorly ventilated room smelled faintly of mildew and bad digestion. For lack of space to stand, Unwin sat on the hard bench built solidly into the walls, while Mounsey stood in the cell doorway, keeping as deferential a distance as the meagre space would allow.

Cheered by reports of the successful and highly visible murder of Saidi, Unwin was optimistic that he'd turned a corner.

'It's on local radio, in all the free papers, and online.' Mounsey handed over his smartphone. Unwin saw a slight tremor in his hand. 'Proof of death.'

Saidi didn't look so cocky bled out on the floor of a nightclub toilet.

'The two girls he took showed up at Tingle Touch salon at around two a.m.,' Mounsey added. 'What do you want me to do with them?'

'Find out what they know, then I'll decide,' Unwin said, scrolling through Mounsey's phone for news of the killing online; it all looked reassuringly horrifying. 'What's the word on the street?'

'Mr Unwin is not a man to trifle with,' Mounsey said ingratiatingly.

Unwin laughed at the unlikely phrasing and Mounsey smiled like he was in pain.

Suppressing a sigh, Unwin said, 'All right, you can tell me the bad news, now.'

'The cash transfer on the cargo *wasn't* made, so the ship is stuck in dock.'

'Fuck.'

'The suppliers are demanding payment,' Mounsey went on, 'and they are quite . . . insistent.'

'Talk to the buyers,' Unwin said. 'If they front the money, they can have the cargo by Thursday.'

The pained look on Mounsey's face became a grimace. 'I'm not sure they will pay for goods they haven't had a sniff at.'

'Course they will,' Unwin shot back. 'They're looking at fifty million in benefits off the back of this one deal.'

Mounsey fidgeted. 'The contract was payment "on delivery", Mr Unwin. I'm afraid it might make you look weak if you ask for a variation of the terms.'

Unwin retrieved the image on Mounsey's mobile of Saidi dead in the nightclub bathroom and thrust it into his solicitor's hand.

'Does that look *weak* to you, Callum?'

Flustered, now, Mounsey concealed the phone in his pocket as if hiding contraband. 'You can't *threaten* these people,' he hissed.

'Use your famous negotiating skills, I won't need to,' Unwin said. 'All I'm asking is they pony up a few million in seed money.'

Mounsey looked so worried that Unwin went on in a slightly more conciliatory tone. 'Float the idea, okay? See what the mood is. In the meantime, keep the pressure on Turner – the sooner I'm out, the sooner I can get the project back on course.'

He saw Mounsey hesitate, and he added, 'You did speak to him this morning?'

'Of course, but—'

Unwin listened to the lawyer's account of his chat with DS Turner and did not like what he heard.

'He refused outright?' Unwin said, his eyes hot with subdued fury.

'He stipulated that he wasn't convinced by the last photograph and is not minded to cooperate further unless he had certain assurances.'

'"*Not minded? Assurances?*"' Unwin repeated, in the same mimsy tone. 'Taken to tiptoeing around the facts like a *lawyer*, has he?'

Mounsey bristled in the fussy way little men do. 'I really don't think that's called for.'

Unwin eyed him with distaste. *Prissy little prick.* 'What does he want?'

Mounsey had the gall to scowl at him.

'My barrister is due to make an appearance in the next five minutes,' Unwin growled. 'So, spare me your hurt feelings and get to the *point*.'

Mounsey turned away, glancing quickly into the corridor, then pulled the door to and edged a little further into the cell, carefully avoiding contact with the walls.

'He says he wants proof of life,' he murmured.

Unwin sucked his teeth. He didn't want it to go this way, but Turner had given him no choice. 'Give it to him,' he said. 'And make sure he knows there are serious consequences for anyone who has the nerve to yank my chain.'

Mounsey gave a delicate cough. 'If I understand you correctly—' The little man drew his thumb suggestively along the line of his jaw.

'*Fuck* no – not the face – the girl needs to earn a living, doesn't she?'

The vicious little bastard looked disappointed, but he nodded. 'Anything else?'

'He'll expect a provable time and date somewhere in the frame. And send me the video when it's done – I'll watch it in my cell tonight.'

Chapter 30

DAVE COLLINS WAS STANDING AT THE BARRIER inside
Canada House. Rick glanced across at him as he signed in at
the desk and took a guest lanyard. The forensic accountant was
doing his best to present a poker face, but the big man's eyes
danced from Rick to the receptionist, and he was practically on
his toes as he waited.

'You're in early,' Rick said.

'Never went home.' Collins's usually pale face was slightly
flushed and although the foyer was decidedly chilly, he kept
plucking at his shirt front as if to stop it clinging to his chest.

'You okay, mate?' Rick asked.

'Good,' Collins said. 'I'm good. But—' He ushered Rick into
the lift and hopped in after, setting the carriage a-judder. 'Best
if I explain at my desk.'

A spare chair requisitioned, coffee offered and declined, Collins
sat down and tugged again at his shirt.

'So,' he said. 'When Mr Kildoran asked for a breakdown of
the key points of evidence for the expert witness to focus on, it
was a little bit tricky, 'cos, as you know, we weren't a task force
assigned to this. It was just me and whoever I could rope in to
do me a favour when they had a half-day spare.'

'Yeah . . .?' Was he about to say they'd messed up? Collins was agitated, but he was making better eye contact than usual, and his grey eyes glittered with feverish excitement, so Rick guessed it must be good news.

'I didn't want to miss anything important, so I reviewed the entire case, start to finish.'

In one night? Rick didn't say it aloud: Collins had almost spontaneously combusted when Rick had passed on the prosecution barrister's thanks and admiration for the work he'd done after King's death. Instead, he let the accountant talk, trying to keep his mind off Jess and on what Collins was telling him.

'We'd already tagged every shell company with a provable link to Unwin,' Collins said, 'ready to freeze the assets they shielded as soon as he was under arrest.'

Rick nodded – these were the protocols they'd adopted over a year earlier, as they made the first tentative steps in the investigation into Unwin's financials.

Collins took a breath. 'So, we were looking at a company in Jersey—'

'A shell company?' Jersey might be a small island, but it had recently been ranked in the top ten worst economies for international corporate tax fraud.

'No, a *real* one,' Collins said, clicking to a screen that showed a nondescript dockside warehouse. 'This is Coutanche Shipping and Storage. Been in operation since the mid-1990s, owned by Marie-Louise Coutanche, a Jersey national.' He clicked to her bio page on the company's website: Marie-Louise was a glossy fifty-something, her dark hair styled in a layered bob.

'Coutanche Shipping came to our attention because Unwin used one of her warehouses as a waystation for his imports – mainly machine parts and agricultural equipment bound for the UK. We thought the company might be writing receipts for stuff that never existed – you know how it works – falsified ships' manifests and bills of lading and faked import-export documents.

Money laundering, basically. But we were able to follow the goods through the supply chain from factory to farm. They were real.'

'I don't get it, Dave – if it's kosher, what's your point?'

Collins's grey eyes danced. 'Mrs Coutanche was joint owner of the company with her husband. Unknown to her, he'd run up huge gambling debts, "borrowed" from the firm, threw good money after bad – usual sad story. Finally topped himself two years ago, leaving her with a firm on the point of collapse and a big tax debt – I mean nearly half a million. She did her best to keep going, but with no capital to cover ongoing costs, she was struggling to bring in customers.'

Rick glanced at the image again. 'Well, things must have looked up, 'cos that looks like couture clobber she's wearing.'

'Flash forward six months and Mrs C's about to lose the house – she's even put the business on the market – then literally *days* before she's due to land in court, her tax debt is cleared, mortgage arrears paid, and Coutanche Shipping is back in business. Which got me thinking – how did she find that kind of money?'

'How indeed?' Rick said.

'I mean, you're gonna think smuggling, aren't you?' Collins mused. 'Undeclared goods, drugs hidden in engine blocks, weapons in among the hardware—'

'But I've never heard of Coutanche,' Rick interrupted. 'So I'm guessing she was in the clear?'

'I'd got as far as checking with the mortgage provider. She told them that the money had come from a casino win.'

'Ironic.' Collins gave him a blank look and Rick added, 'Given that the business was almost ruined through gambling.'

'Oh, yeah,' Collins said, clearly not getting it.

'Big win, too.'

Collins nodded eagerly, back on familiar ground, now. 'And I was on the point of looking into it, but – sorry, mate – back then, your case was low priority. I got assigned a multi-asset pensions fraud, so I asked a colleague to handle Mrs Coutanche.'

'And?' Rick said, knowing he sounded impatient. Almost nine-thirty and he still hadn't heard back from Mounsey; they would be heading into court very soon, and if Unwin hadn't agreed to his demand for proof of life by then, he would be faced with a very long and anxious wait until lunch break.

Collins carried on, oblivious: 'Last I heard, this colleague was talking to Interpol.'

'Last you heard?'

'I was focused on the pensions fraud for seven, eight weeks? When I got back to *your* case – it'd be about this time last year – things had moved on. To be honest, Coutanche Shipping didn't even cross my mind – and even if it had, I'd've thought the same as you – that she'd been checked out and cleared.'

Rick nodded; it had got pretty full-on last autumn. By the end of July, they had established the money trail between the banker and the contract killing of Wilson. Making the connection between Unwin and the contract hit on Haskins was more complicated, but they'd had that data trail pinned down by last autumn and their focus had shifted to consolidating the evidence they already had.

Collins broke into his thoughts: 'So, I'm checking back through the docs last night, I find a reference to Marie-Louise Coutanche, and I think, "Oh, yeah – the shipping boss whose luck turned," and I think I'll just take a quick squint at the report. And I'm a bit miffed to discover that Mrs Coutanche's so-called casino win hasn't even been looked into.'

'Why not?'

Collins tugged at his shirt again and dug a finger inside his collar for good measure. 'Like I said, Rick, this was never an SFO-led investigation. We took our lead from you guys.'

Rick straightened up, hearing the underlying message. 'Are you saying the Coutanche line of inquiry got shut down?'

'Yep – and fair enough as far as the shipping angle goes – I mean, it's hard to prove a shipment's been used to shift contraband *after* the event.'

'True.'

'But the casino win should have been as easy as looking into her tax returns,' Collins said. 'Jersey doesn't have land-based casinos – none of the Channel Islands do. So, wherever Mrs C won it she'd have been taxed on it: there's forms to fill in, receipts given out. And with a win that big she'd be mad not to claim back the tax. The last thing I said to my colleague before I handed over the file was, "You want to check with HMRC, see if she made a claim".'

'What's this colleague got to say for himself?'

'I'd like to know!' Collins exclaimed. 'I hadn't seen him for a bit, so I went looking. Couldn't find him. I asked HR if he'd been reassigned. They said he's gone – packed it all in.'

Rick sat back in his chair. 'Huh.'

'What I thought,' Collins said. 'I mean what would you call it?'

'Sinister' was the word that came to Rick's mind. 'Who shut down the line of inquiry?' he asked, and his voice sounded muffled to his own ears.

'That's the weird thing. There's no name on file; it just says "discontinued".'

'Weird,' Rick echoed stupidly, when all the time that word *sinister* kept insinuating itself into his thoughts.

'By now, I'm *well* curious,' Collins went on. 'So, I'm looking up Coutanche Shipping's website – as you do – and of course, they've got a Facebook page. It's all official and corporate, as you'd expect, but I thought maybe she'd have a Friends' page where she'd mentioned her big jackpot win. Short version – I find her page and she hasn't set her posts to private.'

'You found the win?' Rick asked, praying that he had.

Collins shook his head. 'I didn't really expect to. But on Monday, Marie-Louise did write a moving piece on the sudden death of her former accountant and old university pal, Austin King.'

Bloody hell . . .

Collins was grinning from ear to ear.

'HR's arsey about giving out personal info,' Collins went on. 'But given the circumstances, I'd be justified asking for a forwarding address and phone number—'

'No.' Rick heard the panic in his voice and hoped that Collins couldn't.

'What?' Collins seemed shocked. 'Marie-Louise Coutanche knew Austin King – she even admits to working with him. Look at it, Rick: Unwin could ship his goods direct from any number of European ports to Southampton or Felixstowe or Hull, so why make a pit stop at Jersey? I dunno – bet Mrs Coutanche could tell you.'

'You don't know that.'

Puzzled by his lack of enthusiasm, Collins said, 'We never do, till we investigate. But if I'm right, Marie-Louise lied about where she got the money to buy herself out of a very deep financial hole – and that gives you bargaining power.'

Rick hesitated, and impatient now, Collins said, 'Austin King is dead, and *you* need someone in the witness box who has direct knowledge of Unwin's trade; that's Mrs Coutanche to a T.'

Rick broke into a sweat. Collins was right: adding in an extra port of call would increase shipping costs; there had to be a solid financial reason why Unwin would do that. And why shut down the SFO's inquiries into Coutanche Shipping when they hadn't interfered with other leads? It all pointed to Marie-Louise Coutanche's firm being vital to Unwin's illegal trade.

Jeez, Rick thought, *if Unwin gets wind of this discussion, he'll see it as a gesture of defiance – and Jess will be the one to suffer.*

He steadied himself and spoke as dispassionately as the screaming in his head would allow: 'You can't be following new leads, Dave.'

'Bollocks to that, mate,' Collins said. 'King was a key witness as well as Unwin's right-hand man. He's been murdered, and you've got a definite link between King and Mrs Coutanche, who just *happens* to own Unwin's preferred shipping company.'

Rick took a breath, and frowned at a point above Collins's head, as if trying to piece the facts together. 'But *Unwin* didn't have King killed.'

'It's new evidence,' Collins insisted. 'The jury needs to see it.'

'That's not new evidence, Dave, it's new suspicions,' Rick said, kindly. 'This case can't stand too many surprises, mate – and King's murder is already one too many. Without your help it probably would've derailed the prosecution's case.'

Collins looked abashed. He hated having the attention on his work – on *him* – and Rick exploited that, though he felt a heel exploiting the man's weakness.

'Seriously, Dave – things were looking shaky till you stepped in. Most of us police on the case need an aspirin and lie-down after a squint at the spreadsheets; Kildoran was practically having kittens about presenting the financials to the jury – he was convinced half of them would call in sick after the first day.'

'Like I said, it's teamwork, isn't it?' Both Collins's hands went to his shirt front, and he plucked at the fabric, his face red and sweating, his eyes anywhere but on Rick.

Merciless in his appreciation, Rick drove his point home. 'I mean it, mate; we could *not* have got through day two without you. And right now, we're all about putting the evidence we've checked and rechecked in front of the jury. We don't want to go asking questions we don't know the answers to – not at this stage.'

Collins hung his head, defeated by Rick's logic. 'What d'you want me to do, then?'

'Stick to the plan. If the SFO decides to go after Unwin's relationship with Coutanche Shipping *after* the trial, I'll support you every step of the way. But stay away from mining new data. It'll only get you in trouble. And if it alerts Coutanche – and Unwin – we'll lose the advantage.'

In the lobby, he shook his friend's moist hand.

Collins looked hurt and perplexed, and Rick said, 'If it makes you feel any better, I'll talk to the superintendent – see what he says.'

Transparent as a child, Collins immediately brightened. 'You'll tell him?'

'Definitely,' Rick lied. 'First chance I get.'

Chapter 31

RICK'S MOBILE RANG AS HE LEFT THE BUILDING and he almost tore the pocket of his suit getting the damned thing out. It was Superintendent Ghosh.

'Where the hell are you? Kildoran expected you at the pre-trial briefing.'

'Sorry, sir. I'm at Canada House – I got a message from Dave Collins – thought it might be urgent.'

'Was it?'

'Not relevant to the trial – something to pick up later maybe, if all goes well,' he said, hedging. 'I can head over to the court now.'

'Never mind – he'll be in full flow by now. But make sure you see him during the lunch break.'

'Will do.'

As Rick ended the call, a text notification came in, sending a tingling shock through his hand.

—WhatsApp, 10s

Rick darted across the road into the relative quiet of Spring Gardens. Sheltering in a doorway, he opened the app and saw Jess on a video link. Her eyes looked huge, and tears spilled onto her cheeks.

'Rick?'

'I'm here, Jess. Are you okay?'

'Do what they say, babe. Please, do what they say.' Someone grabbed her by the hair, and she yelped, seizing the man's wrist with both her hands. 'Get off me, you pig!'

The man dumped her in front of a TV screen; BBC News 24 was playing. 'Read it,' he said.

She read the crawler at the bottom of the screen and told Rick the date.

Rick examined the room around her. The skirting and covings seemed the same; they hadn't moved her. He just hoped that Sam's people were tracing the call.

Stalling for time, he said, 'I can't read the caption – let me see it in focus.'

Still holding on to Jess's hair, the man gripped her left wrist, pulling it behind her. His face came into shot for a second. He was masked.

'Wait – what are you *doing*?' Jess yelled.

A second man took hold of her right wrist. Something gleamed in his hand.

'No. NO! Don't you fucking DARE!' she screamed.

Rick stupidly tried to change the angle of the phone to see what they were doing.

'Whatever you're planning – stop. I'm doing everything I c—'

Jess arched, flinging her head back, catching the first man on the jaw so hard that Rick heard his teeth click.

'Bitch!' the man yelled.

She lashed out with her feet, but the second man – also masked – pulled her in close, clamping her right hand in one huge paw. She tightened her fingers into a fist.

'Open it,' he growled.

'Are you fucking *crazy*? *Oh God*,' she shrieked, 'Rick, make them stop.'

Rick saw what was in the man's free hand.

Oh, Jesus.

'Stop,' he shouted. 'There's no need for this. Stop!'

The men continued to grapple with Jess.

'Open your fist; I'll take just the first joint,' the second man said. 'Piss me about, I'll take the lot.'

Jess set up a terrible keening, inarticulate at first – a wordless mewling, like a frighted infant – then, 'Pleeeeease Rick . . . Please, give them what they want.'

'You can have it,' Rick said. 'Are you *listening*? I'll get what you want. I'll get Mrs Yalman – just *don't hurt her.*'

By now, the man had uncurled Jess's fist, had her pinkie finger in his grip.

'Why are you doing this?' Jess cried. 'Whyyy? Oh*please*Godoh*please*don't – n-n-noooo—'

'Stop!' Rick yelled over her: 'Stop, you bastards – stop! I'll fucking *kill* you!'

He heard a sickening crunch and a scream of pain.

Jess went limp. Simultaneously, the second man stumbled out of shot, cursing, and the first man said, 'What the f—?'

The line went dead. A second later, Rick's phone buzzed; a text – from Mounsey.

—Proof of life, it read. Now, get the job done.

Chapter 32

RICK STARED AT THE MESSAGE, his breathing harsh, his eyes burning. He began to thumb in a reply, then cancelled. Better if Mounsey didn't see him coming. It was nine-thirty-five; the court wouldn't be in session till ten – if he flagged a taxi, he might just get to the Old Bailey in time.

Slipping his phone into his jacket pocket, he rubbed a hand over his face; it came away wet.

'Shit,' he murmured. 'Shit.'

He stepped out of the protection of the doorway into the street and was immediately confronted by two men – one big and muscled like a weightlifter, the other shorter and wiry. The bigger of the two held his hands up.

'Need a chat,' he said.

Unwin. 'You made your point,' Rick said, taking a pace towards the man. 'You do *not* want to mess with me right now.'

'Five minutes,' the man said, backing away slightly, giving himself room to manoeuvre. 'Then you'll be on your way.'

The second guy had edged to his left.

Rick pointed at him. 'You. Stand still.'

The smaller guy took another step and reached for his arm. Rick batted his hand away, and the big man came in fast. Rick brought his right hand up, turning as he made contact, but the guy moved with him, light on his feet.

Rick pulled his right fist back, ready for a kidney punch, but the speed of the taller man again forestalled him – he moved like he was on rollers. And his hands were *fast* – he blocked and parried, turned and spun faster than Rick could counter. A sudden, sharp impact sent him staggering, and before he could recover his balance he was cuffed and stuffed into the back seat of a limo.

His head boomed. He couldn't make sense of what was happening. Little and Large sandwiched him between them in the centre seat, while a third man drove, screeching away from the kerb amid a flurry of car horn blasts. They zipped past the blinding white expanse of Trafalgar Square and on to the Strand, turning right at the church of St Martin in the Fields. In a surreal moment of confusion, Rick thought they were taking him to the Central Criminal Court. But the driver scooted left at Aldwych and headed towards Holborn, weaving in and out of the traffic like a maniac.

Rick's stomach lurched with the speed and nausea from the blow to his head. He was almost relishing the thought of throwing up on his captors when the car swerved neatly to the kerb, into a disabled parking spot.

The big man hauled him out of the car and set him on his feet.

Rick gained his bearings, realising that they were on the edge of one of the hundreds of garden squares that dotted the capital. Through the black iron gates, he saw a man, dressed casually in a dark woollen bomber jacket, a black newsboy cap and sunglasses to ensure anonymity. He wore his backpack slung over one shoulder, like a cool tech-type on his way to work.

Sam.

What the f—

Sam shot him a warning look over the rims of his shades, then glanced to the big man and without a word spoken, Rick was released.

He marched towards his brother, intent on violence, but Sam strolled forward, his hand out, ready to shake Rick's as if they were business associates. 'I *do* apologise for the mix-up,' he said, his voice rich and cultured, with no trace of Sam's native cockney.

He clasped Rick's arm and neatly turned him, slipping his own arm through the crook of Rick's, steering him away from the men who waited at the gate.

'Bloomsbury Square,' Sam said, in the same plummy accent, loud enough for the men to hear. 'London's oldest garden square. It dates back to 1665 – did you know?'

'What. The. *Hell*—?' Rick tried to shake free, but the movement brought on another wave of nausea and he stopped.

Sam patted his brother's hand. 'I could hardly let you burst into the Old Bailey on the rampage, could I?' he said mildly.

'What are you, now, a mind reader?'

'I saw what they did to Jess,' his brother said quietly. 'I'm truly sorry.'

Rick looked hard into his brother's face; he seemed sincere.

'You recorded it?'

'We did.'

'Show me.'

'Rick, I don't think—'

'Just the end, where he's—' He broke off, taking a few breaths before going on: 'I think the animal with the shears nicked himself.'

'We'll check.'

Rick began to object, but Sam interrupted him.

'No. You do not need to see that again. We're close, and I promise you, I've got my best people on it. But you should never go in angry. Bring anger to an equal fight, you've already lost.'

'Well, thanks for the homily, but if you're talking about your goons, two on one is not equal.'

'I was speaking in broader terms, but it serves as an example: with your skills, you could easily take on two men. But not when you're blinded by panic and rage.'

Sam released Rick's arm and peered at his face. 'That'll bruise,' he said, and Rick again became aware of the throbbing pain around his right ear and temple. 'Can you hear all right?'

'I can hear fine,' Rick said, over the booming that seemed to reverberate inside his skull.

'Good. Then listen carefully.' Sam began pacing again, leading Rick along the central pathway to the wide paved oval at the centre of the square. 'We narrowed Jess's location to the northern edge of Kensington, edging towards Holland Park. And Novac's mother says that her son – who, we are told, is a *very* good boy – hasn't been home for a couple of days because he's "minding a famous actress while she's filming in London".'

Rick's stomach tightened at the cruelty of the lie.

'A lovely place near Hyde Park, she says. Practically a mansion.'

'Well, what the hell are we waiting for?'

'An address,' Sam said. 'I have people looking for Novac's car. I'm waiting on the mobile phone signal trace, which will give us the location within a one-fifty-metre radius. And the heritage architecture nerds are still trawling their contacts for that building with the ornate plasterwork. We could have her safe in a matter of hours.'

'Okay. Okay . . . But give me something to do, Sam – *please.*'

'Go to the court, keep your one o'clock appointment with Mr Kildoran—' Rick looked at him sharply and he raised one shoulder. 'Yes, I'm monitoring your phone calls as well as WhatsApp. Reprehensible, I know – but look at it this way: it saved you from a gross error of judgement.'

Rick laughed in spite of himself. 'You're unbelievable.'

Sam's mouth twitched. 'I know. Find an opportunity to exchange a few words with Mr Mounsey,' he went on. 'Tell him Mrs Yalman will not be called this week—'

Rick shook his head. 'I've been thinking about this. It won't work; if Kildoran decides to call her, he'll prep his team and Unwin's insider will tell Mounsey – he'll know I was lying.'

'Tell Mounsey that Kildoran knows he has a mole on his team.' Another glib lie. 'Whatever he's told his minions, in *reality*, he will keep her in reserve until you've completed your evidence.'

That felt like a gut punch. 'Sam – I can't—'

Sam touched his arm lightly. 'You won't need to,' he said. 'They just need to believe that the trial is about to fall apart, and you're the only person who can guarantee that will happen. They'll have their guard down, and that will give us the advantage.'

'Only if we find Jess before tomorrow.'

'Have a little faith, Rick.' Sam took a deep breath of London air and looked around him. 'Glorious, isn't it?' he said. It was another fine autumn day, and the trees, glowing gold and yellow and copper, filtered the sun's rays so that the garden beneath was lit like a church. With no breath of wind, the leaves quietly gave up the ghost, and fluttered to the pathway at their feet.

Sam stirred the gathering litter with the toe of his shoe. 'October blood,' he murmured.

Rick looked askance.

'Dylan Thomas,' Sam said. '*Poem in October*.'

'I take it back,' Rick said, 'The Sam I knew thought poems were for birthday and Valentine's cards. You *have* changed.'

'Not all of it for the worst,' Sam said.

'Yeah, but you and poems? You hated poetry in school.'

'I was an ignorant youth. But a person can change a lot in thirteen years, Rick – you only have to look at yourself to see that.'

'*I* haven't changed,' Rick said, offended.

Sam shot him a shrewd look. 'At fifteen, you were a scared kid who thought he had to fight everyone to make them respect you. Now you're commanding the respect of the senior ranks, effectively leading a major investigation way above your pay grade. You've learned the art of persuasion.'

Rick didn't like to admit that often it was Sam's voice whispering in his ear, teaching him the art.

'This isn't about me,' he said, refusing to be deflected. 'You're

190

saying you just woke up one morning and decided you liked poetry and art galleries?'

Rick had been imagining the worst for his brother for thirteen years, and he was genuinely curious how Sam had defied all rational predictions that he would be in prison or dead before thirty.

'Oh, I'm a work in progress,' Sam said with a smile. 'But it began with Theo Lockleigh. When he wasn't loan-sharking or supplying drugs to bored Sloanes with more money than sense, he was a lawyer – a good one. Public school educated – minor league, not one of the Clarendons – but they still dust you with that surface shimmer of wealth and confidence that it takes to be a convincing politician, businessman—'

'Con artist?' Rick supplied.

'Transferrable skills,' Sam said, clearly revelling in the banter. 'Ersatz class and self-assurance will carry you a very long way in this world.'

'I can see the money-making possibilities would be powerful motivation,' Rick shot back, surprised to find himself smiling. He could picture the scene: Sam, watching mannerisms, trying to learn by rote the social interactions that would be to his advantage, a look of intense, almost avid concentration on his face. When they were kids, Sam could imitate most people after ten minutes of first acquaintance, down to their posture and the way they moved their hands.

'You do a lot of waiting around in my work,' Sam went on, 'and there's nothing so obvious as a man who is waiting. If you don't want to be rumbled, you have to learn to blend in. It takes a *lot* of study and practice to seem to be what you are not. But I discovered that I rather *liked* reading and art and socialising in fine surroundings as if I belonged there.' He clapped his hands. 'So now you know everything.'

'I doubt it.'

Sam chuckled. 'Even so, you'd better trot off to the Old Bailey, or people will think you've lost interest.'

Rick experienced a flash of recognition: in childhood when he'd worked himself to a fury over some injustice, Sam would distract him with stories, make him laugh, keep him talking until the rage was spent and he could be rational. But now that he'd cooled down enough to resist going in swinging his fists, Rick felt an unexpected dread at the thought of facing Mounsey.

Perhaps Sam realised it, because he asked: 'Incidentally – what *did* you plan to do when you found Mounsey?'

'Tear his balls off and feed them to him,' Rick said, feeling a cramp of anger, and with it, the welcome return of his courage.

Sam tugged his ear. 'It's a colourful image. You might want to keep it in mind as you tell him what he wants to hear. I've found that kind of visualisation extremely helpful in my line of work.'

Chapter 33

Tuesday, lunch break at the Old Bailey

RICK HAD FINISHED HIS LUNCHTIME consultation with Kildoran; Mrs Yalman was slated for Thursday afternoon. The prosecutor saw him to the door of the break room and Rick saw Mounsey talking to one of his assistants in the corridor. He drew Kildoran outside for a moment, positioning himself so that Mounsey was bound to see Kildoran's face.

'You're happy with the jurors' response to the expert witness, then?' he asked, lowering his voice.

As expected, Kildoran frowned – hadn't he just said exactly that, not five minutes earlier? 'Perfectly,' he said. 'She unfolded a tale a ten-year-old could follow.'

Rick nodded slowly, keeping his back to Mounsey, and Kildoran's frown deepened. 'Do *you* have any concerns, Sergeant?'

'No – I just wanted to be sure Austin King's murder won't derail the hearing.'

Kildoran tapped him briskly on the shoulder. '*Nil desperandum*,' he said.

'Oh, I'm a glass half-full type,' Rick said. He turned, ready to leave, surreptitiously checking Mounsey.

His assistant had gone, and the solicitor was now talking to a man dressed in the uniform of court security. Clean-shaven, with a shock of wiry blond hair, he had the build of a weightlifter past his prime, running to fat. They were deep in conversation, and the expression on the lawyer's face implied a level of authority over the man. Just then, the guard spread his hands, palms up – a gesture of appeal and vulnerability. His left hand was bandaged. Rick's heart picked up pace; could this be the bastard who cut Jess?

Rick took a step towards the solicitor, and Kildoran said, 'Is everything all right, Sergeant Turner?'

Rick didn't answer – he could barely hear the lawyer's words for Jess's screams reverberating in his head. He sidestepped, but Kildoran was quick for a big man, and he blocked the way.

'Rick?' The use of his first name snapped him out of it. 'He's an objectionable little shit,' Kildoran said, 'but you can't let him get to you.'

'No, of course, you're right,' Rick murmured, grateful for the intervention.

He turned and walked away. When he heard the break-room door close, he stopped and stood with his back to the wall, staring at his burner phone as though checking his texts. He switched on the camera and, looking away for a second as though distracted, snapped a shot of the security guard.

He sent the image with a short message to Sam, and a moment later the guard finished his chat with Mounsey and headed in the direction of the cells.

—Will have him followed / get a tracker on his car, Sam texted back.

Rick pocketed the phone. Now he needed to find a way to bump into Mounsey without attracting the attention of Kildoran, his acolytes, and a host of police acquaintances and colleagues coming and going from the courts. He needn't have worried.

194

As he stood undecided in the busy corridor, a woman in a black suit walked towards him.

'Mr Mounsey's compliments,' she said. 'Cojean, five minutes.'

Rick knew the café; it stood on the corner of Ludgate, only yards from the rear of the courts.

Mounsey was already there when he arrived, standing two ahead in the queue. Rick ordered a white Americano and stood to one side near the solicitor, but Mounsey didn't speak, and Rick wondered if this was just another power play.

To hell with that, Rick thought; Mounsey had called the meeting – he should start. Mounsey's order was placed on the counter, and he edged past Rick with a polite smile, taking his time at the trolley, picking up napkins, stirring sugar into his coffee, and when Rick joined him, he finally broke the silence.

'So, Mrs Yalman will be called on Thursday. When can I expect details of her transport schedule?' He licked the foam from the stirrer and Rick wanted to grab it and ram it in the little bastard's eye.

But Sam was right – Unwin needed to believe that Rick had capitulated – and as Mounsey was Unwin's eyes and ears, he needed to make the little prick believe it. So he said, 'You won't need it.'

Mounsey arched an eyebrow.

'Kildoran knows you've got a mole on his team.'

'I hardly see how that's relevant—'

'He fed his team a line. The lady will not be called; you've got me instead.' He watched the petulant look on Mounsey's face fade to haughty indifference.

'Satisfied?' Rick said, acutely aware that Mounsey hadn't challenged his accusation. Unwin really *did* have someone inside Kildoran's chambers.

Mounsey carefully replaced the lid on his coffee cup and fixed his gaze on Rick, his pallid eyes wide and unfocused, as if Rick was a ghostly image, fading to nothing.

'That depends on what you plan to say.'

'You'll get what you asked for,' Rick said quietly. 'You don't need to hurt her again.'

'Is that a bruise?' Mounsey countered.

'You're not listening; your boys fucked up this morning. I want—' He broke off. 'I'm *asking* for your reassurance that it won't happen again.'

'Go thrashing about like a wild animal, you're likely to be injured,' Mounsey added, as if Rick hadn't said a word.

'Don't mess with me, Mounsey,' Rick warned, hearing a rasp in his voice. 'They'd better not fuck up again. They had better keep her safe. They'd better wrap her in cotton wool and feed her delicacies and cups of fresh mountain dew—' He stopped, noting the rising anger in his voice, and only went on when he was calm enough to add in a conversational tone, 'Because anything else happens to her, I'm coming after all of you.'

Mounsey tried to brazen it out. 'That would not be wise.'

'Every . . . last . . . one of you.' Rick waited until he saw the faintest quiver of uncertainty at the back of the little man's eyes before he picked up his coffee cup and left.

Chapter 34

Tuesday, early afternoon

BACK AT HAMMERSMITH, RICK WENT through the motions, updating DCI Steiner and Superintendent Ghosh on the Unwin trial, explaining Kildoran's next moves, passing on the prosecutor's optimistic assessment of the financial expert's effect on the jury, giving them the official line on Mrs Yalman's expected appearance in the witness box later in the week.

In the Incident Room, he set about typing up a summary, anticipating that Steiner would want the details again in writing. Few desks were occupied, yet Rick felt eyes on him. He scanned the room and saw DS Stott peering at him from behind his computer screen.

Rick lifted his chin in greeting, and sat at his own desk, burying himself in writing up his notes. His nerves jangled, and he kept flashing to Jess struggling with her captors, screaming for help he was powerless to give. He needed action, but there was nothing he could do; he wanted to get out of the office, but he'd spent a lot of time out in the last two days, and it would be hard to justify yet another disappearance. He had no choice but to rely on Sam and be ready when he was needed, so he might as well stick around and be visible for a few hours. Even so, it didn't stop him checking his burner phone every few minutes.

An hour and a half crawled by at an agonising pace, and finally he began to see an end to the paperwork and report-filing that had backed up during his absence. He stopped to take a breath, and a paper cup appeared at his elbow.

'White Americano, no sugar.' Jim Stott. 'Haven't seen you around much, mate.'

Rick stifled a debilitating wave of gratitude for the gesture of friendship and accepted the coffee with a nod of thanks.

Gotta get some sleep, Rick, Sam-as-mentor told him. *Can't have you welling up over a Costa coffee.*

'It's been hectic,' he managed.

Thankfully, Stott seemed unaware of his embarrassing surge of emotion. 'I thought they hadn't called you, yet.'

'Strategy meetings,' Rick said. 'Briefings, updates – you know how it is.'

Stott's brow twisted, more in pain than irony. 'Not really, Rick. I never fronted anything as big as this.' He glanced towards the door. 'Talking of front – Steiner carrying her weight, is she?'

Rick picked up his coffee cup. 'Leading question, your honour.'

Stott laughed. 'Going all right, though, is it?'

'Kildoran's quietly confident.'

'Well, that's gotta be good, right?' Stott took a sip from his own cup. 'When *are* they calling you, then?'

'People keep asking me that,' Rick said.

A spasm flickered across Stott's jaw. 'If you'd rather not say—'

You could try not to sound so arsey, Sam's counsellor voice whispered in his ear. *Now you've hurt his feelings.*

'It isn't that, Stotty,' Rick said, making an effort. 'Just – my guts turn to liquid every time someone mentions it,' he improvised.

Another laugh. 'Come off it! It's not like you're an Old Bailey virgin. Be a walk in the park for a lad like you.' Then, still grinning: 'A walk in the park holding the hand of your best girl.'

Rick stared at him hard, and the smile faded from Stott's face.

Easy, Rick, not everyone's out to get you. He's joking – trying to get back in with his star pupil.

Rick took a breath and told Stott what he wanted to hear: 'I'll keep it in mind.' Adding with an effort at a smile, 'Thanks, Stotty.'

Stott dismissed his thanks with a wave of his hand. 'But get some sleep for Gawd's sake – you can't stand up in front of a jury looking like Kung Fu Panda.' He peered closely at the side of Rick's face. 'Is that a bruise?'

'Training accident,' Rick said, touching his right temple lightly.

Stott's eyebrows shot up. 'Wow – you got time for the dojo?'

'Late-night session,' Rick said. 'Stress relief.'

Stott snorted. 'Well, I'm impressed, but I'm not sure the judge will be. And you've never been the clumsy type, Rick, so if you're suddenly getting pummelled in your classes, there must be something throwing you off your game.'

Shit, Rick thought. Mounsey had noticed, Jim Stott had noticed, so other less friendly minds would too. Perhaps his stoic front had slipped a little, because Stott eyed him with concern.

'Look,' he said, 'I know we've drifted apart these last two years, but I'm here, Rick. Ready to listen.'

It was tempting; Stott had always given good counsel.

Stott was staring at him, waiting for him to speak, a puzzled frown creasing his forehead at the delay, but at the instant Rick opened his mouth to tell Stott everything, his phone rang.

'Dave Collins,' he said with an apologetic smile. 'Sorry, mate. Got to take this.'

Chapter 35

'BLOODY HELL, RICK, YOU COULD'VE WARNED ME!' Dave Collins was shouting; Rick had never heard him so angry.

'Sorry, mate,' Rick said, 'I'm not with you.'

'Your superintendent.' Collins was breathing hard into the mic of his phone. 'He had a go at me – I mean this is my job – it's what I do. And I don't appreciate being—'

'Whoa, wait . . .'

Stott had wandered off, but was obviously earwigging, so Rick stepped outside the Incident Room.

'Slow down, Dave,' he said. 'Take a breath.'

He heard the forensic accountant take a huge gulp of air.

'All right,' Rick said. 'Now, start again – why's he had a go at you?'

'He didn't like the idea of me looking into Coutanche Shipping.'

Maybe it was the knock on the head, or maybe it was lack of sleep, but Rick couldn't make sense of what Collins was saying.

'He blew his top,' Collins went on. 'Told me to stop digging into Coutanche's background – called me a bloody liability.' He took another ragged breath. 'Threatened to tear me a new one.'

'*Ghosh* said that?'

An admin assistant glanced at him as she passed, and Rick moved further away from the office door.

'That, and worse,' Collins hissed.

'Are you sure it was him?'

'What d'you mean? Why *wouldn't* it be him?' Rick heard a note of panic in the accountant's voice. 'The call was from your switchboard. I checked.'

Of course he'd checked – Rick's paranoia was based on current circumstances, but Dave Collins's was a constant hum in the background of his psyche.

'The thing is, Dave,' Rick said, 'I *did* speak to the superintendent, but it didn't seem the right time to bring up Coutanche, so I haven't told him.'

The line went silent, and for a second, Rick thought that Collins had hung up.

'Dave? D'you want me to have a word with him now?'

'*No.*' Collins's voice was raised an octave.

'It's no problem, I'm sure I can straighten this—'

Collins shushed him. 'Stop! Do not say another word!'

Oh, hell . . .

'Meet me,' Collins whispered. 'Where it all started. Same time, same place.'

'Wait – I'm not with you. I don't know—' But Collins was gone.

Rick stared at his phone for a second. What the *hell* was that about? And what did he mean by 'where it all started'?

The first time he'd met Dave Collins was at Twickenham Police Station. That was the day Ghosh had sent Dave out of his office and berated Rick, practically denouncing Dave as mentally deficient. And all the while poor, brilliant, socially crippled, analytic genius Dave stood outside the room, listening to every soul-crushing insult. There was no way Rick could see Collins voluntarily setting foot in that place ever again.

He speed-dialled Collins's number; it went straight to voice-mail.

I don't know where he means, or when— The constant terror of what might be happening to Jess pushed Rick to a state of near panic. The walls seemed to close in on him and he blundered through the fire escape doors onto the stairwell. Close to blacking out, he bent forward, clasping his knees.

A sudden *boom* from below warned him that someone had opened the outer door onto the rear courtyard, and Rick heard them climb the stairs. The smell of a takeaway meal wafted ahead of them, the aroma of chips sparking a memory that snapped Rick back to his long chat over a pub meal with Collins all those months ago.

That was where it really started – at the Bear & Stag.

Okay, so now he knew where and when Collins wanted to meet. But why would Ghosh get so agitated over Coutanche? How could the Jersey shipping company hurt their trial? And how had he even found out? Which brought him to the other unanswered question – was it really Ghosh who had made the call?

Rick took a breath and exhaled slowly; there was one sure way to find out.

He knocked at Det Supt Ghosh's door and waited for the okay before going in.

'Sorry to bother you, Guv,' he said, with a slight dip of his head. 'Did you try to ring Dave Collins, a few minutes ago?'

Ghosh frowned. 'The forensic accountant? Why would I—?'

'He had a call, but they didn't leave a message,' Rick said. 'Thought it might've been you.'

'It wasn't,' Ghosh said. 'Anything else?'

'No, that's it,' Rick said. 'Thanks, Guv.' He backed out before Ghosh could ask any more questions.

Rick made his way slowly back up to the MIR, thinking through what all of this meant. Ghosh's bemusement seemed genuine. So who had rung Dave? And how did they know that Dave had been looking into Coutanche Shipping? The SFO ran random checks on the use of their resources – it was standard practice in law enforcement. But any misuse would be investigated internally – and with checks and counterbalances, issues like doing dodgy searches could take a very long time before they were acted on. Yet, whoever spotted Collins's searches on Coutanche had been on to him in less than an hour. Which meant that both he and Dave Collins were under surveillance.

It seemed that Dave's paranoia was entirely justified.

Chapter 36

BY MID-AFTERNOON, RICK TURNER was at another safe location with Sam, having texted the bad news about the threatening call to Collins. Sam had taken a room on the third floor of a busy tourist hotel near Earl's Court, and as instructed, Rick used the fire escape stairs to reach it.

'Ah, Rick.' Sam stood at the door of the room, one hand on the door, the other flung wide, and for an awkward moment Rick thought he was offering a hug, then Sam stepped aside and ushered him through.

The coffee table had been cleared of brochures and ornaments, and a laptop, tablet and several photographs lay on its surface.

Rick picked up a shot of a grand-looking terrace in red brick, decorated with an ornate plaster moulding.

'Well?' Sam said.

'It certainly *looks* like it,' Rick said. 'But the plaster's whiter than the image Unwin sent me, and that pattern looks more like a bunch of feathers than a palm tree.'

'The pargeter expert tells me that the plasterwork varies from one building to the next along the row,' Sam said, picking up the tablet and swiping through a series of close-ups showing a variety of grapevines, feather plumes and leaf patterns in bright white pargeting. 'But fortunately for us, only *one* building has the palmette design.' He swiped to one more image before handing the tablet to Rick.

The plaster had the same creamy hue as the photograph Jess's abductors had sent to Rick's phone, and the pattern was identical.

'That's it,' he said, forcing the words past a sudden constriction in his throat. 'Where?'

'Kensington,' his brother said. 'In Kensington Walk. It's a stone's throw from Kensington Palace, as it happens. But of course, it's the row *opposite* this building that we're interested in.'

'Well, what are we waiting for?' Kensington was ten minutes' drive from their location and Rick wanted to get out there and storm the place – bring Jess home without a second's delay.

'There are things we don't know,' Sam said. 'The target building is four floors; each floor is subdivided into apartments, some of which will probably be sublet.'

Too much uncertainty. Rick slumped onto the arm of the sofa. 'We need an apartment number,' he said.

'Can you help with that – do you have access to databases?'

'For a private property, we'd usually check the electoral register – but judging by the photos, this place is empty, so that's out. Second option: an online search of the Land Registry. But Unwin buries his assets *deep* – it took Collins months to trace ownership of just a fraction of his real estate.'

Sam's eyebrows lifted a fraction. 'So, Collins might be able to help.'

'No, Sam.'

Sam cocked his head.

'No. Forget it, I'm not asking him.'

'Because . . .?'

'I can't believe I have to explain this to you. I've failed to report an abduction; I've gone AWOL during the biggest trial of my career;

I've lied to my bosses, prosecuting counsel, and my colleagues; I've searched the police databases without authorisation, misused other police resources – practically torn up the PACE rules. If I'm found out, I'm finished. Don't get me wrong, I've made my peace with that – but that's *my* career, *my* choice. If I involve Collins, everything *I've* done reflects on him. I can't ask him to take that risk.'

'Yes,' Sam said calmly, 'you can. And he can refuse. *His* choice.'

Rick shook his head.

'I can pay him.'

Rick choked back a laugh. 'It isn't about *money*. Dave Collins is like your pargeter expert, only with numbers. For him, it's about patterns – finding them and discovering where they break down. But he works within a strict set of criteria: if it's not in the rules, Dave won't do it.'

Sam raised his shoulders. 'Yet he went looking for the Jersey connection.'

'Yeah, but that wasn't strictly out of bounds – and it got him in trouble. He's had a warning. He was already paranoid; now he's *terrified* and paranoid—'

'So, use that,' Sam said, as though he'd missed the obvious. 'Ask him is he going to let the London Met make the rules for the SFO. Ask him who would call him pretending to be your superintendent. In whose interest is it to keep the prosecution in the dark?' He paused. 'We both know the possibilities are extremely limited, and they all point to Unwin. If your friend Collins wants to get out from under this, he *has* to help us.'

'I can't ask him,' Rick said doggedly.

'Is this him needing the rules, Rick, or you?'

'What's that supposed to mean?'

'With your brains, you could have done anything you wanted, yet you chose the police, which, let's face it, is heavily reliant on rules and hierarchy. Ever asked yourself why?'

Rick tossed the tablet onto the pile of printouts. 'Don't start with this, Sam.'

'Every game, ruck, caper and scrape we ever got into as kids, you always demanded a set of rules. You know why?'

Rick stood. 'Don't try to psychoanalyse me.'

Sam held up his hands. 'I'm just saying you like clarity. If you don't know *instinctively* that something is right or wrong, what do you have to guide you if not the rules?'

'I know the difference between right and wrong,' Rick said, hearing the defensiveness in his tone.

'Despite what you think, so do I,' Sam said. 'But you can't reduce life to a set of simple rules, Rick.'

Rick felt a hot rush of anger. 'It's a bit late to lecture me on morality, pal.'

'I'm not lecturing you – I just want to make you see sense. After everything you've been through to get this case to trial, do you *really* believe that your police colleagues abide by the rules?'

'Most do,' Rick said.

'Including those involved in the first botched investigation into Kirk Wilson's death? Or Haskins's drowning? And how do you account for the initial apathy of your bosses to investigating Unwin?'

'Lazy policing, I'll grant you—'

'You're being obstinately naïve. Rick.'

'No – you've got a twisted view of humanity.'

'If you don't believe the evidence of your own eyes, let me tell you from personal experience: people follow the rules when it's easy, or if it suits their purpose. Give them a way to break the rules that won't get them caught – better yet, a way that pays – and they'll tear up the rule book and use it to light the fire of their ambition.'

Rick shook his head.

'The few good, honest types who never took a bribe or so much as filched a paperclip are the exception,' Sam insisted. 'And the higher you go, the bigger the transgressions. Those at the top see themselves as above the petty diktats that keep the grimy masses in order.'

Rick couldn't help smiling. 'Sam, you sound like a Marxist.'

Sam shot him a sideways glance. 'Oh, I'm far too wealthy for that. I *am* an out-and-out realist, though. Which brings us back to Collins's dilemma: he's in danger whether he helps you or he doesn't. In reality, he's in greater danger if he doesn't.'

'How d'you work that out?'

'If Unwin goes free, your friend will live in fear for the rest of his days. But if you find Jess, get her to safety and send Unwin to prison, you neutralise the threat; Collins can sleep safe at night.'

'You're exaggerating. If Dave drops Coutanche Shipping, they'll leave him alone.'

'Kirk Wilson was murdered over a few photographs. And what did Jess ever do to Unwin?'

Rick's shoulders sagged; there was no denying the logic.

'I couldn't tell him the truth,' he said, feeling himself weakening. 'He'd be working blind.'

'Blinkered, maybe,' Sam said with a twitch of his mouth.

Rick hesitated.

'Come *on*, Rick; I can't act until we know exactly where Jess is. It's not as if I'm asking him for a set of blueprints – although if he could get the apartment layout, it would be *most* welcome.'

Rick folded his arms and stared at the images on the tabletop. 'Okay.'

'You'll do it?'

Rick nodded, feeling sick to his boots.

'You've already arranged to meet Collins?'

'Yes.'

'What time?'

'Five o'clock.'

Sam stared at him, and it seemed to Rick that he was making mental calculations, working out strategy, deciding on complex logistical factors. 'Let me know his answer either way, as soon as you can,' he said. 'I'll keep working for a solution at my end. I have people watching the place; they all have photographs of

Unwin's crew. If they can pinpoint the apartment, the room – even the window – they will.'

Sam's phone rang as Rick took one last look at the fancy plaster carvings on the tablet screen.

The caller spoke for a few seconds and Sam said, 'Odd in what way?' Then: 'Talk me through the timeline.'

He listened, and his expression changed from perplexed, to sombre.

Rick stared at him, but he held up his finger as if to say, *Wait*.

'Good work.' Another pause. 'I'll let you know.'

'Problem?' Rick asked.

Sam gave him a quick smile. 'Nothing to change our plans.'

Chapter 37

Tuesday, the Old Bailey, end of session

MOUNSEY STOOD JUST INSIDE UNWIN'S holding cell. The judge had sent the jury home for the day, and they were waiting for the prison transport van. The door was almost shut, and Mounsey was nauseated by the stale air.

Thomas Unwin glared up at him from the niche seat in the wall. 'Coutanche?'

'The Fraud Office bean-counter has had a reprimand, and a warning,' Mounsey said. 'He won't be any further trouble.'

'You sure of that?'

'He'll be looking over his shoulder for months after the scare your Met contact put into him.'

'And the girl?'

'She'll live.'

Unwin sucked his teeth. 'Put some detail on that.'

'She fainted, that's all.'

'She did a hell of a lot more than that, judging by the video.'

'Ah, I thought you meant—'

'Detail,' Unwin repeated, and made it sound like a threat.

'Her finger is injured, as instructed, but she won't lose it.'

'Not exactly "as instructed", is it?'

Mounsey pursed his lips; this constant needling was tiresome. 'Not quite,' he conceded.

'There's a numpty walking these corridors with a bloody *bandage* on his hand.'

'She was—' Mounsey cleared his throat '—feisty.'

'Twice her weight and he came off worse than she did.'

'Yes, well, there will be no repetition—'

'Still waiting for the detail, Callum.'

Flustered by the use of his given name, Mounsey said, 'First aid has been administered, together with a sedative to keep her calm and compliant. Peace has been restored.'

'Complaints from the neighbours?'

'None. The apartment below is empty, and an elderly – and rather deaf – man lives in the one adjacent.'

Unwin jerked his chin. 'Anything else I should know about?'

Mr Unwin had been irascible ever since he'd heard about the mess Norland had made of organising proof of life. But Mounsey felt he could hardly be blamed for the debacle – a simple snip with a sharp blade was surely not such a difficult task?

He should probably tell Mr Unwin about the bruising to DS Turner's face but decided it would not be wise to mention it. If the sergeant had had an altercation with one of Mr Unwin's crew, Mounsey would deal with it himself.

Instead, he shared the good news that Mrs Yalman would not be called that week, and emphasised Turner's cooperative tone.

'He even tried a court rehearsal at home, yesterday evening,' he added.

'Any good?'

Mounsey smiled. 'Somewhat stilted, perhaps. But with a little polish it promises to be an entertaining and highly satisfactory performance.'

'And he's definitely up this week?'

'So he says.'

Unwin must have picked up on his slight emphasis on 'he'.

'Is there a difference of opinion on that?' he said. 'What does Kildoran's pup say?'

'*His* story differs from the sergeant's. Apparently, prosecuting counsel knows we've got someone inside his operation.'

'Does he know who it is?'

'I don't think so – I gather Kildoran is just acting from an abundance of caution.'

Unwin didn't speak, but Mounsey read the disgust on his face. After a few moments he rubbed his hands palm to palm, as if wiping the dirt from them. 'Well, he's no good to us now, and with Turner fully on board, we don't need him. Cut him loose – but make sure he knows to be discreet.'

Mounsey inclined his head.

Down the corridor, voices were raised, and doors clanged open; the prison transport must have arrived.

'Is there anything else I can do?'

'You can get me out of here.'

'I'm doing everything in my power.'

'It's taking too long.'

'Less than forty-eight hours so far, Mr Unwin.'

'Do I need to remind you that I've been banged up for six months already?'

'Of course not. And I sincerely do *not* mean to trivialise your discomfort,' Mounsey said, thinking, *Oh, dear, he really is out of sorts.* 'But we were hoping to gain leverage over Turner at an earlier stage. As you know, despite our best efforts, that didn't work out, so the best course of action was to wait until the trial, when we could control the variables. We have eyes and ears at strategic points in the system; Turner is in a cooperative mood. I am confident that he *will* bodge his testimony – and he'll give us prior knowledge *and* access to the PA, in the unlikely event that *she* is called before he is.'

Unwin nodded, seeming more at ease.

'We—' Mounsey cut himself off. He *had* been about to say, 'we can't lose', but Mr Unwin was a superstitious man, who in matters of chance, believed in random luck with the innocence of a child and the obsession of a gambler. So he began again: 'We should discuss what should be done with Turner after your release.'

'Done with him? We'll keep using him – he'll be a valuable resource.'

'I'm less sanguine about that. He may, indeed, be a problem after the fact.'

'We'll have him on misuse of police computer resources, corruption, misconduct in public office – and that's just for starters.' Unwin smiled. 'He'll be good as gold.'

Now that he seemed in a better mood, and the guards would be removing him to the prison van soon, Mounsey felt safe to bring up one final pressing matter.

'I spoke to the um, buyers during the lunch break,' he began diffidently, 'and I'm afraid they were not receptive to your proposal.'

He saw the gathering storm in Unwin's face and the bunching of his fists. He seemed to expand and fill the space. 'They know I'm good for it.'

Mounsey passed one soft finger pad over an eyebrow. 'They suggested that you might solve the problem of access to your funds by appointing an alternative executor.'

Of course, he had suggested just such a course of action to his client two days earlier, and Unwin had declined.

Unwin did not respond well to slurs against his wife, so Mounsey knew better than to repeat the buyers' comment that if Unwin couldn't trust his wife or his lawyer, why should they. But his boss's continued silence suggested that he was not about to change his mind and Mounsey himself was seized by a fit of pique.

'They think you're trying to make them pay in advance for the consignment so that you can fund your legal expenses,' he burst out.

'That's bollocks.' Unwin looked shaken, as well he might.

Mounsey wouldn't demean himself by offering himself as executor again, so he said, 'What would you like me to tell them?'

The guards were outside the door, now, calling Unwin's name and number.

'Tell them they're wrong! I'll sort it, but it's complicated.'

The door opened and the guard asked Mounsey to step outside.

'A few stages to be gone through, that's all,' Unwin said, standing.

'Sir, I must ask you to step outside,' the guard insisted, raising his voice, and this time Mounsey complied, feeling a perverse satisfaction in the mounting anxiety in his boss's tone.

'We'll talk about it tomorrow,' Unwin called over his shoulder as he was led away.

Chapter 38

AT FIVE P.M., AFTER TAKING A TORTUOUS ROUTE from his meeting with Sam and switching his phone off in the underground, Rick Turner arrived at the Bear & Staff. He'd stepped out of Leicester Square station into a brief shower, but by the time he'd reached the pub the sun was shining again. The nights had drawn in since the clocks were turned back, and the sun was low in the sky. It cast a golden glow on the street and sent cascades of wet leaves from the maple trees across the road onto the shivering puddles at his feet.

Collins was sitting at his usual table upstairs. He looked miserable, but it seemed that the scare hadn't harmed his appetite: his plate was piled with what looked like a double order of chips and he was halfway through a steak pie. He gave Rick a baleful look and carried on, working his way through the food with a stoicism that made it seem like a duty to be fulfilled.

The room was empty, except for a middle-aged couple seated near one of the windows. The man reached to pick up a Big Bus Tour leaflet at the woman's elbow and murmured something about their next 'adventure'. Rick sat so that he could keep an eye on the stairway and the couple, but they seemed oblivious to him, placidly working their way through their meal and occasionally exchanging a few words.

Rick gave Collins the time he needed to gather his thoughts and a few minutes later the accountant pushed away his plate and wiped his face with a napkin.

'It wasn't your boss who phoned me, was it?'

'I don't think so,' Rick said.

'Who, then?'

'I don't know, mate,' he said honestly. He kept going back to the bewildered look on the superintendent's face when he'd asked about the call to Dave, and the more he thought about it, the less he knew if it was faked. It seemed to Rick that he'd lost the knack of seeing through others' lies to the truth.

Collins crumpled the napkin and dumped it on his plate. 'Well, whoever it was called me a liability.'

'I know. That was out of order.'

'One of Unwin's lot?'

'Someone on his payroll, anyway,' Rick said.

Collins's forehead creased. 'Police?'

'Seems likely.'

A man's head popped up at the top of the stairway at the far end of the room and Rick tensed until three women followed him. Their accents marked them out as tourists, and he breathed easier.

'If I'm being monitored,' Collins murmured, 'you must be, an' all.'

Rick nodded. *You have no idea how closely, my friend.*

'What do they *want*, Rick?'

'For the prosecution case to collapse,' Rick said truthfully.

'Well, that's not gonna happen,' Collins scoffed. 'Didn't Mr Kildoran say the numbers expert had the jury eating out of her hand?'

'He did.'

Collins slumped in his seat like an unhappy Buddha. 'I don't see how me looking at Coutanche Shipping would change that.'

'Me neither. But it does underline the point that the company is important to Unwin.'

Collins reached for his glass and sipped his beer thoughtfully. 'I'm not a liability, Rick.' Sometimes Collins got stuck on minor details.

'You're the foundation this case is built on,' Rick said, understanding that for Collins the quality of his work anchored him in a world he found hard to navigate.

Collins took another sip of beer, avoiding Rick's eye.

Now would be the time to deploy Sam's strategy, reminding Collins that the Met didn't tell the SFO what to do, that his best defence against Unwin was attack. But Rick couldn't be sure that his friend really would be safer that way; it might be better if he kept his head down and did as he was told. As far as Dave Collins knew, his investigation – the accounts he'd deciphered and the money trail he'd traced from them – had already ensured that Unwin would go to prison. In reality, it *should* be enough to secure a conviction – it was too much to ask him to go further, to risk so much.

'He called me a *liability*,' Collins said again. 'I'm the best investigator the SFO's got.'

This wasn't bragging; Collins could spot a dodgy payment in an invoice by what most would see as intuition, but it was in fact an uncanny intuitive ability to identify any unnatural frequency of certain digits in a payment. He knew what he was good at, and he hadn't the guile for false modesty.

I can't ask him.

'Fuck 'em,' Collins said.

'What?'

'I'm going to keep digging into Coutanche.'

'No, Dave—'

'It's my *job*, Rick,' Collins said, his pale eyes suddenly ablaze.

Stop putting him off and give him something useful to do! The inner voice was Sam-but-not-Sam.

Rick looked away.

'When people look away, it means you're talking too much, and they want you to shut up. Or it *can* mean they're hiding something,' Collins intoned in a voice not at all his own, and Rick looked at him, startled. 'They taught us oddballs non-verbal clues at school.' He paused, frowning. 'Or is it cues?'

Rick smiled. 'Bit of both.'

'So . . .?'

Rick thought it through. They really did need that apartment number. The question was how to present the request so that Collins wouldn't be implicated if things went sideways.

'Coutanche could tip our hand,' he said at last. 'But there is something you *can* do.' He hesitated again and Collins shifted impatiently, his chair creaking in complaint. 'I won't lie to you, mate – there's a degree of risk, even in this, and you need to understand there could be consequences.'

The big man glanced down at his ample girth. 'Well, I'm not built for your kung fu moves, but as long as it doesn't involve climbing drainpipes or kicking down doors, I'm your armchair ninja.'

'Well, all right,' Rick said, feeling as if a physical weight had lifted from his chest. 'There's a man on court security.' He heard the tension in his voice and took a breath, exhaling slowly. 'He's a bit too cosy with Callum Mounsey.'

'Why does Unwin need someone like that?'

Rick shrugged. 'He's probably making sure Unwin is well looked after in the cells. And that isn't all of it. I haven't told anyone on the team, but I think Unwin's got an insider at the barrister's office.'

Collins stared at him, wide-eyed. 'You've got to tell your boss.'

'I would, but you know Ghosh – he likes evidence gift-wrapped and delivered to his door. I think they're arranging meetings at this swank apartment in Kensington.' This was Rick's first lie.

'Who – the mole and the security guard?'

'And Mounsey.' The second lie. 'I've seen them going into the building at various times, but it's a mansion house, divided into apartments, and I don't know which one. I want to get surveillance set up, but without an apartment number, it's hopeless.'

'Don't you need a warrant for covert surveillance?'

'Inside the flat, yeah. But I'm thinking, if I can get a camera into the public areas – stairs and corridors, say – show them going to and from – no one's gonna burst a blood vessel over me bending the rules a bit. And if I gather the intel we need for a warrant, we could legally sneak cameras *inside* the apartment.' By now, he'd lost count of the number of lies he'd told.

'What's the address?'

Rick gave him the number of the building in Kensington Walk.

'So, you're asking me for the flat number?'

'Can you get it?'

Collins rubbed his forehead hard with one hand. 'I can't use office resources – not while they're watching me.'

'If anyone can do this under the radar, it's you, mate.'

The accountant watched the bubbles rise in his glass for a minute. 'I could try the Land Registry.'

'Unwin wouldn't have the property registered under his own name, would he?'

'Not likely,' Collins said. 'But he does have some registered under his shell companies.'

'Surely there's scores of those?' Rick had waded through the documentation, so he knew just how bewildering the dead ends and misdirects were along the money trail.

Collins nodded. 'And some of the shells are contained within other shells.'

'Like babushka dolls,' Rick said.

'Strictly speaking, they're *matryoshka* – mother dolls,' Collins said, his fastidious mind constitutionally incapable of letting the common error pass. 'You've heard of the Panama Papers?'

Rick nodded. 'A bunch of journalists blew open an international shadow economy sheltering billions of dollars for the super-rich. Governments fell.'

'Criminals hide their identities by appointing a nominal director or "beneficial owner" of their shell companies – supposed administrators who do the day-to-day running of their shell companies,' Collins said. 'In reality, the "beneficial owner" will be a cleaning lady, office typist, or building caretaker who's willing to take a couple of hundred dollars for signing documents and asking no questions. Given that most of Unwin's shell companies are registered in the British Virgin Islands where the minimum wage is six dollars an hour, a few hundred is a big payday.'

Rick nodded, remembering.

'But it doesn't matter what it says on the documents – it's all blah to cover up the real owners' identities. The "beneficial owners" don't really *own* anything. And only the *real* owner can *create* a transaction.'

'So,' Rick said, 'let's say Unwin decides he wants to buy Apartment X in Kensington Walk.'

'He sends an instruction to Hugenot at Laligne Bank,' Collins said, ''Cos Hugenot manages Unwin's shell companies. Hugenot gets in touch with his branch in the British Virgin Islands – which might be nothing more than a shopfront in a strip mall with a couple of phones and a secure fast broadband connection. His "branch manager" prints off the necessary forms and tells the fake beneficial owner-slash-cleaning lady to leave off dusting and sign on the dotted line. She goes home a couple of hundred dollars richer, having authorised the transfer of *millions* of dollars' worth of funds on Unwin's behalf. Unwin doesn't touch the money, but since he's the *real* beneficial owner of shell company, he now owns the apartment – safely hidden from the tax authorities behind the shell.' He flashed a quick smile and Rick saw excitement fizzing in his friend's eyes.

'So you know how to make the connection between Unwin and the shell?' Rick asked.

'Right!' Collins took a triumphant swallow of beer.

'How?' Rick asked. 'I mean the cleaning lady signs the documents, so Unwin is still hidden behind the shell, and his name isn't on the property's paperwork, either. How do you identify this *particular* shell company as belonging to Unwin?'

Collins set the glass down again and leaned forward. 'It's obvious, isn't it?'

Rick's shoulders slumped. 'Not to me.'

Collins looked so disappointed in him that Rick went on the defensive: 'Gimme a break, mate. The expert witness just spent an entire *day* going through this stuff with the jury. I wasn't there for much of it, and frankly, I'm knackered. So, I'm sorry, but I really *don't* know how it helps us.'

'It's the emails!' Collins exclaimed. 'Hugenot's *secret* account, not his official company one. If you're right about the apartment, there will be an email from Unwin to Hugenot, telling him to transfer funds from one of his shell companies to pay for the property in Kensington Walk.'

Rick shook his head. 'You're talking about a bundle of emails as thick as a brick, and you just said you can't look through the files at work.'

'I don't *need* to.'

Rick ran a hand over his face. 'Well, you'd better explain to me in words of one syllable exactly how you're going to find *one* email in over a *year's* accumulated evidence without access to your works computer.'

The skin under the forensic accountant's eyes flushed pink and in a sudden leap of imagination, Rick said, 'You're not telling me you memorised that lot?'

'God no, I'm not eidetic,' Collins said, as though that would be *weird*.

'So . . .?'

Collins took a breath and gazed at a point somewhere off to Rick's left. 'I get anxious sometimes.'

Rick tilted his head. 'About?'

'My data. One time, the IT department decided to upgrade security – wiped my entire F-drive. I lost six months of work.' He had to take a couple of breaths to calm himself before he could go on. 'And, you know – cyber-attacks do happen . . .'

The shame on Collins's face told Rick the rest. 'Jesus, Dave – you made copies?' After he'd told Sam that Collins would never colour outside the lines.

Collins shushed him, wild-eyed.

'I swear, not to do anything you know, *illegal* – I mean, it's not— I-I wouldn't . . . This is just, you know – for peace of mind,' Collins gabbled, holding both sweating palms up as if Rick might suddenly produce handcuffs and arrest him. 'It's under AES-256 encryption – that's *military* grade, Rick. O-on a Wi-Fi-disabled laptop, which is never – I mean *never* – connected to the web.'

Rick suppressed a smile. 'Good to see the paranoia's working for you at last, mate.'

Collins managed the ghost of a smile. 'Sod off. Anyway, I wasn't wrong about them being out to get me, was I?'

'You were not, my friend,' Rick said in great earnest. 'I hate to sound ungrateful, but I've got hours, rather than days and there must be *hundreds* of emails in those documents.'

'Thousands,' Collins corrected, like it wasn't a big deal. 'I've got an algorithm that'll search for key words. Shouldn't take more than an hour – maybe less – once I've got it running.'

'And will you be able to jump straight on it?'

'As it happens, the SFO's too tight to pay me for the all-nighter I pulled to get that stuff ready for the trial. I was thinking I'd take time owed.'

'Good man,' Rick stood, feeling more hopeful than he'd dared wish when he first walked into the pub.

'Before you go—' Collins rummaged in the shoulder bag on the seat next to him and handed Rick an old mobile phone and a new SIM card, still sealed in plastic. On the back of the packaging, he'd printed a mobile number. 'Ring me only on that number,' he said. 'Don't use my regular number. And *no* texts.'

Chapter 39

RICK TURNED HIS PHONE BACK ON AT EARL'S COURT. He'd been out of touch for nearly two hours, and he'd sweated every second of it. He held his breath as he checked for WhatsApp messages, releasing it in a grateful whoosh when there were none. He'd received two voicemail messages from DCI Steiner between four-thirty and five-fifteen p.m. Listening to the first message, he realised that Kath Steiner was stressed and pissed off in equal measure. She'd been trying to reach Rick at Southwark Crown Court, but nobody had seen him. Steiner would like to know where the hell he was. The second voicemail was terse and left no room for argument: 'Call me as soon as you get this. And head back to base. You're wanted. Now.'

He dashed off a quick text, saying he was about to dive into the underground, and he'd be there in twenty minutes.

When Rick arrived, DCI Steiner was talking to Jim Stott in the Incident Room.

She turned as Rick entered and said, 'Well?'

'Sorry, Guv?'

'What did Kildoran say?'

For a second, Rick scrambled to make sense of the question; finally, he realised that she was asking for an update on the trial, 'He said he's happy – it's going better than he could've hoped.'

'That's funny,' Steiner said. ''Cos when he rang just after four, looking for you, he said he hadn't seen you since the lunch break.'

Heart pounding, Rick looked her in the eye. 'I've just come from his chambers.'

'So, he'll have told you they want you in bright and early tomorrow – you're first witness on the slate.'

'Yep.' He couldn't have managed another word if he'd tried; it was like a chasm, fathoms deep, had opened up at his feet.

'Well, I hope you're prepped and ready.'

'Been practising nightly,' Rick said, feeling DS Stott's eyes on him. 'That all, Guv?'

'No. That bruise.' Steiner touched the side of her own face. *Bloody hell.*

'Training injury, wasn't it, Rick?' Stott said.

'That's right, Stotty.'

'Well, it isn't a good look in front of a jury,' Steiner said.

'I don't see what I can do about that,' Rick said. He was tired and sore and sick with worry and the DCI's posturing was beginning to chafe.

Steiner began to bristle, but Stott tapped Rick on the arm. 'I bet your Jess will know what to do. Actress, isn't she? Saw her in *EastEnders* a while back. Or was it *Emmerdale*? What a looker!' The crooked grin on his face made Rick wonder if he'd been drinking.

Steiner sighed, irritated by the interruption. 'Just – sort it,' she said, walking away.

Rick shook his head, mouthing an obscenity, but Stott wagged his finger.

When the DCI was gone, Stott scanned the room. It was well after six and there were only two others at their desks by this time, but Stott drew Rick further away and lowered his voice.

'So, is this for real – they're calling you in tomorrow?' The slightly sweet odour of half-metabolised vodka on Stott's breath confirmed Rick's suspicions.

'You heard the guv'nor.'

'Yeah, but—'

'What?' Rick asked, his skin prickling.

'Well, what with Kildoran's chambers having sprung a leak . . .'

'Who told you that?'

He rolled his eyes in the direction DCI Steiner had just gone. '*She who must be obeyed.*'

Rick lifted his chin. 'Oh. Okay. Well then, yes – it's real.'

'D'you think Unwin'll walk, Rick?'

'Not if I can help it.'

Stott eyed him thoughtfully. 'Maybe it would be better if he did.'

Rick stared at him. 'Why would you say that?'

'King was under Unwin's protection, and they got to him. Now, admittedly, with Unwin in prison pending trial, it was a safe hit. Safe-ish, anyway. But think about it, Rick – whoever got to King could've arranged a fall, an overdose, a stumble into the path of a bus. The problem with any of the above is, the potential for misinterpretation.' He was slurring slightly. 'But a *gun*, suppressor, a double-tap to the head?' He spread his hands. 'Put 'em together, they practically *scream* professional hit.'

'Stotty, what are you trying to say?'

Stott glanced over his shoulder.

Rick had a clear view of the two detectives at their desks. 'They're not listening, mate.'

Even so, Stott turned his back fully to the others in the room and spoke in a whisper. 'Whoever took out the contract on Unwin's right-hand man wanted to send a clear message: Unwin is finished. And anyone from his crew with ambitions to fill his shoes might want to think twice.'

'So?'

'I'm thinking, if Unwin *does* get out, maybe that *same* someone who took care of Austin King will take care of *him*.' Rick saw something avid and calculating in the older man's eyes.

'The *law* will take care of him,' Rick said, choosing not to enlighten him on Saidi's bloody fate.

Stott seemed to shrink at those words, and his shoulders rounded. 'That's what I thought you might say. But life isn't always as simple as you'd like it to be, son.'

'What the hell is going on with you, Jim?' he demanded.

The older man reared back as if Rick had threatened him. 'Me? Nothing. Just talking bollocks, like usual.' He flashed a smile so sad it could break your heart.

'Jim—'

Stott turned abruptly and walked away.

Rick called after him and heads went up.

Back off, Rick – don't push it, Sam the counsellor told him.

He watched Stott slouch out of the room. Now was not the time – not with Jess still in Unwin's hands. But it did imply there was a conversation to be had, and when this bastard thing was over, he would sit down and have a serious conversation with Jim Stott.

Chapter 40

AT HOME AFTER DINNER, RICK DUG out the scanner from where he'd hidden it under the kitchen sink and set about scanning the house for bugs. He didn't find anything new, which was reassuring: Unwin must believe he was continuing to cooperate. He checked his watch and thought about going for a run, but his head was still hurting, so he made a cheese sandwich, read his notes carefully, and did another sham rehearsal to please whoever was listening at Unwin's end. Another nervous glance at his watch, then he picked up his mobile phone to make sure; it really was only nine o'clock.

'It's gonna be a long night,' he murmured.

He tried watching TV and gave up after surfing a dozen channels and making sense of none of them. Then he picked up the burner phone Dave Collins had given him, willing it to ring. When that didn't work, he decided to take a shower, dressing in dark sports gear and running shoes so that he'd be ready if the call did eventually come. An hour later, he considered calling Dave to see how his search was going but decided that would be a bad idea. Instead, he turned off the lights and lay on the sofa, thinking it might do him good to take a short nap, but sleep eluded him.

* * *

Jess is dancing. Totally lost in the moment, her body responds to the dreamy psychedelia of the band's opening number. Abruptly, the drummer jacks up the pace, the bass guitar growling over the melody, grinding through a raw, buzzing riff. She opens her eyes, throws her arms wide. Her face is ecstatic; she seems lit from within. She seeks Rick out in the crowd, turns her back on the stage and flings herself at him, wrapping her arms around his neck, her legs around his waist.

'I fucking LOVE this band!' she yells in his ear.

They had met for coffee at three p.m., just five minutes from the police station. She had momentous news, she'd said. Couldn't wait till evening.

Rick thought that she'd finally snagged a part in a TV show. But before she'd even sat at the table, she said, 'Creeper's on at the Apollo tonight – and guess who's got tickets?' Grinning, she waved the evidence under his nose.

'I'm a detective,' he deadpanned. 'I think I can guess.'

'Come with me.'

'I can't, Jess; I've got too much on.' It was six weeks to the Unwin trial, and he was working twelve hours a day.

'*Two hours*,' she said. 'One and a half if we skip the intro. It doesn't start till seven – *way* after you're supposed to finish – and it's practically on your doorstep.' With one finger on his chin, she turned his head. 'Look. See the big building you pass on the way to the Tube every day? Ever wondered what it was for?'

'Enough of the sarcasm.' He laughed.

She fanned her face with the tickets, her eyes dancing, and he reached to squeeze her hand gently. 'Look, I'm sorry to say this, Jess – but horror's really not my thing.'

She tilted her head back and laughed, then covered him with kisses in case she'd offended him. 'Rick, my darling, what *have* you been doing all your life?'

'Okay,' he said, laughing as he fended her off. 'Tell me what I said.'

'It's not *Creepers* the horror film, it's Creep*er*, the coolest rock band since My Chemical Romance.'

'Your chemical *what*?'

'Seriously?' she said, dissolving into helpless giggles. 'Baby, you've got to get *out* more!'

He took a breath, intending to let her down easy, but she leaned across the table and placed one finger on his lips. 'Imagine – you'll be able to tell your friends, your kids, your *grand*kids you saw them in the vampiric goth-fusion freaking flesh!'

Rick demurred. Jess cajoled, bullied, counselled – and finally convinced him that two hours of jet-engine-loud eardrum pounding was exactly what he needed to give him focus. She was wrong in that. Watching her abandon herself to the music was what he'd needed.

'Jeez, this is better than sex!' she screams. Suddenly, she opens her hands, throwing her whole body backwards and he holds her tight, fearing she'll fall.

Her eyes, so alive with excitement, widen in terror and she pleads, 'Don't let me go!'

She's no longer in his arms. Two masked men have her, and she's writhing, screaming, 'Oh*please*Godoh*please*dooooon't—'

A sudden jarring beep startled Rick awake. Heart thudding, he reached for his phone, rapping his knuckles painfully on something hard. Stupid with tiredness he struggled to one elbow, staring wildly about him, finally realising he was on the sofa; he'd hit the coffee table. Could he have dozed off? Still, the insistent beep of an alarm sounded. With a sudden jolt, he realised it must be the burner phone he'd bought to stay in touch with Sam.

But Sam never rings, he texts.

Rick reached for the unregistered mobile, anyway. Nothing.

Then he remembered the burner phone Dave Collins had given him in the pub.

He could hear its persistent beep, but his head felt stuffed full of cotton wool, and the only light in the room came from the streetlamps, their pale light filtering through gaps in the window blinds. He rolled off the couch and felt around the sofa, eventually locating the phone under the table where it must have dropped as he'd startled awake. Aware that Unwin's crew were listening, he declined the call, and went out into the back garden. The sudden cold was like a slap in the face; a blustery wind penetrated the lightweight fabric of his running kit, and clouds scudded across a thin crescent of moon. He looked at his watch: it was 1:30 a.m. – he had slept for two hours. Shaking the grogginess from his sleep-sodden brain, he rang Collins back.

'Why didn't you pick up? Is something happening? What's that sound?'

Dead of night, and Collins was wide awake, and wired.

'Sorry, mate. I'm outside – in the garden – it's just the wind. Didn't want to take a chance talking in the house – you know, in case . . .'

'Right,' Collins said. 'Right – good decision.' For Dave Collins, it was a foregone conclusion Rick's house would be bugged. 'I've got that address,' he added.

Rick listened. It wasn't as straightforward as he'd hoped, but Collins talked him through his strategies and explained his rationale, and at length Rick was convinced. Finally, Collins gave him a case number for the Royal Borough of Kensington and Chelsea website.

'Fantastic, can you text that to me?'

'Not a chance, mate; texts are retrievable. We never had this conversation.'

'Okay, I get it,' Rick said.

'It's over to you, now,' Collins said. 'Let me know how it goes, yeah?'

'Sure,' Rick said. 'I really appreciate this, Dave—' He stopped, realising he was talking to dead air. His armchair ninja had vanished.

Rick switched phones and sent a text to Sam telling him he had the apartment number. Sam texted back:

—Can you get out without anyone who's watching seeing you?

Rick recalled the many times as a teenager he'd snuck out for one of Sam's escapades.

—Yeah, he texted —I can do that.

Chapter 41

Wednesday morning, 2 a.m. day 3 of trial

ANOTHER HOTEL. BIGGER THIS TIME, and higher end than the last – a conference venue with a casino tagged on to one end. Sam had chosen well, Rick thought; their own late-night activity wouldn't attract attention among the constant comings and goings of gamblers.

Sam opened the door to an executive suite. His laptop, phone and tablet were set out on a coffee table near the window; two sofas faced each other either side of the table. The curtains were drawn.

'Coffee?' Sam said.

Rick accepted gratefully, and they sat opposite each other, the coffee table between them.

'You have the apartment number?' Sam asked.

'Eight,' Rick said.

'It's registered to Unwin?'

'Be serious, Sam. He's dodged the law for twenty years – he's not likely to make his assets that easy to find,' It was an evasive answer, but Rick wanted to build the picture, dropping in a few persuasive arguments along the way before broaching the bad news.

'Dave checked the apartments against the Land Registry. Then he cross-referenced with the electoral register.'

'I can't see millionaire landowners listing their properties on an open register,' Sam said.

'You'd be surprised. Not all were on there, but between the two registries, he was able to confirm that six of the apartments are owned by individuals or couples who look legit. Of the three remaining, one is owned by a big tech company, one by an aparthotel chain. Apartment eight is the *only* property owned by a foreign entity.'

'A foreign entity?' Sam's eyebrows twitched at the phrase.

'An offshore shell company based in the British Virgin Islands.'

'Ah,' Sam said. 'A buy-to-leave . . .'

'The beneficial owner is a former Barbadian, but his role is nominal – he just signs the documents that keep the money train moving.'

'So how can we be sure this is the right place?'

'It so happens that this foreign entity also used Laligne Bank to manage its shell companies,' Rick said. 'The RBO sent an email to the bank requesting a money transfer to pay for the apartment. And he's had multiple interactions with Unwin.'

'The RBO – that's *real* beneficial owner – you have a name?'

'Yup.' Collins had given him the name Konstantin Popov – not that it meant anything to Rick, and the man had no online presence, so they were none the wiser.

'You're investigating him?' Sam probed.

Rick shook his head. 'We didn't have the resources – our focus was on the two contract killings. But we do have full access to Unwin's computers and phones, and according to the records, Unwin ordered several payments to this same shell company over the past two years.'

'Okay, direct link.' Sam looked at him expectantly, and Rick knew that he was waiting for a name.

'Forget it, Sam,' he said. 'I'm not hooking you up with a Russian mafioso.'

The Russian mafia connection was the bad news, but if Sam was daunted by the idea of forcing entry into a Russian gang leader's property, he didn't show it. Instead, he gave Rick a winning smile, cupping his chin in his hand. 'How interesting. You're sure he's Russian mob?'

'I think it's a good bet.' Rick paused for a second or two. 'Convinced, yet?'

'It's persuasive,' Sam said. 'But I'll want something more concrete before I send my men in to kick down doors.'

'All right, how about this: apartment eight looks out over Kensington Walk. It's on the third floor which, if you happened to snap a photo from the main living room, is at the right level to catch a shot of the plasterwork on the building opposite.'

'I take it the Russian isn't in residence at the moment?' Sam said.

'It's currently shown as unoccupied.'

'So, he loaned the place to Unwin?'

'It's listed as immediately available for a three-month rental period.'

'How much?' Sam asked.

'Thinking of taking a city break?'

'No . . . I'm wondering why Unwin would think it worth the risk of sneaking in there without permission.'

Rick pulled up the estate agency's website on his phone and found the listing before handing it over.

Sam gave a low whistle. 'Saving a rental of 85k a month would certainly be tempting if money were tight. And I should think Unwin's imprisonment and trial has put a sizable dent in his wallet.' He scrolled through the agency ad-shots. 'But using a Russian mobster's *pied-à-terre* to keep a kidnap victim hostage? He'd have to be desperate.'

Rick shrugged. 'It's a buy-to-leave. The owner probably hasn't even set foot in the place; why would he care?'

'I've worked alongside these types for a long time, Rick. Believe me, too much is *never* enough. They would come after Unwin for every penny of the rental they're owed – with interest.'

'Even though the place was lying empty?'

Sam shot him an amused look. 'I thought you said *I* was the communist?'

Rick suppressed a smile. 'We agreed you don't qualify. But the owner *is* Russian—'

'And no more Marxist than me or you. My bet would be Russian vory.' He glanced at Rick. 'You know they go way back to before the Bolshevik revolution?'

Rick nodded. 'Survived purges by Lenin *and* Stalin – they're the cockroaches of the criminal world – indestructible.'

'Think virus, rather than cockroach,' Sam said. 'Since the turn of the century, they've adapted and diversified. They have influence at the heart of the Russian state and across Europe – as well as from upstate New York right into Northern Canada. They may not have their thieves code inked into their skin anymore, but it runs just as deep.' He nodded as if settling an internal argument. 'They'd take Unwin squatting on their property as an intolerable mark of disrespect.'

Sam returned his attention to Rick's phone. 'It says here that apartment eight has five bedrooms and two entertaining rooms.' He stopped and squinted at Rick. 'Those floor plans on my wish list . . . I don't suppose Dave came through on that?'

'Next best thing.' Rick spun Sam's laptop around and searched for the Royal Borough of Kensington and Chelsea website, then tapped in the case number Dave Collins had made him memorise. 'The apartment was upgraded and refurbed two years ago,' he explained. 'And as it's part of a listed building, the development needed planning permission – which meant submitting full plans.' He turned the monitor so that his brother could see it. 'That includes floor plans, diagrams, dimensions – the lot.'

'Your Dave's a keeper,' Sam said in admiration. He clicked through the apartment layout, thoughtful, serious, his eyes darting to different areas of the screen, pinching and enlarging sections, resetting them before clicking to the next room plan, his concentration fierce and absolute. Finally, he took a breath. 'We can work with this.'

'Good,' Rick stood. 'Can we go now?'

Sam laughed. 'Not so fast,' he said, catching Rick by the wrist. 'You always did have a problem with impulse control, Rick, old son.'

Rick looked into his brother's eyes. Was Sam really was making a joke of his eagerness to save his girlfriend after she'd been dragged off the streets, terrorised and mutilated?

'Wasn't me who vanished off the face of the earth on impulse, though, was it?' he said in quiet retaliation.

Sam let go of his arm and brushed a fleck from the pristine twill of his trouser leg. 'There were extenuating circumstances.'

'It's not like you to tiptoe around the facts,' Rick said, adding savagely, 'There was a dead man with a knife through his chest.'

He was shocked by his own words and was perversely satisfied to see a reciprocal flash of anger in Sam's face.

The burner phone buzzed in Rick's pocket, and he answered it with a warning look to his brother.

'Problem, Dave?'

Sam sat back on the sofa, the anger gone in an instant, replaced with calm, dispassionate interest.

'Sorry, Rick. Sorry . . .' Collins sounded breathy and anxious. 'Couldn't sleep – wrong time of day. Now, I know you told me not to – but before you go off on one, just listen – I've been careful, okay?'

Sam must have seen it in Rick's face because he sat forward again, a question etched in the quirk of his brow.

'I'm *not* working from the office,' Collins said. 'And I used proxy servers and VPNs via Tor – every keystroke is encrypted, anonymous, and I swear, I've been from China to Alaska and back via Belgium with these searches.'

Rick's heart seized for a second. 'You kept digging, didn't you? Dave—'

Collins kept going: 'I want you to know this isn't something I'd normally— I mean, I stick to the rules, so I wouldn't – I mean I don't—' He took a breath. 'But they're coming after me when I'm just doing my *job*. I got a right to fight back, haven't I?'

Rick swallowed against the sickening image of Jess struggling with the man who cut her. But this wasn't just about him and Jess anymore: Collins himself had been threatened; he needed to understand the danger he was in. 'They're on to you, Dave,' he said. 'If they find out about this – if your *bosses* find out—'

'It's *okay*,' Collins said. 'Trust me, they won't find out until it's too late.'

Rick took a few calming breaths, aware that Sam was watching him with concern.

'You ready?' Collins asked.

'No. But go ahead.'

'A cargo ship named *Junara*, owned by Coutanche Shipping, has been tied up in the Jersey docks since Sunday. It was supposed to ship out to Southampton on Monday, but there's been a delay over payment.'

'King was murdered before he could make it,' Rick breathed, and his brother tilted his head as if straining to listen in.

Killing Saidi had looked like overkill until you put it in the context of a major international deal about to go sideways, Rick thought. *Saidi had made Unwin look weak, and in the process, had jeopardised what must be a highly valuable shipment.*

Rick couldn't help saying, 'What the hell is on that ship?'

'Yeah, *right*?' Collins's voice bubbled with excited laughter. 'I was thinking the best way to find out would be to track where it came from.'

'And?'

'It shipped from a newly built port in Russia two months ago.'

'Russia,' Rick said. 'So . . . drug trafficking?'

'This is in the eastern regions – not really poppy-growing territory,' Collins said. 'But a large reserve of rare earth ore was

237

recently discovered there – hence the new port. And get this – they started exporting purified rare earth metals two years ago.'

'Right at the start of our timeline,' Rick said. 'But why rare earths?'

'They're not *actually* that rare,' Colins said. 'Only—'

'Dave,' Rick interrupted. 'It's after two in the morning, and I've got to testify first thing, so—'

'Sorry, mate. Sorry,' Collins said.

'I meant why's it worth his while? Drugs are more Unwin's style, aren't they?'

'Think of it this way: pure rhodium is *seventeen times* more valuable than gold.'

'Jeez . . .'

'Avoid import duty and VAT, you could save twenty-five per cent of your costs. And industries worldwide are *fighting* over this stuff, Rick.'

'There's a shortage?'

'*Technically*, no,' Collins said. 'But they're used in everything from green energy to electric cars and mobile phones – and China, which controls ninety per cent of production, is messing with the market. This year alone, car production lines have been stalled, solar panel manufacture is backed up, and wind farms have been put on hold because they just can't get the parts.'

'Ideal conditions to drive black market trade – and desperate manufacturers aren't likely to ask awkward questions,' Rick said.

'Especially if they're getting what they need at bargain basement prices. It's a smuggler's dream,' Collins said. 'High value product, hard to detect—'

'So a sniffer dog might miss the stuff?' Rick cut in, thinking about the failed joint force raid last year.

He heard a snort of amused surprise. 'Dogs are trained to sniff out people, animals, drugs, weapons. These metals can be disguised as ordinary machine parts – the dogs'd walk right past them.'

'Do we know where this stuff is headed?' he asked.

'Too risky,' Collins said. 'I'd need to send a query to the harbourmaster's office and that might alert the shipping owner.'

'Understood. Dave, this is brilliant work.'

'That's not all,' Collins said, and Rick heard a rare crow of pride in his friend's tone. 'I've been looking for images of Konstantin Popov.' The real beneficial owner of the apartment where Jess was being held. 'He's camera-shy, but I did find a reference to the same name in a trial for cat-converter thefts—'

'Dave?'

He heard Collins take a breath. 'Long story short: the court case collapsed – witness intimidation – but a blogger tracked down a picture of Popov from his Russian navy days.'

Rick used his own phone to access the blog. His spine tingled from the nape of his neck to his tailbone: he was looking at the mystery Russian from Kirk Wilson's surveillance images.

'Fuck me . . .' Rick breathed. 'You know what this means, Dave?'

'We've got 'em, Rick. We've got 'em all!' He could hear the grin on Collins's face.

Sam waited till he'd closed the phone, then he tilted his head and said in a tone of perfectly measured irony, 'Good news?'

'If we finish the night in one piece, it could be huge,' Rick said.

'We have over an hour, if you care to share . . .'

Rick brewed fresh coffee while he decided how much he should say. He told Sam about the shipment – naming neither the ship nor the port – and the rare earths that were probably on board. He didn't need to tell Sam about the value of the metals; it seemed that he had investments in both rhodium and palladium.

'Unwin tapped into the mother lode,' Sam said. 'Industry *and* governments worldwide are desperate to get their hands on rare earths – without them, they haven't a chance in hell of meeting their clean energy targets.'

'For years, Unwin was importing drugs, dabbling in human trafficking, and he ran a chop shop,' Rick said. 'A few years back, there was a major epidemic of car exhaust thefts. You could park your car, nip into Tesco for a pint of milk and a KitKat, come back five minutes later to find the catalytic converter ripped out from under your car.'

'I read about that,' Sam said. 'Seems a scrappy way to earn a living.'

'Worth their while, from what Collins just said. Russian gangs were heavily involved, and we were sure that they were using Unwin's chop shop to get at the valuable innards, but we could never catch him in the act.

'Then a shipping company owner suddenly gets thrown a ladder out of the deep, deep hole her husband dug her company into with gambling debt. Coincidentally, that's also when Unwin went into the import-export business and started hobnobbing with the big boys of industry and commerce.'

Sam nodded. 'The men in Kirk Wilson's surveillance photos.'

'One of whom owns the apartment we're about to raid.'

Sam's eyes lit up. 'Ah, the mystery man is Russian mob – they switched from exporting stolen car parts to importing the pure stuff!'

'Right,' Rick said. 'So Unwin takes a pole-vault up the food chain, from small-time East End geezer to international smuggler with friends in high places.'

'Until you rain on his parade,' Sam said. 'No wonder he's got it in for you.'

'You don't have to sound so thrilled,' Rick said.

Sam smirked. 'Dave Collins is quite the phenomenon, isn't he?' he said, adding, 'Remind me to stay on the right side of your armchair ninja friend.'

Rick looked up sharply, the coffee cup frozen halfway from the table to his lips. 'Armchair ninja?'

Sam returned a blank look.

'Dave used those exact words to describe himself in a confidential chat I had with him.'

'Really?'

Rick returned a steady look and after a few seconds Sam puffed air and raised his hands in surrender. 'I had you followed – *for your own protection*,' he added with force.

Rick recalled his meeting with Collins in the Bear & Staff and the softly spoken couple planning 'adventures' on London tour buses. 'The middle-aged tourists in the pub,' he said.

'They're *actually* in their early thirties,' Sam said, 'but they do age up well.'

Rick shook his head in disgust.

'Come on, Rick – you were planning to publicly castrate Mounsey at the Central Criminal Court yesterday morning – I was doing you a favour.'

'A *fav*—' Rick didn't know if he was more furious or outraged. 'My boss wants to know why I'm walking around with a stonking great bruise on my face – thanks for that. And you keep trying to drag my colleagues into this mess, intruding on their privacy, manipulating them like it's some kind of game.'

Sam was implacable. 'If work isn't fun, it's time to give up,' he said. 'And don't you know that play stimulates creativity?'

This surprised an incredulous chuckle from Rick. 'Unbelievable,' he gasped, laughing, despite himself. 'You're *literally* unbelievable.'

'See – we're having fun,' Sam said. 'And for the record, I have colleagues to protect, too.'

'Fair enough,' Rick said. 'But I need some action. So, please explain to me – what the bloody hell are we waiting for?'

'A propitious moment,' Sam said. 'I have a van in the street; if anything happens – if anything *at all* changes – they'll let us know. But as police, you will know it doesn't make tactical sense to go straight in. The best time to make a move will be four a.m.'

When the human body temperature is at its lowest and they were likely to be deep asleep. It made sense to time the raid to their own physiological and psychological advantage, but Rick didn't think he could sit still and wait for another two hours.

'What do you suggest we do in the meantime?' he asked.

Sam gave him an appraising look Rick recognised from when he was a kid. 'Since sleep seems out of the question, we'll memorise the floor plans and work out a strategy.'

'And if something *does* happen?'

'I have three men in the surveillance vehicle, ready to act, and transport waiting here,' Sam soothed. 'It's less than five minutes door to door.'

'All right,' Rick said, rubbing a hand over his face and into his hair, wincing at the tender spot where Sam's goon had slammed him in the head. 'Do we know how many are on-site?'

Sam reached for the tablet, lying at one end of the table. 'Two personnel have remained in the apartment since we started watching the place, but Oliver Norland comes and goes.' He showed Rick an image of a chunky man with thick, light-coloured hair.

'The court security prick who cut Jess,' Rick said.

'My people say he's nursing that left hand, so he shouldn't be too much of a problem.' Sam swiped to the second image.

Rick stared at a lean woman dressed in chinos and a soft-shell jacket; her hair was fastened in a tight braid, and she looked alert and fit.

'I don't know her,' he said. 'But the "battle braid" and the way she holds herself shouts military.'

'Mara Solomon, former Royal Highland Fusilier, served in combat in Afghanistan. Currently gun for hire.' Sam zoomed in to a shadow inside the woman's unzipped jacket. 'Literally.' Solomon was wearing a paddle holster on her waistband, the butt of a pistol just visible.

'My men will target her – and leave Norland alone, too.'

Rick studied Norland's face, committing it to memory.

'Do you hear me, Rick? You are to stay clear of Norland,' Sam repeated.

'I will. If I can.'

Next up was Tommy Novac, Unwin's trusted minder whose

old mum thought he was looking after a famous actress. Tommy was standing on the steps of the building, smoking a cigarette.

'Tommy took the stub with him after finishing his cigarette, like a good boy. Nobody has been in or out since then.'

Two men, one woman. Unwin's trusted minder, a violent thug who couldn't pass the police entry-level tests, and an armed, combat-trained soldier. Rick slid the screen to Norland's image. 'This one's the wild card,' he said. 'No discipline, according to someone I trust.' He recalled the way Norland had grovelled to Mounsey. 'A classic bully, so—'

'Don't underestimate Oliver Norland,' Sam said. 'Noted.'

He retrieved the tablet and swiped through a few more images. 'I wanted to show you a character who visited Callum Mounsey's office last evening.'

The shot pictured a man in suit pants and wool jacket. Greying hair cropped short, colour heightened, hair beginning to recede. Rick saw in the rounded stoop of his shoulders the resentment and humiliation of a strong man brought low.

Rick felt suddenly hollowed out. It was DS Jim Stott.

'You know him?' Sam asked.

Rick didn't answer.

'I'm thinking police.'

He felt Sam's eyes on him.

'Yeah.'

'Someone you work with?'

Rick barely heard him. He was scrambling to remember the details of his last conversation with Stott, feeling his heart throb in his throat.

Stott had known that Jess was an actress, but Rick had told no one in the job what she did for a living. Even more unsettling was his old mentor's glib lie that he'd heard about the mole in Kildoran's chambers from DCI Steiner, when Rick had told only two people: his brother and Callum Mounsey.

Jeez, how did I miss this?

'When was this taken?' he demanded.

'Six-forty p.m.,' Sam said.

After their tête-à-tête back at base. What had he said that would bring Stott to Mounsey's door? He stared at the picture; the solicitor seemed angry, and Mounsey rarely showed any emotion. Had Rick given Stott the impression that he was about to renege on his 'arrangement' with Unwin? Could Stott have been reporting this apparent change of heart to Mounsey? After all, he'd told Stott that the law would deal with Unwin. But Rick had the strongest impression that Stott was spying for Unwin under duress – hadn't he implied that he wanted Unwin dead?

'Rick,' Sam said sharply, 'is there something I need to know?'

'Did your people pick up any chatter – any signs that they were increasing security or changing routines?'

'If they had, we'd have moved in earlier,' Sam said equably, as if reasoning with a neurotic child.

'In that case, no. It's something I'll have to deal with later, but it's not anything you need to worry about.'

Sam watched him for the longest time, but at last he gave the briefest of nods and turned again to the floor plans of apartment eight.

Chapter 42

AT THREE-FORTY A.M., Sam's mobile phone buzzed.

'Is it ready?' He listened to the answer. 'Okay, send it up in five.'

Rick had been dozing on the sofa. 'Send what up?' he asked.

'A drone.'

'Whoa, wait!'

Sam said, 'All due respect to your armchair ninja, I won't go in blind.'

'Those things are as loud as a car – it'll wake the whole street!'

'No, it won't. It's state of the art – not much louder than a mosquito whine – and it has an IR-night camera, with no extraneous lights. It's safe, Rick.'

Rick stared at him.

'What?' he said.

'How come you have access to all of this?'

'Gadgets are what makes the internet worth the hassle.' Sam laughed.

'It's not just the gadgets,' Rick said, thinking, *that wasn't the question*. 'It's the people, information, the surveillance vehicles. The *money*.'

'I told you about the money. And you would know more than anyone that I've moved in dubious circles all my life.'

'Yeah,' Rick said. 'Ever since Lockleigh.'

'Oh, since *well* before that – like I said, I moved up in the world when I hitched my wagon to Theo Lockleigh.'

'That mentorship didn't last though, did it?'

'It didn't.' Sam gave a careless shrug. 'I got cocky, and I got caught.'

It was a police sting operation. They had given Sam a choice: incriminate Lockleigh or go to prison. Sam hadn't hesitated to save his own skin.

'You give Lockleigh a lot of credit for your – I don't know what to call it – metamorphosis?'

Sam thought about it. 'Evolution. It took a long time to get here. And Theo deserves the credit for setting me on the path of self-improvement – he rubbed the edges off, showed me what life could be like, encouraged me to study.' He laughed. 'I actually took night school classes – can you believe it?'

'You were always clever,' Rick said. 'But I don't get how you could betray Lockleigh.'

'To survive,' Sam said.

'Then just walk away, leave everything?'

'You can always make new allies, find new friends.'

'Leaving behind old allies and new enemies?'

'Is there any other option?'

'In your circumstances, I suppose not. But if that's what you did, then why are you here now?'

'We've been through this, Rick.' Sam got to his feet and began emptying items from a backpack he'd tucked in the corner by the window. 'You're family.'

'That's not an answer; I was family every day of the thirteen years that we heard nothing from you.'

Sam set two bundles of clothing side by side on the sofa he'd just vacated.

'But you show up within hours of Austin King's murder and Jess being kidnapped.'

Sam glanced at him. 'You're back on that? You still think I abducted Jess?'

'You're doing it again – trying to divert me from my question by asking your own,' Rick said.

For a long five seconds the brothers glared at each other. Then Sam relaxed.

'All right. I'll tell you what you want to know if you satisfy my curiosity on one point.'

Rick threw up his hands. 'Why does everything have to be a negotiation with you?'

'Just one question, Rick.'

'Go ahead, ask it.'

'What made you show up at Haskins's hotel room?' Sam asked. 'You said it wasn't your case – why would you be sniffing around an accidental death that was none of your business?'

Rick recalled the sudden dread he'd felt, standing at the bathroom door, certain that he'd find Sam was lying dead in that bath. 'Are you sure you want to hear this, Sam?'

'One hundred per cent.'

'If you really want to know, it all goes back to that night.' They both understood that he meant the night Sam had murdered one of Lockleigh's thugs. 'Six years, Mum kept vigil for you,' Rick went on. 'Missing persons charities, newspaper ads, appeals in the *Big Issue* – you name it, she tried it – short of calling in the police.'

Sam paled. 'You told her about—?'

'No – I would never do that to her. But she knew she couldn't involve the police – Dad told her to stop looking. He said, "When you do find him, it'll be in an alley or a ditch somewhere, and it won't be pretty."'

Sam paused in the process of putting on a black soft-shell jacket from one of the bundles. 'Did he, now?' he said, an almost fond smile on his lips. 'Didn't stop him moving up west, did it Rick? Didn't stop him taking my money.'

'He thought you owed him for all the crap you put them

through over the years. Anyway, what was he supposed to do? You made the family name toxic on the estate. The few who weren't scared of you hated your guts.'

'Bam-Bam Sam was who I *needed* to be on the estate to protect you and Mum – it was a front – I thought you knew that.'

Rick shook his head. 'Mum and Dad were always on edge; they lost friends, their standing in the community—'

'Community! Is that what you'd call it?' Sam finished shrugging on his jacket and zipped it up. 'I gave them a decent place to live,' he said, his voice harsh with emotion. 'Somewhere *you* could grow up without having to watch your back.'

That much was true. Sam had given him the chance to be a different person, to walk down the street without constantly having to watch doorways and alleyways for signs of danger. Sam had lifted him from the barren concrete and scouring winds of their flat in Lewisham and planted him in the rich loam of the house Rick thought of as his first true home.

Rick had done everything he could to be the good son their mother had wanted in Sam, to chain the monster he knew was in his own DNA. He'd got a degree, while the kids he'd grown up with on the estate drifted into dead-end jobs or unemployment or criminality. He'd volunteered as a special constable while other students pissed away their weekends at parties. He had obeyed the rules, studied hard, and was one of the youngest in his borough to pass the sergeant's exam. But he was too angry to grant Sam any of the credit: their mother had never got over his disappearance, and only two years after Rick made detective, she was dead.

Sam was packing his mobile into his pocket, a Maglite torch, a pair of gloves.

'Six long years,' Rick said again.

'I was doing everyone a favour,' Sam said. 'You most of all.'

'Mum stopped looking for you because she was afraid Dad was right.'

Sam shook his head, dismissing him.

'I watched that thought eat away at her,' Rick said. 'You know she died of cancer?'

A spasm creased Sam's face for a second. 'I do,' he said quietly. 'But I still don't hear an answer to my question. What sent you to Haskins's hotel room, that night?'

'Mum gave up,' Rick said. 'But I didn't. I skimmed police reports and listened to emergency service chatter on a scanner during my off-duties, looking for men who'd died violently. Men about your age.'

Sam raised his gaze to Rick's face.

'I've turned up at so many coroners' inquests the staff mistake me for a reporter. I've been thrown out of crime scenes mortuaries from Hounslow to Dagenham looking for you.'

Sam's shoulders sagged. 'Oh, Rick . . .'

Sam's compassion only made him angrier; Rick didn't want sympathy, he wanted his brother off guard. He wanted the truth.

'I wasn't interested in Haskins's murder, I was looking for *you*, Sam. But here's the weird thing: when I told you about the body in the hotel bath – how posed it looked – right off, you said, *Death of Marat*.'

Immediately Sam dropped the concern, and the barriers went up. 'Well, you did describe the scene vividly.'

'Don't do that. Don't take me for an idiot. You said, "Death of Marat", like it was a no-brainer.'

'What's your point, Rick?' Sam said, his eyelids half-lowered.

'Was it a joke at the expense of some donkey of a detective? You always were a smart arse.'

Sam looked suddenly bored. 'Are we really going to do this now? I thought we'd called a truce at least till you get Jess home safe.'

'You're the one who keeps picking at that scab. I can't help wondering if it's professional vanity – that this is you, worrying that you missed something – or got too cocky. Again.'

Sam glanced at him, wary, now. 'You're making a big leap

from my admittedly prurient interest to – well, what exactly *is* it you're suggesting?'

'You show up out of nowhere after thirteen years with your bottomless money pot, your shady contacts and your gizmos and surveillance tricks. All clued up on Austin King and Thomas Unwin. What am I supposed to think?'

Still watching him, Sam said, 'In my business, it pays to be well informed.'

'That's what's eating me: what exactly *is* your business, Sam?' Even now, Rick couldn't bring himself to ask outright: *Are you a killer?*

'I do what I always did, Rick. I solve problems, fix situations.'

'Problems like Austin King?'

'Bullet in the brain, wasn't it?' Sam said blandly. 'Lacks the finesse of Haskins as Marat, dead in his medicinal bath.'

'Was that an admission?'

'An observation,' Sam said.

'When we were kids, you used to say you created bespoke solutions for individual problems, do you remember?'

Sam gazed at the ceiling. 'With your memory for words, you should have gone into acting. It's quite phenomenal – probably what makes you good police.'

Another attempt at deflection. 'Is Unwin your next problem-solving exercise? Is *that* why you're helping me – so you can get close to Unwin?'

Sam laughed. 'If that *were* the case, it would make my job a lot easier if I left Jess exactly where she is – Unwin on the streets would be far more accessible than Unwin in prison.'

Rick flashed to Jim Stott, to his sly suggestion that Unwin would feel the full force of justice if he did get out.

'Why did you show me that photo?' he asked.

Sam seemed nonplussed. 'Which one?'

Rick picked up the tablet and flicked through to the image of Stott. 'This one.'

'Because he turned up at Mounsey's office,' Sam explained patiently. 'And if he *is* police, he could be a threat to—'

'If! You can identify an unknown mercenary in less than a day, and now you're trying to make me believe you can't find the name of a bent copper from your own pocket police?' Rick held his brother's gaze till he looked away.

'I know his name is Jim Stott,' Sam said quietly. 'I know he's on the Unwin inquiry.'

'And you couldn't just tell me that? See – this is why I can't trust you, Sam.'

Sam shook his head. 'The fact is you trust too easily, Rick. I showed you the picture because I wanted to warn you that the people you *think* you can trust are not to be trusted at all.'

'Tell me about it.'

'As I said before, I'm here to help *you*,' Sam went on, and the quiet control in his voice told Rick just how much emotion was at the back of it. 'Jess and the others don't mean a thing to me one way or another. You know me – I never really gave a shit about anyone but you and Mum. And to set the record straight, little brother, Mum stopped looking because she found me – or rather, *I* found *her*. When Mum got sick, I was there, every day, at the hospital. When she was buried at Putney Vale, I was there.' His voice roughened and he coughed, before adding, 'And I'm here, now.'

Rick stared at him in shocked silence. A hundred questions assailed him, and he didn't even know how to begin. 'You're lying,' he managed at last.

'No,' Sam said. 'I'm not. I'm sorry she didn't tell you, and I'm sorry you kept looking for me. But Mum made me promise to say nothing and stay away.'

Rick felt a band of constriction around his chest. 'When?'

Sam frowned. '*When*?'

'When did this happen?'

'When you transferred to CID.'

Rick closed his eyes for a second. 'That would be when she first got her diagnosis. Why would she *do* that?'

'Because it wasn't safe.'

'For you,' Rick said, anger and resentment warring in his chest.

'For *you*, Rick. Mum thought I was a bad influence. She was right. She said you'd got your life together, that you were building a career. She wanted that for you more than anything.'

'She said you went through a rough time after I . . . left,' he added softly. 'Didn't want you all stirred up again.'

Sam's mobile buzzed, jarring them both.

'The intel is good – it's the right apartment,' Sam said, glancing at the screen. 'Your decision, Rick – are we doing this, or not?'

Rick stood. 'Let's go.'

'It could get messy, and if you're determined to continue in the police, you might feel compromised.'

'I already am,' Rick said. 'Everything I've done since I got the first message that they had Jess has put me on the wrong side of the law.'

'Then you'll have to gear up like the rest of us.'

'What kind of gear?'

'Protection. Disguise.'

'All right,' Rick said.

Sam shoved the second bundle of clothing at Rick. 'The sports kit is okay as a base layer,' he said, focused, professional, all trace of filial emotion gone. 'But wear the jacket, neck gaiter and baseball hat. And leave your phones here.'

Rick emptied his pockets of the three phones he now carried and donned the clothing.

'Be aware there's CCTV on the corridors and at all exits.' Sam looked at Rick appraisingly. 'And you might want to hunch a little.'

'I could limp, if you want,' Rick said.

'That won't be necessary,' Sam said smoothly, adding with a twinkle that said he'd recovered his good humour, 'Just try not to stand out.'

Sam led the way down an internal fire escape to the back

of the building. A black van was parked at the gate. Rick recognised the logo of a prestige security firm, but on closer inspection he saw a few air bubbles in the lettering and guessed that they had faked it using vinyl stickers. Clever – that particular firm's logo in Kensington would reassure, rather than unsettle.

Sam slid open the side door and Rick climbed in. He recognised the two men occupying the bench seats on the left of the van as Little and Large, the two who had bundled him into a limo and brought him to Sam the previous day. They were dressed in black and wore high-spec body armour over their jackets.

Rick sat facing them, and the smaller man reached under his seat and handed a set each to Rick and Sam.

'Helmets and visors are in the rack above your head,' he said.

'Visors?' Rick looked in question to his brother.

'There's no street CCTV, but a number of properties do have smart doorbells,' Sam explained. 'Which will record unidentifiable men in full assault gear moving efficiently and with minimal noise into the building. A police exercise, maybe? We'll have the advantage of surprise, and we'll do all we can to execute a bloodless takedown of the hostage-takers.'

'And if it *does* get messy?' Rick asked.

'It will be dealt with.'

'No cowboy tactics, no civilian involvement,' Rick warned.

'Goes without saying,' Sam answered.

'Yeah, well, I'm saying it.'

The two brothers locked gazes.

Finally, Sam nodded. 'No civilian involvement.' He took a pistol handed to him by the taller of the two men and screwed a suppressor in place. It was a Glock 17; standard issue for most UK police forces. Using 9mm ammo, it couldn't have been the weapon that killed Austin King, but judging by the armoury Sam had at his disposal, it didn't exonerate him, either.

'Hope for the best, prepare for the worst,' Sam said, misinterpreting the look. 'Are you firearms trained?'

'Yes.'

Sam offered him the gun, grip first, but Rick shook his head. 'I'll pass.'

'I can't let you go in unarmed.'

'Got a Casco baton? I'll use that.'

Sam hesitated, then glanced at the smaller man. He reached around to the side of his utility belt and passed Rick a black nickel-zinc-plated, police-grade baton. After a moment's thought, he unhooked a couple of pairs of plasticuff restraints from his belt and handed those over as well. Rick accepted them with a nod of thanks and stuffed the baton into his trouser pocket and the cuffs into his jacket.

The big man passed a tablet to Sam. 'Drone footage,' he said.

Two of Unwin's men were sprawled on sofas in the large, almost empty, sitting room. Rick recognised Tommy Novac and Norland, the tow-headed court security guard. Both were asleep, Norland nursing his bandaged hand across his chest, his hair dazzling white under the infra-red camera. The drone operator swept right and left. There was no sign of the mercenary, nor was Jess in the room.

'We'll split up on entry,' Sam said. 'You two, plus two more from the surveillance van will clear the other rooms; Rick and I will deal with these two.'

Both men nodded. The smaller man spoke briefly into his chest mic, relaying instructions to the second van, and after that, not another word was spoken.

They drove slowly through the narrow streets of Kensington, past red Victorian mansions and white Edwardian houses, rows and terraces reserved for the stratospherically wealthy. Executive cars were parked kerbside of houses with gleaming paintwork and polished brass doorknockers. Turning left at Palace Gate the driver skimmed the edge of Hyde Park, in darkness but for the ghostly, white wash of light from the LED streetlamps and the hotels on Knightsbridge Road tastefully lit for the benefit of their genteel guests.

Another left turn brought them to their destination.

Chapter 43

Wednesday, 4 a.m.

THE ROAD WAS JAMMED NOSE-TO-TAIL with high-end vehicles. The van driver, a grey-haired man in his fifties, passed a couple of empty bays outside buildings bearing the flags of foreign countries.

'Sorry, Boss,' he said. 'I wouldn't want to use those bays – they're reserved for diplomats' cars, and the embassies are shit-hot on any infractions.'

'Well, we certainly don't need that kind of attention, Lawrence,' Sam said mildly.

'I'll drop you outside and wait in the club car bay,' Lawrence said. 'It's just around the next bend, about forty metres down on the left.'

'Very well.' Sam glanced at the others. 'Gear up, gentlemen.'

His neck gaiter masking the lower half of his face, the helmet obscuring the rest, Rick jumped from the van after the others and saw that Little and Large had POLICE emblazoned in reflector patches on their backs.

'Wait,' he said, grabbing Sam by the arm. 'Are they—?'

'It's *days* too late for that question,' Sam said.

He was probably right: whether these men were mercenaries impersonating police, or *actual* police on a highly illegal op was immaterial. He just had to hope these men knew what they were doing.

Rick turned to the sound of another door sliding open, and three more men joined them from a nondescript grey van parked across the road.

The front door was surprisingly easy, and they were inside the wide hallway in seconds. A grand stairway led to the upper rooms, with an old-style elevator off to the left. One of the men diverted, opening the outer concertina gates to prevent anyone using the lift, then he rejoined the group climbing the stone stairs. They were quiet and efficient, all of them were armed, and one man carried an 'enforcer' – effectively a manual battering ram. Jittery with the flood of adrenaline, now, Rick was thinking if they had to use it, it could wake up half the occupants, the police would be called, and if they were, it was game over.

On the third floor, they strung out along the corridor while the group leader tried his picklocks on the apartment door. After half a minute, he nodded, turned the door handle and swung the door open, allowing two men in ahead of him, then followed on.

Two of the crew headed left, two right. Rick and Sam stood at the centre door into the sitting room. The leader counted down on his fingers. On three, they burst through the doors.

Tommy Novac seemed to *levitate* off the sofa – on his feet before he was fully awake – fists raised, protecting his head and body, like the ex-boxer he was. As he was nearer, Rick should have dealt with him, but the court security guard had rolled off his sofa and seemed to be trying to scoot behind it. Rick lunged, grabbed the man's ankle, and gave it a fierce yank. Norland fell on his face, bringing his injured hand up just in time to save himself from a broken nose. He screamed in pain and, twisting to look up at Rick, he kicked out with his free leg.

Rick held on to him, giving the foot a sharp wrench. Another cry of pain and, with the prisoner struggling face-down again, Rick bent, grinding one knee in the small of the man's back, while he grabbed the injured hand and, ignoring the thug's agonised screams, felt in his pocket for the swift-cuffs.

He roared at Norland to hold still, but he would not give up, reaching with his good right hand, trying to secure a hold on the sofa leg to give himself leverage.

The cuffs were caught in his pocket lining and Rick glanced down for a second. He heard Sam's voice, muffled by the gaiter he wore over his mouth, and assumed he was yelling at Novac. When he looked up again, Norland had brought his right hand from under the sofa, bringing a gun around and over his left shoulder. It was aimed at Rick's face.

Two muted coughs, and something wet spattered on Rick's visor. Norland went limp and the gun clattered to the block floor. Sam stepped up quickly and kicked the gun away before turning to Rick.

'Are you hurt?' he said, his voice urgent, his eyes intense with anxiety.

'I'm fine,' Rick said.

'You can let him go now,' Sam said.

For a second, Rick wasn't sure what he meant. Then he looked down and saw that he still had the dead man's hand in his grip. He lowered it, grateful that he could not see Norland's face. The bullets had blown a gaping hole in the back of the man's head.

He swallowed hard and pivoted on the ball of his foot to take in the rest of the room.

Tommy Novac was kneeling on the floor. A black hood covered his head.

One of Sam's men appeared in the doorway, gun raised, and Sam said, 'Stand down.'

He lowered his weapon and Sam asked, 'Is the target secured?'

A nod, then the man stood aside, and two more operatives escorted the female mercenary – also hooded – into the room. There was still no sign of Jess.

Rick glanced at Sam. 'Where is she?' he asked, forcing the words past a pain in his chest.

No one answered until Sam gave a terse nod, then the man Rick thought of as Little said, 'Last door on the right.'

Sam stopped Rick before he'd taken two steps and handed him a handkerchief. 'Best not to spook her,' he said, and Rick remembered the spatter of blood on his visor.

Wiping it, Rick headed out of the room, and heard Sam give instructions to Little to arrange 'cleaning services'.

When he got to the end of the hall, the door was closed, and Rick had a sudden superstitious feeling that he didn't want to open it.

A hand on his shoulder startled him and he turned, ready to fight.

'Easy,' Sam said. 'She's fine. You can go in.'

Jess was seated on the edge of the bed, her hands clasped between her knees. She was trembling violently.

Large stood beside her, feet apart, gun holstered.

'Jess?'

Her head snapped up, and Rick saw a look of terror on her face. *The blood*, he thought. *The blood on my visor.*

He snatched the helmet off and said again, 'Jess?'

With a cry of anguish, Jess flung herself into his arms, sobbing. Rick calmed her, turning her to gently guide her from the room. Sam was watching him from the doorway and Rick caught a look of compassion in his brother's eyes.

Rick kept Jess in the hallway while Sam returned to the sitting room. He addressed Mara, the ex-fusilier, by name. 'Your part in all of this is finished,' he said. 'It's no longer your fight. Now, you know how this goes if you cooperate. And you know how it goes if you don't.'

A pause, then Rick heard the mercenary say, 'You won't get any trouble from me.' A few seconds later, she was led from the room, offering no resistance.

Through the open door, Rick could see the hooded figure of Tommy Novac, stilling kneeling.

Sam said, 'Tommy, if you want to see your mum again, you need to follow Guardsman Soloman's example.'

Novac stiffened. 'If you've—'

'She's perfectly safe, at home, being well looked after,' Sam said. 'No harm will come to her. And if you behave yourself, you have my word that you will be released in good time and in one piece.'

Novac nodded, then he began hesitantly: 'You know, this isn't what you—'

Sam touched his shoulder lightly and he flinched.

'I don't care,' Sam said. 'I just need to know if you're going to be a problem.'

'No,' Novac said, shaking his big head under the hood like a bear. 'I won't be a problem.'

Holding tight to Rick, Jess watched as the two men, still hooded, were steered across the hallway and out of the apartment.

Sam and the small guy came into corridor from the sitting room, closing the door after them.

'Where's the other one?' Jess demanded. 'Where's the bastard who did this to me?' She held up her bandaged hand.

'He's not your concern,' Sam said.

She tried to shake free, but Rick held her close. 'Come on, Jess,' he said, urging her to follow the others.

She balked. 'I want my phone. He's got it,' she shouted, still struggling. 'And I'm *not* leaving without it.'

Rick looked helplessly at Sam.

'Calm yourself,' Sam said sharply, and she subsided. Then, to Little, he said, 'Would you mind?' as if it were a minor inconvenience, having to search the dead man's pockets.

The short guy ducked into the main room again and, returning a moment later, he handed Jess's phone to Sam.

She snatched it from him and then apologised, offering Sam an embarrassed smile.

'Oh, don't worry yourself,' Sam said indulgently. 'I understand how important an actress's phone is. Office, showcase, electronic lifeline.'

He raised a hand to encourage them to the door, but Rick faltered.

'What will you . . .?' He glanced towards the sitting-room door.

'We'll have the place shining like a new pin in no time.' Sam might have been referring to a teenage party that had got out of hand instead of the abduction and imprisonment of a woman that had ended in a bloody shoot-out. And if he harboured any worries about the body leaking blood onto the hardwood floor, Rick couldn't read it in his face. 'We'll leave no trace,' Sam finished.

For reassuring words, they didn't feel very reassuring.

Chapter 44

IN THE VAN HEADING BACK TO THE HOTEL, Sam sat opposite Rick and Jess, watching them with a curious look on his face that Rick couldn't quite read. Jess clung to him, and he held her tight, calming her, murmuring reassurances that she was safe, that it was over, that she needn't be afraid anymore.

After a few minutes, Rick looked through the windscreen and saw that they were still some way from their destination. 'Are we switching hotels again?'

'Just working out a few wrinkles,' Sam said, ever the enigma. 'Are you feeling better now, Jess?'

She turned her huge brown eyes on Sam, and Rick felt her sigh run like a tremor through the core of his own body.

'I'm – I'm much better, now Rick's here.'

'Good.' Sam gazed at her solemnly. 'Do you think you could answer some questions?'

She gripped Rick's jacket with a little mewl of fear. 'Oh, I couldn't go through it – not yet. It's too . . .'

'I understand, it's been an ordeal. Just a couple of questions to help Rick – to keep him safe.'

Rick began to feel uneasy. 'Sam, what are you—?'

'Simple questions about the morning you were abducted,' Sam said, his full attention on Jess. 'For Rick's sake.'

'Of course,' she murmured, her voice small and childlike. 'For Rick.' She glanced up and Rick felt a searing joy to have her with him again, to feel the warmth of her body against his.

Sam smiled encouragement and then called through to the driver. 'Would you mind giving us some privacy for a few minutes?'

'Sure, Boss.' Lawrence lifted the centre console armrest and reached inside for a pair of wireless headphones. He turned them on, and they heard a burst of music, but Sam waited until he had slipped them over his ears before he began.

'On Monday, you had your first audition at eight-forty-five a.m., and left the venue at around nine-twenty. Does that sound right?'

She snuffled. 'Yes.'

'Rick, you received the first WhatsApp message at nine-thirty – correct?'

Rick nodded, wondering where he was going with this.

'And the men who abducted you picked you up at around nine-twenty-five.'

'I suppose . . . it must have been. I was just wandering; it went so well, I was buzzing – needed to move – I didn't really watch the time.'

'Not to worry,' Sam said in that same warm, kindly tone. 'We actually have CCTV footage, which confirms that it was indeed nine-twenty-five. A white Ford Focus van with stolen number plates stopped kerbside next to you on Shoreditch High Street. And when they moved on, *poof*, you were gone.'

Rick felt Jess shift uncomfortably next to him. There was an odd edge to Sam's tone, and clearly Jess heard it, too.

'Can this wait?' he said. 'She's clearly distressed.'

'Almost there, Rick.' Sam kept his mild, relentless focus on Jess. 'Then the production team got a text – purportedly from Jess – at ten-twenty a.m., saying that you'd been mugged.'

'*Sam*. We know all this, why are you—'

'But that's not right, is it, Jess? Do you want to tell him, or shall I?'

'T-tell him *what*?' she stammered. 'I don't know what you're—' She looked up at Rick, appealing to him. 'I don't know what he wants . . .'

'The time was out by an hour – the text was sent at *nine*-twenty, not ten-twenty. Can you explain that?'

'No – I mean yes. You've got it wrong,' she said. 'I sent the text at ten-twenty.'

'Oh, you sent it yourself?'

'No,' she said, flustered, 'I meant *they* did – you're confusing me. He's getting me all mixed up. Rick—' She stared up at him, but Rick looked past her to his brother, a terrible dread settling on him.

'I sent a tame police contact to check on the audition time and to verify when Jessica left,' Sam explained. 'The producer's PA was very apologetic. It was the end of British Summer Time on Sunday,' Sam said. 'The clocks should have been turned back an hour. But the wall clock in the church hall where you auditioned hadn't been reset. The PA happened to glance at the clock when the text came through and mistakenly noted the time of Jess's text as ten-twenty.'

Rick's stomach flipped over, recalling the phone call Sam had taken on Tuesday afternoon. 'Talk me through the timeline,' Sam had said, his mood suddenly sombre. And when Rick had asked if there was a problem, he'd said, *Nothing to change our plans.*

Of course, he would want proof – Rick had made it abundantly clear that if Sam had said it was raining outside, Rick would insist on opening a window and sticking his head out to be sure.

'It was only later, when the PA looked at the text again, and noticed the time stamp, that she realised it had been sent an hour earlier than she'd first thought.' He watched Jess, his expression curious, rather than angry. 'You know what that means, don't you, Jess? You sent the text saying that you'd been mugged five minutes *before* you were abducted.'

'I *didn't*. They're lying.'

He smiled softly, almost sympathetically. 'Why would they lie, Jess?'

'I don't *know*.' She gripped Rick's arm fiercely, appealing to him. 'Ricky, please – why is he *doing* this?'

'I suppose you didn't want to miss your big chance at a regular spot on a TV series,' Sam said. 'The audition really did go well, didn't it?'

Rick carefully disentangled himself, gently prising Jess's fingers from his arm.

'You don't believe *him*?' she cried. 'You know he's a liar – you said it yourself, for God's sake!'

'We could clear up the confusion in a minute.' Sam remained unruffled, reasonable, as if he merely wanted to settle a mild dispute. 'You have your phone right there. Shall we check?'

Jess licked her lips. 'It's locked – they changed the PIN.'

'Thumbprint should still work, though, eh, Jessica?' Sam said, dropping one eyelid in a roguish wink.

Rick reached for her, and she sagged gratefully against him, but he felt in her pocket and withdrew her phone.

She snatched at it, and he held her wrist. 'Don't fight me, Jess,' he said, his voice harsh with emotion.

She was deathly pale, now, her hand ice-cold as he guided her thumb to the icon.

He found the text in seconds and it was just as Sam had predicted. He handed the phone over, unable to say the words. Sam looked at the text and with a nod of acknowledgement he began scrolling through the rest, then switched between apps while keeping up a steady flow of chatter.

'Goodness, you are quite the social butterfly, aren't you?' he said. 'All these photographs!' Chuckling, he turned the camera around, skimming through a few to demonstrate, then returning to his idle examination of her photo gallery.

'You waitress between acting jobs, don't you, Jessica?'

Jess gave a resentful shrug; her head was down now, and her hands limp in her lap.

'And you've been to Thomas Unwin's house several times, haven't you? In a waitressing capacity.'

Rick saw her breath quicken, but she spoke in a dull, uninterested monotone. 'I don't know – they just ferry you to the venue, you waitress and then they take you home.'

Sam named two dates when she went to the same house. 'Unwin's house,' he said.

'If you say so.'

'You didn't recognise him?'

'There were over a hundred guests. I didn't—'

'You didn't recognise the host – even though he was the subject of Rick's investigation?'

'Me and Rick hadn't even met when I did those jobs,' she protested.

'True enough.' He glanced at Rick, underlining the fact that she'd changed her story. 'But then Unwin gave you a job at his club.'

Her mouth set in a stubborn line.

'And it seems he was taken with you, because he offered you a much bigger, better-paying job, more in line with your talents.' He paused. 'You met Rick in a pub, yes?'

'So?'

Rick stared at his brother, his mouth dry. If he could, he would have told Sam to stop, to let him out of the van – he didn't want to hear this.

'That would be, what . . . a few months ago?'

'Three,' Rick said, and his lips felt numb. 'Mid-July.'

Sam began scrolling through Jess's photos again. 'It was a set-up, that little *fracas*, wasn't it, Jess? The groper who turned nasty; Rick being on hand to step in and protect you.'

She turned again to Rick. 'You'd take the word of a liar and a criminal over me? You'd take the word of a – a killer?' The venom on her face made him recoil. 'You saw him stab a man to death.' Her voice rose to a scream. 'Why would you even *listen* to him?'

Rick's mind flew back to the morning he'd told Jess about the stabbing and felt sadness gather like a solid stone around his heart. 'You were so angry when I told you that,' he said. 'I was terrified you were going to leave me. But you know what you said, Jess – your exact words? "God, I *so* effing wish you hadn't told me."'

'Because I saw how it *hurt* you, Ricky . . .'

He shook his head. 'You wished I hadn't told you, because you knew you had to tell Unwin, or whoever your handler was.'

'No, no, *no!*'

'Maybe you didn't need to. I know the house is bugged, Jess. I just never thought that you were the one who bugged it.'

She shot a bitter look at Sam. 'His lies have got you all twisted up, Rick. I would *never*—'

'Oh, my, this one's a peach!' Sam laughed, eyes still on Jess's phone, and Rick felt beaten down by his ruthless good humour. 'Rick said you were *magnificent* that night. Fearless. You even broke the handsy little creep's finger in the tussle.'

She glared at him, tears still brimming, but her eyes dark with hate.

'And here's the proof.' He turned the screen again.

Jess, with a smile to break your heart, cheek-to-cheek with a man, also smiling, his hand held in front of his face, showing off his pinkie finger, splinted and strapped to his ring finger.

Rick recognised the smiling man as the groper in the pub the night he'd met Jess.

'Well, it's good to see there were no hard feelings,' Sam said. 'I suppose as a fellow thespian, devoted to the craft, he'd regard minor injuries as an occupational hazard – a badge of honour, even.'

Jess began quietly sobbing.

Rick found himself reassessing her rescue. The look on her face when he came through the door of the bedroom – it wasn't terror – Jess was horrified to see him. She must have thought he knew what she'd done. He recalled, also, the look of pity in his brother's eyes. He'd thought that it was for Jess, but it was for him.

'You got drunk the night before your audition,' Rick said. His tongue felt thick, and his voice strangely dull. 'You never do that.'

'Were you worried about how the "abduction" would go?' Sam wondered.

She shook her head, tears falling into her lap. 'I was scared. When I saw that stuff online about King being shot … . I'd met him – at parties, the club – God, I was *so scared*, Ricky.'

But she hadn't seemed scared that day – she'd seemed *thrilled*. 'You said you wished you'd been there.'

He saw a flash of temper. 'You expect me to feel sorry for him? He was a pig.'

Sam clicked his tongue. 'Now you're contradicting yourself.'

She flushed, caught in another lie.

'You quizzed me on how King's death would affect Unwin's prosecution,' Rick said. 'Did you know they were listening to us, Jess? Is that why you kept asking me those questions about the trial?'

She bowed her head again.

Another snatch of the conversation came back to him. Why had she been so keen for him to confide in Jim Stott? Was it so that Jim could pass on information to Unwin?

'You know,' Sam said, 'I've been wondering why Unwin put you up in such luxury when he might as easily have kept you in a warehouse – or one of his massage parlours, maybe.' He cocked his head, considering. 'But he *is* known to pander to his wife's little fancies – I'll bet he'd go easily as far for his mistress.'

Jess's head came up, her eyes wide with alarm. 'No!' She nursed her injured hand. 'Look what they *did* to me!'

'Oh, I'm sure he thought twice about it, but he *badly* needs to get out,' Sam said. 'And give him his due – he didn't mark that lovely face.'

'Jesus.' Rick stared at her aghast. 'Was *everything* a lie?'

She shook her head, choking and hiccupping. 'No . . . No, Rick.' She looked across at him, her face tear-stained, her eyes swollen from crying. 'I genuinely fell for you.' Her lips twisted into a smile made grotesque by her mixed emotions. 'How could I not?'

Sam was watching her with a complex blend of amusement and contempt.

Rick moved to sit next to his brother, and she reached out to him with her injured hand. 'You believe me, don't you, babe?'

'No,' he said, thinking he should feel more. 'It's quite a performance, but no. And even if I did, you betrayed me, Jess. I could never trust you again.'

For the first time, she looked truly afraid.

Sam tapped the driver on the shoulder and Lawrence removed his headphones. 'You can drop us at the car,' he said.

Lawrence drove out from the maze of narrow streets he'd been cruising for the past ten minutes, onto Kensington High Street, headed west for a couple of blocks, then ducked left again, parking up in a residential street. The door slid open, and a man and a woman climbed inside.

Rick recognised the nondescript couple from Bear & Staff who'd sat quietly by one of the windows eating their meals and discussing bus tours during his last meeting with Dave Collins.

The woman smiled; the man did not.

'She's all yours,' Sam said, picking up his baseball cap, ready to leave.

Jess gasped.

'Wait a minute,' Rick said. 'Sam – you can't—'

Sam nodded to the man who had just entered, and he slid the door closed again.

'They'll keep her incognito until it's safe to release her,' Sam said. 'She will not be harmed' – he glanced at Jess – '*if* she cooperates.'

'Will you?' Rick asked her. 'Cooperate, I mean?'

'You bastard,' she spat. 'You and your sanctimonious creed: "Follow the rules", "do the right thing". It's all front. You don't *feel* it.' She was yelling now. 'You use the law as a surrogate for your conscience, because, you know what? You don't *have* one, Rick. You broke your *rules* a hundred times over the last few days. You broke a *thousand* more building this case you're so obsessed with. You saw *him* stab a man to death and you did nothing, you *fucking* hypocrite.'

'*Enough.*' The threat in that one word from Sam silenced her in an instant. He looked at the man and woman in turn. 'If she's any trouble, handcuff her. If she raises her voice, gag her.' Then, looking at Jess, he said, 'You're fortunate. It's Rick's decision that you're unharmed. *I* am not so forgiving.' He stared at her till she shrank from him. 'Your safety is contingent on your cooperation. Are we clear?'

She nodded meekly, avoiding his eye, but as Rick stood, she caught his arm.

Rick eyed her coldly until she dropped her hand. 'You should disappear, after they let you go,' he said. 'Unwin will probably think that you let me know where to find you.'

'Oh, I'll make sure he does,' Sam said, sliding the door open to let Rick out first. 'By the time I've finished, Unwin will be convinced that Jess ruined his chances of freedom.' He gave a little mock shiver of excitement. 'Won't he be *thrilled*?'

Chapter 45

NEITHER BROTHER SPOKE ON THE SHORT trip to the hotel.

Inside the room, Sam removed the holster from his waistband and placed it on the coffee table, then began packing the few possessions he'd brought with him.

Rick leaned against the door and watched him.

'So,' Sam said at last, 'you told her.'

'I did.'

'Do you think she told Unwin?'

'It's possible.' Rick paused; now was the time for complete honesty. 'And if she didn't, I've no way of knowing how long ago the audio devices were planted at the house.'

'Okay.' Sam seemed to accept the fact without rancour. 'Have you decided what you'll do – about work, I mean?'

'I haven't even decided what I'll do in the next few *hours*,' Rick said. 'It's five-forty, I'm due in Kildoran's chambers at eight o'clock, and I don't know if I have the gall to stand up in front of a jury and tell them I'm there to uphold the law.'

'Don't overthink it, Rick. You did what you had to in order to prevent a criminal from perverting the course of justice.'

Rick ran a hand over his face. 'A man died, Sam.'

Sam's eyebrows twitched. 'He was doing his damnedest to kill *you*.'

Rick nodded. 'But you told me to leave Norland to you, and you were right – I went in angry, and would have lost the fight, if . . .'

'I read somewhere that we humans make around thirty-five *thousand* decisions in a day – you're allowed to make the occasional bad one,' Sam said.

'Please, Sam, don't joke about it; I screwed up, and a man lost his life.'

'Well,' Sam said, 'rather him than you.' He stared at Rick for a few seconds before going on in a more serious vein. 'Don't allow the what-ifs in life to paralyse you, Rick.'

Rick had to see the logic in that, but he couldn't help saying, 'It still doesn't sit right, covering up his death.'

'If you reported it, do you think Jess would back up your story?'

Rick hung his head.

'Let me know when you've made your decision,' Sam said. 'But it'd be a pity to let Unwin get away free and clear after all this. I'll keep the burner for a few more days in case you need to contact me. If you need money or a place to stay, I can help.'

Rick nodded his thanks. 'How will I know that you've released Jess?'

That earned him a sharp look.

'I expect she'll call you. But I sincerely hope you won't consider letting her back into your life.'

'I meant what I said, Sam.'

'Good.' Sam frowned and Rick could see that he wasn't sure if he should say what was on his mind. Finally, he took a breath: 'You know what she is, don't you?'

'I know the label,' Rick said. He had read a thing or two about psychopaths over the years, trying to understand his brother. 'But I wouldn't have believed it of her until thirty minutes ago.'

'I'm sorry, Rick,' Sam said. 'Truly I am.'

Sam went to the bathroom, leaving the pistol on the coffee table.

Rick stared at it for some moments, undecided. Sam had helped him get out of this terrible mess and saved his life into the bargain. But on the drive back, he'd been taking stock, and flashes of Haskins's body kept coming back to him, the man's arm artfully draped over the edge of the bath. And Austin King – Sam had come back into his life just hours after King was found shot dead, and although Sam had made one of his conversational evasive manoeuvres, he hadn't exactly denied the murder. He'd described his job as 'fixer', and that moniker had a special significance in Rick's investigations. It had been cowardly to shy away from asking outright if Sam had killed those men. He wasn't exactly blameless, himself: *could* he go back to work after what he'd done – suspecting what Sam had done? What of Norton – and the man Sam had slaughtered without hesitation thirteen years ago?

He picked the weapon up, still unsure.

Coming out of the bathroom, seeing the gun in his hand, Sam looked so sad, so *lonely* that Rick almost changed his mind, despite the years he'd spent watching his parents in despair, despite the constant nightmares he'd suffered, revisiting the murder he'd witnessed. But in the end, what hardened his resolve was remembering widows like Mrs Wilson, and angry, bewildered children like little Ethan, left to struggle after Sam and men of his ilk 'fixed' situations for the Unwins of the world.

'Sit down, Sam,' he said, stepping away until his brother was seated.

'I haven't told you how we got Unwin on conspiracy to murder Charlie Haskins,' Rick said.

'Oh, I'm fascinated by the body in the bath,' Sam said. 'You really don't need a gun to make me listen to that tale.'

'Mrs Yalman literally handed me the evidence of Unwin's involvement in Kirk Wilson's murder,' Rick said. 'But there was nothing about a hit on Charlie Haskins in the bank documents. Why would there be? Haskins was Unwin's financial adviser.

Killing him was a business decision on Unwin's part – punishment for stealing from him.'

Sam sat quietly, but Rick knew he would be ready to pounce the moment he let his guard down.

'Then I noticed the term "bulletproof" repeated in some of the emails between the bank CEO, Unwin and King – one internal memo referred to "BulletProof" like it was a nickname. Mrs Yalman said it was what Hugenot called Thomas Unwin, and that got me thinking. You've heard of EncroChat?'

Sam gave him a wry smile. 'It's an encrypted phone messaging app favoured by criminals across Europe – a kind of *anti*social media platform. It got hacked by the law, ironically. Dutch and French police installed malware and gained access to messages even before they were sent. After EncroChat was hacked, catching criminals became a lucky dip for law enforcement agencies.'

'To be fair, some of them as good as sent out invitations,' Rick said. 'Taking selfies, sharing birthday snaps, pictures of their new cars.'

'Astonishing, isn't it,' Sam said. 'Why use an encrypted network, code names, VPNs, and then share personal information on it?'

'They think they're invisible,' Rick said, with enough emphasis to warn Sam that he had no need to feel smug. 'Since you're so clued up, you'll know that when EncroChat was put out of business, others sprang up. WireChat, for instance. But – you've guessed it – WireChat has also been infiltrated.'

Sam remained self-consciously blasé, but Rick sensed a heighted tension.

'About a week before Haskins was murdered, someone calling himself BulletProof contacted an assassin. BulletProof offered twenty-five K for Haskins's "eradication".

'We found the text on one of Unwin's burner phones – he hadn't even bothered to delete it. Oh, and another text on his phone had an image attached of Haskins, dead in the hotel bath. Collins found a payment for the *exact* amount transferred from one of Unwin's shell companies, minutes after that image was sent. Would you like to know the hired assassin's code name?'

'I'm agog.'

'He goes by "The Fixer".'

'So you had Mr Unwin bang to rights,' Sam said, as though "the Fixer" meant nothing to him. 'And the hit man?' he asked.

'Well, you tell me, Sam.'

'I really don't think there's anything I *can* tell you.'

'We already know the Fixer murdered Haskins,' Rick said. 'If I asked Collins to pull up WireChat messages addressed to the Fixer, d'you think he'd find King's name? Or Saidi's?'

'I don't know, Rick. What do *you* think?'

'I think I should take you in,' Rick said.

'No,' Sam said. 'You shouldn't.'

'You've as good as admitted to the murders of Charlie Haskins and Austin King.'

'I made a few astute observations.'

'We have a witness who saw you at King's hotel.'

Sam's eyes hardened. 'Reliable, are they? I mean, did they get a good look at this *assassin*?'

He knows damned well that the gunman who shot Austin King stood behind the waiter.

'What did this shooter sound like?' Sam persisted, dropping the plummy English tones and reverting to cockney vowels. Rick understood the message: Sam was a chameleon; if they put him in a line-up, he would look nothing like the portly, middle-aged man the waiter had encountered, and if they made him say a few words, he would make sure he sounded like a London cab driver.

'Get any CCTV of him? Or maybe your tech ninja traced the payment – I mean, where did it go after it was paid out from Unwin's shell company?' Sam's good humour seemed restored – he might even be having fun.

After first contact, the assassin had directed Unwin to a

chatroom routed through a VPN on an encrypted browser. The money was untraceable; in fact, they didn't even have an idea *how* the killer was paid.

'You were always the Fixer,' Rick said stubbornly refusing to admit defeat.

'Oh, Rick, that's lame – I was also Bam-Bam Sam, Chauffeur Sam, Samuel Turner, business associate and *Mister* Turner, antiques collector by proxy for Theo Lockleigh.' He smiled at the memory and even sank back onto the sofa. 'Have you ever been to Sotheby's on a sale day? It's pure theatre – magnificent!' He folded his hands in his lap and said in a kinder tone, 'Fixer is a generic term – like "gaffer" or "roadie".'

That was Sam all over: an answer for everything.

'Of course, you *might* say that you saw me shoot Norland, but that would put you at the scene. I, however, was never there. I have thirty people who will swear I was hosting a wine tasting in Fleet Street until one-thirty a.m. and remained chatting with two dear friends until . . . let's say, four-fifty.' He mulled for a moment. 'Yes, that should do it.'

'You can do that?' Rick said. 'Pluck an alibi out of thin air?'

'Haven't you been paying attention these last few days? "Hope for the best, prepare for the worst",' Sam said, quoting himself. 'And FYI, that alibi took over twenty-four hours to finesse – I knew it would have to stand up to close scrutiny.'

'Smug bastard. You had this planned from the start.'

'I told you, Rick – you trust too easily. I, on the other hand . . .' He lifted one shoulder and let it fall.

Rick brought his left hand up to support his gun hand.

'Norland is gone,' Sam went on. 'No one will be surprised that he moved on – he was a waster, and no one will miss him. The apartment was deep-cleaned before my crew left, so there will be no forensic evidence of him there, either.'

'What about the man you stabbed – d'you think you can you make him go away, too? Maybe I can't prove the others, but that's one body you didn't "disappear". You were seen running from the scene with blood on your hands, Sam.'

Sam tilted his head. 'I was, but did anyone report what they'd seen to the police?'

'There was a post-mortem, an inquest – there'll be evidence under lock and key somewhere – there was a lot of blood, you'll recall.'

Sam's eyes darkened. 'Trust me, Rick, you don't want to go down that path.'

It didn't sound like a threat; in fact, he looked more sorrowful than angry. A sudden sigh seemed to release all the tension from his body. 'What were you even *doing* there that day, Rick?'

'Looking for you,' Rick said. 'When you grassed up Theo Lockleigh, I knew you'd be offered witness protection. But that wouldn't be good enough for you, would it?'

'I know a lot about the crummy accommodation reserved for your brave star witness,' Sam said with a rueful grin. 'I *lived* in it – or something just like it.'

Rick lifted his chin, absurdly pleased that he'd read his opaque brother right: he'd never intended to stand up in court and testify against his former boss.

'But what made you think I'd go back to the flat?' Sam asked.

'I got to wondering why you kept the old place on when you moved us out to Putney. I mean, you could've kept an eye on the estate by paying a few spies, or by sitting in your car to watch the goings-on. You could even have walked around the place openly, like the cocky bastard you were. But you kept the flat. Even after Lockleigh was arrested you *still* kept it on. The police came looking for you in Putney, after you gave them the slip. I reckoned you'd want to get out fast, and in style. To do that, you'd need cash. You were always good at planning, Sam – you had to have money stashed somewhere, and the old flat was the obvious choice.'

'Nicely reasoned.'

Rick nailed him with a look. 'It's my job.'

'It wasn't your job back then,' Sam observed. 'You were fifteen years old.'

'Well, I'm not now, so don't bloody patronise me. D'you remember that time Dad had a go at you – said you'd spend the best part of your life in prison?'

He saw from the withdrawal of eye contact, the bitter smile, that Sam remembered it well.

'I *begged* you to stop.' Rick had been too young, then, to know that people like Sam never stop until they're made to. 'You said, "Never gonna happen, Rick."'

Sam nodded, his face lit with a softer glow of reverie.

'Plan A was not to get caught, and when inevitably you *were*, plan B was not to *stay* caught. And if that meant giving up Lockleigh, so be it.'

'What was I supposed to do?' Sam asked. 'Go to prison for *Lockleigh*? The man was a menace to society.'

Rick couldn't tell if he was joking.

'But you worked out where to find me, picked up my old baseball bat and took a stroll down to the old gaff,' Sam went on. 'How long did you keep watch?'

'Five days.'

Sam clapped his hands delightedly. 'I was your first stakeout!'

'Yeah, well, I wasn't the only one staking the place out, was I?'

'No,' Sam said, serious again. 'That was an error on my part.'

Lockleigh had eyes everywhere. Tenement looked onto tenement, landings looked down on landings, and the scruffy square of concrete below was visible to every tenant in the block. Motivated by the price on Sam Turner's head, the jackals on the estate had kept watch night and day.

'They must have seen you coming from half a mile away,' Rick said.

'Yet *you* managed to evade Lockleigh's boyos.' Sam appeared to have forgotten the gun pointed at him. 'That's always puzzled me – did you have help?'

'Who was going to help me? I had no friends there, Sam,' Rick said. 'I spent my first ten years hiding in the shadows.' He might have added that it was only after Sam had taught him some street moves that he'd been able to step out of their home unafraid.

'I didn't mean to make it so tough for you, Rick.'

Sam seemed genuinely regretful – not for what he'd done, but for the effect it'd had on Rick and their mother. Sam had always known right from wrong, but – what was it that Jess had said? – he just didn't *feel* it. For Sam, there was no shame in being found out – no pain in the acceptance of guilt – and he would do just about anything to avoid punishment. That was why Sam killed the man in their flat that day. He'd done it calmly, with cold, calculating accuracy and no compunction. None at all.

Sam roused himself as though Rick had spoken his thoughts aloud: 'You saved my life that day. You do know that don't you?'

An image flashed before Rick's eyes of Sam poised with the knife over the unconscious man's chest. He heard again the faint hiss of the blade slicing through flesh, the sickening crunch when it hit cartilage and bone, the boards beneath. The horrible sucking sound as Sam withdrew the knife from the man's chest.

He remembered yelling, 'What are you *doing*?'

And Sam – tense, but controlled – saying, 'Giving us time.'

Looking at his brother thirteen years on, Rick saw that same tense alertness. The gun's weight was beginning to strain the muscles of his shoulders and forearms, but Rick steadied himself.

'You didn't have to kill him, Sam,' he said. 'I'd laid that poor bastard out cold – he couldn't hurt us. But you checked his pulse and then you *stabbed* him.'

'Yes,' Sam said, 'I checked. Yes, I stabbed him. But do you remember the CPR?'

Rick remembered every detail. And of all the awful things he saw that day, the CPR was the worst. Sam, his fingers laced one hand over the other, both palms down, compressing the man's chest like a seasoned medic.

'Go home,' he'd said. 'Stay out of sight.'

Rick was frantic. 'No. I have to call the police.' He'd fumbled his mobile from his pocket, but Sam slapped it out of his hands.

'Don't be a moron, Rick.' He'd snatched Rick's phone up with his bloody hand and pocketed it, then took up where he'd left off.

'What's done is done,' he'd said, punctuating each word with a chest compression. 'Involving the police won't help anyone.'

Rick wanted to shout, 'Stop – you're making it worse!' but he couldn't speak. He couldn't take his eyes off the blood leaking through Sam's fingers, spurting at first, then diminishing. All the time, Sam had issued a steady stream of instructions, keeping up the pumping action of his hands.

'The police will come looking for me. Tell them you don't know where I am. Tell them you know nothing – because you *saw* nothing. You weren't even *here*.'

And Rick had stood there like an idiot, watching his brother squeeze the life blood out of an unconscious man. The memory kept him awake at nights, roused him, sweating and fearful in the small hours, tormenting him with guilt.

'Are you asking me to believe you did CPR to *revive* him?' Rick said. 'You think I'm that gullible?'

'No,' Sam said, his eyes on Rick. 'No, he was definitely dead.'

Rick couldn't make sense of it. 'Then why—'

'The gun you have in your hand is linked to other gangland murders,' Sam interrupted. 'If you bring me in, you will have to surrender the weapon.'

He's doing it again – changing the subject – trying to stop me from thinking about what really happened. There's something I should know, and he doesn't want me to know it.

Sam went on: 'I do *not* want my name linked to those killings. Believe me when I say, if you send me to prison, I won't last a week.' He gave Rick a sad, self-mocking smile. 'You see, I swim with sharks, too, little bruv.'

Rick faltered. *Do you really want to send Sam to certain death? He saved your life – your career, if you still want it.* This was his own voice – not Sam's, or his parents' – and it scared Rick a little to know that he would so easily deny the law and reshape the rules to his own purpose.

'Come on, Rick,' Sam coaxed. 'What's done is done.'

Rick had a sudden dizzying flash of recognition. Catapulted back for the thousandth time to that horrible day, Rick recalled Sam placing his fingers on the man's sternum, feeling the ribs on the left side, counting audibly, 'One, two, three . . .' Finding the exact position of the heart before he'd slid the knife in with cold precision. God, that blade was so sharp!

'What's done is done,' Sam had said. Then: 'I can fix this.'

Rick's stomach clenched and he felt a wave of sweat from his head to his chest – cold, clammy and debilitating. The CPR made no *sense*. The ground seemed to fall away, and it felt like he was teetering on a dark and dangerous cliff edge.

'He was dead before you cut him, wasn't he?' Rick gasped.

The realisation struck him with such physical force that the gun was suddenly too heavy to hold. He slid the safety catch on and laid it on the table. It rattled with the tremor of his hand.

'It was me,' Rick whispered. 'I thought I'd knocked him out, but I killed him.' He stared, horrified, into Sam's face. 'The CPR was to make him bleed, to make it *look* like he was still alive when the knife went in.'

Sam 'the Fixer' had been fixing the situation for Rick, not for himself.

'Rick, don't do this to yourself,' Sam said.

But a second startling realisation jolted Rick. 'You made sure you were seen, didn't you?'

Sam looked away. 'It doesn't matter. It's history.'

'Why, Sam? All these years I thought you'd killed him in cold blood. Why did you take the blame?'

For a few long seconds it seemed that Sam wouldn't answer, then he sighed. 'You walked through that den of wolves with nothing but a baseball bat to defend yourself. My kid brother who never wanted to hurt anyone. You wouldn't even have *been* there if weren't for me.'

'Don't try to make me sound like a hero,' Rick said. 'I piled in on that poor mug because he made me feel like a useless kid – hit him harder than I needed to because I felt humiliated.'

Sam shook his head. 'You saved my life. Look—' He dragged his shirt from the waistband of his trousers and showed Rick a neat, four-inch scar.

'He stabbed you?'

Sam tucked in his shirt. 'I was already weakening when you showed up.'

'But I'm the one who killed him – I should've—'

'You stopped him from killing *me*. And if you hadn't stopped him, he'd have finished the job – maybe gone after you, too.'

'But I've blamed you for *thirteen years*,' Rick said, overwhelmed by the injustice of it.

'I had to get out,' Sam said. 'And I knew I wouldn't be coming back – not while Lockleigh was alive. I *wanted* you to believe I'd killed him. I could live with your contempt, Rick, but I couldn't have forgiven myself if I'd let you turn yourself in.'

The pain and grief over the death of his parents, Jess's and Jim Stott's betrayals, the fear and exhaustion of the last few days, descended on Rick like a crushing weight, but more devastating was the sense of loss. All those lonely, terrible years he had obsessively sought out his brother in the faces of dead men; had despised Sam when he should be thanking him.

As Rick stared, Sam doubled and trebled, his image fracturing, blurring, and Rick's chest constricted till he couldn't breathe. His legs began to buckle, and Sam was suddenly on his feet, gripping his shoulders, holding him up.

'It's all right,' Sam said. 'It's okay.'

Rick bent his head, ashamed of the years of unwarranted rage against his brother, embarrassed by his tears, and Sam pulled him into a hug. 'I saved your future, but you saved my *life*,' he said, with a fierceness that only imperfectly masked his own emotion.

Chapter 46

Wednesday, 9 a.m., the Old Bailey: day 3 of trial

STANDING AT THE OPEN DOOR of his boss's holding cell at the Old Bailey, Callum Mounsey remarked that Mr Unwin seemed relaxed, almost happy. He sat at ease in the narrow alcove that served as a seat, his eyes sparkling with suppressed glee.

'So this is it, then. He's up first.'

'Indeed.' Mounsey tried a smile, but the muscles of his face went into a kind of spasm, and he had to cover his mouth.

'What?'

With that one word, a darkness seemed to gather in the room and all gaiety fled.

'A . . . situation has arisen.'

Unwin's gaze did not waver, and for the first time in their long association, Mounsey felt in physical danger from his employer. Nevertheless, he stepped inside the cell and eased the door to.

'I had some difficulty raising the um . . . *custodians* this morning.' He thought it wise to say nothing about the increasingly frantic nature of his attempts to make contact.

Unwin's glare could have burned through concrete.

'I sent someone to the apartment; the key didn't work, so he rang the bell.' He cleared his throat. 'The door was answered by "a big, angry Russian" – I'm quoting.'

Unwin blinked involuntarily. 'The Russians know I used their gaff?'

'It would seem so,' Mounsey managed.

'Fuck.'

Mounsey watched his boss's chest rise and fall, rise and fall.

'The girl?'

'No sign.'

'Her mobile?'

'Switched off or gone entirely.'

'And the crew?'

Mounsey shook his head.

'What about your court security guy?'

'Didn't show up for work this morning.'

'So . . . Are we thinking they moved her?'

Mounsey stared back at him, marvelling at Unwin's self-control, but not underestimating for an instant the danger if Unwin reached flash point. 'It looks likely,' he said. 'Do you want me to reach out to th-the owner?' He heard his slight stumble, and knew that Mr Unwin would too, but even in the closed quarters of the holding cell, he would not say Popov's name – a Russian vory whose power extended across national boundaries and continental divides.

'No,' Unwin said. 'No contact. Wait for him to make the first move. As far as Turner's concerned, we've still got her.' He nodded to himself. 'We go with the original plan.'

He hesitated, and Mounsey was surprised to read an unfamiliar uncertainty in the man. It was quickly subdued. 'He's prepped?'

'Yes. Rehearsed like a good boy,' Mounsey said, on firmer ground, here. 'From what I heard of his run-through, he will practically admit to fabricating evidence. He got an early night, didn't stir till six this morning, and has been with prosecuting counsel since eight o'clock.'

'All right,' Unwin said. 'All right. If the lads got out safely, they might have the girl stashed somewhere. And if Russians have her, they'll be in touch. I need to know which it is, so I know how to handle Turner. Get one of your staff to find out if the lads are still operative. And find out if she was moved – street cams should help.'

Mounsey didn't have the nerve to tell Mr Unwin there were no street cams in Kensington Walk. He would ask his police contact about getting access to smart doorbells, see if they would yield anything useful.

'I'll see to it,' he said. 'Anything else?'

'Nah. I'll deal with the rest when I'm out.'

When I'm out. Mounsey couldn't help but admire the man's irrepressible optimism.

A guard tapped at the door. 'You're up, Unwin,' he said.

The courtroom was filled to capacity. Unwin sat in the dock, a square, panelled box high above the narrow table that accommodated both the prosecution barrister and his own defence team and ran at right angles to the judge's bench. The dark wood panelling and green leather upholstery added to the air of gloomy solemnity.

Unwin glanced at the twelve jurors, then allowed himself a moment to take in the spectators squeezed into rows to their right and above, in the gallery. Minutes later, the prosecution barrister called his first witness of the day: Detective Sergeant Richard Turner. This was the moment Unwin had been waiting for. He heard a rustle from the reporters crammed into the benches behind him. He knew that some of them would have a restricted view. He, on the other hand, was practically at eye level with the judge, and he had full command of the raised double row of seats that housed the jury to his left as well as the witness box tucked in the corner between the jury and the judge's bench.

He watched Rick Turner make his way to the witness box. He looked gaunt and nervous -- and was that a bruise on his right temple? Unwin leaned forward and coughed, trying to attract his attention, but Turner avoided eye contact and Unwin had to suppress a smile, noticing that the detective's hand was shaking as he raised it to take the oath. Then Turner lowered his right hand and looked directly at him.

What Unwin saw in the young sergeant's eyes cut him to the bone.

Chapter 47

'THINGS ARE LOOKING UP FOR YOU, LASER.'

Pavel Lasovsky has been enjoying the luxury of a snooze, knowing that it will not be interrupted by Thomas Unwin. But Unwin will be back in time for dinner and the respite will be short, so he can't see how things could possibly be looking up.

He peers up at the screw. 'How is that, Boss?'

'You got a visitor – a lady – a real looker, by all accounts.'

Lasovsky raises himself to one elbow.

The screw snorts a laugh. 'Don't get too excited – it's your sister.'

Laser has only brothers in his family, and anyway, he hasn't filled out a visiting order form since he was locked up, which means this visit has been arranged by someone with money and influence. Someone high up wants something from him. Well, maybe he can get something in return. Sharing a cell with Thomas Unwin has been a living hell; maybe the someone who arranged this visit can organise a change of cellmate.

Besides, he has been in prison for almost a year and has craved the gentle solace of a woman's company for so long that it feels like a dull ache in his heart. He swings off the bed and straightens his sweatshirt over his jogging bottoms. There is a hole at the neckband, but he knows that this screw won't wait for him to change into his one neat shirt, so he jams his feet into his trainers and checks his hair in the clouded metal surface of the wall mirror before hurrying out of the cell.

His 'sister' waves from across the hall and his stomach flips; it is like sunshine has pierced the plexiglass windows and brought colour into the room.

She is a brunette, which is his preference, dressed in a creamy-white coat, open at her creamy-white throat. The dirt in this sordid place doesn't seem to touch her. He revels in the admiring, envious, *hungry* looks from other inmates as he walks towards the woman. She's so clean she *glows*.

She embraces him, and the shock of physical contact feels like an electrical jolt. She whispers to him in his own language, and he's flooded with such sudden emotion and gratitude, it makes him want to cry. He is acutely aware of the shabby prison-issue jogging pants and his ragged sweatshirt, which is baggy on his spare frame and so long that he has to turn the cuffs back, like a child in a borrowed uniform. But she doesn't seem to notice.

She sits and smiles, looking into his eyes and telling him exactly what he wants to hear. For ten minutes they talk, and he feasts his eyes on her, watching her pretty lips shape the words of his homeland. She smells like roses and fresh air; her hair is glossy and soft, and he has to press his hands flat against the table to stop himself from reaching out to touch it.

As she leaves, she embraces him a second time, briefly – a chaste, sisterly kiss – then circles her long fingers around his skinny wrist and gives it a friendly shake. He keeps his head down leaving the hall, doesn't look back, doesn't respond to the sly comments of the screw who escorts him to his cell, or the wolf whistles of the men who've heard that Laser's visitor was a stunner. He doesn't even look up as the cell door slams shut and is locked. Even then, he sits with his hands between his knees, feeling the woman's kiss as a tingle below his right cheekbone.

He waits until he's sure that the screw has walked away, then he takes the few steps to the tiled area at the end of the cell. Here, trembling, he crouches behind the panel before turning down the cuff of his sweatshirt to retrieve a small, folded sachet.

Chapter 48

Wednesday, late afternoon

RICK GAVE TESTIMONY FOR NEARLY THREE HOURS before lunch and another two after. Kildoran was delighted. Drawing him to one side after the judge closed the session, he told Rick that the jury loved him, assuring him that another morning – at most a day – in the witness box should complete his part in the proceedings. Rick had never seen the lawyer so elated, and it pained him to put a damper on this high point in the trial, but he had to warn Kildoran that he might not be able to trust everyone on his staff.

Kildoran was too experienced a barrister to let it show in his face, but Rick saw a stillness settle on the man's shoulders.

'That's a serious allegation, Sergeant,' he said quietly.

'*Allegation* is putting it a bit strong,' Rick said. 'I have no clear evidence. But the defendant's brief apparently knew I was on the slate for today before I did.'

'And you know this because . . .?'

'He told me.'

One bald eyebrow hitched. 'He approached you?'

And then some, Rick thought, but he let Kildoran draw his own conclusions from his steady gaze.

The lawyer loosened his stance and smiled, but Rick knew that he was taking in every one of his pupils and interns as they cleared away the day's papers and tidied up the detritus of coffee cups and lunch wrappers.

'Do you have any idea who?'

'Sorry, no,' Rick said, then: 'Do you?'

'I might,' he said. Anyone watching them would be forgiven for assuming they were exchanging a few self-congratulatory words, but Rick was close enough to see the hard look in the man's eyes. 'As for Callum Mounsey – he has a reputation for trying to rattle the opposition, and this isn't the first time he's been implicated in an attempt to pervert the course of justice. But he's a slippery little Essex eel; keeps slithering off the line every time.'

'I'm particularly concerned about Mrs Yalman's safety,' Rick said. 'I'll talk to my boss, but—'

'I'll take care of this end.' Kildoran offered Rick his hand and raised his voice for the benefit of the others, even inserting a chuckle of laughter: 'Now, for God's sake, go home and get some rest – you look like you need it.'

Rick went next to Hammersmith, where he was congratulated warmly by Detective Superintendent Ghosh, and with less enthusiasm by DCI Steiner. He told them about the possible breach in security, leaving them to work out that the leak could just as easily have come from their own team. Ghosh said that any future decisions on the witnesses should be kept between Kildoran on the one hand and the three of them on the other. Ghosh would deal direct with the team providing protection for Mrs Yalman.

As he and Steiner headed out, he called Rick back. Steiner shot him a resentful glance, and Ghosh made a point of asking Rick to close the door.

'Do you think the leak has come from Kildoran's chambers?' he asked.

'I couldn't say, sir,' Rick said, wondering why he hadn't asked the question with Steiner in the room.

Ghosh glanced at the door. 'Well, for now, I want you to report to me first – I'll decide how much you can tell DCI Steiner.'

'Um . . .'

'I know – I'm putting you in a tricky position, Rick. But until we're sure it hasn't come from here, I think we need to be extra careful.'

Rick could tell him right now that Jim Stott was probably on the take, and he should tell his boss about the ship, currently stuck in Jersey with millions of pounds' worth of stolen and illegally imported rare earth metals on board. But he wasn't sure that Ghosh could be trusted, either. Dave Collins had done the bulk of his sleuthing about Coutanche on the dark web, and Rick needed to find a way to persuade the authorities to search the ship without implicating Collins or placing him in danger.

Back at his desk, he got a text on the burner from his brother:

—Congrats – glad you saw sense.

Rick suspected that Sam would continue to be the voice in his head, speaking up from time to time when he needed Sam's worldly-wise perspective. But future advice from his revised superego would likely speak with the rounded tones of an Oxbridge graduate.

A moment later, the phone buzzed a second time. Sam again:

—Sorry, couldn't resist. That image I showed you – the 'something' you said you'd deal with later? He slept in his car last night.

Jim Stott is sleeping in his car?

Stott came through the door of the Incident Room at that very moment.

'Ricky boy! I hear congratulations are in order,' Stott said, and although he was smiling, it didn't reach his eyes. 'That's gotta be worth a jar or two, right?' Stott added, looking almost wistful.

He looks anxious, Rick thought. He shelved the idea of travelling a few stops along the Piccadilly line to see Dave Collins; now might be a good time to have that talk with his old mentor.

Ten minutes later they were in a bar on Shepherd's Bush Road. Stott insisted on buying, and came back to their table with two pints, despite Rick having asked for a half. Stott downed a third of his pint before setting the glass on a coaster and adjusting it just so.

'How're you doing, son?' he asked.

Rick gave him a sharp look at the use of 'son', and Stott laughed nervously.

'I only ask because it must have been a stressful week – it can't have been easy, facing Unwin down.'

Rick took a sip of beer. 'I presented the evidence, Stotty. I don't see that as facing him down.'

'No, but—'

Rick cocked his head, ready to listen to a clarification, but it seemed that Stott didn't have anything to add.

Stott gave a humourless chuckle, realising that his glass was already empty, and hauled himself out of his chair to order another round. When he returned a few minutes later, he was carrying two more pints, and Rick guessed by his high colour that he'd had a couple of shots to fortify himself at the bar.

Rick reached into his jacket pocket for his wallet.

'Put your money away. I told you – these are on me,' Stott said, setting the drinks down. 'How's Jess – all right, is she?' He sipped his pint, but Rick saw the sly, sideways glance.

'Been meaning to ask you about that,' Rick said.

'About what?'

'You, being so in the know about Jess – about her being an actor – stuff like that. Seeing as I haven't mentioned it to anyone.'

Stott took another swig of his beer – to steady his nerves, or to give himself time to think. 'I told you, I saw her on the telly.'

'Not on *Emmerdale* or *EastEnders*, you didn't.'

Stott licked the foam from his upper lip. 'One of the soaps, anyway – *Doctors*, maybe.'

'Taken to watching afternoon TV, have you, mate?'

Stott gave three, short, unconvincing coughs of laughter, 'Ha-ha-ha,' like a character in a cartoon. 'Nah,' he said. 'Maddie watches that stuff – records it when she's gotta go out.'

'How is Maddie?' Rick asked.

'Oh, you know Maddie – she's *fine*,' Stott said.

Rick heard a bitter note in the word 'fine'.

'Give her my love,' Rick said. 'If you see her.'

Stott was drunk, but he wasn't so far gone that he wouldn't hear the sarcasm in his tone. He glared at Rick over the dregs in his glass. 'What's that supposed to mean?'

Rick held his gaze. 'Well, with you dossing down in your car, I was thinking you might not see her at all.'

'*What?*'

'Maddie kicked you out, didn't she?'

'Rubbish! No. What makes you . . . Who told you that?' Stott stumbled over the denials.

'A source.' Rick took a five-by-four print from his wallet. 'You'd know all about sources, wouldn't you, Sarge?' He laid the photo on the table. It was the one Sam had shown him in the early hours: Mounsey, talking in a friendly manner to Jim Stott.

Stott lost colour so fast that Rick thought he might faint.

'It's not what you think, Rick.'

'I know what it is, Jim.' Rick placed one finger on the print and slid it across the table. 'And you know what you've got to do.'

Chapter 49

Wednesday evening, Unwin's prison cell, after lockup

LOCKED IN HIS CELL AFTER A DISASTROUS DAY in court, Unwin was feeling queasy. He had made up his mind to give Mounsey access to one of his bigger funds, get the shipment out of Jersey and into Southampton. He hated having to trust the little weasel, but he didn't have any other option, and he'd feel better once the money started to roll in.

As he retrieved his phone from its hiding place in the mattress it buzzed in his hand. For a giddy moment he thought it might be a good omen: he'd been on the point of ringing his lawyer and it was Mounsey himself on the line. He was quickly disappointed; Mounsey had called with bad news. Unwin listened, anger rising in him, churning his stomach till the acid reflux was like a sharp, painful stiletto, driven from his solar plexus to below his left ear, settling in as a throbbing pain at the angle of his jaw.

'So *Rick Turner* got Jess out,' he said.

'There's no way to be certain.'

'The Russians would've said something by now if they had her,' Unwin said. 'And given that Turner stitched me up like a kipper in court today, I'd say it was a fair bet,' Unwin interrupted. 'How the fuck did he do it?'

'I'm afraid I am entirely at a loss,' Mounsey said. 'I've been unable to raise the – ah – custodians, or Jessica.'

'What about CCTV?'

'A security firm's van pulled up outside the building at four-oh-two this morning. I'm sorry to say that its presence obscured a camera on the opposite side of the street. They left some twelve minutes later, and twenty minutes after that, a van marked "Warp Speed Cleaning Services" arrived.'

'A clean-up,' Unwin said, massaging the sensitive area at the join between his throat and his jaw.

Mounsey gave a noncommittal grunt. 'The cleaning service does not exist and, while the security firm does, they insist it was not one of their vans. Our police contact confirmed that the number plates were faked.'

'And *no one* saw *anything*?'

'Apparently one of the residents saw five individuals in white coveralls, masks and hoods, leaving the apartment at around six-thirty. They were carrying cleaning kit and what looked like hi-tech machinery. The gaffer said they'd had an infestation of moths, but it had been taken care of.'

Unwin took a quick peek at his cellmate, quivering behind the modesty panel that housed the toilet facilities. He had let the scrote know that he was in for a bad night as soon as he'd returned from the Old Bailey. Eyes shut and music blasting through the earphones into the narrow, empty space between his ears, Laser was on his best behaviour – hadn't budged an inch in the past ten minutes.

Satisfied that he would not be overheard, Unwin said, 'It's even more urgent that I get out – the Russians have a presence, here.'

'We've still got the other thing on Turner.' He meant the knowledge that Turner had watched his brother kill a man and had failed to report it. 'Go with that.'

'The admission happened before we had audio equipment in the house, so we don't have anything recorded,' Mounsey reminded him.

They had bugged the house hours after Turner had confessed to Jess, but although she had tried many times to get him to say more, he'd shied away from further discussion.

'We've got *her* on record; she signed a statement, didn't she?'

'Turner proved strongly resistant to the leverage we had over him when we had his girlfriend.' Mounsey sounded genuinely regretful, 'And without her to verify the statement, I'm afraid it would not be taken seriously – by him or his superiors – should you decide to take it that far.'

'Fuck. Fuck!' The chance of a lifetime – to move into the upper strata of his world, make real money and this *nobody* kept getting in his way. 'I swear, when I get out, I'll end that little fucker myself!'

Unwin sensed a movement on the floor of the cell and, looking over the edge of the bunk, he caught Lasovsky looking up. His eyes, too large in his emaciated skull, shone in the dim light filtering through the cell window.

'Don't look at me, you bleeding *turnip*,' Unwin commanded, and Laser flinched. 'Look away. NOW!'

Laser crossed his arms over his head, as though he expected blows to start raining down.

Unwin lay back on the bed. *God, my guts hurt.* 'I want her found,' he said, when he felt calmer.

'Mr Unwin, I'm sorry to say that may prove imposs—'

'*Don't*,' Unwin interrupted. 'Do *not* tell me that. Get your thumb out your arse and *do* something – I don't care what it takes. *Find* her.'

Mounsey didn't answer and for a second, Unwin thought the hissing in his ears must be a fault on the line. His arm started to cramp, and he switched the phone from his left hand to his right, opening and closing his fist to ease the tightening of his chest muscles.

It didn't help, and when he cursed softly, Mounsey spoke at last.

'Mr Unwin, are you quite well?'

'Do what I pay you for, Mounsey,' Unwin said, suddenly losing patience with the little man's strangulated voice. 'I want news of the girl by morning.'

He killed the call.

Without warning, he felt his heart crushed in his chest, his chest turned to stone. *Can't breathe. God, the pain!*

Laser sensed rather than saw the movement off to his right. *What the fuck?*

He crouched smaller. 'I'm not looking. I'm not looking!' he yelled. '*Please*, I didn't look at you!'

Suddenly Unwin was coming at him. He felt the rush of air and opened his eyes soon enough to glimpse the man launch himself off the upper bunk. With a yell of terror, Laser scooted out from his corner of the stall as Unwin crashed to the floor, clutching his left bicep with his right hand, 'Need a doctor.'

Laser Lasovsky looked down at him.

'Laser . . .'

'Can't hear you, mate,' Lasovsky yelled over the music blasting through his earphones. 'Anways, I'm not even supposed to *look* at you, am I, so—?' He shrugged. 'But if I *was* to take a little cheeky peek, I'd say you was looking a little bit grey. Might even be having heart attack.'

'Help . . .'

Unwin reached for his ankle and Laser stepped back. '*Poshol tih*,' he spat. 'Screw you.'

Chapter 50

RICK BEGAN ROOTING OUT THE LISTENING DEVICES as soon as he got home. He considered frying them in the microwave, but in the end, he stamped on each of them and then packed them into a carrier bag, ready to dump them in a bin on his way to court the next day. That done, he started boxing up Jess's stuff ready for her to collect when Sam released her.

His stomach churned, recalling how badly he had misjudged his brother. All these years he'd thought Sam had fled his crime and abandoned his family. For thirteen years Rick had thought himself the moral one – had been so sure that he was the better man.

Even over the last few days, he'd told himself that he'd acted outside the rule of law only to save Jess. But thinking about it now, he realised that he'd had no serious qualms – only an uneasiness that breaking the rules had proved so easy. Maybe Sam was right – maybe they really were alike – both born with a broken moral compass. Sam might well be a psychopath, but it was part of a continuum, and Rick was beginning to wonder where he lay on the scale.

An hour later, he'd finished boxing up Jess's laptop, tablet, her headshots, cosmetics and costume jewellery, emptied the bathroom cabinet of anything remotely feminine, and bagged her jackets and coats from the hall cloakroom. Back in the bedroom, he fetched down a clutch of dresses from the wardrobe. With a stab of grief, he recognised the dress Jess had worn the night they'd met.

Feeling the shimmering silk in his hands, anger displaced the sorrow. Impulsively, he snatched up a bin bag and jammed the clothing, hangers and all, inside.

His phone buzzed in his trouser pocket and, ditching the bag, he took out the phone. It was Detective Superintendent Ghosh.

Frowning, Rick slid the icon to 'answer'.

'You're not driving are you, Rick?'

'No, sir,' Rick said, with a sinking feeling of dread – this must be serious.

'Bad news, I'm afraid. Unwin is dead.'

'*What*? When?'

'He was found collapsed in his cell, an hour after lockup,' Ghosh said. 'His cellmate, lying in his bed not two feet from the body, says he didn't hear a thing.'

'Do we know how?'

'Prison doc says a heart attack, but after King's assassination, I'm thinking the worst.'

Rick took a breath. 'What happens to the trial?'

'It'll be suspended initially, but ultimately it will be terminated.' Ghosh gave a growl of frustration. 'Sorry, Rick, this is a bloody nightmare. But we'll follow through on the other suspects – and we've a strong case for pushing the SFO to do more.'

Rick was thinking of Mrs Yalman, facing terrible fear and disruption to her life; after all she'd gone through, they owed her at least that much. His mind raced from her to Wilson's widow and her son, Ethan.

'Will it affect the hit-and-run prosecution?'

'No,' Ghosh said. 'That should be unaffected.'

'Has Kildoran been informed?'

300

'He's next on my list.'

'So – sorry, sir, it's the first time this has happened to me – do I turn up in court in the morning?'

'I was coming to that. Normally, the prosecutor would inform the judge of the death of a defendant in an active trial, and a death certificate would be sufficient proof, but this is an exceptional case, Rick. It's rarely done, but the Crown Court *can* require a police officer to identify the dead body as the defendant, and I think it would be a wise course of action. Would you be up for that?'

'Of course,' Rick said, still dazed. 'Just let me know where and when.'

'I'll ask the pathologist to contact you direct – he should be in touch this evening. He'll be able to give you more details about the exact circumstances if you've any further questions.'

Now would be a good time to mention the illicit shipment of rare earth metals sitting in a port in Jersey, but who to trust? He still couldn't decide if Ghosh was clean – hadn't he tried to block the original investigation into the two murders?

He did bring Dave Collins on board. This was Sam's voice in his head, and Rick countered with: *Yeah, but that was when he thought Collins was an idiot.*

He needed time to think, and he would not drag Dave into this without warning. It was only after he'd hung up that he realised that neither of them had mentioned DCI Steiner.

He speed-dialled the forensic accountant and got an empty line. For a moment, Rick thought the connection had dropped.

'Dave?' he said. 'Are you there?'

Collins let out a *whoosh* of air. 'God, I thought you'd – that they'd . . .'

'No, I'm fine—'

'Then why'd you ring my mobile?' Collins demanded. He sounded more jittery than angry.

'I thought it would be more private than the landline,' Rick said, rueful that some of Dave's paranoia had rubbed off – although on the basis of the past few days, maybe he should call it caution, rather than paranoia.

'Unwin's dead – possibly murdered.'

'Okay,' Collins said.

Rick had expected more. He couldn't work out if Collins was being cagey, or uncharacteristically laid-back.

'We need to talk,' he tried again. 'About the – other evidence.'

A silence, then, 'Still got that pay-as-you-go?' Collins wouldn't want to describe the mobile he'd given Rick as a 'burner'.

'Yeah.'

'I'll ring you in five.'

Rick raced downstairs and fished the phone out of his jacket. The bag of broken listening devices waiting for disposal at his front door caught his eye and he suffered a sudden qualm.

Sod it. He shrugged on his jacket and let himself out the back door. Standing in the middle of his lawn in the freezing cold, under a crescent moon, Rick picked up on the first buzz of the phone.

'You didn't seem surprised when I told you Unwin was dead,' he said.

'Yeah, well, that's 'cos something weird is going on with Coutanche,' Collins said. 'One of Unwin's shell companies I planned to follow up on after the trial has Marie-Louise Coutanche named as beneficial owner. Now, you know how that goes – she's not the *real* beneficial owner, but she signs the documents so money can get moved about. Anyway, I set up an algorithm to watch for activity, and I got a ping a few minutes ago. It just received a *humungous* wadge of money. The exact same sum went *out* of the company's coffers thirty seconds later.'

Rick's heart missed a beat.

'I can't trace where it went,' Collins continued, 'but I've got screen grabs of the amount on record – seven-point-five *milli*on – as well as the time in and out.'

'Is that enough to get the rare earths shipment moving?' Rick asked.

'Plenty.'

'Shit. It's happening,' Rick said.

'Yeah,' Collins said. 'So, what are you gonna do?'

'I don't know, Dave. If word gets to Coutanche Shipping that they're about to be raided, could they make a run for it?'

'The ship's been anchored offshore since the payment was delayed,' Collins said. 'If they get spooked, they could definitely ship out into international waters before Border Force can board it.'

'Bloody hell,' Rick murmured. 'I don't want to risk that, but *I* can't mobilise a Police and Border Force raid – I'd need someone much higher up the food chain – and the obvious choice would be Ghosh.'

'You don't trust him?'

'I don't *know* if I trust him.' Rick's explosion of breath fogged in the moonlight.

'Dude,' Collins said. 'Welcome to my world.'

'Well, nice as it is to "share", this isn't helping.' Rick winced as the words came out of his mouth – Collins was sensitive, and the sarcasm was uncalled for.

But the accountant surprised him again. 'When you trust no one, decisions are actually easier,' he said.

'Okay, I'll bite,' Rick said. 'Metaphor,' he added quickly, sensing Collins's confusion. 'I meant to say please explain.'

It took a second or two for Collins to unmuddle his thoughts, and perhaps banish the image of a ravening police sergeant with teeth bared, but he finally began: 'If trust is an issue, you go with facts and statistical chances, instead of the emotions and uncertainties. And there are things you can do to reduce the risks – if you don't mind hurting people's feelings,' he added.

Perversely, Rick suddenly felt on more solid ground. 'All right,' he said. 'Start with the facts.'

'So . . . the shipmaster has put in a request to dock, which means they must have some stuff to offload. The good news is it's much harder for a ship in dock to bugger off. There's a bit of a backlog right now, and being so late at night, they probably won't dock until tomorrow afternoon at the earliest. Which is also good.'

'So delay is good,' Rick said.

'It's also inevitable at this end,' Collins said. 'I need to put everything I've got under the radar onto the SFO databases before we tell anyone.'

'How soon could you do that?' Rick asked.

'If I head into work now, I could *maybe* have it done in time,' Collins said doubtfully. 'But if I get pulled off this to do other work—'

'Refer them to me,' Rick said. 'I'll think of something to hold them off.'

'Do I tell them Unwin's dead?'

Rick thought about it. 'Only if you have to – the less people know, the better.'

'All right,' Collins said. 'I'll make a start. But every query I raise on the system, every data set I enter could set off alarm bells for whoever's watching.'

The picture of DS Stott chatting with Callum Mounsey flashed into Rick's head.

'With Unwin dead, my guess is that any insiders he had on his books will be distracted – they might even run for cover,' Rick said. 'As soon as all the intel's on your office systems, copy me in on everything in a single mailing – it'll reduce the chance of alerting anyone who's watching.'

'The hard part is knowing who we tell,' Collins said.

'I still haven't worked that one out, mate.' Rick rubbed a hand over his tired eyes and gazed for a moment at the white sliver of moon.

'I suppose that's where the stats come in,' Collins said. 'Whoever threatened me to lay off Coutanche pretended to be Superintendent Ghosh – statistically, he's more likely to be clean.'

'Maybe,' Rick said. 'But it's not like Unwin would've had staff meetings, so your caller might not be clued up as to who's on his payroll.'

Collins was quiet for a while. 'Okay. The biggest risk is the shipmaster being warned of the raid in time to get the ship out of harbour. So we wait for the ship to dock and hold back from telling anyone what's on it till the last minute.'

'Good thinking,' Rick said. 'Do you have anyone you trust at the SFO?'

'Depends what you mean by trust,' Collins said.

'I'll rephrase,' Rick said, smiling despite himself. 'Choose the person you distrust the least. When you give me the go-ahead, I'll talk to Ghosh at the same time, browbeat him into getting someone from Border Force on the line who has some clout. He can't say no – even if he is in Unwin's pocket.'

'They'll need to lock down the crew and cargo,' Collins said. 'If the containers with the rare earths unload, we could lose them.'

Rick was about to hang up, when Collins said, 'Wait – when did Unwin die?'

'They found him in his cell an hour after lockup, so I suppose about eight-thirty?' Rick said.

'Well then, there's one more weird thing.'

'Go ahead.'

'Anyone can pay money into that shell if they've got the payment details,' Collins said, 'but only Unwin should be able to instruct a payment *out* of it. When the money went in, it should have stayed there – Unwin already being dead.'

Rick didn't know how to respond, and when he tried, he realised that Collins had already hung up.

Freezing cold, now, he headed inside and heard his personal mobile ringing where he'd left it on the meter cupboard in the hall. He picked it up in time to see that it was Maddie Stott.

'Hey, Maddie,' he said. 'It's been a while.'

'I know, Rick, and I'm sorry. Things have been . . .'

'Yeah,' Rick said. 'I gathered.'

'So, you know he's been drinking heavily.'

'Yes.'

'Well, I kicked him out yesterday.' She sounded defensive, even angry. 'And now I'm thinking maybe that was a mistake.'

He heard the slight crack in her voice on the last word and realised that she was using the anger to keep from breaking down.

'You've got to look out for yourself and the kids, Maddie.'

'I know,' she said, 'I know. But he just rang me, and he sounded terrible. Kept telling me he loved me. Said he'd done his best to protect us, but he couldn't handle it. I'm worried, Rick.'

'Ah, Jeez,' Rick sighed. 'I think this may be partly my fault – he reached out to me, and I was pretty hard on him.'

'No, this has been a long time coming,' she said. 'He's changed, Rick – you must have seen that. I can't get through to him – haven't been able to for over a year – but he'll listen to you. Will you call him?'

'Did he say where he was?' Rick asked.

'No—' Her voice rose sharply, and she paused, choking back the emotion. 'He – he wouldn't say.'

That sounded bad. 'It's okay. I'll ring him. I'll do it now.' He didn't tell her not to worry or try to feed her the lie that everything would be fine. Maddie was an ex-cop; she knew better.

Looking around him at the bags and boxes piled up in the hallway, Rick wondered how things had got so bad so fast. He scrolled through his contacts to Jim Stott's number and stared at it, trying to decide his approach. It needed to be strategic; Stott thought he was out of options – how could he persuade him otherwise? A five-minute pep talk over the phone wouldn't do it, that was for sure; they needed to speak in person.

Rick's mind flew again to Maddie's revelation, during one of their alcohol-fuelled Friday night curry sessions. Tapping her husband smartly on the nose, she'd said, 'Cur-i-osity – that's *your* biggest strength.'

Rick hit the 'call' icon. He knew what he was going to say.

His first two attempts went straight to voicemail, but he hung up and tried again without leaving a message, and on the third try, Stott picked up.

'Something's come up,' Rick said, not giving him the chance to speak. 'Where can we meet?'

'Meet? What the hell are you on about?' Stott sounded drunk and tearful. 'You told me I was done not three hours ago.'

'New development.'

'So, tell me.'

'Has to be face to face.'

'Fuck that.'

'Up to you, mate,' Rick said. 'But it could be in your favour.' He waited. For ten agonising seconds, he waited, refusing to break the silence. Then his phone pinged with a text. It was a hotel address.

'Room five-oh-four,' Stott said, and hung up.

Chapter 51

THE DOOR OF ROOM 504 WASN'T FULLY CLOSED. Rick saw that a pen had been trapped at the bottom of the frame, preventing the latch from locking. His heart thudding hard, he deployed the Casco baton Sam's oppo had given him, holding it close to his body over his right shoulder while he gently eased the door wider with the tips of his fingers. If this was a trap set by Unwin, he wasn't going to walk into it blindly.

Jim Stott was seated at the far end of the room on a sofa behind a coffee table. Rick swung the door wide, checking right and left before stepping inside and sweeping the bathroom.

'S'all right, mate,' Stott said. 'S'just me, here.' He sounded drunk but seemed less tearful now.

Rick kicked the pen away and closed the door, flipping the security latch in place.

The glass coffee table was stacked with cartons of Chinese food. A twelve-pack of Peroni lager had been broken open and six bottles placed in a wine cooler; two empties sweated on the tabletop. A bottle of Famous Grouse whisky stood three-fifths down, and Stott held a tumbler of the stuff in his right fist.

'Join me,' Stott said with an expansive gesture that sloshed whisky onto the furniture. 'After you've put the weapon away, of course.'

'Nah, I'm okay, Jim.' But he collapsed the baton and shoved it in his trouser pocket.

'You're sure?' He dug into one of the cartons and plucked out a dumpling. 'It's Yauatcha.' Stott's favourite Chinese eatery. 'Thought I'd treat myself,' he added through a mouthful of food.

Rick thought it had more of a vibe of the condemned man's last meal than a treat, but he didn't comment, just dragged the chair from the dressing table-cum-desk and sat opposite.

Stott nudged a carton of crispy duck rolls to him, and Rick took one, just to keep him happy.

'Heaven in a pancake.' Stott grinned, setting his own beer down and passing Rick a bottle from the cooler.

Rick took it and placed it on the glass of the table.

'What's the occasion, Jim?'

'Well, you should know, mate.'

Rick wasn't sure if that meant the photo of Stott in the company of Mounsey, or the new developments in the case. Jim Stott always had been good at drawing out information with ambiguity.

'Going-away party, then,' Rick said, using Stott's own tactic against him.

Stott's eyes dulled, but he braced after a swallow of whisky, and when he spoke, it was with abrasive cynicism. 'Kath Steiner out in the hall, is she? Waiting for you to do the heavy lifting, so she can sweep in when it's all done, then it's "Off you go, DS Turner, I'll take it from here."'

It was a fair imitation of Steiner's polished tones and in a moment of clarity, Rick said, 'It was you who put the fear of God into Dave Collins, wasn't it?'

Stott scratched his nose, smirking. 'Between you and me, I've given Ghosh some of his finest moments.'

'You think this is funny? You scared the shit out of Dave and not five minutes later, you're dropping hints about Jess to me, pumping me for information, telling me you're ready to listen.'

Stott looked instantly crestfallen. 'Look, I am sorry I did that – he's all right, is Dave – and I really *did* want to help you.' He sighed. 'You want the truth, I got a call from – let's say from someone in Unwin's employ – I was to put Collins off Coutanche—'

'And you jumped right to it.' A sudden realisation brought Rick up short. 'Collins had only just found the link between Unwin and Coutanche that night, but you knew all about it? How deep in this are you, Jim?'

'You're giving me more credit than I deserve.' Stott rubbed a hand over his face. 'Fact is, I don't even know who or what Coutanche is.' He stared at his hands. 'I just do as I'm told, Rick. It makes me sick – physically sick. But I'm out of options.'

'There's always options, Jim.'

'Really? You're saying that to me after what *you've* done?' For a second, he caught a glimpse of the old Stott, canny and hard as flint, staring back at him.

Having finished clearing his house of bugs less than an hour ago, Rick wasn't about to make a full confession to the corrupt cop sitting across the table from him. 'I'm not with you,' he said, eyeing him coolly. 'What have I done, Stotty?'

The older man wavered, dropping his gaze. *Shame, or fear?* Stott reached for his drink and took a greedy gulp, then set the glass down with a self-deprecating grimace.

'I'll admit I'm vague on the details. But I know you didn't tell the brass that Jess had been abducted.'

'Would've been a lie if I had, wouldn't it?' Rick said, leaning in.

'Yeah, right . . .' He smiled his lopsided smile.

Rick watched him, waiting, and Stott seemed to realise that there was something he hadn't understood, but he struggled to make sense of it.

'What?' he said. 'D'you mean, she wasn't . . . That she— Was Jess *part* of this?' He looked genuinely shocked. 'Rick, I . . . I don't what to say.'

'Nothing to be said, mate. If anyone is interested enough to

310

ask, Jess went off with some college friends, stayed away for a few days.' He shrugged. 'It's a bit of a non-story, really.'

'So the cleaning service parked outside the Kensington gaff . . .?'

Rick's anger flared. 'You seem to know an awful lot for someone who just does as he's told.'

Stott held up his hands. 'No – *listen*, Rick. I'm only told what I need to know at any particular point in time. I knew they had Jess because I was supposed to keep an eye on you. But I was only told about the Kensington house because they knew she was gone, and Unwin wanted street-cam footage. Don't look at me like that – you've seen how easy it is for the likes of Unwin to get inside your life.'

Rick shook his head. 'What the hell happened to you, Jim?'

'You really want to know?' He stared into his glass for so long that Rick thought he'd nodded off, but then he began to speak: 'We agreed when Maddie fell pregnant with Billy that she'd stay home, look after him. It's bad enough *now* for women in the Met – it was even worse back then.'

'I can believe it,' Rick said. Sexism was rife in the Met – even sexual harassment – yet some perpetrators had been promoted, rather than punished.

'Anyways, I was the one supposedly going places,' Stott went on. '*I* was the ambitious one, destined for the higher ranks.' He sighed. 'I don't know what happened, I just got . . . stuck.' He spread his hands, and the light caught his gold wedding band. He turned it on his finger, continuing his narrative.

'By then, Jason had come along, and I wanted *so* much for them – and for Maddie. I made a couple of rash investments: storage units – remember those? They were supposed to be guaranteed earners back then. And, well, you know about the time-share.'

Rick nodded. The time-share was never finished. Their money had been tied up for last five years and was surely dwindling by the day as the litigation went on.

'You know the boys are both in private school – Jason's on a scholarship, but not Billy. I was already behind with his fees, overtime had dried up – just paying the mortgage every month was getting to be a struggle. We could maybe move Billy to a sixth-form college – it'd be an upheaval, but he only had a couple of terms to go. But if we took *Billy* out, would they cancel *Jason's* scholarship?'

'Am I supposed to feel sorry for you?' Rick asked. 'You're telling me you lived beyond your means and when things got tight, instead of moving to a cheaper house and sending the boys to a state school like millions of other families, you turned to a criminal to bail you out.'

'You don't understand – you get a private school education, you start life halfway up the ladder.'

Rick stood impulsively. 'Listen to yourself, man. You betrayed everything you've ever worked for so your kids could get a *foot on the ladder*?'

'Nah, it wasn't like that. Come on, Rick, siddown, let me explain.'

'No, I think I've heard enough, mate.'

As Rick began to move away, Stott reached under one of the sofa cushions and pulled out a gun.

Rick's heart rate spiked; every hair on the back of this neck rose, and his skin tingled from his scalp to his fingertips.

He tried to speak, but all he could manage was a croak. He cleared his throat and tried again: 'Is this your latest need-to-know instruction?'

Stott gazed at him, and Rick saw the weight of immense sadness in his eyes. 'If you think I'd do that to you, of all people—' He shook his head. 'Well, you never knew me at all, son.' He waved Rick off – thankfully, with his empty hand – and at that point, Rick knew he couldn't leave.

'All right,' he said, 'I'll hear you out, but you've got to put the gun down, Jim.'

Stott looked at the gun in his hand as though he wasn't sure how it got there. It was a revolver, and all Rick could think was, *There's no safety on that thing.*

'Please, Jim,' he said, 'you're making me nervous.'

Stott eyed the gun with distaste, and then laid it down on the table to his right. The gritty crack of metal on glass made Rick wince.

'Go ahead, I'm listening,' Rick urged.

'Ah, what's the point – it's such a fucking cliché,' Stott said, and he sounded so despairing that Rick readied himself to lunge for the gun if he reached for it. But Stott sat slumped on the sofa for thirty seconds without saying a word.

'Jim,' Rick said. 'Talk to me.'

Stott lifted his glass.

'Without the booze – just for a minute, eh?' Rick said.

Stott took a large swallow.

'For God's sake, Stotty . . .'

Stott slammed the glass down on the table, then, in an abrupt change of mood, he laughed softly. 'I don't know why I'm so pissed off with you – it's not like *you* did anything to me.'

He passed a few moments in silence, and Rick got the impression he was putting his thoughts in order.

'Here's the thing,' he began at last. 'Couple of times I got home not – well – not entirely sure *how* I'd got there. Then, this guy comes to me. He's distraught. We're neighbours – lives right opposite – Jason and his youngest are in the same year at school. His eldest boy is seventeen and the lad's arrested on a drink driving charge. He's got a provisional acceptance to study law at Oxford, and a conviction isn't going to do him any good when it comes to final selection. So, Dad says, is there anything I can do?'

Rick had a gloomy sense of where this was going.

'I knew I had no right to judge, given my recent record for driving one over the eight, so I say get your son a good solicitor – he might be able to put forward a Special Reasons Argument, get the kid off. But that's not good enough – Dad doesn't want to leave anything to chance. I tell him there's nothing else I can do, and the guy makes a tentative offer – he can pay me for my time.

'Ten thousand quid – two terms' worth of fees – enough for Billy to finish the year – solve all our money worries.' Stott shook his head, and Rick read self-disgust on the man's face.

'The evidence went missing and the lad got his place at Oxford,' Rick finished for him.

Stott huffed a laugh. 'And I was naïve enough to think that was the end of it.' He sighed, interlacing his fingers palms up. 'A few months later, the guy comes back with a new request – something small – nothing I could really say was the depths of criminality – and there's good money in it, so . . .' He shrugged. 'This went on for I think nine or ten months. Then there's a request I balk at. I politely decline, and he comes on a bit heavy, so I *forcefully* decline. Same day, I'm heading into a pub for a swift half before I head home, and this car pulls up right by me – coming in fast and aggressive, you know?'

'Unwin?' Rick asked.

Stott shook his head. 'I never had direct contact with Unwin, but I recognised the weasely little man in the back of the limo.'

'Callum Mounsey,' Rick said.

Stott raised his glass in salute and took another mouthful of liquor.

'Two big thugs get out and persuade me into the car. Unwin's brief opens a laptop and shows me some video footage. It's dark, but it looks like my house, and I'm thinking is this a threat against my family?'

Rick saw anger and outrage in Stott's face.

'Then I see my car pulling into the drive; *juuust* graze the gatepost.' He stopped, shook his head again. 'Who am I kidding? It was a miracle I didn't knock the damned thing over. I fall out of the driver's seat, weave up the steps and let myself in.'

314

Stott glanced up at Rick but couldn't quite make eye contact. 'I'm about ready to throw up at this point. I say, "How did you get this?" and that little creep pontificates about how my neighbour – this is the guy whose kid I bailed out – was concerned about damage to his car, so he'd mounted a spy-cam on his house. I've got to be honest with you, Rick, I lied. Said I had a bad case of the trots – was desperate to get to the toilet. No one was hurt, the damage was to my own property, what's his problem?' Stott pinched his upper lip between his finger and thumb and gave a wet laugh. 'The next clip was like a replay of the first – except instead of clipping the gate post, I hit the neighbour's car, damaging his rear offside lights and dinging his bumper. I get out, check the damage, drive my car into the garage to hide it.' Tears seeped from his eyes as he told the rest.

'Mounsey reminds me that the next day, my neighbour had asked if I'd seen anything, and I said no. Of course, he had this denial on video. Mounsey lists the charges that could be brought against me and the consequences for my career. But he tells me that this neighbour is *grateful* for the favour I did for his son – and Mounsey's client is a generous man – everyone stands to gain from the . . . association.' He paused to guzzle the rest of his drink and pour another. 'Yeah, that's what he called it – the "association".'

Rick had always thought it was his promotion that caused the rift between him and Jim Stott, but now he realised that Maddie had started calling Rick the 'designated driver' after Rick had shopped an idiot colleague for drunk driving. It must have been around that time that Jim had started getting into scrapes driving home with a skinful of ale inside him.

Stott was staring into his refill. 'Thassit – the full story, son. I did someone a favour, and they took my life.'

'No,' Rick said sadly. 'You gave it to them, Stotty.'

Stott sniffed and wiped the tears and snot from his face with his hand. 'You may be right. But I'm taking it back.' He reached for the gun.

Rick's left hand snaked out, gripping Stott's, forcing it to the table before he could raise the revolver.

Stott glared at him, refusing to relinquish the weapon.

Rick calculated the distance: with the table between them, he didn't have the reach for a punch to the body or throat.

'Give it up, Jim,' he growled.

Stott's face contorted into an agonised grimace. 'S'what I'm trying to do, mate.'

He leaned forward to prise Rick's hand from his and without warning, Rick launched into a head-butt. Stott's head snapped back and he brought both hands up to his injured nose. Rick followed through with a hard shove, sending his former mentor sprawling onto the sofa.

In one smooth movement, Rick took the gun and emptied it of bullets. He placed the weapon on the floor beside him and the bullets on the table.

'Bastard!' Stott yelled. 'You broke my bloody nose.'

'Here.' Rick tossed him a couple of paper napkins and while he watched Stott dab at his injured face, he said, 'You'd really do that to Maddie and the boys?'

'Like they give a shit,' Stott moaned.

'I'm about sick of this self-pitying crap!' Rick shot back. 'You know why I'm here? Maddie called me. I haven't seen her in – what – two years? But she'll call someone who's become almost a stranger because she's worried about you and she's not too proud to ask for help.'

'She kicked me out, Rick – you were right about that.'

'Well, do you blame her?'

Blotting the last of the blood from his upper lip, Stott said, 'Honestly? No.' He sighed. 'I don't really understand why she didn't do it sooner.'

'She loves you, you pillock. It's the drunk she hates. Get help – therapy, a twelve-step programme, whatever it takes, because she's worth fighting for, Stotty.'

Stott balled up the napkins, hiccupped a sigh and rubbed his chin hard. 'It's a nice idea, but I can't see how me being sober will making a hell of a lot of difference after Unwin releases what he's got on me. Drunk or sober, I'm a corrupt cop; the DPS will stick my head on a pikestaff at New Scotland Yard as an example to others.'

'Unwin won't be causing you any more problems,' Rick said quietly.

Stott, snorted, then winced with the pain; the bridge of his nose was already badly swollen and would need to be reset.

'D'you think a man like Unwin can't run things from inside?' Stott demanded. 'You're dreaming, son. I'd lay odds he's got at least one prison guard on every shift catering to his needs. "Mobile phone? No problem, sir. Cell need cleaning? Consider it done. Special food concessions? We're here to help."'

'You're not hearing me, Jim,' Rick said. 'I wasn't lying when I said something had come up that could be to your advantage.'

Stott squinted across the table, his eyes still watering from the damage to his nose.

'Are you listening, Stotty?' Rick said. 'Unwin is out of the picture. Permanently.'

He saw hope flicker in Stott's eyes like an uncertain candle flame. 'He's dead?'

'Good and dead.'

Stott slumped back on the sofa and wept silently for a few moments, but then he straightened up, anxiety creasing his face. 'Thing is, Rick, it's like I said, I didn't ever meet Unwin – I only ever saw his solicitor.'

'Mounsey will have his own fires to fight,' Rick said, thinking about the money funnelled through Coutanche's shell company to release the ship. 'He isn't likely to be interested in you – if anything, he's more likely to come after me.'

Something sly and calculating flashed across the old dog's face.

'What's he got on you, then?'

Rick smiled. 'Nothing. And that's the way it'll stay.'

'Good,' Stott said, serious again, his emotions still swept on the high seas of drunkenness and relief. 'Good . . .' He stared at his hands for a while, then took a breath and blew it out slowly. 'So . . . am I under arrest?'

'No.'

He bit his lip. 'Are you gonna report me?'

Rick's gaze dropped to the bullets lying between them.

'No, I'm not going to report you, Sarge.'

Stott's head snapped up at the use of his title. 'You're not?' He seemed afraid to acknowledge his sheer good fortune.

Rick shook his head. 'But I expect you to put your papers in tomorrow.'

Stott stared at him, his eyes wide with shock. 'I can't *retire*.'

'Course you can. You're on the old PPS scheme – and you've got your thirty years in. Take sick leave till your notice is done – I know you've got time owing.'

'But, Rick—'

'That's non-negotiable, Stotty.'

Stott's shoulders drooped, but he nodded. 'All right. Okay . . . I know it makes sense. And I'm grateful, Rick, honest I am.' He puffed out his cheeks. 'What a bloody night, eh?' He rubbed his hands as though preparing for work. 'Well, I suppose I should get that revolver back into the evidence store,' he added, holding out his hand.

'Not a chance,' Rick said.

'I've got to. It'll be missed. Come on . . . you can keep the ammo,' he added, his tone wheedling.

Rick smiled. 'We're both older and wiser than that, Stotty.' He retrieved the revolver and stood to leave. 'You can keep the bullets – I'll take the gun.'

Chapter 52

Wednesday, late evening

RICK LEFT ST THOMAS' HOSPITAL MORTUARY as Big Ben chimed the quarter-hour after eleven. He'd confirmed that the body was, indeed, Thomas Unwin, and had an informative chat with the pathologist about the circumstances of his death.

A bitter wind swept across the Thames as he crossed Westminster Bridge; the glow of the clock tower gave a false sense of warmth, and his eyes watered in the cutting blast. Traffic noise was loud, even at that time of night, so he didn't hear his burner phone ring, and he was only alerted to the call by its vibration. The only contact on that phone was Sam. But Sam preferred to text, so Rick hesitated, his thumb hovering over the icon for a few seconds. Then he swiped right to answer and clicked to speaker before raising the mobile to his ear.

'It wasn't me,' Sam said.

Turning right onto Embankment in search of somewhere quieter, Rick glanced around, half-expecting to see his brother smiling at him from some street corner, taken aback by his disappointment that Sam was nowhere in evidence. An unfamiliar wave of nostalgia followed on as he realised that, for all he knew, this might be the last contact he would have with Sam for another thirteen years. On impulse, he said, 'Can we meet?'

'I'm in the middle of something,' Sam said, sounding regretful. 'But I'll ring you before I leave – that's if you'd like.'

'I would,' Rick said, making an effort to sound casual, although the words 'before I leave' had made his stomach cramp. He wanted to say, *Don't go*, but that would sound needy, so instead he told Sam that he'd just come from identifying Unwin.

'Surely his wife would do that?'

'Let's say the high-ups wanted corroboration from an unbiased source.'

'Hah, that would be a neat get-out-of-prison trick, wouldn't it? Very Arsène Lupin . . .'

A silence followed, and Rick feared that Sam would use the awkwardness as an excuse to end the call, so he asked, 'Any theories on who would put out a contract?' he asked.

'You're assuming it *was* murder?'

'Looks like it.'

'Well, then, your guess is as good as mine,' Sam said.

'I doubt that.' In the pause, Rick could picture the smile chasing across his brother's face.

'The Unwins of this world make the kind of friends you wouldn't want as enemies,' Sam said at last. 'He was a big fish in a small pond for a long while. But with the rare earths racket he swam into shark-infested waters. His arrest wounded him – and sharks can scent blood in the water a mile off.'

He was right, of course. Even before the trial opened, Superintendent Ghosh had hinted at a raft of follow-up investigations if they got a successful conviction. And with the full resources of the Serious Fraud Office to back inquiries, there were potentially dozens more international criminals Unwin could have taken down with him.

'You're saying it could be anyone?'

'What was the cause of death?' Sam asked.

'The prison doctor said it was a heart attack, but the pathologist thinks it could be poison.'

'Good luck with that – the medics argued for months over the precise chemical used to poison the anti-corruption lawyer who stood up to Putin. I believe they agreed on Novichok in the end – the Russians do like their nerve agents . . .'

'So, you think it was the Russians?'

'Based on our earlier chat about Unwin's disrespect of their property – and let's not forget, that rare earths cargo stuck in port would be a powerful incentive.'

Rick didn't tell him that it looked like the ship was about to be liberated.

'That said, Novichok is more your government-sponsored poison of choice,' Sam mused. 'Tricky to handle, difficult to dispose of any excess safely – almost impossible in a prison, I should think. So, unless Unwin had dealings with high-level Russian politicians, I'd be inclined to discount it. Did anyone else fall sick?'

'Not that I know of,' Rick said, but he would be sure to ask that staff and inmates were medically checked. 'His solicitor brought him his lunch personally at the court. He died shortly after lockup, so if it *was* poison, it was most likely administered in the prison.'

'Then I'd be looking at his stash of tea, or Pot Noodles – *so* easy to contaminate, and it doesn't take much to do the job.'

'Much of *what*, though, if not a nerve agent?'

'Fentanyl is easy enough to come by,' Sam said. 'Even better, *car*fentanyl – that stuff is five thousand times more potent than heroin.' Sam paused, and Rick sensed that he was finding the conversation professionally stimulating.

'Russian organised crime bosses are good to their own, and they would have access to prisoners, guards, administration, health care staff – any one of whom might be recruited. But the simplest approach is often the most efficient and elegant.'

Interested that he defined ways of killing as 'elegant', Rick asked, 'In this context, that would be . . .?'

Rick heard the blast of a tugboat horn from Sam's phone, and a second later, more faintly, the same mourning tone and pitch was carried to him on a gust of wind. He stared downriver and saw the lights of a barge being towed towards Waterloo Bridge, less than a mile away. The arches were underlit in blue and lilac at this time of night, and the blurred figures atop it were mere silhouettes. Was Sam there, watching him?

'Russian hitmen – and women – do tend to favour the rather aptly named "heartbreak grass"', Sam was saying, 'which is known for causing cardiac arrest.' He paused, adding suavely, 'So I'm told.'

Chapter 53

Five days later

AFTER ANOTHER TWELVE-HOUR STINT at the office Rick Turner was planning a hot bath, a takeaway and an early night. In the four days since the joint NCA and Border Force raid on cargo ship *Junara* in Jersey, he and Dave Collins had briefed Interpol, HM Revenue and Customs, and representatives of the British Intelligence Service. The cargo had been bound for a recycling plant on Romney Marshes. Officially, the company salvaged rare earths from scrap hi-tech goods, but HM customs and the NCA found a quantity of high-grade refined rare earth metals with an estimated full market value of eighty *million* pounds, which the company couldn't account for. Apparently, their legit operation was a cover for the far more financially rewarding off-the-books import and distribution of stolen rare earths, smuggled through customs as machine parts and base metals.

Toxicology had identified 'significant quantities' of gelsemine in Unwin's blood, urine and kidneys. An alkaloid related to strychnine, it was abundant in heartbreak grass. They had Sam to thank for its speedy identification – it would have taken weeks if he hadn't suggested they look for it. More traces of the stuff were found in the mug Unwin had used to brew tea at the start of lockup. His cellmate 'Laser' Lasovsky swore ignorance, but the prison service had discovered that he had no sister and the woman who had visited him on the day Unwin died had vanished. The formerly friendless and destitute inmate was also better clothed now than he had been since his incarceration almost a year ago.

Rick's phone rang as he left Hammersmith Police Station; it was an unknown number.

'Congratulations – Mum would have been proud.'

'Sam,' Rick said, experiencing a jolt of happiness hearing his brother's voice.

'I'm in Covent Garden,' Sam said. 'Come to dinner; my treat.'

Rick checked his watch; it was nine p.m. 'It's getting late,' he said doubtfully. 'It'd take me half an hour by cab from where I am.'

'All right, I'll meet you halfway. There's a little bistro in Chelsea – fifteen minutes door to door, and it opens late.'

'I'm not really dressed for a Chelsea bistro,' Rick said. 'Will they let me in?'

'Oh, this place is very laid-back, but the menu is *fabulous* – they serve Colchester oysters – and it stays open till midnight.'

Rick realised he was ravenous, but he didn't fancy the idea of oysters. 'Do they do steak?' he asked.

'They do,' Sam said. 'Frites, too – for the philistines,' he added with dry humour. 'Call me when you're nearer.'

Rick began hunting for a taxi. 'Okay, what's the address? Sam?' He was talking to dead air.

He made good time and after a follow-up call to confirm the address, stepped out of the freezing night into the warmth and light of the bistro. Taking up the entire floor space of what had been an old carriage works, the place had what the tourist guides called a 'rustic' vibe. Concrete floors and open rafters strung with fairy lights, charmingly mismatched tables and chairs.

The smell of food reminded Rick that he hadn't eaten since

snatching a sandwich at lunchtime, and he watched hungrily as a waiter passed, carrying plates of food.

The manager swept him up, guiding him directly to Sam's table, already crowded with a variety of small dishes, and Sam waved him to his seat.

'Dig in,' he said. 'You looked half-starved in the courtroom last week; haven't you been eating?'

'You sound like Mum,' Rick sniped back, then realised fully what Sam had said. 'You were in the courtroom?'

'Briefly,' Sam said, digging with relish into a dish of dressed crab. 'I wanted to see the look on Unwin's face as you gave your evidence. Don't worry, I was unrecognisable.' He chewed and swallowed. 'And *you* were impressive.'

He shoved dishes at Rick and lifted a bottle of wine, ready to pour him a glass. Rick covered it with his hand, and Sam frowned.

'I insist – drink beer for the rest of the night by all means – but this *particular* St-Émilion has powers to grant strength to a weary soul and cure a broken heart.'

Rick chuckled. 'He jests at scars that never felt a wound.'

'Well, look at *you*, quoting Shakespeare,' Sam said, pouring a generous measure.

'You pick up a thing or two, dating an actress,' Rick said with a grin. They clinked glasses and Sam raised his eyebrows, waiting for Rick's assessment of the wine.

'Actually,' he said, 'it's not bad.'

Sam chuckled. 'They'll be ringing the bells in thanksgiving at Château Angelus.'

'Still wouldn't mind a nice craft beer, though.'

Sam sighed and by some magic, a waiter appeared at their table. Rick wolfed samples of food from each dish, and it was only when he came up for air that he realised Sam was eyeing him narrowly.

'So,' Sam said. 'No scars?'

'None that won't heal.'

'And how is the lovely Jessica? I understand she picked up her belongings yesterday.'

'Hardly said a word.' Rick's tired brain caught up a moment later. 'You're still having me watched?'

'Jessica – not you.'

Rick nodded slowly. *He's still looking out for you.*

'No words of penitence?' Sam nudged. 'No pleas for forgiveness?'

'Honestly, Sam?' He stared at the plum-coloured wine in his glass. 'I think she's pissed off she didn't get paid for her big performance.'

'Hm,' Sam said. 'For what it's worth, I think she did care for you.'

Rick shot him an incredulous look. 'Are you trying to talk me into giving her a second chance?'

'You weren't tempted?'

'She once called me a puritan for holding Jim Stott to too high a standard.' Rick lifted one shoulder. 'Maybe she's right, as far as Jim goes – he screwed up and got hooked by a master manipulator. But Unwin didn't have anything on Jess. *She* wasn't coerced. *She* wasn't threatened. She betrayed me for *money*.'

'Money *can* be a powerful incentive . . .' Sam said. 'You know, in *The Merchant of Venice*, Jessica – daughter of Shylock – betrays her own father, steals his money, even denounces her religion – yet her lover calls her wise, fair, and true.'

'Well, that's just twisted,' Rick said.

Sam laughed. 'I know, what was he *thinking*? But I guess even the Bard is entitled to an occasional off-day.'

The food was wonderful, the sound of jazz in the background mellowing, and Sam was brilliant company.

They ate companionably, exchanging war stories from both sides of the legal divide, and listening to Sam spin his yarns – heavily redacted to protect the guilty – Rick had a powerful urge to apologise again for the blame he'd placed on his brother's shoulders, for the years he'd spent simultaneously raging against him and yearning for him. But that was the rationale of a maudlin drunk.

Sam hadn't been there to witness the bitterness and heartache of those years. Why would he care? Rick didn't doubt that his brother was capable of emotion: he'd demonstrated anger, joy, vengeful-ness – even familial affection – in the last ten days. But regret? That would require empathy and despite all of Sam's astonishing resourcefulness, empathy was one quality he lacked.

You know what she is, don't you? Sam had said of Jess. He might equally have said it of himself. *Odd,* Rick thought, *that the two people I care about most are borderline psychopaths.*

A good hour later, happily alcohol-infused, he finally turned to the case.

'So,' he said. 'Unwin . . .'

'Have you established how he died?' Sam said.

'Heartbreak grass.'

'A Russian hit, then.'

'Like you said.'

Sam raised both hands. 'Not guilty, your honour.'

'Relax,' Rick said. 'It wasn't an accusation.'

'Oh, in that case, you're most welcome. Interesting that they got to him first,' he added almost to himself.

Rick stopped in the process of mopping his plate with a chunk of bread. 'There was more than one contract out on him?'

'Only the one, as far as I know,' Sam said. 'I gather the *actual* assassination was more in the nature of a favour for a favour.'

Rick's mind flitted to Lasovsky, whose life had become so much easier over the last few days. 'So, who took out the contract?'

'Unknown,' Sam said. 'And it came via an unusual middleman – a rather brutish individual I personally wouldn't trust to keep order at a nightclub, let alone broker a high-profile hit.'

Rick blinked. 'Was that an admission?'

'Oh, let's not do this dance again,' Sam said.

Rick watched him, coolly, thinking back to the day before.

When Jess came for her belongings, she'd plucked a battered coffee table book out of one of the boxes and dumped it on the hall floor. 'That scruffy thing isn't mine,' she said. It was a book on art.

After she'd gone, Rick thumbed through it and found notes pencilled in the margins. It wasn't Jess's handwriting, it was Sam's. The centre page held a full-colour image of Marat, lying dead in his bath. On the facing page, the author had given the history of the image, some of which Sam had quoted verbatim to Rick. A marginal note in Sam's handwriting read, 'A decorous murder', the very words Sam had used when Rick first described Charlie Haskins's murder scene.

Which meant two things: Sam really had started on his path of self-improvement long before he'd disappeared, and Sam was the contract killer who had posed Haskins's body to create that 'decorous murder'.

But even if he had proof, Rick wasn't sure he would act: thirteen years ago, Sam had fled a murder he didn't commit, had assumed the blame to save Rick from imprisonment and guilt. Five days ago, Sam had saved him again, and Rick had no intention of turning his brother or himself in for that killing. Norland's disappearance, like Haskins's murder, would remain a mystery.

The silence between them had gone on for some time, and Rick realised that Sam was weighing up how much he felt he could safely say.

At last, he began: 'I understand why you would want a fuller explanation—'

'No,' Rick said. 'I'm good.'

'You're—?' Sam looked almost comically perplexed.

'But it was you who tipped the Russians off about Unwin using the apartment, wasn't it?'

'You didn't give me the name of your mystery Russian, remember?'

'Sam,' Rick said, 'don't be obtuse. With your "sources" I don't suppose it took you long to find out.'

The spark of humour in Sam's eye told him that he'd guessed right.

'Men like Unwin aren't sporting in defeat, Rick. And since you'd decided to proceed with the trial as planned, there was a strong chance he would come after you again. I couldn't take that risk,' Sam said. 'But it seems he'd made new enemies of old friends – if the Russians hadn't got to him, there were clearly others waiting in line.'

Rick nodded, accepting it as the truth. 'One last thing . . .'

Sam cocked an eyebrow.

'Who's the broker you wouldn't trust as a nightclub bouncer?'

Sam laughed. 'Nice try. But I'm afraid I must protect my sources; it's a question of mutual trust.' He picked up his cutlery and began eating again. 'Speaking of which, have *you* worked out who you can trust, yet?'

'Dave Collins.' Rick took a breath. 'You.' He saw a slight hitch as Sam raised the fork to his mouth.

'That's . . . good to know,' Sam said.

There was thirteen years of heartache and regret behind that one stilted sentence, and it seemed that Sam couldn't bring himself to meet Rick's gaze.

'Jury's out on Ghosh and Steiner.' Rick pushed on through his own emotion. 'Although it was Ghosh who pressed for the ship seizure – and he's delighted with the outcome.'

'As he should be,' Sam said, quickly regaining equilibrium. 'Tons of stolen rare earths worth millions; exposing a conspiracy involving Russian gangs and British bankers – not to mention netting Thomas Unwin. That's promotion gold, Rick.' He took another sip of wine, openly appraising him. 'But I'm sensing you have reservations?'

Rick was thinking about Collins's parting salvo that payment for the rare earths had come out of one of Unwin's shell companies *after* Unwin was dead.

'The ship was at anchor for days after Austin King's murder – he was topped before he'd had the chance to make payment on the cargo,' Rick said. 'Then, hours *after* the hit on Unwin, the cash transfer happened through a Coutanche shell company, which in reality was one of Unwin's. The money should have been stuck there, because Unwin was – you know – too *dead* to give instructions to complete the transaction.'

'But payment *was* made, nevertheless,' Sam said.

'In seconds.'

Sam stared off into the middle distance for a second. 'Was his wife a signatory?'

'No. And his solicitor didn't have power of attorney, either.'

Sam's eyebrow twitched. 'As I said, money is a powerful motivator – but it would take a *lot* of money to arrange a fraudulent transfer on that scale.'

Rick nodded. 'The deposit was Russian money – we're sure of that. But someone had to authorise the transfer out again – and I very much doubt that Unwin would have given free access to the Russians.'

'I'd be looking at Mounsey,' Sam said.

'We are. Mounsey received frequent calls from an unknown mobile number in the past few weeks – probably a burner Unwin had hidden in his cell. That's long gone, but if he gave Mounsey authorisation codes to his accounts, I wouldn't put it past the little shit to go way beyond his remit, transfer money he wasn't supposed to touch.'

'Almost makes me want to stick around, see if your armchair ninja can run this to ground.'

'Why not? There's a spare room going begging at our house,' Rick said, only half joking. 'We could make a second attempt on London Zoo – if you've got the nerve.'

Sam laughed. It was joyful, natural laughter, and Rick couldn't help but smile.

'It has been fun, hasn't it?' Sam said.

'I think we have different definitions of the word,' Rick said. 'But, yeah, it's had its moments.'

Sam beamed. 'God, I've missed you.'

Rick was too stunned to reply. For a few seconds they looked at each other, and Sam's smile faded. For once, it seemed that he was struggling to find the right words.

'*What?*' Rick said at last.

'I wanted you to know I'm sorry I couldn't be around when you needed me,' Sam said.

Rick scratched the back of his neck, embarrassed, but decided he'd own up to it anyway. 'You were – kind of.'

Sam tilted his head, waiting for an explanation.

'I sometimes hear your voice in my head. Giving me advice, pep talks and that.'

'A kind of superego?' Sam glanced at the ceiling. 'Oh dear, I don't think I'm ideal as the voice of your conscience.'

'Yeah,' Rick said. 'That's what I keep telling myself.'

He caught a softening in his brother's eyes, perhaps even a gleam of emotion.

'You're moving on then,' Rick said, seeing the inevitability of it.

'Things are a little . . . hot for me here, just now,' Sam said.

'Why d'you do this, Sam?' Rick asked, mortified to hear his teenaged self speaking. 'With all your money, you could do anything you want.'

'Retire to the Bahamas and hope to die of a heart attack before the boredom kills me?' Sam softened the sharpness of his words with a smile. 'No thanks. Anyway, I need the exercise.'

Rick shook his head. 'It was always the adrenaline rush you needed.'

'Can't live without it, Rick,' he admitted, still smiling. He rapped the table, suddenly brisk. 'I'm off to the little boys' room; why don't you order coffee – I'll have a cappuccino.'

Rick ordered and waited five minutes, then another two. As he stood to find out what was keeping Sam, the manager came over. 'I hope you enjoyed your meal, sir. Mr Holland had to leave, but he's settled the bill,' he said.

Rick was about to say he'd made a mistake, until he realised that 'Holland' must be another of Sam's aliases.

'And he asked me to give you this.' The manager handed over a slip of paper, and Rick sat down again to open it.

'Good times, Rick. We make a great team. I hate goodbyes, so I'm afraid I've done the cowardly thing again and sneaked off. But I promise I'll be there, in your head, giving good counsel. I've texted you a link to a forum. If you ever need me, send a direct message to "The Fixer". But make sure you use a VPN to access the Tor browser; you'd be surprised how many are caught making that rookie mistake.'

Rick checked the burner phone. Sure enough, the link was there, along with a final message:

—I've ditched the phone. A bientôt. ~Sam.

A Letter from M. K. Murphy

Thank you so much for choosing to read *Dead Man Walking*. I hope you enjoyed it! If you did and would like to be the first to know about my new releases, you can follow me on Twitter, Facebook and Instagram. My website has occasional blogs on writing and also 'Shelf Indulgence' – where I post reviews of books both new and old. Do sign up to my newsletter for up-to-date news ahead of the crowd – and the odd giveaway.

Bringing books from inception to realisation can be a long, hard road, and the idea for *Dead Man Walking* first came into being in 2016. My agent, Felicity Blunt, had asked for a few possible storylines for submission as TV pitches, and while on holiday in Cornwall, in a slightly damp fisherman's cottage on a very wet day, I was noodling and doodling. Often my stories are triggered by a strong, often shocking, image in a daydream or even a nightmare, but this novel was different from the start. Out of nowhere I wrote a single sentence: 'The best criminals are those who never get caught.' At that point, I didn't even know who'd whispered those words in my ear, yet the entire story was built around that one phrase. It was as if it had a gravitational force, pulling in characters, scenes, situations and plotlines, and each new addition to the outline made me want to know more.

As I say, the outline was for a TV pitch, and getting anything commissioned on TV is incredibly tough. *Dead Man Walking* wasn't taken up, and I set it aside. But that didn't stop me thinking about it. I was strongly drawn to the central characters – you know how it is when you've been thinking about an old friend, wondering how they're doing, and feeling bad that you haven't been in touch? That was how it felt. Even worse, I'd left Rick in terrible jeopardy! I *knew* that at some point I'd have to write the story as a novel . . . So when I found myself with time on my hands I came back to it, and in the autumn of 2021 I submitted a draft to my agent. I wrote, 'I hate an unfinished project, so I went back to *Dead Man Walking* and have just finished. Would you be interested in taking a look?'

And here we are, with Rick Turner having fought his way through that awful peril while trying to bring a dangerous man to justice – making enemies and finding new friends along the way. I hope you liked how it turned out, and if you did, I'd be immensely grateful if you would leave a review. I always love to hear what readers think, and it helps new readers discover my books too.

With heartfelt thanks,

M. K. Murphy

Social media links:
Twitter: @murphynovels
Facebook: @murphynovels
Instagram: @murphynovels
Website: www.margaret-murphy.co.uk

I've written under my own name and three pseudonyms over the years, in genres ranging from domestic noir, through forensic, to detective fiction, and by some technical wizardry beyond my comprehension, my brilliant webmaster, Steve Bennett, has brought all of them under one virtual roof. Do have a good rootle through my backlist – you might find something you missed first time around!

Acknowledgements

So many people have brought their energy, expertise and considerable skills to make this book happen that I scarcely know where to begin. But I'm going to give it a try . . .

I am delighted that *Dead Man Walking* has found such a good home at HQ Digital. Abi Fenton's enthusiasm for the novel, determination to bring it to a global audience, and her vision for Rick Turner's future investigations and exploits are beyond exciting, and I'm thrilled by HQD's innovative and agile approach to seeking out the ideal readership for the series.

Some time ago, feeling frustrated and pigeonholed as a writer, I decided that it was time to look for a new agent. The first I contacted at Curtis Brown was focusing on debut writers, and as I already had nine titles under my belt, I was technically disqualified. But he recommended me to a young agent who was just beginning to build her own list. It was my great fortune to sign with Felicity Blunt. From the outset, Felicity was open to any and all ideas I had for new stories, heroes and antiheroes, styles and settings. She has been supportive of my forays into different forms, subgenres, and even ways of working, supporting my adventures – even an experiment in collaboration – with the perfect blend of pragmatism and optimism. It has been, and continues to be, a joy working with an agent whose ambition matches my wildest dreams.

But in comparison with my other works, *Dead Man Walking* has a very different setting, style, voice and pace, and I confess I experienced a slight quiver of anxiety asking Felicity if she would like to see a novel I'd reworked from a TV pitch. I should have known better: there were no quibbles, qualms, or barriers, only enthusiasm and positivity. Of course, there was also strategic hardheadedness – which meant there were changes to be made – many of them – and I won't lie, some were arduous and even painful to achieve. But I am proud of the result, and grateful for her input, and for the suggestions and comments of her superb team.

A special mention here for Rosie Pierce: questions have such power in editorial process, and at a crucial stage in redrafting the novel, your questions were particularly apposite and honed to the best advantages of the story – thank you. Finally, the book to film team at Curtis Brown rallied round *Dead Man Walking* even before the final draft was written, and their commitment in sharing their enthusiasm with TV and film producers has been awe-inspiring. They brought this book to the attention of so many brilliant production companies, and somehow found my ideal. Special thanks to Anna Weguelin from an occasionally skittish author for her ability to convey excitement and passion while maintaining a zen-like calm.

Finally, and crucially: Murf, for the patience, support and love you've shown me over the years you deserve a ruddy medal!

Dear Reader,

We hope you enjoyed reading this book. If you did, we'd be so appreciative if you left a review. It really helps us and the author to bring more books like this to you.

Here at HQ Digital we are dedicated to publishing fiction that will keep you turning the pages into the early hours. Don't want to miss a thing? To find out more about our books, promotions, discover exclusive content and enter competitions you can keep in touch in the following ways:

JOIN OUR COMMUNITY:

Sign up to our new email newsletter:
http://smarturl.it/SignUpHQ

Read our new blog www.hqstories.co.uk

🐦 https://twitter.com/HQStories

📘 www.facebook.com/HQStories

BUDDING WRITER?

We're also looking for authors to join the HQ Digital family!
Find out more here:

https://www.hqstories.co.uk/want-to-write-for-us/

Thanks for reading, from the HQ Digital team